The Fig Orchard

A NOVEL

LAYLA FISKE

Rancho Publishing LLC

THE FIG ORCHARD is a work of fiction. Names, characters, places, villages, schools, businesses, houses of worship and incidents either are the product of the author's imagination or are used fictitiously. Any resemblance to actual persons, living or dead, structures, institutions, business establishments, events, or locales is entirely coincidental.

Fiske, Layla.
The fig orchard : a novel / by Layla Fiske.
p. cm.
ISBN 978-0-9894554-0-4

1. Women peasants--Middle East--Fiction. 2. Midwives
--Middle East--Fiction. 3. World War, 1914-1918--
Fiction. 4. Middle East--Fiction. 5. Domestic fiction.
I. Title.

PS3606.I854F54 2013   813'.6
                               QBI13-600088

Author's website: www.laylafiske.net

Book design by Frankie Frey

Printed in the United States of America

In memory of my grandmother

Mariam

Midwife to so many

The Fig Orchard

PROLOGUE
Palestine
1896

AS THE FIGS HUNG ripe and honeyed on a hillside high above the Jordan River and the whisper of an early autumn breeze danced lightly between the wild roses, Nisrina Huniah's soul, in all its beauty, descended from the heavens. She arrived suddenly and unexpectedly, in her father's orchard amongst the baskets and cuttings of a late harvest. And on that very same day, in that very same orchard, by God's will and inexplicable wisdom, her mother's soul sadly departed.

There were no doctors in their small village and the midwife, a gray-haired woman who walked with a stoop, her face to the ground, was gone—called to a neighboring town to help in the delivery of twins. She'd left early that morning before the sun had risen, traveling partially by foot and partially by cart. Before she left she gave instructions to her husband, a toothless man who nodded as she drove away, that she would not return until she'd seen the two babies brought safely into the world.

Sabra Hishmeh was the only midwife in Beit el Jebel, and to the villagers her word was sacred. One sideways glance from those deep, dark, wrinkly old eyes would make even the strongest of men shudder and shake, their blistered bravery slipping away like a delicate blossom on a hot summer's day. For Sabra Hishmeh had been given the gift—the secret of life. A wisdom learned from a very young age as she watched her mother and her mother's mother practice their trade throughout the provincial village. Talented midwives in their own right, they urged and compelled, pulled and prodded until an innocent babe would relinquish its hold on his mother's aching womb, finally venturing into the light of a newborn day.

With the exception of a very few, most members of the village could proudly say that they had been guided into the world through the able hands of either Sabra Hishmeh or her mother before her.

And they knew that if their sons and grandsons were to live to see life outside the womb, they had better take heed of the wary instructions of this ancient, gifted woman.

But even in her capableness, Sabra was only one woman. One midwife. She could not be in two places at the same time. So when her work with the twins was finally done and she had, at last, returned to the silent, somber streets of Beit el Jebel, it was too late. Nisrina was a motherless child and her father was enraged. Not only had his beautiful wife been taken from him, but he was left with a daughter.

A daughter! What's a man to do with that?

The gentle wind, uncommonly cool for that sullen September morning, carried with it a gray mist that had slowly descended upon the small village. Like a mother swaddling her newborn child with a blanket of dew, it crept softly in, along the crags and crannies of the rural Mediterranean town. And as it traveled amidst the olive and the fig trees, the pomegranates and the palms, it silently deposited tiny, water-filled teardrops on branches and leaves, on fruits and flowers, leaving behind a glistening haze that clung to the ridges and mountainsides. Trespassing into each crevice and rise, it worked its way through the orchards and vineyards that covered the lush green hills; and as it did, it cast an ominous gloom over the town. A gloom which lasted for seven long days and seven long nights while the people of Beit el Jebel mourned the loss of a good and gracious woman.

As they mourned, they also talked. Telling tales filled with mysteries and false notions. Behind closed doors and in places where women would gather, where they could candidly speak their minds, words were being whispered of the poor mother whose life was so tragically taken. Rumors and innuendos were exchanged as the ladies of the village traveled back and forth into town fetching water from the common well, their bare feet stepping lightly over stones and brambles, while jugs filled with water balanced gracefully on their heads. They could be seen, bent-in, close together, wives and mothers, sisters and aunties crouched around their outdoor *taboons*, the domed shaped ovens hissing and steaming as they baked their bread to a warm golden brown. For although no one would openly admit it, not wishing to bring the curse of the evil eye upon their homes, many believed that before its birth, the sacred soul in heaven could willfully choose not only the day of its birth, but also the day of its death. And perhaps the dearly departed wife of Isa Huniah, God rest her soul, had, from the gates of heaven itself, known a secret so horrid, so tragic, that she could not live with it another moment, nor divulge it to any living soul; and so, without pomp or discord, she'd taken this opportunity to make her sudden departure from the world.

Of course, the thought that Nisrina's mother had actually decided to leave of her own accord was a preposterous supposition, and if asked, the townspeople would have explicitly declared it so. To state otherwise would be blasphemous and contrary to the teachings of the church, and all the bearded Orthodox priests in their blackened robes and their golden regalia would be heard the next Sunday morning preaching the sermon of God's indeterminate will and man's insignificance in the hierarchy of the divine. And as the clerics walked, slowly and deliberately down the aisles of the majestic Syrian Orthodox Church carrying their large, ornate, golden crosses and swinging their vessels of burning incense, the smoke rising up as prayers into heaven, the fragrance encircling the pews and rafters, signifying God's grace pouring into their souls, they'd somehow know what the people were thinking, and the looks they would cast upon their congregation would bring great shame to their flock for having such irreverent thoughts.

Nevertheless, tongues, indeed did wag, and after much whispering and sordid speculation, the people of the village could come to only one possible conclusion: Isa Huniah who now stood alone in his home, his young daughter fed by a wet nurse, his aged mother washing his clothes and cooking his meals, must have done something very terrible in his life that was finally seeking retribution. Of course, no one knew for sure. They could only surmise.

But one thing was certain—the poor child who came into the world had come at a price, her soul a burden to bear.

PART ONE

1910 – 1917

They thought I could not hear their whispers, but I could.

Walking into town to fetch water from the well, my fingers clasping tightly the soft, petaled folds of my grandmother's skirt, my face buried deep within its linen calm.

I could see them from the corners of my eyes. Wives and mothers, sisters and aunties, crouched down in their long-hemmed thobes, their cheeks bright red from the hissing steam of the fiery taboons where they baked their bread over smooth, round rocks carried up from the bank of the river's edge.

The words that formed on their lips were unmistakable.

"Motherless child."

That's what they called me.

They'd shake their heads and make their pitied sounds as their tongues clicked sharp against the roofs of their ruffled mouths, their sideways glances piercing hard into my ravaged soul.

ONE

Childhood's End

NISRINA WOKE UP IN a pool of blood. The red liquid seeping from her groin had covered her sheets, her gown and the inside of her legs. She doubled up, the pain overwhelming, the odor pungent and stale. She knew what it meant. She'd heard the other girls in the village with lowered voices, their eyes averted as they whispered to each other—"It came to me!" or "Has it come to you yet?"

More than once she'd seen her stepmother privately washing the bloodstained rags that she pushed up tight between her legs each month, and she knew it was only a matter of time before she, too, would need to keep a supply of clean rags in her drawer. When she bathed, she noticed that her breasts had grown fuller, larger, to hurt actually; and for the last few days she felt a heaviness below her belly button that wouldn't subside.

So when she woke that morning and saw the fresh stains, bright red, with a sticky moistness all around her, she knew—it had finally come to her.

Her father left long before daybreak, taking his sons into town to sell the latest crop of grapes. Relieved they were gone, Nisrina called out to her stepmother.

Esma, seeing her stepdaughter's circumstance, promptly took her nightclothes and the sheets from her bed and threw them into the kitchen fire. Together, the two women stood in the center of the room mesmerized as they watched the flames rise up, surrounding and engulfing the cloths. Laden with the apprehension of child-hood's end, the fabric smoldered and curled as the fire's fury devoured the soiled linens. The stench, heavy and searing, quickly spreading through the room.

Esma opened the windows and doors allowing the fresh morning air to drift in, its cool moist breeze diffusing the harsh, rancid odor. They watched as the red blood slowly became indistinguishable from the flames; and as the weave surrendered to the heat, its shape changed—shrinking, curling, twitching about, until all that was left was a soft form of black soot that vaguely patterned the shape of cloth.

When there was nothing left to watch, the embers smoldering, the sudden overwhelming warmth of the room subsiding, Nisrina turned to her stepmother, "Is this the custom, *yumma*? To burn the sheets of a first menstruation?" It seemed so wasteful; she wondered why Esma hadn't just washed them. Perhaps it was the need for physical cleanliness, she thought to herself, or maybe a form of spiritual purification—the flow from the first menses laden with ancestral sin.

Mystified by the burden of her transitioning body, Nisrina had been taught nothing of womanly ways, a subject that was always left to half-heard whispers and clouded undertones. But even so, she remembered no ritual like that which just occurred in Esma's kitchen.

"You will understand these things when you're older, Nisrina. For now it is best that we say nothing to your father. Not a word. Agreed?" Esma's eyes opened wide beneath her furrowed brow, and she held her stubby forefinger up against her tightened mouth as if the act alone would seal both their lips. To Esma, discretion was paramount. She saw no need for her husband to know of the blossoming change in his young daughter.

Surprised that her stepmother would keep such a secret from her father, Nisrina nodded. These were the sacred things of womanhood, and in these most private of matters she assented to the older female's judgment. The cramping in her abdomen made her legs feel weak and the muscles in her back ached terribly. But seeing the look in her stepmother's eyes, the purse of her sun-parched lips, and the way she repeatedly ran her roughened palm up over her brow, she felt it wiser to ask nothing more. Tucking the mystery back into the recesses of her mind, she prepared her bath, hoping to one day understand the surreptitious burning of the bloodstained cloth.

Of course, Esma had her own reasons for burning the sheets, however none so lofty as Nisrina's innocent imaginings. Her intentions were simple—she relied heavily upon Nisrina's assistance in raising her four rambunctious sons. She depended on her help with the daily chores of farming life, with the cooking and cleaning. She marveled at the courage and ease in which the young girl learned new tasks, and she didn't want to lose her.

She'd just recently taught Nisrina to twist the neck of a chicken and meticulously pluck the feathers from its body. She showed her how to cut the fowl into manageable pieces for cooking over the fire, and noted how Nisrina held the knife lightly between her fingers, carefully removing the tough, outer membranes without piercing its tender flesh.

Her stepdaughter's coming-of-age was something she'd dreaded for years and she couldn't risk letting her husband see the evidence. Esma knew only too well that Nisrina had been her father's curse since the day she was born, reminding him daily of the wife he once loved and lost. And now, Esma, not much older than Nisrina herself, beset and overwrought with the responsibilities of four young children, a farm, and a demanding husband, dreaded the outcome this news would bring. No, she did not want her husband to know of his daughter's transition into womanhood. It simply would not do. She was not ready to lose the help and companionship of the girl. Not now. Not this soon.

TWO

A Visitor

THE TALL, STATELY WOMAN returned the demitasse cup to its delicate saucer. Dressed in curious attire, a woolen suit buttoned up tight around her neck, her purse tucked neatly in at her side, she patted her lips with the handkerchief she held loosely in the palm of her left hand.

Smiling graciously, she thanked her hostess for the Turkish coffee, "*Salaam adaykee,*" she blessed her hands in Arabic. "I've never tasted such delicious coffee."

Thankful for the coolness of the stone block house that provided a respite from the searing Mediterranean heat, Mrs. Arden, sitting upright and proper, studied the wife of Isa Huniah as she busied herself in the kitchen. It was really a large one-room house, and like so many of the simple homes in the village, the "rooms" existed merely by virtue of the placement of furniture: a table here, a sofa there, partitioning each section into small enclaves. Most homes, built without heat or running water, housed a crude fireplace, an area carved out in the wall with a thick stone hearth, the huge blocks stacked so closely together that when finished, the stonemason, who took great pride in his work, would boast how no man could slip even the thinnest of blades between two blocks.

The indoor fire was used to heat the room or cook a light meal. However, for the daily task of baking bread, the village women preferred the *taboon*, an outdoor oven centered amongst a cluster of homes. The *taboon*, commonly shared by several families, was a favorite gathering spot for the isolated village women. Made of dirt and straw, its dome shaped structure offered a small vent at the top by which steam could escape. And as the steam escaped from the top of the *taboon*, it also escaped from the mouths of frustrated wives and mothers as they'd meet to gossip and share their private thoughts. They'd fire up the inside of the ovens two or three times a day, fueling them with animal dung or olive remnants, peels and seeds left behind after pressing the rich, fragrant oil from the fruit. Then they'd gather around chattering and spouting, laughing and clucking, as they watched their flat, round loaves bake to a rich golden brown, the bread finally taking the shape of miniature mounds and valleys as it cooked atop small, smooth stones brought up from the river bed.

But now with a guest in her home, Esma Huniah could not run out to the *taboon* on the premise of needing a fresh batch of bread. The news of her visitor would have to wait. For the time being she remained in her kitchen stooped over her indoor hearth, tending to her caller's needs. As the fire in her kitchen burned, its heat rose up and swirled around her face, giving a flush to her plumpy, round cheeks. She was preparing another pot of *kahweh Arabiyah* for the tidy lady. Stirring the thick Turkish-style coffee in its small copper vessel, she minded it carefully, nestling it deeply into the red, hot coals; and as the liquid began to rise to the brim, just before it boiled over, she would quickly lift the pot from the fire until the bubbles calmed and subsided. She watched it boil and simmer three times over, lifting and replacing the hot *ibrik* the way her mother had taught her to do and the way she, in turn, would soon teach her stepdaughter.

Mrs. Arden observed how very young her hostess was. She admired her long, flowing *thobe*, the caftan-style dress meticulously embroidered with scenes of the countryside, minute pictorials of trees and plants that represented her village. Over the dress she wore a simple, white apron which she'd often grab to dry her hands. The guest noticed every detail and she surmised that the peasant woman's simple garb, clearly hand sewn, must have been made before she'd given birth to her children. She saw how the fabric bunched and pulled as it struggled over her enlarged bosom, and how it stretched tightly over her upper arms, the threads fraught at the seams.

Esma was unaware of her guest's scrutiny. Her kitchen was her palette, her coffee her art. Chatting away, she pinched a cardamom pod firmly between her two fingers until it cracked, then dropped it into the boiling coffee grounds at just the precise moment, allowing the aromatic spice to merge with the dark, thick liquid, pulling its essence from the seed slowly and gently to avoid any bitterness.

As the rich scents of coffee and cardamom drifted through the room, Mrs. Arden observed how the cheeks of the young woman's face puffed and deflated with each word she spoke. And when Esma would occasionally stop and smile at the prim and proper spinster who watched her through her spectacles, the strange lady took note that her hostess' smile was both genuine and endearing.

The Quaker woman had, in fact, been dreading this visit for some time. She'd heard that the man of the house, Isa Huniah, could, on occasion, be most unreasonable. A bit wild and unpredictable, they warned her, given rise to a volatile nature and quick temper that could possibly be attributed to the many hardships he'd suffered over the years.

But now, as she sat sipping her second cup of freshly brewed coffee and enjoying the warm generosity of a Middle Eastern kitchen, she slowly began to relax.

In her well disciplined hospitality, Esma Huniah offered her visitor another serving of fruit. Holding the basket in front of her guest, she insisted that she make another selection, a fig or pomegranate perhaps? Mrs. Arden stared at the huge bowl overflowing with pomegranates, apples, figs and oranges. She eyed the walnuts and dates scattered randomly between the fruit, and her mouth watered a bit, but she held up her hands, shaking her head in respectful protest.

With a big toothy smile and several uncomfortable chuckles she enthusiastically declined the offer. Thanking her host profusely, she explained that the sweet grapes, picked fresh from their vines, and the repeated servings of *ma'mool*, the date-filled butter cookies sprinkled lightly with powdered sugar that she'd just moments ago consumed, were more than her appetite could bear, and now, stuffed to the brim she couldn't possibly eat another bite. No. No. Not another bite. She thanked the kindly woman who stood before her for her generous hospitality and blessed her hands repeatedly in her finest and most formal Arabic.

Esma Huniah, after several attempts to encourage her guest to eat more, finally and a bit begrudgingly, acquiesced to her refusal. Making a disapproving sound from a place deep within her throat, not quite a grunt and not quite a hum, she returned the bowl to the center of the table. Then, wiping her hands with the towel draped loosely over her shoulder, she reluctantly sat down on the chair in the center of the room, a hard wooden piece that forced her to sit upright, her esteemed visitor seated comfortably on the soft velvet sofa adjacent.

Tilting her head to one side, Esma smoothed out her skirt and patted the bun at the nape of her neck, half-hoping her husband would walk in and half-hoping he wouldn't. She could hear her stepdaughter, Nisrina, just outside in the garden, hanging the wash and chastising her young half-brothers, a roguish lot that had more energy between them than the rays of sun that endeavored to dry her wet clothes.

Nisrina had always been a quiet girl, never giving Esma any trouble, obedient and demure. Still, Esma worried for her. She knew her husband had never forgiven his daughter for causing the death of his beloved Tahirah, and in her estimation, the harsh indifference with which he treated the child was far worse than the occasional beatings she herself endured under his roof. Although she'd never met his first wife, the villagers whispered of how the child so resembled her mother. The large obsidian eyes cast deep within her alabaster skin forever haunted her father, a reminder of the heartache that devoured them both.

But today the attentions of Isa Huniah's wife were elsewhere. The American lady, who sat so dignified in Esma's sitting room, her skirt to the floor, her knees pressed tightly together, had originally introduced herself as one of the Directors of the Religious Society of Friends, a group of American Quakers who were opening schools throughout the region. And only now, after partaking in coffee, refreshments, and general conversation, did she mention that in an effort to encourage the education of young girls in the Holy Land, she was going from home to home, through the rural villages found scattered amongst the hills and valleys of the Jordan River, meeting with families, discussing their curriculum, soliciting, and encouraging parents to send their daughters to the renowned GBSCR, the Girl's Boarding School for Cultivation and Readiness, that had opened two years earlier in the northernmost village of Dar el Qamar.

"I understand you have a daughter," Mrs. Arden finally added, sniffing gently into her handkerchief. She stated it in such a spontaneous, matter-of-fact manner, as if it were merely an afterthought and hardly the main purpose of her visit, the conversation hovering delicately between the weather and the abundance of fruit in this year's crop. Of course, the two women had briefly discussed Esma's sons and how the eldest had just begun his primary education at the Friends Boys School in Beit el Jebel, the other boys possibly to follow when they were older. They'd also talked about the baking of bread and the making of stew, the spices and oils that Esma preferred to use to give them just the right flavor. But never had she expected to discuss Nisrina with this stranger, the impropriety disturbing.

Esma sat frozen in her chair not knowing what to say. She was gravely concerned by the matron's remark. Nisrina was a girl—too young to be married, but too old to play loosely in the streets with the other children. She'd hoped that this was just a social call from the dignified Quaker woman, but, if she'd been honest with herself, she would have had to admit that she was a bit concerned when she learned that her visitor was from the Religious Society of Friends. Not for reasons of faith, for they were a fine group of Christian people; no, it was more of a vague feeling, perhaps it was because she knew that they were known for their steadfast commitment to the field of education, a concept that the Huniah family did not wholeheartedly embrace, and especially not for women.

Mrs. Arden had casually shown up around mid-morning, walking past the gate that led to the Huniah compound and right up to the front door where Esma had been working—washing windows and cleaning the stone threshold. She'd greeted Esma with "*sabah el kheer*," a pleasant good morning, followed by a sincere "how-do-you-do?" She'd said that she was just passing through, visiting many families in the community and could she stop for a chat?

Esma was taken by surprise. Occupied by canning and fruiting, she'd not been to the *taboon* to bake bread for several days and had not heard of the Quaker woman's visitations. Nevertheless, in keeping with the customs of her village, she welcomed the stranger into her home with the gracious hospitality befitting a queen. Her thoughts concerned only with whether she had a sufficient amount of coffee ground fine that day and if she had enough *ma'mool* left in the canister to serve.

And now, the woman's candid declaration of the purpose for her visit, followed by her question regarding her husband's daughter, carried an intention that was not to the liking of the poor farmer's wife. What she'd wondered when she first saw the fine lady standing so upright, so self-assured on the path to her door, had now become quite clear.

Hearing the Director's words, Esma's eyes went wide, the smile on her face beginning to melt as if she were made of softly plied wax and the candle maker, in a moment of distraction (possibly an errant child or a farmer come to share the news of a watermelon that had grown twice its size) had absentmindedly abandoned her in front of a hot fire to waver and bend—melting and merging into a disjointed assemblage of facial features that no longer resembled the farmer's chubby wife.

Esma was sure of one thing—her husband out working in the vineyards, would not be pleased by this visit. He'd already woken tense that morning, plagued by an unusually large infestation of wasps threatening to devour his crops, the insects singling out his sweetest, ripest grapes to satisfy their voracious appetites. And now, as her visitor raised the subject of his young daughter, she was convinced that it was for the best that he was not present.

The farmer's wife tried to smile, to continue the pretense of enjoying her company, but the grand lady had stepped over the boundaries of protocol. Esma knew what would come next and she dreaded the discourse, for she was only too well aware of her husband's position on the subject. Education for women? Whatever for? Their sons, yes, of course, sure, why not? One day they might all go to school, the oldest already attending the boy's school sponsored by the Quakers. But Nisrina? No. That was not an option. He was vehemently against it. Her husband's words consistently reflecting those she'd heard from her father—"Schooling for girls? Absolutely not! It can only have one result and that is to bring grave discord to the family." She could see her father's face getting red, his eyes puffing out, "No man wants a woman who's too smart. All she needs to know is how to cook and clean, to darn and sew, and most importantly," he would shake his forefinger in front of his face, "to obey her husband at all times! A woman's purpose in this world is to make a man comfortable and to give him many sons!"

At just that moment, while Esma Huniah wrestled with her thoughts, deciding which words she'd choose to dissuade further discussion on the subject, her husband burst into the room with the fury of a man on fire. Obscenities were pouring from his mouth, his shirt sleeve torn wide open. Screaming at the top of his lungs, he held his arm up high and extended like a red hot iron. Trailing three steps behind him was Nisrina trying to calm him, followed by her four younger half-brothers who were jumping wildly about, whooping and hollering and swishing imaginary swords. Each one proclaiming that they would have sliced the wasps in two had they attempted an invasion of one of their limbs. With raised voices they argued as to who would be the bravest in slaying the insects that had so viciously attacked their father.

As they exploded into the room, the Quaker woman jumped to her feet, knocking over a vase full of lilies that had been carefully placed on the table beside her. Clutching her purse to her breasts, she looked on in horror, the circus parading frantically before her.

Esma, realizing the severity of the situation, immediately ran to the kitchen. Grabbing a clay bowl from the shelf, she bent over, dipping it into a large vat of vinegar she kept tucked under the counter. She proceeded to pour the acetic liquid over her husband's swollen arm, his bellows still piercing her ears. But his angst was too great—brutally he brushed her aside, knocking her to the floor where she slammed hard into the wall alongside a basket of ripened tomatoes. Unaware of her circumstance, he plunged his aching arm into the barrel of vinegar. There he kept it, drowned and secluded while his howlings and vulgarisms unabashedly continued.

As the pain of the venomous bites slowly subsided, he at last settled down, his disjointed murmurings cloaked by the slush of the soak. Esma, Nisrina, the four boys, and the Quaker woman breathed a collective sigh of relief. Even Ashtart, the calico cat who'd wandered in through the doorway and taken cover between the soft folds of the sofa, began to ceremoniously lick her left paw, a reminder that she, too, could use some attention. When Isa Huniah finally pulled his arm from the vat, still swollen and red, Esma tenderly wrapped it with rags soaked in vinegar.

It wasn't until he'd been seated in his favorite chair, his feet elevated on a three-legged stool and a cup of Turkish coffee in front of him, his bandaged limb lying gingerly on the armrest, that he finally noticed the visitor who was now standing quietly in the far corner of the room.

"*Mashallah!*" He exclaimed as he saw the upright lady standing so poised and so patient. "Please accept my humblest apologies. I didn't know that we were honored with such an esteemed visitor." He could tell by her dress and her stature that she was a foreigner and most likely one of high standing in the community. "Please excuse my harsh words dear lady, but as you can see, I have been unjustly accosted by varmints in my own garden." He waved at his wounds with his good arm in an attempt to explain what was now quite obvious to all in the room.

"Nisrina," Esma directed, her voice serious, her smile insincere, "please, take the boys outside. Your father and I need to speak with our visitor."

Nisrina looked at her stepmother and then at the Quaker woman. She noticed how well dressed the stranger was, very modern and western in her styling, yet still she carried herself with humility and grace. She admired the confidence the woman exuded as she stood there so calmly, so strongly in front of her father, and she pondered the purpose of her visit to their home. But one glance at her father's face and she knew she mustn't hesitate. Obediently, she herded the boys outside, leaving through the back door which she softly closed behind her. Perhaps too softly, leaving it ajar just a bit, just in case.

"Isa," Esma began, addressing her husband, "Allow me to introduce you to our visitor. This is Mrs. Arden, she is a Director from the Religious Society of Friends, and she has come on behalf of the Girl's Boarding School for Cultivation and Readiness, the one in Dar el Qamar."

Isa Huniah's eyes narrowed. The smile with which he'd greeted the stately lady, now gone from his face.

"She has asked about Nisrina," his wife whispered softly, knowing there was no need for further words.

"I see," Isa Huniah said looking away. "And what exactly are your intentions in inquiring about my daughter? Do you have a betrothal in mind for her? If so, then I'm sorry to disappoint you, but my daughter is only fourteen and has not yet come of age."

He bent down and took a long, slow sip from his cup, the inhale echoing hard against the soundless room.

Mrs. Arden responded in a quiet voice, calm and considered. She enunciated each word clearly, her Arabic precise, poetic, "Firstly and most importantly, Mr. Huniah, I would like to thank you and Mrs. Huniah for your most gracious hospitality. I am happy to be in your beautiful home and honored to sit with you and your kind wife; my thanks and blessings of peace are extended to you and your family." She paused, as they nodded their appreciation, their heads tilted graciously to one side. "But more specifically, I am here to talk about your daughter, Nisrina, who I believe would benefit greatly from what we have to offer at the Girl's Boarding School for Cultivation and Readiness." Smiling broadly, she added, "We have an excellent program." She articulated the word *program* in such a way as to give it special significance. "I was hoping that I could persuade you to allow her to enroll in our school. I assure you that it is of the highest quality, attended by daughters from some of the finest families . . ."

Isa Huniah did not let her finish. He interrupted, waving his good arm towards her in a dismissive manner. "Madam," he began, "Thank you for coming to our home. We are honored to entertain such an esteemed guest in our sitting room." Now it was Mrs. Arden's turn to smile and nod her assent. "However, we are *fellaheen*. Simple country farmers. And Nisrina is an essential part of our household. Esma needs her help in the kitchen, and the boys, God bless them, they are quite a handful for my young wife." He puffed up his chest, clearly proud of his progeny and his ability to have sired such prolific offspring. "And there is me, too, you see. I need Nisrina's help in the fields. There are fruits to pick and much soil to turn. No. Schooling is only proper for boys, dear lady. Only for boys," he attempted a smile, a sickened look enshrouding his face.

"But Mr. Huniah, my dear sir, let me explain . . ."

"No, no." Looking down at his lap, he again gestured dismissively, as if he could just shoo the director away like a troublesome fly. "There will be no schooling for Nisrina. Not for a girl. She gets all the education she needs right here at home, cooking and sewing and cleaning. Right here with her stepmother and me." He patted his wife's hand, smiling condescendingly in her direction.

"But, she is such a bright girl," Mrs. Arden interjected. "It would be a shame not to cultivate that gift."

"The simple truth, dear lady," he went on, "is that we are a poor family. We can barely meet the expenses of sending our eldest son, Josef, to one of your schools, much less our daughter. And as you know, he is not my only son. I have four. Four sons!" His chest puffed up again as he held his head high, sniffing in deeply through his nose. "I have three more spirited boys following right behind Josef, clever young lads that we also hope to send to your school one day. But Nisrina? No. Out of the question." He looked away, his gaze resting in a spot outside the window.

"Yes, I understand," replied Mrs. Arden nodding, "I understand. And we've come prepared for those who cannot afford our school. You see we have scholarships." She rounded her mouth as she said the word *scholarships* to give it special emphasis, implying that she had the solution that would make all the difference, something that would instantly change the farmer's position on the subject. "We have heard high words about your Nisrina, sir," she continued, "We've heard that she is very bright, and our school is prepared to make special considerations, an unprecedented opportunity, I might add. We have available a scholarship that would cover all costs: her education, her room, and her board at our facility."

Mrs. Arden smiled, quite pleased with herself. How could they resist such a proposition?

"I see," said Isa Huniah. He took another slow sip from his coffee, appearing thoughtful, as if he were allowing for the proposal that this Quaker woman so boldly placed before him.

Esma began to fidget in her chair. Would her husband actually consider approving this venture? Was he so taken by the offer that he would resign from all he believed? The position of women that he'd always held sacred? She'd heard nothing less since the day she was born. Esma scratched her head and looked out the window at the orchards and vineyards of the Huniah farm. She saw the tattered fencing and weakened groves, the fig trees grown wild and unpruned for years. Her husband refused to hire help, insisting he trusted no one; and her days were consumed in her home and her vegetable garden, ensuring enough food to feed her growing family. She saw her sons through the window, running wildly in the yard. Josef was carrying a large stone, threatening to throw it at his younger brother. How would she cope without Nisrina?

She held her breath as her husband slowly replaced his fragile cup on its saucer.

Finally, he looked up, his eyes skewed in a monstrous way. Relinquishing all pretext of civility, Isa Huniah spoke frankly to the Quaker woman, "I'm sorry to disappoint you, Madam. But you must understand that no daughter of mine will ever leave this home until the day her husband takes her, and even then, only after a substantial dowry has been paid!"

Rising, he held out his hand in a sweeping gesture, and, as if by command, the American woman also rose to her feet, her worried eyes following the direction of his outstretched arm.

He promptly escorted Mrs. Arden to the gate of his compound, "Please, come again anytime, our door is always open." He now spoke softly, pleasantly, as if all was well and they'd just finished a cordial visit.

Pausing one more time, he turned to face her, his timber reversed, his finger pointing up to the heavens, "However, you must understand, this subject that you have opened in my home today—it is forever closed. Not to be raised again. And quite frankly, if you don't mind my saying so, I do not appreciate your putting such high-minded ideas into my young daughter's head, not now, not ever. Do I make myself clear?" His eyes stared into her brain with a merciless glare.

Mrs. Arden was not intimidated. She fiercely looked back at her contender. Her eyes were moist, reddened with fury; the desperation in her face exceeded only by her grave disappointment. Determined, she willed herself to speak, to try one more time to convince the stubborn farmer to reconsider his daughter's fate, "But, Mr. Huniah, you don't understand. Things are different for women now. Think of her future. You are doing your daughter a grave disservice . . ."

She was not allowed to complete her thoughts, as the large iron gates through which she'd just passed, closed with a clang only inches from her face.

THREE

Lost Dreams

IN THE GARDEN, NISRINA stood beneath the canopy of an enormous bougainvillea. The one planted the day her mother joyfully whispered in her father's ear that a child was growing inside her womb. At the time it was a small bush, its limbs short, the trunk frail and bent, but the blooms were a glorious shade that blanketed the branches in a glistening burst of crimson color. It delighted his wife, the smile on her face causing the sun to rise in the eastern sky.

Isa Huniah, his heart on fire by the news of a child, a son, no doubt, wanted more than anything else to please his pregnant wife. So he lovingly planted it outside the back door for her to enjoy as she worked in her garden. And now, years later, its branches had grown thrice their size as they twisted and turned, wrapping themselves around the wooden arbor that he'd so painstakingly built in its honor, the never-ending blossoms bursting in a stunning explosion of scarlet hues.

As a young girl, Nisrina had wondered why her father, in his rage and despair had not ripped out the bougainvillea when her mother had died, only to find out that he indeed did try.

Her grandmother told her the tale of how screaming and blaring, he grabbed the sorry plant by its tender base and pulled it and tugged it with all his might, cursing the sharp pointy thorns that pierced and bloodied his hands. Then, throwing the branches and blooms alongside the house to wither and die, he turned his back on the pitiful sight, vowing that such frivolities would never occupy his time again. But by miracle or fate, no one knew why, the plant took root once again, growing back thicker and stronger than ever before.

The old women of the village, shaking their heads and wagging their long, crooked fingers in front of their faces, warned him of the vengeance of the evil eye, telling him that it was surely a sign from the heavens of which he must cautiously take heed. Perhaps the spirit of his poor wife lived on through its beauty, taking residence nearby to watch over the daughter she'd so heartbreakingly abandoned. So with reluctance and dread, he allowed the plant to stay, giving it neither notice nor nurture, and mockingly it continued to grow. He finally acquiesced to its existence, but turned his head when he passed through the door, shunning its brilliant beauty from his eyes.

Now, standing in the shelter of this grand plant, close to the door left ajar, Nisrina felt a quiver run down her spine. As she stood with her head bent, watching a trail of ants carry bits and pieces of a dried, dead spider off to their lair, she heard her father's voice, "No. There will be no schooling for Nisrina. Not for a girl. No. No."

The splintering words pierced her brain, shattering wide into a kaleidoscope of colors. She closed her eyes, the blinding glare of the sun reflecting harsh off the white stone walls, the birds chirping wildly in the branches behind her. Her ears filled with a sudden, deafening rush as a mighty wave pulled her far, far, out to sea.

She steadied herself against the arbor's hard, round pillars, her thoughts racing back to only two days earlier when her best friend, Lamia Saleema, a girl, one year younger than herself, and from a neighboring farm, had breathlessly come running up the path to her home.

"Nisrina! Nisrina!" Lamia called out to her, scurrying through the gate. "I have such news! I have such news!"

Nisrina, hearing the shouts, ran out to greet her good friend, "What, pray tell? What is it Lamia that you should come to my father's house without your headscarf on and your hair left loose!"

Lamia carelessly threw her head back and laughed, a loud hearty sound, the sun reflecting gaily on her teeth, her unshorn hair sparkling brightly under the ray's light.

"I have such news!" She repeated again, trying to catch her breath.

The moist sweat was dripping from her brow and down the sides of her enlivened face, beads forming on her upper lip. She mindlessly wiped them away with the back of her hand.

"It's the lady, Nisrina! The lady from the Friends school . . . the Quaker woman . . . she has invited me to be a student in her classroom, the one in Dar el Qamar!"

Lamia, dancing on her tiptoes, had grabbed both Nisrina's hands in her own, "God willing! And the best news . . . the best news my dear friend, is that my father has agreed! He is sending me to *madrasa*, to school! To learn to read and write! I have been awarded a scholarship! A scholarship, Nisrina! I am going to Dar el Qamar, to a boarding school especially for girls!!"

Lamia began jumping up and down, taking Nisrina into the air and back again.

"*Mashallah*! This is wonderful news, *ya* Lamia! I am so happy for you!"

Nisrina was truly delighted for her friend and a bit curious as to how such great fortune had come her way. "How did this come about? You must have shown such promise, perhaps in church, during your recitations? No?"

"I don't know, Nisrina. I'm not sure, but, I was thinking, maybe you too . . . maybe the grand lady from the Society of Friends will come and speak with your father, *Enshallah. Enshallah* we shall go as two sisters seeking knowledge of the world! Would that not be a wonderful thing?"

"Oh, yes," Nisrina replied trying hard not to get her hopes up, but failing miserably at it, "That would be wonderful, indeed!"

The two girls were giggling, their hands covering their mouths. They began dancing around in circles, their bare feet leaving patterned imprints in the soft, dry dirt. They sang songs, words they'd invented about their journey to the girls' school and what grand women they would become.

Lamia had a wide, round face that seemed to sit directly atop her chest. When she turned her head it was always in concert with her shoulders as if God, in all His greatness, had been quite busy the day He created her and in His haste had failed to give her a neck. Her torso was thick, her arms and legs short, which resulted in a squatty appearance as she moved about. But what Lamia lacked in grace and form, she more than made up in an earnest and kind disposition.

Nisrina envied how Lamia so closely resembled her mother—the way they both laughed loudly from a place deep within their bellies, their mouths opened wide, showing all their teeth.

Her heart ached as she wondered if perhaps she, too, bore a resemblance to her mother, the lovely lady she'd only heard tales about. Then Nisrina would recall her grandmother's words whispered in her ear late at night—a kindly voice, softly reminding her that she looked more and more like her dear mother with each passing day.

Lamia was like a sister to Nisrina. Their two families shared a *taboon* and their mothers loved to gossip about the comings and goings of the townspeople while they waited for their breads to bake. The two girls would sit quietly alongside the older women, listening to their stories and learning life's lessons from the tales they told. At times they'd sneak off and tell stories of their own. With youthful enthusiasm, they discussed their hopes for the future— wondering who they might marry and how many children they'd have. Nisrina wanted four children and a husband who would treat her kindly, while Lamia declared she would have no fewer than six, and her husband had better beware if he dared to look at her askance.

Lamia was often sent to Nisrina's house with baskets full of lemons or apricots, her family's trees often producing more than they could eat, preserve or sell. And in turn, Nisrina carried grapes and figs to Lamia's house, lingering a while to enjoy her friend's company and to help with chores as they chatted non-stop.

They'd talk about the predictions of the old seers, the ladies who would open fortunes by reading the dark tapestry of coffee grounds left on the sides of an overturned cup—the breath of the drinker transferring its essence into the small demitasse, casting a spell and creating a pattern with a story to tell.

Although too young to have their fortunes read, Nisrina and Lamia would sit, huddled close together on the edge of the women's circle, watching and listening as the women were told of great things to come: opportunities for travel, or a visit from a mysterious stranger; sometimes unexpected funds might be coming their way, or a child lay growing in a young wife's womb. When it came time to have their cups read, the single women would lean in with bated breath, anxious to hear if a winsome suitor might be in their future.

The seer, calling out her predictions from the lacy pattern lying deep within the cup would say to them, "Look here . . . I see a man with a long beard and a beautiful mustache. Do you see?"

She'd point a crusty finger, hovering it lightly over the edge, "He's wearing a fez hat, right there . . . can you see him? Here is his torso. He has long arms and strong legs. I'm sure of it. And here is a camel, he's riding in on a great beast!"

Nisrina and Lamia would giggle, exchanging glances as they'd watch the optimistic spinster lean in closer, her head finally colliding with the seer's; her eyes straining to see the mysterious figure in the cup who might one day be her husband.

If God is merciful, he will be a kind and prosperous man, the hopeful one would think to herself, but to the others, she'd only blush and whisper demurely, "*Enshallah*, God willing."

But now with the hot sun beating down on her back, Nisrina was glad that Lamia was not there to hear her father's words, or to see how he so swiftly and rudely escorted the Quaker lady out of his home. She was even relieved that her four half-brothers had run off through the trees in pursuit of Ashtart, the feline that so protectively patrolled their orchard. She could hear them yelling and laughing in the distance as she continued to watch the lone trail of ants on their journey with the spider.

She recalled every word that Lamia had spoken that day—the day she came to her home with her breathless news. Nisrina envied the look on her young friend's face, so animated and thrilled. With such unleashed elation, she'd not taken the time to replace the scarf that'd blown from her head, and instead left it strewn on the road below.

She could see in her mind's eye how they had danced around and around at the thought of pursuing an education together and she could still hear the light-heartedness of their joyful laughter.

As she remembered these things, Nisrina debated whether she would tell Lamia about the prim and proper lady who had come to her home. The visitor who had sat so upright and sure in her father's sitting room and had so eloquently spoken words of high-minded encouragement. And she wondered whether she could find the strength to confess to her friend that they would not be colleagues traveling to Dar el Qamar after all; and that their dream of being two sisters-in-spirit seeking an education was simply not meant to be.

FOUR

Holy Communion

DESPITE WHAT HE'D TOLD the Quaker woman, Isa Huniah had been anxiously awaiting the change in his daughter. Fourteen years had passed since the tragic day that Tahirah, his first wife, lay bleeding in his orchard. But his memory was fresh, as if it had happened only the day before.

He'd been working quietly, calmly, on the far mound near the end of the road, clipping the season's last fruit, making plans for the future. The most easterly vineyard that stretched on the rise needed rest, and he'd hoped to expand the old farm, move it farther out, past the stone fence onto near, rocky slopes. He envisioned a son working close by his side and his chest burst with pride—the boy would be strong, with his mother's sweet smile and his father's sharp wit.

Then he heard the scream, Tahirah's voice calling out, frantically pleading for him to come. He dropped his knife and ran hard down the hill. Through the brushes he chased, sliding fast past the trees. He'd ventured too far east and now had to wind his way back to the sound of her cries. With legs fired hot, his chest aching for air, he struggled to reach her in time.

But it was too late. She lay there motionless, surrounded by blood. Her eyes opened wide, staring up at the heavens. She'd given birth to a daughter who'd cost her her life, the beetles and flies invading the torn placenta which lay half within her and half outside.

Isa blamed not himself for Tahirah's demise. He failed to consider that his wife should not have climbed the hill that day to work in his orchard. He refused to believe that he ought to have seen the signs of impending birth and call for the midwife. No, it was much easier to curse the child who lay helplessly between the grasses and jasmine growing wild beneath the tree.

Be it from guilt or propriety, no one knew why, but Isa Huniah reluctantly agreed to keep the female child, his face cold and distant at the sound of her cries. His body tensing when he saw her smile.

The ancient women of the village, who remembered the past, claimed that Tahirah Zabaki was, in fact, not Isa's first love—that there'd been another sweet thing long before her. No one knew the girl's name or the family of her birth, but they whispered that when, as a young boy, he had come home all bloodied and bruised, he could be heard cursing the man who gave him the beating, swearing to one day seek his revenge. When his father, whose vision was fading, had asked him the whereabouts of his earnings and the fruit cart he'd taken to market that morn, the boy released a glare that could only have come from the devil himself, sending a shiver through the old man's spine, so depleting and vile, that he never broached the subject again. And by the time Isa had finally met Tahirah, even the old ladies with flapping tongues had quieted their chatter, burying the dubious story deep in their minds.

After Tahirah died Isa took a new wife, Selwa, who too, died in childbirth. Their son tragically stillborn. And when the midwife handed him the lifeless boy, so silent and pale, Isa Huniah fell to his knees unleashing a sound so violent and base, its tremors shook the very foundation of heaven. Howling wild like the jackals that crept amongst the fettered brambles and pointed boulders of the dark, cold night, the son he'd always wanted was taken before he could feel the warmth of his soft, sweet breath.

The days and weeks that followed were dark and dreamlike in the Huniah household. Drinking and carousing late into the night, Isa remained in town, storming and screaming. Such fury and pain was expelled on the world, until the sun itself took fear to rise.

His young daughter, watched over by her grandmother, remained anxiously quiet in her small wooden chair, her face pressed up tight against the shutterless window, her eyes ever hopeful. There she'd stay for hours on end, waiting and wondering. Having lost a second mother, she worried that her father might never return, and as she waited and watched her eyes grew sadder and wiser.

Then, as the pain of his losses had softened, Isa Huniah met Esma—a strong, young woman of sturdy stock who came from a neighboring village. It was a warm summer's day and his yearnings were high. She was plain and simple, sporting an ample bosom that quickly caught his eye while visiting a purveyor of farming supplies.

Unaware of the gossip surrounding his past, Esma's family consented to their marriage, and in the four short years that followed, Esma gave him four healthy sons. Isa Huniah at last, could hold his head high and walk proudly through the town. The outrageous rumors of a torrid past and vengeful retributions finally put to rest.

And now, with his daughter past her fourteenth year, he was watching and waiting. He'd noticed along with the other men of the village that Nisrina was becoming a beautiful young woman, her body growing round and full; and he knew that she would bring a good price, a strong dowry in her marriage. He was aware that if a girl had passed her prime she would have difficulty finding a suitable husband and the people would talk and whisper of the whys and whats of her virtue, bringing much shame and discomfort to the family. Upon confirmation of her womanhood, Isa Huniah was prepared to act.

Esma and Nisrina's secret did not stay hidden for long.

In the Spring, on the Day of the Lord's Rising, the Huniah family sat in the back of the Syrian Orthodox Church, their heads solemnly bowed in prayer, the melodic tones of Gregorian chants filling the chamber.

It was time for Holy Communion and two bearded priests standing straight and poised in front of a golden altar, signaled to the congregation. In unison the worshippers rose to their feet.

Dressed in his finest white gown, laced with glittering braids and sacred embellishments, the first priest raised a basket of bread to the heavens as he called out to his flock, "Take, eat. This is My Body, which is broken for you unto the remission of sins."

The second priest followed. Holding a large brass chalice filled with rich red wine, he lifted it high up over his head, "Drink of it, all of you. This is My Blood of the New Testament, which is shed for you and for many, for the remission of sins." Their voices rang out with blessings and prayers until the bread and wine within the basket and vessel, were infused by the Holy Spirit, becoming the body and blood of Christ himself.

As the congregation proceeded to the altar to receive Holy Communion, Isa Huniah noticed his daughter still seated on the pew. Furrowing his brow, he motioned for her to come quickly and join the rest of the family. He'd been up all night nursing a sick, old ewe, his patience worn thin. He had no time for disobedience, particularly not in the church.

Esma saw her husband's displeasure and she knew she could hold back the truth no longer. She'd already risked his rage by keeping his daughter's secret for as long as she had. They were in the house of the Lord. The time had come.

It was well known that a woman in her time of menses could not, by the laws of the Orthodox Church, take the sacrament of Holy Communion. Their faith held that a woman's flow is a representation of the fallen nature of mankind and in that state, could not take into herself the sacred body and blood of the Lord Jesus Christ.

Esma reached out, gently touching Isa's arm. He turned and looked at her, studying his wife's silent gaze. She lowered her eyes, quietly shaking her head.

Like a fox on the hunt, he turned back towards his daughter. His senses were enlivened, his hair stood on end. He sniffed the air, the smell of incense pervaded the room, but that was not the odor he was seeking.

He sniffed again, his nostrils flaring wide.

The scent was unmistakable, how had he not noticed it before?

Finally, he thought to himself. Finally he smelled the change in his blossoming daughter. His mouth curled up, his eyes on fire—at long last his broken heart would be vindicated.

As the entire congregation witnessed Nisrina Huniah seated alone on the wooden bench, her family marching proudly to the communion altar without her, their mouths fell open, their eyebrows lifting high to the tops of their heads. They began to whisper and murmur, the sounds of the throng echoing loudly over the strong Gregorian chants.

But Nisrina refused to acknowledge the commotion. With flushed cheeks, her eyes remained fixed on her hands folded neatly in her lap, while the sound of her grinding jaw rumbled deep in her ears blotting out the roar that now filled the chamber.

Isa Huniah wasted no time. Finally able to respond to the many inquiries he'd received over the years, he moved swiftly and decisively spreading word through the village. His daughter was comely and had caught the eye of more than one suitor. And now as the news passed from farm to farm, they came to pay their respects—the highest bidder, the wealthiest family winning the hand of the young maiden.

FIVE

Betrothal

FROM THE FIRST TIME he'd seen her, he was smitten by her beauty and grace.

She was delicate, with a hint of mystery. Her dark hair, peeking out from under her headscarf contrasted with her milky white skin. Most women from the village were *samarra*, born dark complected and swarthy. But Nisrina was *baathah*, a girl of light complexion, a rare feature for a daughter of Arab descent. A trait she'd inherited from her mother whose family had migrated from the northern hills of Syria, finally settling in the verdant landscape near Beit el Jebel. It was a quality that bewitched and intrigued the young man.

He saw her in church, a young girl staying close by her stepmother's side. He watched how she patiently cared for her four half-brothers, the rambunctious boys squirming on the hard wooden pews. And although she always kept her dark, almond eyes cast downward in grace and humility, never daring to look up or gaze at the other parishioners for fear of seeming too brazen or bold, Jabran noticed her; and he promised himself that one day he would take her for his wife.

A gentle man with kind eyes, Jabran Yusef always approached life in a slow and thoughtful manner. The youngest son of the Yusef family, he worked in his family's orchards, his olive skin darkening to a deep tan, his hands stained from the richness of the fertile Mediterranean soil. He was handsome and tall, his stature bringing him much respect and admiration. Mothers found reason to bring their daughters across his path in hopes he would take notice, and fathers nodded respectfully when he entered a room. But despite the urgings and hopeful wishes, Jabran waited for the young Huniah girl to grow into a woman.

Nisrina was told to leave the room.

The elders of the Yusef family had come to her home to ask for her hand in marriage. An *itulab* was about to take place. Seeing her father's solemn expression, her heart started pounding, the blood draining from her face. She knew better than to ask any questions or speak her mind. With trembling hands, she reached for the door and stepped outside. She took no heed of the warm sun or the gentle Mediterranean breeze that greeted her. She didn't notice the children playing in the yard, nor did she hear their calls beckoning her to come join them. She simply turned, and with bare feet ran as fast as she could in the direction of the fig orchard. In no time at all, she found herself on the hillside where she'd been born so many years ago, and she sat down beneath the canopy of the giant fig tree where her mother had taken her last breaths.

There Nisrina waited, her hands wrapped tightly around her knees, her lower lip bleeding where she'd bitten down so hard. From that vantage point she could look through the trees, down to her small stone house. She saw the loquat tree that grew outside her bedroom window, so filled with the small round succulent fruit, that the branches hung heavy, nearly touching the ground; and she saw the jasmine vine that trailed along the western wall, now covered with tiny white blooms, the scent so sweet it sang to her each morning.

She watched and waited, clenching her teeth over and over as her thoughts raced wild.

Curious about the man who'd shown interest in her, her imaginings wandered to the future—to a home she'd never seen and a family she didn't know. She saw her husband and her children in her musings. He would be handsome and strong, she thought to herself. Loving and gentle. Wise and patient. A giant of a man in every respect. She envisioned her future home filled with joy and laughter, with orchards that stretched over the hills and into a valley, full and lush. She would have a garden of her own, where she'd grow tomatoes and zucchini, onions and eggplants. She closed her eyes as the visions danced their way through her hopeful innocence.

The clouds moved silently overhead as she woke from her musings. Her heart was racing; she'd heard voices trailing up from the courtyard. Hiding behind the trunk of the massive tree she looked down at the house. They were leaving. Several older men walked out the door bidding her father farewell. She saw them bow to one another, enthusiastically shaking hands, nodding and smiling. She noticed one man in particular, the largest of the three who was short and wide. He stood off to the side, his hands clasped tightly behind his back. She noticed how he rocked back and forth on his heels, and her father's furtive glances in his direction.

They left as suddenly as they'd arrived.

Finally, she heard her stepmother's voice calling her to come home.

Nisrina entered the darkened house, her eyes slowly adjusting from the bright sunlight. Her father was standing tall and proud near the center of the room, a triumphant look spread wide across his face. Her stepmother was gazing out the window, but when she heard the door open she turned her face away, disappearing into the shadows of the kitchen.

Isa Huniah motioned for Nisrina to come and sit on the ground before him. Like a fragile leaf, lifted and tossed by the eastern wind, she knelt down beside her father's sandaled feet. She studied his face, longing to reach up and wrap her arms around his shoulders and press her cheek against his chest. She ached to call out and tell him she loved him and beg his forgiveness for taking his wife. She wanted to say that she would gladly give up her own life if it would deliver Tahirah back to him. She wanted to plead with him, to ask him to hold her and to hear him say that he loved her in return. But she knew it was futile. Those were words he'd not tolerate, and things he'd not give. So her lips remained sealed and her eyes remained steady. Out of respect or fear, she wasn't sure which, she stayed silent. Waiting. Knowing that her father must be the first one to speak.

Looking straight ahead, his face void of expression, his massive arms crossed in front of his chest, Isa Huniah finally cleared his throat, "Nisrina," he began, "As you know, you are a woman now. Your body has told you that you are ready to bring forth children; you are finally able to honor a man and give him the greatest gift of all, the promise of a newborn son. But first, you must have a husband—someone who'll provide for you while you raise his children." He tapped his fingers restlessly on the arm of the sofa. "The time has come for your betrothal, and as such, I am proud to inform you that I have given you to the Yusef family of Beit el Jebel. As is our custom, their family will make the preparations for your wedding ceremony. You will be wed to their youngest son, Jabran Yusef ibn Farooz and you will go to live with him in the house he has built in his family's compound."

He paused for a moment as if thinking about his next words, then with a staccato voice he flatly stated, "Never. To. Return. To. This. House. Again." He was shaking his finger in front of his face, "Understood?"

Nisrina let out a small gasp, air suddenly seeming in short supply, her eyes were wide, her body trembling. Although she'd expected it—to actually hear her fate so decidedly, so coldly sealed, sent a shiver up her spine. She did not know this man who would become her husband, nor did she know any other member of the Yusef clan. Perhaps she'd passed him on the street once or twice near the village square, or maybe she'd stood beside him in the *souk*, the grocer serving his sister before finally turning to assist her. She did not know and would never ask.

Her father glanced down for a moment. His eyes were cold, his expression bland. He quickly returned his gaze to a spot that hovered just above her head, "The Yusef's are *fellaheen*, simple country people as we are, and therefore you should have no cause to develop any airs from this betrothal. They are a hard working family with successful orchards and you will be expected to work alongside them. You should be honored that they have come asking for you."

He paused again, his thoughts distant, his eyes glazed over. Finally he continued, "They have promised me a generous dowry in exchange for your hand, and this quite frankly, has pleased me." He sniffed inward, "Your stepmother will prepare you for your responsibilities—how to serve him and be a good wife."

He looked down at his daughter. Her gaze remained fixed on the red Persian carpet upon which she sat, and she stared at the rough, crusty toes of the man she called father. She could feel his eyes burning into the back of her head, but she dared not turn to face him.

She nodded her compliance.

He reached out and put his hand on the top of her head. But it was not the gentle touch she longed to feel. His grip was firm, unrelenting. He forced her face upward to his, "Remember Nisrina," he said, his voice menacing, his gaze piercing straight through her, "do not shame me."

She saw the look on his face, the hard cold line of his lips, and she shuddered beneath his grasp.

He said nothing more. His expression telling her the conversation was over.

Calling to his wife to bring him his water pipe and a fresh cup of *kahweh Arabiyah*, Isa Huniah rose to leave, to sit outside in the garden under the shade of his favorite olive tree. There he could relax and contemplate both his past and his future. He was pleased that his daughter would be living in the Yusef compound. The retribution so sweet, he thought to himself. Nisrina had taken the life of his first wife, her mere existence a daily reminder of his painful loss. She deserved the likes of the Yusef family, and they deserved her.

Nisrina watched him walk out the door. The room suddenly silent. The air tight and still.

Sitting alone on the rug at the foot of the sofa, she felt herself falling into a dark chasm—the molten floor opening up before her, the walls caving in.

She closed her eyes, squeezing them tightly with all her might.

Then pressing her face hard into the palms of her hands she prayed.

She prayed that the spinning would stop, the churning would calm. She pressed them again and again, harder and harder, until she could no longer feel the pain that seared through her soul. Perhaps it had not really happened, she thought to herself. Perhaps her father's words had been only a dream and she would soon awaken to find herself in the familiar warmth of her tattered old blankets, with the smell of coffee brewing strong in the kitchen.

But when she opened her eyes, she could no longer see. The glare of the far window blinded her, her tears blanketing her sight through a misty haze. The darkened room, once familiar and comforting, held only shadows and whispers of words now past. Her cheeks were wet, her breath uneven. Harbored by the ruins of her home, she turned towards the sofa and buried her face within its cushions, the soft velvet fabric caressing her skin.

The next day Esma took Nisrina into the courtyard; she needed assistance in grinding the wheat. Nisrina helped her stepmother carry the basket of grain to the milling stone where together they filled the large lower portion with handfuls of the golden beads. When sufficiently filled, Esma attached the small wooden lever into the hole of the upper stone, and with both her hands, began turning it round and round, the sound of the crushing wheat crackling and droning as the two stones flattened the grain for the coming week's meals.

Nisrina sat close to her stepmother. Esma was the only mother she'd truly known and although she understood that her loyalties were primarily to her four sons, Esma had always been kind to Nisrina. Today, the day following the news of her betrothal, she took special solace in her stepmother's presence—in the sound of her voice and the smell of her skin. She knew her time in the Huniah household was short-lived. She would soon be given to another family, never allowed to consider this her home again. And if she should return, it could only be as a visitor, a stranger.

The two women silently listened to the hum of the grinding grain. The wind was still, not a leaf stirred. Two oversized pigeons pecked at each other in the gravel nearby. Their necks bobbing and dipping, they valiantly fought over a single, fat worm that had the misfortune to stick its head out between a patch of yellowed weeds.

Finally, Esma stopped working the wheel. Turning to her stepdaughter she spoke in a quiet voice, serious and plain, "Nisrina, I will tell you what my mother told me the day of my betrothal. As a good wife and mother, you will be expected to work hard. To cook, to sew, and clean for your family. You will be expected to raise your children in the sacred teachings of the church, keeping them safe and close by your side at all times."

Nisrina nodded as Esma paused, wiping the sweat from her brow.

The older woman sighed and shook her head, lifting the heavy stone from the grinding wheel, placing it on the ground beside her. Nisrina watched her stepmother's thick, calloused hands as they neatly scooped the finely ground flour into a waiting bowl.

Finally, Esma turned back to her stepdaughter, her eyes large and her brows furrowed. She wagged her finger in front of her face, the powdery grain that clung to her nails floating softly through the air like down from a pillow, "You must always keep your home clean and tidy the way that I've taught you, eh?"

Nisrina nodded. These were things she knew.

Esma refilled the stone. She was about to turn the wheel again, but stopped and took a deep breath, the palms of her hands now resting flat against her thighs. She looked straight into Nisrina's eyes, her own dark orbs intense and powerful, "And Nisrina . . . above all else, you must remember this . . . always do whatever it is your husband asks of you. Whatever that might be. Do you understand?"

"Of course, *yumma*," Nisrina smiled, glad to finally be given some instructions. "Like you always do for father."

"Yes, Nisrina," her stepmother sighed, "Like I always do for your father."

Esma lowered her eyes and turned her head away, her thoughts flashed back to the days of her own youth, when, like Nisrina, she too wondered what future lay ahead for her. She recalled her mother's face when she first told her that Isa Huniah, a farmer from Beit el Jebel, had come to her father and asked for her hand in marriage. She remembered the thrill and the terror of being an anxious bride, of knowing that everything in her life was about to change.

She glanced sideways at Nisrina, debating whether she should say more. Was it wise to speak her mind, be candid and frank? She thought better of it and held her tongue. Seeing the fear and antici- pation in the young girl's face, she simply shook her head.

Wiser to say nothing, she thought to herself, wiser to say nothing more—the rhythmic hum of the grinding stone the only sound as Esma resumed her work, crushing another batch of wheat between the two hard rocks.

SIX

Marriage

IT WAS WHEN JABRAN took the blade and sliced it across his thigh, his blood oozing through the open wound and running down his leg, that Nisrina knew she would love this man until her dying day. With a big smile, he quickly tore the sheet from their bed and wiped it across his bleeding flank, the red liquid transferring to the center of the cloth, soaking into the fibers, yielding a perfect, round stain—the unmistakable mark of a virtuous woman. With a mischievous wink to his new bride, he opened the door a small crack and passed it out into the dark of the night, into the courtyard and on to the boisterous group of villagers who hovered outside their front door.

Hours earlier, while the sun stood high over the Mediterranean sky, Nisrina found herself veiled and bejeweled before God and the golden altar of the Syrian Orthodox Church. With eyes cast downward, her face turned modestly away, she stood obediently beside the tall, dark, stranger whom she'd soon call her husband. She silently clenched her jaw, over and over again, her legs trembling as the priests and townspeople gathered noisily around her.

Their curiosity piqued, scores of villagers had pushed and shoved their way into the candlelit alcove of the sanctified chamber.

The women, dressed in their finest *thobes*, embroidered gaily with greens and reds, gold and turquoise, heads covered and carefully wrapped in their best scarves, smiled widely as they called out their greetings to one another. The men waited outdoors, inhaling their smokes with heads close together, their voices animated, their arms moving wildly in the air. Huddled in groups, they watched the comings and goings of the guests, lingering until the final moment when they'd reluctantly stamp out the hand-rolled Turkish tobaccos on the rough stone steps and take leave to enter the church.

As the priest took his place at the front of the church, hushes were heard and the crowd quieted, anxious to witness the holy matrimony of the motherless girl to the youngest son of the Yusef family.

Not wanting to miss the smallest detail, the guests stretched their necks to view her hands and wrists, so beautifully stained in a delicate, lacy pattern of red henna. They nodded to each other making small sounds of approval as they admired the fine linen *thobe* she wore, noticing the elaborate floral embroideries on her bodice and matching jacket.

Nisrina felt the cool, hard, weight pressed against her face from the coins that had been sewn into her headdress. Her heart was beating ferociously in her chest, but her hands were steady. She could feel her palms moist, and secretly worried that the whirling in her head might never stop. But as the villagers watched and the priest proudly posed, she stood dutifully still, motionless, as she listened to the chantings and prayers of her marriage ceremony.

Nisrina sensed the heat of the man who stood beside her, and she smelled the musty scent of his mortal form. She watched surreptitiously from the corner of her eye as his hand reached out to take hers. Jabran entwined the smallest finger of his right hand with the smallest finger of her left, their skin touching for the first time. She felt the warmth of him, noticing the rough, coarse nature of his flesh as a sigh escaped her lips.

According to custom, the couple circled the golden altar three times while crowns, attached by a single white ribbon, balanced lightly on their heads. They listened as the priests chanted words that joined them in God's love—Jabran to a woman he did not know, and Nisrina to a man she'd never met. And as they followed the holy ritual with chaste spirits and loving souls, the motherless child from the house of Huniah and the humble farmer from the house of Yusef softly and silently gave their hearts away.

It was dark by the time the ceremony and the mealtime celebrations had ended. The women of the town led Nisrina in a torch light procession through the village escorting her past the shops and the open market, through the town center and beyond the well, their voices ringing out in the cool night air, ceaselessly and unmistakably chanting blessings for good health and many strong children.

Jabran, who'd left earlier, waited at home for his new bride. Hearing them approach, he smoothed back his hair and straightened his *thobe* as he paced back and forth in the sparsely lit sitting room. The small stone home had been built for the new couple within the walls of the Yusef family compound. Located on the outskirts of town, the compound contained a horseshoe arrangement of homes clustered around a large, open courtyard. It was a rustic enclave with dirt paths, benches, and gardens scattered between an abundance of fruit and olive trees. The trees, some hundreds of years old, provided shade to the family and their guests during the hot summer months.

At the head of the women's group was Mona, the eldest female of the Yusef family. Approaching the entrance, Mona knocked three times on the large wooden door of her brother's new home. As they waited for the door to open, Nisrina noticed the tall entryway and delicate patterns carved into the freshly cut wood. She'd heard that the Yusef family had engaged an old cabinetmaker from their village to carve the likeness of the orchards and hills that surrounded Beit el Jebel. And now as she stood before the giant door, she marveled at its magnificent beauty. She could see the rise and fall of the landscape, the sharp cuts into the wood, sanded smooth and sinewy. As her eyes wandered over the surface, she saw the rise of a mountain, and imprinted delicately at the top of the mountain was a massive fig tree, its branches reaching out to the far corners of the wood, the leaves large and comforting. Her eyes moistened as she thought of the old tree under which she'd been born. She wondered if her mother, looking down from the heavens, could see her now, and she hoped she was happy for her.

The door slowly opened and Nisrina's eyes grew wide as the women of the village ceremoniously delivered the new bride to her waiting husband. As she left the candle-lit procession, disappearing into the cool, darkness of her new home, she could hear their voices outside growing louder and stronger, their songs and lululululu-ing tongues flapping out a high-pitched sound from deep within their throats. She knew the villagers would remain in the courtyard, their calls increasing in intensity as they collectively urged the new couple towards a blessed consummation.

Entering the darkened room, the sounds from the courtyard faded to a dim, hazy hue. The vinegary odor of women's sweat mixed with spiced, garlic charms quickly dissipated as the soft, sweet smell of jasmine greeted her senses. Nisrina's head swooned, the heady aroma engulfing her, softening her. But her languor was short-lived. She heard a thud as the large wooden door closed solidly behind her, the click of the latch speaking final and firm.

Her heart raced.

She sensed his presence. He was close. Looming.

Her head jerked slightly to the side, away from where he stood. Her body shivering beneath her elaborate gown.

Nisrina had left her father's house and had entered her husband's abode. No longer the daughter of Isa Huniah, she was now the wife of Jabran Yusef.

A stranger in his home, she kept her eyes averted. She passed through the darkened space feeling the heat from his body so near, hearing the pulsing rhythm of his breath—heavy and labored. He moved to the side allowing her to pass. Afraid to meet the gaze of the man to whom she now belonged, her eyes searched around the room, taking in her new surroundings.

The room was filled with flickering shadows cast by a single candle perched lonely on the stone mantel. Her eyes were drawn to a second light fluttering softly from a separate room at the far end of the house. A separate room? What a grand home this must be! Her thoughts struggled to wrap around its meaning. Through the low, narrow doorway she saw the foot of a bed, and her heart beat wildly. She heard her husband's body shift quietly in the dark, and then his soft, deep voice echoed within the hollows of her ears.

"*Marhaba*," he welcomed her in, motioning for her to enter his bedroom.

She crossed the threshold like a spirit lilting lightly through the air. Numb from fear, she could not feel her feet on the cold stone floor, nor recall how she finally reached the far corner of the room. Jabran motioned for her to undress. He watched as his bride removed her elaborate headdress. The *smadeh*, an embroidered cap with a stiff padded rim covered by rows of coins sewn into the fabric, represented the generous gifts bestowed upon his new bride. Jabran was pleased. Proud that the villagers had given so graciously of their silver and gold to welcome his young wife to his family.

He admired how Nisrina lifted the heavy adornment so cautiously, careful not to dislodge the numerous coins attached to the rim, and he wondered if he should reach out to help her. But she gave no indication of needing assistance and he hesitated to be so bold. With her eyes still cast downward, her gaze to the floor, she carefully removed it from her head, and as she did, her rich brown hair pulled out from its bun, falling loosely in a cascade across her shoulders.

Jabran could hear the women outside singing and clapping as Nisrina slowly and self-consciously turned away from him. She took off her jewelry, her stockings and her shoes. As she did, he noticed her hands and feet, dyed in an intricate lacy pattern of red henna—the tattooed markings of a bride's beauty.

Finally, he saw her remove her wedding gown which was richly embroidered with colored threads and detailed panels. She carefully laid it across the chair that stood alongside their bed. He watched her from the corner of his eye, trying hard not to stare at the marvelous beauty only steps away. Her face was modestly turned toward the wall, her back and hips delicately curved, her legs white and shapely. In that moment, as he watched her in her nakedness, he realized how truly small and fragile this young girl was and a surge ran through his body.

Until this time, Jabran had only seen Nisrina from afar, usually in church or across the marketplace at the local *souk* as she assisted her stepmother in managing her young half-brothers. Her confidence had been seemly, and her hand with the roguish boys, gentle. He had watched and waited as he saw the young girl grow from a child into a woman. Over the years, many matchmakers had tried to pair him with other girls from the village, those who'd come of age, but he continually refused their proposals for he knew that his heart had been lost on the quiet, demure daughter of Isa Huniah.

Although he had never spoken with her or exchanged an inappropriate glance, when it came to matrimony or matters of the heart, he could think of no other. And he promised himself that when that girl whom he watched from a distance finally came of age, he would take her and her alone as his beloved wife.

When the news of her availability was recklessly spread through the village, he panicked, fearing that another might win her before he could make a proper proposal. He promptly went to his father and told him that he would have no one else, that it must be Nisrina Huniah, the daughter of Isa Huniah, the farmer of figs and grapes. His father, overjoyed that his son had finally shown an interest in matrimony, and anxious to bequeath him an orchard of his own, gladly gave his blessings along with a large and fruitful dowry for her father.

But now, as the groom stood alone with the angel of his dreams, as he realized that there were no others to distract or disrupt, he noticed her anxious breath and how she intentionally avoided his gaze. He prayed that she would not hear his pounding heart or see the beads of sweat that were forming on his brow. And as he watched her self-consciously remove her adornments, he hoped that she would not turn around and notice his apprehensive face or sense how much he wanted to hold her close to him. His body ached in a way that he had never known possible, and he hungered to tell her that he would always honor her. He would treat her with kindness and respect, and be a gentle, understanding husband. But he could not find the words nor did he have faith that if he opened his mouth there would be a voice with which to speak; and so, reluctantly, like a ghost lingering in the shadows of her heart, he said nothing. As she had done moments before, he, too, turned his face to the wall and quickly changed into his nightshirt.

As he moved, Nisrina turned to face him. Her cheeks were flushed with raw anticipation as she stood naked beneath her muslin-colored cotton bed gown. It had been specially embroidered by her stepmother, the delicate florets of crocheted lace running full along the width of her neckline, drawing subtle consideration to her full, erect breasts. As she searched her husband's silhouette, she realized that she knew not what to expect from this man. She had been given no instructions other than to obey his wishes and to please him in all respects. She had learned from gossip and whispers around the *taboon*, that the women who lay calling and singing outside their door would not leave until a sheet, stained with the blood from between her legs, was given to them in proof of her purity. She'd been warned that the act to produce this evidence would be painful indeed, and that she should nevertheless be prepared to endure. But she knew nothing else.

Her mind drew blank as she stood silently before him, her breath coming rhythmically now in short waves like the moon's coursing action on the ocean's floor. And like the dutiful tide, she surrendered her will, awaiting his direction, his sacred command. It had grown quite dark outside and the light from the single candle in the room cast a flickering glow on her face while the long silhouetted shadows danced tauntingly against the stone wall. Trying not to stare, she furtively watched him undress.

He removed the sash from around his waist, then pulled his gown up and over his head. It was a large tunic-styled *thobe* made of fine gold-striped cloth. She noticed how once removed, he dropped it carelessly to the floor, slipping quickly into a loose night shirt that fell just below his knees.

Glancing shyly as he changed, Nisrina became aware of the sinewy strength of his legs and buttocks. Quickly, she turned her head away, her heart fluttering, her groin growing surprisingly moist. But when he finished changing and moved to approach her, wanting to take her into his arms and lead her to his bed, their bed, she began to shake all over—such violent shaking, the likes of which he'd never seen. Before he could reach out to her, to hold her in his arms and tell her that all would be well, rivers of salt were streaming down her cheeks.

Nisrina realized that all she wanted was to be back in her home, sitting by the familiar stone hearth, the one in which she had memorized every chink and imperfection. She wanted to sit with her stepmother, her father and her four silly half-brothers and feel the warmth of the fire as she worked quietly on her quilting. She wanted to smell her stepmother's cooking, the garlic and curry, the cinnamon and allspice. And she longed to hear her tender, sweet voice call her to come help in the kitchen.

But instead, she was in this strange house with this strange man who had shown her his thighs and his buttocks. She was ashamed. This is not how she was raised. Her body shook so violently that her face twitched and her teeth chattered until finally her legs gave out from under her. She could hear the women outside in the courtyard. They continued on with their clapping and calling, their unceasing sounds of encouragement only adding to her mounting distress. She wanted to scream to them to disperse. To call out for them to quiet down, go home and let her return to her former life. But all she could do was rattle and cry, the tears flowing freely from her eyes.

"Nisrina, please, do not be distressed." Jabran was beside himself with worry. He could not stand to see the woman of his dreams so unhappy and he wondered what he might possibly do to console her.

"I . . . I'm so sorry," she cried, burying her face in her hands. She was sure that this was not the way she was supposed to act, but she knew of no other. If only she could stop her shaking, but the harder she tried, the tighter her muscles grew, the tremors increasing with each passing moment.

"Nisrina, please, come sit here beside me. I won't hurt you. I promise." Jabran reached down and lifted her up from the hard stone floor. She noticed how strong he was as he easily carried her onto the side of his bed.

"I'm sorry, sir, I just want to go home," she said between her tears.

"But you are here. This is your home now," his voice was soft, reassuring.

"How can this be my home? Where is my father? Where is my stepmother? Where is my bed and my chest of clothes?"

"This is your home now Nisrina," he repeated. "This is your bed. See, you are sitting on it. And my father will now be your father and the memory of my mother, God rest her soul, will be the memory of your mother."

His last comment only made Nisrina cry harder, remembering her own mother who died giving her life. She began to pray to her spirit, asking for guidance and intercession. She wished she could be back under the giant fig tree in her father's orchard, the one from whence she first came into the world, and under which her mother had so rapidly departed. And then she heard her husband's voice again. It was soft, gentle.

"We are kindred spirits, Nisrina. You and I. You see, we have both lost our mothers. This is a sad tale indeed."

He had caught her attention. Nisrina wondered if his mother had also died giving birth to him. "How did your mother die?" She finally asked, her voice a whisper.

"She died years ago. She was a splendid woman. Beautiful and kind. The doctors said her cough was too strong causing the blood in her chest to burst forth, the explosion delivering her straight to the gates of heaven. No one could say why. Some blamed it on the heat of too much ginger in her stew; other's surmised that perhaps she'd had too many yearnings which finally took hold and carried her away."

"Why Sir? What yearnings would such a grand lady have?" Nisrina's curious nature had begun to calm her.

"I saw her suffer, Nisrina. I saw how my father's philandering ways caused her to lose her smile. I was just a young boy at the time, but wise enough to understand the actions of a careless heart. I tried to comfort her, but it was to no avail. Helplessly, I watched her confidence fade and her joy rub thin." He was shaking his head, lamenting the memory. "I think she died of a broken heart."

Hearing these words, Nisrina turned to face him, compelling him to go on.

"Don't misunderstand me, I love my father very much and I will always honor his name, but his actions are not my actions, nor will they ever be . . . they caused my mother much heartache, much suffering. She could no longer hide her sorrow. The truth of her circumstance was written on her face. Such transparency told me that she had a pure soul."

He turned his head away. Now it was his turn to feel distressed, the sting of his reminiscences still paining him.

Forgetting her own miseries, Nisrina put her hand on his back and patted him tenderly. Her body had stopped shaking and her tears had subsided. Through her fingers she could feel the strength in his shoulders and her hand rested there, sensing the warmth of him.

Jabran was comforted by her gentle touch. His body ached to take her as his wife, but his mind was strong. A calm and measured man, he understood the fragility of her innocence.

"Nisrina, I can see that you understand suffering and I want you to know that I will never cause you any pain. Not tonight, not ever. I want nothing more than to hold you and make love to you, but instead, I suggest that we wait for our time of intimacy. I want you to want me, as much as I want you. I will wait for you. I will wait for you to tell me that you love me and only then will I take you and make love to you. Do you understand?"

He gently turned her face to his and she saw the love and gentleness in his gaze.

"But the villagers. They are waiting. Your father. Your family. What we will tell them if we don't have the stained sheet to show? What will they think? I couldn't bare the shame of it. Oh, my father!" Her eyes widened with fear as she recalled her father's final words to her.

"Hah! Easy!" Jabran jumped up and ran to the kitchen. He pulled out a knife and lifting his dressing gown, he ran the blade crossways against his thigh and sliced a gash into his leg. As the blood seeped out, he grabbed the sheet from his bed and pressed it firmly against the bloody wound.

Nisrina watched in wonder. He did this for me, she thought to herself, and as she witnessed his bravery, her lonely heart expanded.

She continued to watch as the thin stream of blood trickled down his leg, and she observed how he cockily thrust the red stained sheet through the opened door, handing it out to the waiting throng. As he did these things, she smiled softly to herself, and as she smiled, her expanded heart filled with love.

The ululating and singing, the clapping and chanting, had been ceaseless since Jabran first opened the door and welcomed Nisrina into his home as his wife. The outdoor vigil of songs and howlings were customary in their village as the women encouraged the new groom to deflower his young virgin bride. And as Jabran passed the soiled sheet out through the crack in the door and handed it to his eldest sister, Mona, an unmarried woman for whom the chance of matrimony had come and gone, she held it out proudly for all to see. Then dancing joyously around the courtyard, lululululu-ing in her loudest and highest-pitched tone, she finally laid it down before her father's ancient feet.

The throng hushed as old Farooz lifted the cloth to study the markings.

Stroking the long gray beard that hung from his chin, he turned the fabric, first to the left and then to the right—examining it carefully, as breathless moments vanished in time. The villagers, now silent and restless, shuffled about—their quiet curiosity anxious for the final diktat.

They were not kept wondering long.

Sufficiently satisfied, Farooz Yusef slowly looked up, a thin smile now spread across his weather-beaten face. Raising his right hand high into the air, he nodded his gracious assent to the throng, proudly declaring his youngest son's manhood and his new daughter-in-law's flawless virtue.

Farooz's eyes, once a deep dark brown, had now faded to a coarse yellowed-green covered over with a milky gray film. Early in his days, his wife, Hannah, had blessed him with five healthy children, the last born far too late in her life. And although he'd had an occasional eye for the women, it saddened him still, when the unrelenting cough crept into her lungs. Her last few months found her weakened and pale, no longer able to make him his coffee or fetch him his skoal. He watched helplessly as her full bosom deflated and her arms grew thin, until finally the coughs that shackled her soul were mere shudders of murky red fluids.

When she left him, he looked to his children for comfort and care. But his eldest, Najeeb, who'd been indulged one time too many, simply turned his dark eyes away from the scene.

The old man wondered, what could be said of a son so completely untouched by his father's lone sufferings? But he said nothing to him in reproach.

The next in line, Jacob, quiet, but meek, buried himself in his work, always out in the fields; while Mona and Dora, two daughters unwed, busied themselves with plans for their poor mother's funeral.

It was only Jabran who sat by his side, tenderly holding his hand. Only Jabran, so young and so pure, who quietly wept against his father's sad chest, and only Jabran who hid in the shed for four days and four nights without a drop of food in his grief-stricken belly.

Farooz wished that Hannah could see her son now—on the day of his marriage, so handsome and tall.

Perhaps she did see, he thought to himself. Perhaps she watched from the heavens above, as the crowd called out blessings doubled many times over. He hoped she approved of her son's choice for a wife, and he shook his head to only himself, as the villagers dispersed tired and weary from days of rejoicing.

Before turning to leave, an elderly woman stopped and stood close by his side. She grabbed his cold hands, her own heated and frail, and looked up at him with an old blackened grin, "Hannah smiles down upon you, Farooz. Hannah smiles down!"

The old man beamed, a soft, crooked smile forming on his face. He nodded thankfully to her, breathing a sigh of relief. Hannah was pleased; he was sure of that now, finally able to give his undaunted blessing to their youngest son.

Happy to hear the crowd melt away, Jabran turned back to Nisrina who stood ready to nurse his wound. Moments earlier, she'd gone searching in the kitchen for supplies. There, she noticed a decorative vase placed carefully on the square wooden table in the center of the room. The water inside was clean, and freshly cut blossoms peeked curiously out over the edge—jasmine, the source of the scent that greeted her at the door. She wondered if her husband had placed them there. She chose not to ask. Finding ointment and clean cloths she returned to his side and carefully began to wash his injured leg. She could feel the fine, hard muscles that rippled down along the sides of his thigh as she applied the healing salve to the open cut. She dared not look up as her fingers surprisingly tingled from the intimacy of her touch.

How his scent intoxicates me, she thought to herself. My head reeling wild in his presence. And the warmth when he nears me grabs hold of my breath. Dear Lord, if this be such what they call a husband, then may my days be long on this earth, and I pray with all my heart that Allah deliver me into heaven a chaste woman no more.

Satisfied with her work, she wrapped the wound tightly, holding his leg until she was sure that the bleeding had stopped.

Jabran sat quietly and watched while she attended to him. He breathed in deeply, drinking in the essence of her being, her sweetness numbing the throb in his leg. He no longer felt pain or sadness, nor would he ever again, for his senses were calmed by the love and passion that now filled his heart.

When she finished, he smiled and thanked her, looking straight into her eyes.

She blushed and responded softly, "Of course."

When there was nothing left to be said, Jabran rose and paced quietly about the room. Thoughtfully, he turned to her and in a gentle voice, asked, "Nisrina, tell me, do you read poetry?"

But Nisrina only put her head down in shame and confessed to her husband, "I'm sorry. I cannot read. My father and stepmother, they needed me at home. I could not take the time away from my chores to attend school. I never learned."

"Ah, yes, of course," he breathed in. "Well, that is of no consequence. You see, I can read. And if you permit me, I shall be your eyes to the written world. I was taught by my uncle, a traveling tea merchant, and before his death he bequeathed to me his many books of poetry and literature."

He walked over to the far corner of the room and pointed proudly to a large collection of books. Some were piled on the floor, while others were stacked neatly on shelves against the wall. "I would be honored to read to you . . . each night if you'd like." He looked at her hopefully, "And, if you permit me, we shall start right now. What say you?"

"I would be delighted to see the world through your eyes," Nisrina smiled gratefully.

Jabran nodded and took from the shelf a very old book. It was large and heavy, bound tightly in deep, dark, red leather with raised gold embossments and tied shut by means of two short leather straps. The pages were yellowed and worn, clearly read many times by its ardent admirers. It was, in fact, an old friend. Jabran's favorite book of poetry containing verses from many of the ancient poets.

Climbing onto the bed, he motioned to Nisrina to join him and she did so without hesitation. He handed her the book to peruse and she held it in her lap for a few moments, her fingers running over the rich lettering. She felt the coolness of the soft, smooth leather through her palms and it took her breath away. She wanted to open it, but first glanced at her new husband, wondering if he would permit her to do so. He smiled lovingly and nodded his encouragement.

Nisrina opened the cover, slowly, carefully, she took a deep breath, her fingers smoothing down the curled edges of the old sepia colored pages. She observed the inked letters, each one forming a word and each word forming a sentence. Although she knew not what mysteries they held, she could smell the warm musty scent that greeted her, and it carried her away to the past, to a world of magic and wonderings. She felt the years of life and wisdoms, of words and stories that wondrously beckoned her from within its pages.

Finally, when the spell had been cast, she smiled up at her husband, the light of the candle dancing patterns across his face. Respectfully, she handed the heavy tome back to its owner. Then quietly, peacefully, she lay down beside him, pulling up the soft woolen blanket thrown over their bed.

Jabran was pleased. He opened the book, and watching her delicate features from the corner of his eye, he began to read aloud:

"I take no form.
My soul has shattered into a never-ending silence that envelops and caresses me.
I am part of no thing; and I am a part of all things.
I am at peace, at home in this vast timelessness.
And even though they seek, they shall not find,
For no one can claim my countenance or look upon me.
I take no form and I rejoice,
For I reside in the heart of eternity."

When he finished, Nisrina's eyes were moist, but she was not crying. He kissed her cheek gently and she touched his face with her fingertips. Together, they lay in their bed while Jabran continued to read to her throughout the night, and Nisrina continued to listen. Like an artist paints with color, he painted with words, and her world opened up. She devoured every sentence he spoke, his voice a song in her heart, until finally they both fell soundly asleep in each other's arms.

SEVEN

The Yusef Compound

ONE MORNING, WAKING EARLY, Nisrina slipped quietly out of bed and put on her *thobe*. Grabbing her shawl, she headed out the front door, wandering through the garden and out past the gate, her bare feet stepping carefully on the darkened dirt path. It was long before dawn and the wearing distractions of the Yusef family had not yet taken their hold on the compound. She followed the winding trail that led up the hill and through her husband's orchard. She passed the milk thistle and mulberry bushes, and pushed her way through the tall green stalks of the anise leaves, their licorice scent lingering lightly as they brushed against her clothes. Then climbing over the boulders that separated the terraced lots, she reached a clearing adjacent to her father-in-law's olive groves. It overlooked a broad, green valley. Not a home or building could be seen for miles.

The changing season brought with it a collective sigh as the heat of summer gave way to chilly mornings and misty haze. Stopping to sit on a large stone beneath one of the trees, she took a deep breath. The moist air cooled her lungs and slowed her pulse. The scent was fresh and the sound of the nightingale could be heard chittering its sharp, hopeful tune.

Nisrina's mind calmed, drifting with the soft petals of dawn.

Throughout the canyons and mountains of Beit el Jebel, leaves had begun to turn to a brilliant display of red and gold, while a burst of autumn wildflowers took hold of the hillsides. It was mid-October and the change in seasons not only meant a break from the hot arid temperatures, but also signaled the start of the sacred olive harvest, a month long event that brought together the young and the old, the strong and the weak, as families joined in to pick, sort and process the revered crop.

The narrow leaves of the olive trees were not affected by the cool fall air. Their silver canopied branches could be seen for miles swishing in the gentle breeze, marking out a rhythmic dance like waves on an ocean floor. In stark contrast, the thick, gnarly trunks of the majestic beasts twisted and turned like the wrinkles on an old man's face.

Nisrina marveled at their beauty, their powerful pose, staunchly standing guard over the small, oval fruit that hung delicately from its branches: the giver of life, the eternal symbol of peace, and the provider of wisdom and fertility.

She lingered a while, watching and listening to the sounds of the world until the rising sun reached out to the morning dew. As the sunlit rays hit the swollen droplets, Nisrina smiled, for they shimmered and sparkled like diamonds from heaven. She sat quietly remembering all that had happened to her. Wondering what her mother would think of the father who raised her without a kind word, and the home she could no longer call her own.

She thought of Jabran, his deep loving eyes and his warm smile. She remembered the rhythm of his gentle voice and the verse he'd recited from his book of poetry. "I am a part of all things," he'd said to her. Then, she heard her mother's voice speak softly in her mind. It told her not to fear—that all would be well, and it brought her peace.

The workings of the Yusef compound were communal in nature. Homes, although separate and distinct, were always open, meals often shared, and tasks collectively assumed. The sheep and goats felt free to wander through the courtyard, sometimes walking through an open door or pushing their noses through an unlatched window, the scents of savory stews and boiling chicken too hard to resist. The women took turns chasing the bleating animals out with broom in hand, "*Yullah! Imshee!*" Mona would cry out to them. "My kitchen is reserved for only the two-legged beasts of this household!"

Even Abu Faraj, Jabran's reliable old donkey was not immune to Mona's harsh temper. When she found him eating her carrots or nibbling the corn growing tall in her garden, she'd grab her long-handled broom and chase him away. Indignant, he'd shake his head and open his mouth to bellow, his loud hee-haws heard all through the valley. But the sharp bristles smacking his hind side would finally discourage him and off he'd run, trampling the tomato and onion plants he passed on the way.

Jabran had purchased Abu Faraj at a reasonable price from a wandering merchant who was visiting Beit el Jebel one hot summer's day. The donkey was carrying an extraordinarily heavy load, bearing his burden in the harsh rays of the noontime heat, and the merchant, an irate man with a short temper, kept prodding and poking the animal to move faster. Abu Faraj, a cross-eyed beast with one ear that stood straight up and another that fell down along the side of his face, had suffered enough harassment. Refusing to obey his master's commands, he sat down in the middle of the road where he remained, his head unmoving, his eyes glazed over as if in a trance.

His fur was a mottled pattern of gray and white with speckled patches of brown and rust on his underbelly. The tip of his nose was covered with freckly black spots that only seemed to accentuate the extraordinarily large front teeth that were housed between his powerful jaws. Such an odd-looking animal, he had not endeared himself to his ruthless master and was mistreated and overworked. But Jabran was a man of his own making. He saw something in Abu Faraj that the wandering merchant could not see. Angered by the manner in which the merchant treated the animal, he offered him a reasonable price to take the beast off his hands. At first, the merchant resisted, but realizing the opportunity to unload the stubborn beast, he finally bartered and argued until the two men reached an amicable agreement. The merchant felt vindicated for he was at last able to profit from the tenacious jackass. And Jabran was satisfied that the donkey would no longer be neglected.

His name meant "father of relief," so called by Jabran in gratitude for the assistance he provided. For as Jabran had predicted, it was all in the handling. And the beast, happy to be under the care of a kindly man, proved to be a faithful and steadfast servant who willingly bore the heavy load as his master tended his orchards and carried his crop into town.

The days were long as the men toiled in their orchards, trimming branches and watering their groves. When they had harvested enough fruit to sell: grapes, figs, apricots and nectarines, they'd transport the crop into town and sell them at the public *souk*.

The women always stayed behind, each one maintaining their separate home. They were masters of their gardens and sages of their kitchens. They'd wake long before daylight to fetch water from the well. They'd feed the livestock, and grind the grain. Clarify the butter and bake the bread. They'd sew and darn and scrub the walls and floors of their stone houses. And as the women of the Yusef family worked, so did Nisrina.

EIGHT

Any News?

IT WASN'T THE HARD work that troubled the newest addition to the Yusef family, but rather the growing anticipation amongst its members that unsettled her so.

Nisrina had been married for almost a year and she'd shown no signs of a growing belly.

Farooz, the old patriarch, had no heirs to inherit his land or care for his aging family. Marta and May, the wives of his two eldest sons had given him no grandchildren, and his own two daughters, Mona and Dora, had never wed. Nisrina, the youthful wife of his youngest son, was his last remaining hope.

Farooz was a shrewd and decisive man. His face was pale and his body once robust was now thin and frail. In his younger days, he'd been known to have an eye for the women and a thirst for good drink, always maintaining that a man's privilege to indulge himself resulted in a happier home. When he spoke, his word was law, no one daring to challenge his self-assured declarations. But despite his steadfast canon, it was commonly believed that Farooz, for the most part, administered his family's rule in a just and reasonable manner.

His eldest son, Najeeb, had a full head of hair, now graying at the temples. A lusty man whose reputation for women and wine had reached his father's ears on more than one occasion, he carried himself with the confidence of a scandalous ram asserting dominance over its latest prized ewe. He was large in girth and sported a thick, broad mustache that he twirled when trying to impress. His eyes were dark and his smile falsehearted. And when she found herself in his presence, Nisrina felt an icy chill run down her spine.

Jacob, the second son, was a fair-minded soul who kept his orchards neat and his paths well-tended. Working hard to please his father and keep his wife content, he held himself in reserve, always following his conscience. He resented his older brother's bravado and his ability to win his father's favor despite his licentious way of life.

As Nisrina moved amongst the elders, she kept her eyes averted. Still, she felt their fiery stares like daggers through her soul. Each time she entered a room she noticed their surreptitious survey of her body. The men said nothing, the impropriety shielding her from their inquisitive voices, but their sly fleeting looks were unmistakable. First they'd peruse her belly and then swiftly, eyes shifting back and forth, they'd glance over the outline of her breasts, being careful not to rest their gaze too long.

They watched and wondered, furtive glances, restive motions, all anxious to see if her breasts had enlarged or if a round bulge could possibly be forming beneath her *thobe*. They'd boldly search her face as if secrets could be revealed from the look in her eyes.

Nisrina's features were fine and delicate, her dark eyes shadowed by a thick layer of lashes. And although she wore the modest *thobe* of the village women, her breasts belied its flowing shape. Embarrassed by the stirrings inside them, the three old men would shift nervously in their chairs and flick the ashes from their cigarettes, until finally they'd turn their faces away.

The women, however, were bolder and had no reason to hide their scrutiny. Mona, in particular, took it upon herself to be the gatekeeper of the Yusef name. Coming close to Nisrina's face, she'd stare directly into her eyes, and twisting her hands in an inquisitive fashion, she'd wordlessly inquire if the young bride had any news to share.

Tall and skinny, like a reed growing up from the Jordan River, Mona was the oldest daughter of the Yusef family. With her bloom long gone, her visage had settled into a permanent scowl reflecting the mainstay of her disposition. Her head was elongated and thin, and the unsmiling lips that perched beneath her long narrow nose, formed a straight line that divided her image into two separate planes. Why she had soured against life, nobody knew, and none dared to ask, for fear of the wrath she might unleash upon them. It was well known that she'd had a few suitors in her youth, but had repeatedly declined their offers, choosing to remain singularly sheltered amongst the pathways and canopies of the Yusef compound. The garden was Mona's greatest passion and she tended it single-mindedly, if not a bit eccentrically. Both neighbors and bystanders had, on more than one occasion, noticed her holding out her hemline as she'd guilefully emit a stream of urine on the ants that invaded her yard, her odd ways increasingly disconcerting to the family and particularly unnerving to its newest member.

Mona shared a home with her sister, Dora, a quiet woman, two years younger. Dora walked with a limp, often relying on a small wooden cane to navigate the rocky paths that traversed their village. Her round cheeks and kindly eyes presented the look of a cherub on loan from the heavens. But the sad, sweet smile that graced her face, and the way she tilted her head to one side when listening to others, gave pause to the inexplicable thoughts she never spoke.

While Farooz's descendants held the more prominent positions in the family, Marta and May, the wives of his two eldest sons, were not far behind. Marta, the wife of Najeeb, was a talkative woman with a triangular face and a large, hooked nose. As everyone suspected, her years for child bearing had long since passed and she found her worth in the art of sewing and darning. She could be seen for hours embroidering garments or mending worn clothes, the members of the family bringing her their pants and *thobes* for patch or darn. Her handmade stitches, so straight and even, appeared as tidy and precise as those from Fareeda Samara's foot-powered apparatus, a contraption, to which Marta swore, she would never succumb.

May, the wife of Jacob, had been attractive and lively in her youth. With thick, dark hair and a large beaming smile, she'd given new hope to the family for siring an heir. But like her sister-in-law before her, the years passed without note, and the disappointment gradually stole her radiance. Now, a shadow of her former self, she moved softly through space, talking in whispers, and directing her energies to the tasks of the kitchen. Her gift was her skill for baking, and she now filled her days making breads and sweet delicacies. Admired much through the village, many women turned to her for lessons or counsel.

Their barren states kept Marta and May from approaching Nisrina on the subject of motherhood. However, their interest was as great, if not greater than those of the others, for they had already lost face in the eyes of the elders. Instead of questioning her themselves, they would stand in the corner of the room nervously wringing their hands, whispering and wondering if the new interloper had finally surpassed them. When they'd hear her say she had no news, they'd exhale sighs of relief and exchange knowing glances. For if Nisrina were pregnant, it would only further substantiate their failure in pleasing Farooz.

Although Nisrina was reluctant to admit it, she wasn't sure how to discern if a child was growing inside her. She'd never been instructed in the ways of impending motherhood and was too embarrassed to ask for an explanation. Her stepmother had given birth to four children, but with each one it seemed that Esma simply grew a large belly while the villagers showered her with blessings. So when Mona asked her for news, she'd just smile shyly and shake her head, when the fact of the matter was—she simply didn't know.

Nisrina walked through the door of her father-in-law's home as the family gathered in preparation for the olive harvest. All eyes turned to her. Jabran, stopping to feed his donkey and chickens, had not accompanied his wife. He'd urged her to go on ahead and visit with the others. And now as she entered the room she was approached by Mona.

"Any news?" Mona asked, boldly pointing to Nisrina's stomach. She was squinting her eyes and turning her head like a bird in search of a worm. All heads turned to stare.

"No. No news," Nisrina mumbled, looking down at her feet. She silently wished that she'd waited for Jabran. When he was with her the others kept their distance, their behavior respectful.

Nisrina had grown accustomed to staring at her feet when interacting with her in-laws. She hated to be left alone with them, and yet as Jabran's wife it was something she could not escape. She knew she must learn to get along with her new family, telling herself each day that maybe today things would be better, but so far nothing had changed.

Farooz, observing their interlude, looked at his new daughter-in-law with a sideways glance. He was building a fire and as he fanned the flames he wondered if Jabran had made a mistake in his choice of a bride. How could she possibly be a good wife and mother? She was far too quiet, far too thin. He remembered Jabran's insistence—only her, he'd said, his voice strong, his stance solid. Farooz had witnessed the clarity in his son's eyes and the determination in his jutting jaw, and the old man knew he could not refuse. Jabran had lost his mother at such a tender age, something the whole family knew had been hard on the boy and it etched a singular notch in the old man's heart.

His thoughts were interrupted by talk of the harvest. Nisrina, grateful for the diversion, tucked her legs beneath her as she sat on the floor to listen. In spite of their endless discussions and painstaking lessons on the subject of picking and processing olives, she was grateful for the upcoming event as it deflected attention away from her still slim figure and wanting condition. She was happy to focus her attentions on learning the whys and ways of the olive tree and its delicate fruit.

Although she'd been raised the daughter of a farmer, Nisrina's father had grown only figs and grapes on his modest farm. And now, the prospect of harvesting acres of olives on her father-in-law's property presented a new and exciting experience for her. Unfamiliar as she was, Farooz decided that it was in the family's best interest for Nisrina to learn the subtle techniques of harvesting.

As the eldest member of the Yusef family, Farooz proudly told and retold stories from the past. He'd gather his family around him, and while they sat in a circle, sipping dark, Turkish coffee, he recited ancient tales of the symbolism and value of the tiny fruit.

"The olive branch has been a symbol of peace since the beginning of time," the old sage began, "Our trees are ancient, planted ages ago," he raised his forefinger up to the heavens to signify the importance of his next words, "possibly, even providing shade during the time that our great Lord walked this earth!"

Najeeb and Jacob nodded in agreement, as did their wives, Marta and May. Although they'd all heard these stories many times before, they always sat respectfully and listened quietly as the elder spoke.

"Our ancestors never went hungry and God willing never shall we. The fruit of the mighty trees puts food on our tables and warmth in our bellies . . . in both good times and bad . . . in times of famine and in times of drought."

Farooz sat back in his chair and closed his eyes as he recalled what the elders had said to him when he was young. "The olive is a rich fruit," he recited. "It provides nutrition not only for the body, but for the heart and the eternal soul."

He stopped again and looked around the room, making sure that everyone was still listening. When he was sufficiently satisfied that all eyes and ears were still engaged, he leaned forward and continued, "Mind you, not only can its rich, aromatic oils be used for cooking and healing, but, afterwards . . . after the sensuous oil is removed, its tiny seed and the fibrous skin are also used. Nothing is wasted," he shook his finger in front of his face, "No, no, nothing. You see, the remnants can be burned as fuel to warm a husband's hearth or cook a family its meal."

He looked straight at Nisrina, wanting to be sure she appreciated all the fine nuances of the precious fruit and would dedicate her attentions to serving her husband. Nisrina smiled and nodded. This was the first time she had heard his stories, and she did indeed find comfort in his words.

When his tales were told and he'd taken his last sip of coffee, Farooz leaned back in his cushioned chair and slowly closed his eyes. Leaving the old patriarch to his private dreams and softened memories, the other family members silently returned to their homes. They knew they would hear the same narrative the next day and the many days that followed until the harvest season was finally over.

NINE

The Olive Harvest

THE DAY OF HARVEST finally arrived as Farooz announced the olives were ready to be gathered. Preparations had been made and supplies carefully laid out. The task was slow and arduous, requiring the assistance of many hands. And as such, the entire Yusef family had gathered together on a cool autumn morning, each household leaving their individual orchards and meeting beneath the trees' broad canopies to help in harvesting their father's trees. Within the terraced landscape that encircled the Yusef compound, the full and rich plants were finally ready to give up their ripened fruit. And Farooz, as the head of the Yusef family, was organizing everyone for the month-long task.

Although it was new to Nisrina, the other family members were quite familiar with the protocol. The farmers used rugged, handmade wooden ladders to reach the tall branches of the old stalwart giants. They mostly picked the fruit with their hands, gathering them and depositing them into a basket they carried at their waist. But for the taller branches they'd use long wooden sticks, specially chosen for tapping the branches. Lightly shaking each bough, the ripened olives would fall with a crisp pitter-patter onto a blanket at the base of the tree. The blanket would then be gathered and bundled, the olives carried away for sorting and processing.

Nisrina was taught the advantages of picking the olives at their ripest stage and even more so, the consequences of careless harvesting. Mona, who'd been put in charge of her training, gave explicit instructions, reminding her over and over again on the proper method.

"Tap only the branches, like this . . . " she'd say in her sternest voice. "Not too hard and not too lightly, and never, ever directly strike the fruit. Do you understand? If you do, then may God help you, for they will bruise, resulting in a bitter crop."

Nisrina would nod obediently, but as she listened to Mona recite the rights and wrongs of an olive harvest, she privately wished that it had been Dora who had been chosen to instruct her. For in the six months that she'd known the two women, she'd found Mona to be quite strict and unforgiving, while Dora seemed softer and spoke with a kinder voice.

"For now I will be the one who climbs the ladder," Mona was saying. "But, when my ancient bones have tired, I will permit you to relieve me, and then you will use the stick to hit the branches," Mona was demonstrating how the olives could be knocked down from the canopy, tapping each branch with a long stick. "But you must be careful," Mona shook her forefinger at Nisrina. "If you hit the fruit instead of the branch, it is the family that suffers when we can't sell them at market."

"I understand," Nisrina replied.

"I'm not sure you do," Mona went on. She had not formed a high opinion of her sister-in-law, and the old maid worried that her youngest brother's wife was only good for her beauty and nothing more. She continued to chastise her, "Let me warn you, young Nisrina, if the olives are bitter, it will be you who is forced to eat them . . . you and your husband! And then he will know that his wife harvested a bitter fruit."

Her narrowing eyes disappeared into their sockets, as she scrutinized Nisrina. She tilted her head to one side, her hands resting firmly on her hips, "Do you want that to happen?" she asked relentlessly.

"Do you want your husband to think that you are a woman who bears a bitter fruit?"

Nisrina's eyes went wide. She was not sure if Mona was still talking about the olives.

"No, Mona, no, I do not want that to happen. I will be careful, I promise."

"If you cannot do it right, you will be delegated to using only your hands, and if so, you do it like this," Mona gathered a cluster of olives between her long, sinewy fingers, gently urging the small round fruit off its branch. Nisrina watched as the green balls rolled eagerly into her sister-in-law's palms, dropping them into the large pocket of her apron.

She nodded, "I will be careful." It was not all that different from the many times she helped her father harvest the figs and grapes from his orchards. She wondered why Mona treated her as if she were just a foolish child.

The morning flew by without event as the Yusef family harvested the abundant fruit. The men had moved on to higher levels leaving the women to toil alone along the steep banks of the lower terraces. Mona and Nisrina worked together. Mona perched high above on the ladder, while Nisrina remained safely on the ground.

But as the hours passed, Mona grew tired, her back and shoulders aching. Climbing the ladder is a feat for younger women, she thought to herself.

"My bones are getting old," she called down to Nisrina. "Do you think you can use the ladder and tap the branches as I've shown you?"

Nisrina was worried. Mona's instructions had been clear, but she was a hard taskmaster and the young girl feared the demanding woman's scrutiny. However, she also knew that she could not refuse the offer for it was an honor to be trusted on the ladder. Brushing aside her apprehensions, she braved a big smile and nodded enthusiastically.

"Exactly as I've shown you?"

"Oh, yes," Nisrina responded. "I've watched you carefully. I'm sure I can do it!" Anxious to see the world from the upper rungs of the ladder, she was pleased to finally be given a chance. The lower tasks such as handing Mona the stick, and gathering and sorting the fallen olives had grown tiresome.

"Very well, we'll see if you have sufficiently learned the methods I have taught you." Mona was reluctant to let Nisrina climb the stepladder, but her head was throbbing and her joints felt as if they belonged to someone else. How had Fatima Mirsheed's body, the town's ancient washerwoman, who limped the streets with swollen knees and crooked limbs, suddenly become her own? She muttered angrily to herself, rubbing her shoulders and twisting her neck from side to side, cursing the selfish years that had stolen her youth.

Nisrina held her breath, her jaw tight, as she began her climb up the rickety, handmade, wooden rungs. Until that moment, she hadn't realized how loud the creaks and groans could sound, but she vowed not to let Mona see the worry in her eyes. Clenching her teeth, she mustered her courage and continued her climb, higher and higher into the branches. She wanted her sister-in-law to be proud of her and tell the others what a fine job she'd done. If she could prove herself during the sacred olive harvest, then maybe the Yusef clan would acknowledge her worth and put aside their concerns of her empty womb.

From a spot high on the ladder, Nisrina gazed out over the tops of the trees.

"I can see for miles!" she called out to Mona. "I see Dora, Marta and May!" Her sisters-in-law were farther down the road harvesting together. She couldn't help but smile as she saw the three women talking and laughing. Taking turns, they were picking, gathering and sorting the fruit. Nisrina wondered what tales they were telling that made them laugh and chuckle so heartily, their voices dancing down the lane towards her, first lilting and light, then loud and earnest. She glanced down at Mona. With scrunched cheeks, her dark brows were drawn close together forming one black line that crossed her face. Her eyes, narrowed and tense, had all but disappeared from sight. Perhaps it was the sun's bright glare that made her wrinkle her face so bitterly. "Pay attention to your work!" Mona called up to her. "Don't be gazing like a dreamer. We have much to do!"

Nisrina's smile faded as she quickly turned back to her work.

Striking her first branch at the exact center of its reach, she heard the clipped pitter patter of olives as they hit the ground. Thrilled by the sound she'd created, another big smile spread across her face and she started to giggle. She looked down to Mona for confirmation of her skill.

Mona was not amused.

"Don't look down at me, you silly girl!" She admonished her, her voice shrill and impatient. "Pay attention to your work!"

"Of course, Mona, I was merely pleased . . . the sound, it is so beautiful, don't you think?"

"It matters not what I think; what matters is that you don't lose your balance and fall down upon my head, God forbid, for then we both shall suffer! Now pay attention! Pay attention, you foolish child!"

"Yes, Mona," Nisrina sighed as she resumed her tapping. She continued to find joy in the sound of the olives falling to the earth, but now she kept her thoughts to herself. When she'd pause to wipe her brow or straighten her scarf, she'd glance down the road, seeing the other Yusef women carrying on with guffaws and slaps to their sides. She secretly wished that she'd been paired with one of them.

When she finished one section of the tree, Nisrina carefully descended. Together she and Mona shifted the ladder to the other side. When they finished the first tree, they moved on to the next one, and then the next and the next. Nisrina had been working for over an hour on the ladder and the sun had now reached its highest peak in the sky. The glaring heat caused both she and Mona to slow their pace. Even the laughter from down the lane had faded.

Although she'd been on the ground performing the easier of the two tasks, Mona was sweating, repeatedly wiping the perspiration running alongside her face. She kept mumbling under her breath that she was no longer a young girl and the work more trying than it had been in years past.

"Let's finish this tree and then pause for lunch," Mona declared as Nisrina climbed up into the branches one last time.

"Wonderful!" Nisrina called back to her, her legs beginning to wobble and ache as she worked to stay steady on the rungs.

Nisrina was balancing precariously on the uppermost step of her ladder, holding on with one hand while the other reached out with the long stick. She meticulously beat the branches as Mona had taught her to do, and each time she did, she would pause for just a moment listening to the sound of olives toppling to the ground.

Spying a far-out branch not yet shaken, Nisrina extended her arm and the right side of her body. As she did, her left foot shifted ever so slightly, but it was enough to throw her off balance. Struggling to maintain her stability, she teetered on the rickety rung. And as she tipped, her rod landed hard against the leaves and fruits of the tree.

Mona's voice pierced her ears, "*Ya Allah,* no, no, no! That is *not* how it is done! You are striking the fruit . . . foolish girl . . . this is exactly what I feared. Don't you understand? Have I not explained it to you, time and time again? You are bruising the fruit!"

Nisrina looked down from the ladder, "I'm sorry Mona, my foot slipped, I thought . . ."

"Only a fool would need to think! You must feel it from your heart," she clapped the palm of her hand hard to the middle of her chest, "here, from your heart, if you are ever to succeed as the wife of an olive farmer!"

Mona continued muttering under her breath, "Never have I witnessed such incompetent work," she said, shaking her head. "How could he bring her into this family? A pretty face cannot compensate for a poor day's work." She continued to shake her head in a disapproving manner, her lips pursed tightly in stern displeasure.

"But I married a farmer of figs. My husband's orchards are filled with fig trees, not olives." Nisrina tried to reason with her sister-in-law, "I only need to know . . ."

She was not given the chance to finish. Mona, at the base of the ladder, yelled up, "I will not listen to such insolent words. You dare talk back to me?! I am the eldest sister! You shall have respect for me, do you hear? Must I teach you how to behave?" She began to shake the ladder, "Get down from there, get down this minute, you foolish girl. You are finished!"

Nisrina's eyes were wet, her lower lip quivering, but she knew better than to argue with her sister-in-law. As the eldest sister in the family, Mona had the highest standing of the women, a position which demanded deference and respect. Nisrina carefully descended, hoping Mona would see the reasoning in her misstep—her foot had slipped, she was not clumsy or irresponsible—it could have happened to anyone.

But Mona was not a reasonable woman. In her fury, she began striking Nisrina with the stick. Blow after blow found her shoulders, her back and her arms. "How do you ever expect to be considered a daughter of the Yusef family if you cannot learn to handle a harvest rod? This is the fruit of life! A gift from God! Such a foolish girl! Such a fool!"

Nisrina, cringing on the ground, turned her face away, downward towards the earth. With arms raised up, she protected her head from the rod that repeatedly pummeled her body.

"ENOUGH!" It was Jabran's voice.

He grabbed the stick just as his sister raised it into the air, and in one swift motion, snapped the wood in two over his knee.

Nisrina turned to face her husband. She had tried her best not to cry, to be brave and endure her punishment, but when she saw him standing there so strong, tears filled her eyes.

"I *saw* her working," he yelled at Mona. "I was watching from above. She was doing a fine job!" His eyes were on fire, emblazoned with rage. "Had you not been so dull-witted, my sister, you would have observed how her foot slipped! Had you been properly tending to the ladder, this unfortunate incident would not have occurred."

"And yet it did happen, brother!"

"Have you no compassion?" Jabran's eyes were narrowing. "This could have happened to any one of us! How quickly you forget, dear sister . . . how quickly you forget the time you hit the tree so hard, an entire branch broke from its trunk; and if you will recall, you were promptly forgiven by our dear mother, God rest her soul." His face was red, his back tall and straight. He was not finished with his pitiless sister.

"You will NEVER strike my wife again! Do you understand? Do I make myself clear?!"

Mona glared back at her youngest brother. She had been cursed with an exacting personality and knew no way other than that of a strict disciplinarian. She felt her behavior was justified and appropriate. She was the eldest female in the family and had jurisdiction over the women and she resented her brother's interference. Prideful, she stood in defiance of him, her stance wide, her fists clenched at her hips. She held her head high, her chin stuck in the air.

Jabran was not intimidated.

"Your job is limited to instruction only!" he continued, angrily tossing the broken branches to the ground, "I will have it no other way."

By now, Nisrina had risen to her feet. She was brushing herself off and straightening her head scarf. Wide-eyed, she stood back from the quarrelling siblings. She had never heard her husband raise his voice in this manner. And now, taken aback by his fury, she did not know whether to smile with relief or cringe with fear. As she watched his angry discourse, she realized how little she knew the man whose bed she shared. Having suffered at the hands of her demanding sister-in-law, she was thankful that he'd come to her rescue. But his rage was unsettling, Nisrina never imagining that this gentle man whom she'd come to love could generate such commanding ferocity.

Jabran turned to his wife and wrapped his large powerful arms around her small torso, pulling her in, close to him. He felt her tremble under his touch.

"It is no matter," she whispered to him, knowing it wiser to keep peace in the family. "She was only trying to teach me. The fault is my own."

"No, Nisrina," Jabran interrupted, "There is a right way and a wrong way to teach, and I will not have my wife subjected to such cruelty, not now, not ever! I have spoken." He turned to Mona, his dark eyes disappearing under his brow, "It is final."

His glare pierced his sister's psyche, until Mona, too, began to tremble. She had gone too far in challenging her brother. She lowered her head, "Yes, my brother. Forgive me. Forgive me." Although she was the older sibling, she knew Jabran had the upper hand. She was only a woman, and not permitted to cross or anger any man, especially one from her family. His word absolute.

Jabran turned back to his wife who had gathered up the cloth filled with olives from the tree. He saw her flushed cheeks and the red marks on her arms from his sister's flogging. With a gentle touch, he bent over and kissed her wounds.

"I am fortunate, husband," Nisrina said quietly to him.

He smiled back with such love in his eyes that Nisrina forgot her pain; and then he lifted her into his arms, placing her gently on the back of Abu Faraj who'd been standing quietly nearby.

"You have done enough work for one day *habeebti*, I am taking you home."

Nisrina did not resist, her small hands holding tightly to the donkey's mane.

With one more disapproving look towards his sister, Jabran led the animal and his wife back to their home.

Unbeknownst to them, Dora, who had gone to fetch water, was resting nearby. Stopping behind the tall green cypress at the far end of the orchard, she witnessed the sorry exchange. She saw how Mona had treated Nisrina, her brother's caring touch, and his wife's words in return.

Dora knew that despite their common parentage, her youngest brother was unlike their father and two older brothers. Jabran had always been a kind and sensitive boy, and it was he who was heartbroken when their mother had died. Now, as she watched him with his new bride, she realized the purity of the young couple's love and was shamed by her sister's harsh ways. Watching them walk away, Dora vowed that she would keep a prayer in her heart for Nisrina and Jabran.

TEN

Hopeful Predictions

WITH THE HARVEST OVER, families gathered to celebrate. The townspeople were comforted knowing that there would be food for the winter, oil with which to cook their meals, and an ample crop to sell at market. Song, dance, food and drink were plentiful as loud, shrill voices pierced the air with festive ululations—women chanting songs for a blessed harvest, good fortune and long life.

Rising from their seats, the villagers danced in a circle, twirling round and round, all the while clapping to the rhythm of the *oud*, a pear-shaped lute played by Ali Farah, the town's old leather-maker. He'd been taught to play as a young boy by his cousin once removed, and now as the swollen wooden belly rested on the musician's knee, his fingers plucked away at the tightened strings as if he were still a young man. Ali Farah smiled as he cradled the instrument's short neck in his arms, his eyes focused on the crowd. The intricate wooden rosettes with mother-of-pearl inlay that decorated the instrument shimmered under the light of the kerosene lamps. And as his fingers moved with tempered speed, the crowd twirled and swooped to the deep, resonating tone.

Children ran freely, dancing and snatching treats from the serving trays set out along the perimeter of the garden, while the old seers, ancient women who'd been given the gift of seeing the future, told stories of joy and good fortune.

Mona and Dora, flanked by Marta, May and Nisrina were gathered together on one side of the courtyard, while their men stood in a row, tall and straight, their arms crossed in front of their chests on the other. They had been smiling and watching the crowd, enjoying the celebrations. Farooz, standing with a big smile stretched wide across his face, was the happiest of all for this year's crop was the largest his farm had seen in many years. An omen he attributed to his son's recent marriage.

At just that moment, when Farooz was thinking contented thoughts, Sana Sendawa, an ancient seer with legs the size of tree trunks, stepped out into the dancing throng. Her eyes had an unearthly stare as she looked beyond to a world no man could see. Her nostrils were flared, her white, wispy hair floating disheveled beneath an old silken scarf. A shawl, tattered and stained hung over her twisted shoulders. But the measures of beauty mattered not to the villagers. It was the wisdoms of her soul that intrigued them. And they stopped to take heed when she entered a room. This opener-of-fortunes, as the old seers were called, began to ululate in her most piercing voice. Conversations hushed and the villagers covered their mouths. Sana Sendawa was moving in the direction of the newest and youngest member of the Yusef family.

"Nisrina Yusef!" she screamed out from across the courtyard.

Nisrina stood paralyzed. Her smile fell from her face, her eyes opened wide. She saw the fortune teller walking towards her, pointing her finger in an accusatory way.

"Nisrina Yusef, daughter of Isa Huniah, wife of Jabran Yusef," the seer continued, "I have news for you!"

Her voice boomed loud and strong.

Ali Farah's fingers stopped in mid-strum, his eyes fixed on Sana. The ladies who'd been twirling and clapping, chanting and singing ceased their revelry to turn and face the old seer.

The crowd was spellbound, their heads moving in slow motion as they trailed to follow the crooked finger that offered its mark.

"I swear by all that is holy," the seer began to chant, her voice dropping several octaves, *"Enshallah,* as God is my witness, I know in these matters I am not wrong."

Nisrina's heart was pounding, her legs grew weak. What message did this opener-of-fortunes have for her?

"Nisrina Jabran Yusef," she continued slowly, enunciating each word with the dramatic flair of a wandering troubadour, her right arm now pointing up high to the heavens, "As God is our heavenly father, our master and commander of all things both great and small, and as certain that He is the designer and creator of the entire world, the universe and beyond, I say verily unto you . . ."

Nisrina held her breath, her lungs about to burst, her legs shaking under her *thobe*.

But Sana Sendawa, with face glazed over, was unaware of Nisrina's distress, "Nisrina!" she yelled, "I see a son growing in your womb!!"

The crowd gasped.

It was well known throughout the village that the Yusef family had no heirs. The fact that Marta and May had not been blessed with children caused the family much consternation, casting a shadow on their marriages and their ability to perform as good wives. Their husbands turning bitter and unforgiving. Jabran and Nisrina were the family's last hope. But no one dared say it out loud, fearing that they would cast an evil eye upon the young couple.

And now this.

Sana Sendawa had never been wrong. But to speak it in public? Voiceless concerns filled the air, the disquiet ever so thick. Would the old lady's words, spoken under the canopy of heaven itself, affect the fate of the young couple? No one could be sure.

All stood silent, transfixed as they watched the scene unfold.

Nisrina's panicked eyes searched for her love. Jabran was on the other side of the courtyard and his eyes quickly met her gaze. He saw the pleading look on her face and how she held her hands up to her mouth, daring not to breathe or speak. She so wanted it to be true, but she was frightened, worried that her thoughts alone might curse the possibility of such an honor. She'd had no inkling. Felt nothing inside her.

Jabran saw the distress in her face and confidently smiled back, giving her one of his mischievous winks. He did not believe in such superstitions. When Nisrina saw his lighthearted grin and the sparkle in his eyes, her anxiety softened like the frost on a warm winter's sill.

As always his tenderness calmed her spirit. She smiled back. First just a tiny smile, still afraid to allow herself to feel such joy. And then as he held her gaze longer, his deep, loving eyes piercing into her soul, her worries dissipated and her smile grew large. A quiet little chuckle bubbled up from her throat. A son. God willing, she thought to herself.

The villagers turned their heads to watch. First to the old woman and then to Nisrina, and back to the old woman again. But Sana said nothing more. She turned disappearing into the crowd as the villagers began their whispers and speculations. No one understood it. But somehow Sana Sendawa knew. She knew even before Nisrina could know. And, as it turned out, the old soothsayer was right.

ELEVEN

Coffee House Chatter

JABRAN SIPPED HIS COFFEE as he listened to the talk in the darkened café.

His quiet was a sharp contrast to the restless mood in the crowded room. He used to enjoy his evenings spent with men from the village. They'd meet for coffee and pleasant conversation. Some would sit huddled close together, silently playing cards and sharing smoke from the hookah, the fragrance of imported tobaccos, rich and fine, thickly melding with the deep dark scent of *kahweh Arabiyah*. Others preferred the sharp taste of *arak,* their bodies numbing to the icy burn of the licorice liqueur. They'd drink warm toasts to each other until the lids of their bloodied-red eyes drooped carelessly and their tongues spun loose.

But things were different now. It was 1917 and times had changed. Discussions no longer centered on the weather or the size of a man's harvest. No one complained of a disobedient wife or their mother-in-law's howling temper. Instead, they spoke loudly, endlessly, of ongoing battles between the invading British soldiers and the Turkish-ruled Ottoman Empire. The war of the world took place far from their village, and yet its shadowing menace lingered strong in the hearts and minds of many.

Each night debates ensued, stretching long into the early hours of the morn. Always strewn with lively conversation and high-minded assertions—each man thinking his position the wisest or shrewdest of them all.

However, throughout their discourse Jabran remained silent. As a farmer and the son of a farmer, he believed that all things had their season and he was content to trust that the future would unfold in its due time. The war was far away. It could not possibly reach the remote hills of Beit el Jebel. Their time spent haggling was futile. Could they not see that they were separate and distinct? In his mind, the men's fears were foolhardy speculations.

Jabran loved his wife and tenderly cared for his children.

Nisrina gave birth to a son as the soothsayer predicted, followed later by a daughter. They called the boy Essam, meaning 'safeguard' in hopes that he would always be out of harm's way. Jabran became known as *Abu* Essam, the father of Essam; and the villagers likewise called Nisrina, *Oum* Essam, the mother of Essam. To have a son was a great honor in their village, a cause for much celebration and rejoicing, and having earned this most valued status, Jabran, like all men with sons, walked high and proud.

As a young boy Jabran assisted his uncle, a tea merchant who toured Europe, Asia and Africa in search of exotic teas for purchase and trade. He traveled alongside him, assisting in carrying heavy loads and running errands. In doing so, Jabran learned the languages of the world and he studied the ways of other cultures. But his uncle, God rest his soul, had long since departed from the earth. Jabran, now married, had an orchard and a family of his own, and in these things he'd found contentment.

In the simplicity of village ways, Jabran understood the value of unyielding restraint and good manners. So when the townspeople of Beit el Jebel would gather at dusk and debate the complex issues of war, he maintained that this was the business of politicians and soldiers and would consistently abstain from discussing such matters.

"The British will prevail," one man was saying. "We are Arabs and the Turks have governed our lands for far too long. I, for one, will welcome the change in governments."

"Yes," claimed another. "The days of Turkish rule will soon come to an end! The British are a more even-handed people. Life will be good under their tenets. I'm sure of it!"

"No!" cried a third. It was Fareed Mustafa, the town's barber, "Impossible! The Ottoman Empire is all-powerful. The English can never survive our climate or understand our traditional ways. We are an enlightened people! Pillars of the earth! It is the Turks that helped make us great. They are a strong and mighty nation! They will win . . . mark my words, my friends! Mark my words!" As he spoke, Fareed waved his arms and stamped his foot, the sound resonating on the stone floor of the old café. But the other men were not intimidated. They raised their voices with lurid remarks and strong objections. It was known by many that his wife's father was of Turkish descent and in defending the Turkish people, he, in fact, was defending his own three sons.

Samir Salah, who had a vineyard that stretched across the eastern slopes of Beit el Jebel, declared that if the Turks ever came for him, he would run into the hills and hide between the rocks with the jackals and hyenas. "I'd rather spend my days with the dogs of the earth than fight alongside the dogs of mankind!" he asserted brusquely, his booming voice echoing hard against the cold stone walls. Many of the young men raised their glasses to him and agreed that they, too, would do the same, proclaiming their loyalties only to the hills and valleys of Beit el Jebel, not to the Ottoman Empire.

Malik, the grocer, was energized by the controversy. An inquisitive man who had difficulty forming his own opinions, he agreed with whoever had spoken last. He was round and plump with a pleasant nature, relishing in the debates and raised voices of the villagers, always encouraging the other men to speak their thoughts.

He noticed Jabran sitting quietly in the corner and said pointedly to him, "Abu Essam, you sit here night after night. You drink your coffee and you listen to our conversations, and yet you always remain silent and reserved. You are a learned man. You have traveled far and wide observing the ways of many men. Pray tell us, what do you think of the situation at hand? As the son of an Arab farmer, are you for the British or are you for the Turks?"

Before Jabran could answer, his oldest brother, Najeeb jumped in, "You will never get a response from my young brother, my dear Malik. You see, Jabran holds himself above such things. In fact, his head is so high, it floats in the clouds. He is a mere dreamer of dreams. His only earthly concerns, besides his orchards and his children, are his poetry, and of course . . . his young wife!" Najeeb mockingly rolled his eyes upward towards heaven.

The café roared with amusement. Najeeb knew his brother only too well.

However, Jabran did not join in their raucousness. With calm voice and measured words, he turned slowly to Najeeb, "I follow what is in my heart, dear brother. And from the look of things, I see that you do too."

Jabran was referring to the scantily clad woman whose legs were sprawled across Najeeb's lap. A woman paid by the establishment to dance, and with painted face and enticing ways, encourage the men to part with their coins. She was called Anisah, meaning pleasant companion. As she sat on the thighs of the eldest Yusef brother, his hands passionately caressed her bosom while his eyes devoured her exposed belly, so round and alluring. Anisah managed to cross and uncross her legs multiple times while the other patrons in the café watched in hungry anticipation, their own loins filled with envy. They couldn't help but notice how shapely and strong the dancing girl was, an attribute she acquired from many nights of twisting and gyrating between coffee house tables. Najeeb whispered something wicked into her ear and she threw her head back in feigned laughter as her raven black hair flew wild across his face. Then she smiled a devilish grin with lips tinted dark by the color of pomegranate seeds.

In spite of his brother's words, Anisah began to kiss Najeeb's face and wriggle restlessly in his lap, while her dark *kohled* eyes glared defiantly over her admirer's shoulder toward the young stalwart man who questioned her licitness.

Enjoying her insolence, the café patrons again raised their glasses, Jabran's retort gone unheeded. But he was sickened by it all. He'd had enough of their pretentious talk, of dancing girls and troublesome politics. He wished for peaceful times when men felt free to work and think, and live their lives without the darkness of a looming war.

He hated the conflict and the changes it wrought. He yearned for a time when thoughts could center on the important things in life—on family and home, and the wealth of a good book.

Tossing his coins on the table, he said his "good nights" and stepped out into the cool evening air, the sounds of the café fading as the door closed behind him. His head ached. He wanted to pluck the heated words of the evening from his mind and free himself from the aggravating noise still etched in his brain.

He longed to hear his wife's sweet voice. To be back in the warmth of her kitchen with the fire roaring and the smell of freshly baked bread wafting through the air. He needed to see his children, to hold them tightly in his arms and hear the stories about their day.

Taking a deep breath, he looked around at the rich valley that lay before him. With the Mediterranean basin to the west and vast desert to the east, Beit el Jebel was protected from the evils of the outside world, and for this he was thankful. He drank in the lush greenery of the rolling hills and the calm quiet of the forested trees, the tranquil silence broken only by the chirping of crickets that hid beneath the low-lying brush, their chatter ringing out steady and reassuring like sentries of the night.

Malik was right, he thought to himself. He'd traveled far in his young life, but he always came back to this peaceful village, this unchanging town, and now as he gazed at the familiar landscape and remembered his family waiting safely at home, he knew why.

With renewed thoughts and a warm heart, the farmer turned towards the empty road and hurried home.

TWELVE

Abduction

JABRAN ROSE EARLY TO the sounds of Nisrina working in the kitchen. Her side of the bed still warm, he smiled as her sweet voice, humming songs of the village, came drifting in through the open door. The smell of coffee, along with crackles and snaps from the hearth, told him that a fire had been lit and this pleased him. It would only be a matter of time before the heat from the flames would warm their small stone house. He was tempted to fight the cool chill in the air, to turn back on his side, pull the heavy woolen blanket up over his shoulders and nestle back into the comfort of his bed. Still dark outside, the idea of a few more winks was tempting, but he knew there was much work to do. Careful not to wake his children, he quietly slipped out of bed and washed the night's slumber from his face.

Nisrina prepared a simple breakfast of olives and *kashqwan*, a hard, yellowed goat cheese, its rich, savory tang melting like butter on the tongue. Moving the vase of jasmine she kept fresh in her kitchen, she made room for the food. She added a hot plate of *manaqish*, well-oiled loaves of flat bread topped with a lemony sauté of chopped spinach and thinly sliced onions. The warm scents awakened her husband's palate and he playfully bowed down to her kindness. He smiled when she took the seat beside him, and reached out to her, softly brushing his hands against her fingertips. Nisrina watched her husband as he broke the *manaqish* into small pieces and dipped them, one by one, into the *labben*, the thick yogurt swirling sensuously around the loaf's crisped edge. She loved the way his lips, so full, a dark red, effortlessly devoured her work. And she yearned to reach out and touch his chiseled jaw as it rhythmically moved—the strong, defined bone-line stirring her still.

Side by side the couple sat in silence, eating the flavorful foods put before them and sipping the fine *kahweh Arabiyah* that Nisrina had made using the techniques her stepmother had taught her.

After breakfast, Jabran rose. There was much work waiting in his orchard and he knew his day would be long. Before departing, he paused in the small alcove centered in the heart of their garden. He stood amidst the narcissus and roses that grew high against the arbored wall, and wishing to bid his wife one final goodbye, he lingered a moment, tenderly wrapping his arms around her shoulders. As he did each day when he bade her farewell, he pressed his lips against her cheek and softly whispered in her ear, "You, my love, are the prettiest flower in the garden."

Nisrina looked up at her husband and smiled, her face radiant, her eyes dark like the night sky. Deep, intense and loving. Six years had passed since they'd spent their first night together as husband and wife, Jabran reading poetry to his young anxious bride, and Nisrina gratefully devouring every word.

Jabran couldn't help but notice that although she was seven months into her third pregnancy, Nisrina was as beautiful as the day they'd first met. She laughed shyly at his familiar words, her eyes demurely averted, her hair falling softly in tendrils around her face— thick, long, a dark shade of brown. In public Nisrina always wore her hair in a bun tied neatly at the nape of her neck, a scarf covering her head. But for him, in their private moments when the world was quiet and time stood still, she let it fall free. He loved how the curls caressed her bare shoulders and he cherished the times when he would get lost in her gentle ways. And now, with her standing so close, he felt the warmth of her love and he knew he could not resist.

He took her face in the palm of his hands and ever so gently, ever so slowly, he kissed her soft, full lips as she melted in his arms.

The sun was beginning to peek over the horizon and it told Jabran that he should be on his way. He gathered his tools and headed off in the direction of his orchard. Approaching the top of the mount, he looked back. He could see his two children, Essam and Jameela, playing outside their home. Essam was his eldest child, his son, his heir. He'd been born a month early according to the midwife's predictions. But over the years, he'd grown tall. Now, barely five years old, his head reached the lower branches of his grandfather's olive trees. Jabran beamed proudly when the people of the village proclaimed how young Essam resembled his father.

Jabran was aware of his wife's love for her children, and it pleased him to see her so complete. He, too, cherished their smiles and marveled at their curious nature. However, Nisrina was first and foremost in his heart. The ground upon which she walked was sacred earth, and the sun that shone against her face, fueled the fire of his loins.

But he was a farmer and a full day's work lay waiting. He smiled quietly to himself and disappeared over the crest into the valley below.

When Nisrina first left her father's home, she was a young girl who rarely ventured from the family's orchards. Journeys beyond her gate were limited to the neighboring farm, her church, or the local *souk*. Since that time, she had grown into a woman, a wife and a mother of two. She'd seen her father buried solemnly and quietly in a plot adjacent to her mother's. When she stood before her father's open grave and laid a single rose upon his casket, she mourned not the death of that poor man, but rather his life. Isa Huniah had died unexpectedly from a ruptured appendix, lasting only four days after he first complained of a nagging pain in his belly. Her stepmother, Esma, now a widow and vulnerable to the idle talk and meddling ways of a tight-knit town, returned to the village of her youth to raise her four boys in her parent's home, the Huniah farm sold as an endowment for her children.

Nisrina learned to be a good wife. She was thankful for a husband who worked hard each day. The trees were beginning to bud, the early harvest looked promising. *Enshallah*, she thought to herself, we should have a good yield this year.

Nisrina never predicted an outcome or proclaimed a glory without the word, *Enshallah*. God willing. Like all the women of her village, she attended church on a regular basis, lighting candles and saying her prayers. Twice a year she would fast, give confession and take the Sacrament of Holy Communion. She faithfully invited the Orthodox priest into her home and he sanctified the house where her family lived. Walking through each room, she would bow her head as he chanted his prayers for safety and long life, sprinkling holy water in each corner—water that had been blessed at the Church of the Holy Sepulcher in Jerusalem. And when he was done, Nisrina would kneel before him, kiss the back of his hand and put it to her forehead in supplication. She would thank him and give a small donation to the church. In matters of faith, she did all that was expected of her. No one could fault her on that account or claim that she had strayed from the righteous way. And for this she felt at peace with the world.

With Jabran in his orchard, Nisrina was content to go about her day. She'd set out that morning to wash her clothes in the large basin outside her home. She left early to fetch water from the well near the center of town and walking along, her two children following close by her side, Nisrina nodded gently to the women she passed along the way, saying her pleasant good mornings with wishes for peace and good health. And they gave warm wishes and blessings to her in return. At the well, she filled her large earthen jug and balancing it on her head, her bare feet stepping lightly on the dirt path, she carried the water back to her home.

The basin full and her clothes immersed, Nisrina began to scrub. Her back ached from the weight of the child she carried within her, and she paused a moment to hear the sweet plaintive song of the woodlark flying overhead. Looking up at the expansive sky, her hands tenderly caressed her belly. My life is truly blessed, she thought to herself. The Lord has given me a beautiful home, a loving husband and two children, *Enshallah*, soon to be three.

Hanging her wash to dry, Nisrina saw Essam and Jameela running up the hill towards their father's fig orchard. Essam, who had full run of the farm, had decided to spy on his father as he worked in his fields, and Jameela, as always, trailed not far behind.

She recalled the first time her son had been placed in her arms. The figs hung sweet in her husband's orchard, a sign of good things to come; and the autumn breeze carried with it the sweet scent of jasmine. Fresh with heaven's pure light, he looked up at her, his eyes searching her face. She touched his fingers and toes, feeling the warmth of his skin, and as she did, she felt a light suffusing her, the likes of which she'd never known. Not even her undying love for Jabran compared to the splendor of that moment. She held his tiny body in her arms, realizing that all along she'd been a ship out to sea, lost in the harbors of nameless ports, searching for a place to belong. But when the child's sweet gaze met her own, an anchor was dropped from her heart and set deep into the dark, rich soil of the earth. Finally grounded, she'd found home. Her years spent as a motherless child, as the daughter of a man who could give her no love, were over. Nisrina had at last found solace in the most unexpected of places—in the precious, sweet eyes of her newly born son.

Her daughter, Jameela, followed two years later. Born round and robust, she was full of life. Her plump body and engaging nature carried her safely from infancy to toddlerhood. And now at three years old, she was beginning to chatter like the bearded old charlatans that sold wares in the marketplace. Her days were filled with laughter and wonderment as she followed her brother wherever he went.

As Nisrina watched them climbing up the path, she called out to them, "Be careful my darlings. Do not cause any trouble for your father, and remember, he needs helping hands, not mischievous ones!"

Hearing her warnings, the two children laughed joyfully. Essam waved back to her, hopping frivolously on one foot, "Of course, *Yumma*. You needn't worry. We are *Yaba's* helpers today!"

And Jameela, attempting to follow her brother's antics, bobbed up and down, with both feet planted firmly to earth. She waved and smiled at her mother.

When they reached the top of the hill overlooking the orchard, the two young conspirators lay down on the ground. Nestling in, between the blossoms of wild narcissus and untamed buttercups, they peered over the edge into the valley below. A gentle rain had blanketed the hills to the west with a carpet of bright red, as the springtime poppies spread their wings, and the cyclamen, sweet and delicate, their visage drifting from dark purple to pale pink and white, peeked out shyly from behind the rocks and boulders.

The children, lying on their stomachs, inspected the scene below. They saw their father. He was working alone today, his farmhand gone into town for supplies. The children giggled and whispered as they watched him tending his crop. They were poachers who would pick his figs and run off with the sweet delights.

Jabran, unaware of the young spectators watching from above, meticulously continued his work. First clearing back the wild spring growth that surrounded each tree and then carefully thinning out the new buds on the ends of the branches. He pruned back the smallest of the sprouts, false blooms that would not produce a mature fruit, and left the larger ones intact knowing they would grow hearty.

The children quickly grew tired of his exacting efforts, and succumbed to the warm sun and the gentle breeze that blew in across the rolling hillside. They lay back between the tall, wild grasses and closed their eyes. The sweet smell of sage hung in the air, seducing their senses, the earth hovering soft in a delicate haze. There they rested, feeling safe and secure in their father's orchard.

However, their solitude was soon interrupted.

Hearing sounds from the field below, they turned back onto their stomachs and, remaining low on the ground, once again peered over the edge.

This time they saw that their father was not alone. Five men, Turkish soldiers with guns, approached from the east.

Jabran froze as he saw them, while his mind raced forward. In spite of his hatred for all things savage, Jabran knew war was an inevitable part of life. Countries throughout the world had been fighting each other since the beginning of time. He'd heard the stories told by the elders, in coffee houses and around the dinner table. Stories passed down from generation to generation. How the vanquishers took with them the land, the resources and the very souls of the people they conquered. And although he knew that he lived in a country that had endured multiple subjugations, he had intentionally chosen to distance himself from the fray, to remain a man of his own making, a man of heart. He'd kept his life simple and unfettered, his days spent in quiet reflection. A scholar who elected to work his fields and love his family.

In spite of his beliefs, it was evident that the time had finally come, the soldiers who'd been merely a concept, were a short distance away. The tendrils of war that once seemed so far had now appeared in his orchard. He realized some choices were not his to make. Life had its own plan. Without warning or prelude, and despite his resolve to the contrary, fate had boldly stepped in and taken hold of his destiny.

They approached.

"*Marhaba*," their leader greeted him brusquely.

"*Marhaba*," he replied cautiously, eyeing their weapons. "Welcome to my home. How may I serve you, my friends?"

"We are not your friends," the leader sneered. They drew their weapons. "And you cannot serve us, but you will serve His Highness, the Sultan, and fight in his honor against the British devils!" The leader spat on the ground, his face twisted in a hateful grimace, the sweat on his brow glistening in the searing heat of the midday sun. The men stunk of the foul stench of war. Their uniforms covered in blood and dirt. Their hair grimy and their teeth yellowed from the stains of Turkish tobacco.

Jabran raised his arms in submission. During the debates in the village he'd heard stories of forced conscriptions into the Ottoman military, men taken from their fields at gunpoint to serve in the Turkish army, never to be seen or heard from again. What had once been only tales of brutality and abductions, discussed over sweets and coffee in the village square, had now in a single moment become his reality. Alone and unarmed, he was at the will of these ungodly men. He knew there was nothing he could do to fight them. If he tried to resist, they'd surely kill him and torture his family. His plans to remain separate and distinct, apart from the masses, were instantly dashed. His only hope would be to sacrifice himself in trade for the safety of his loved ones. But he was given no chance to negotiate.

Abruptly, and without further notice, his thoughts were interrupted by a searing pain that shot through his body as the butt of a rifle plummeted deep into his stomach. He fell to his knees, the air forced from his lungs by the terrible jolt. He couldn't breathe. Couldn't speak. He felt a vicious kick to his ribcage, and then another and another as his body fell flat to the ground.

A soldier lifted him up by his armpits and dragged him across the field. Then, slowly, as his breath returned, he whispered, his words barely audible, "But my family, my children . . . we are Christians . . ."

"Silence, infidel!" the Turkish leader sneered, making no attempt to hide his scorn for the self-serving Arab. "You are a subject of the Ottoman Empire and His Highness, the Exalted Sultan Mehmed V commands your loyalty! You are one of us now." And with that, they tied his hands tightly behind his back and dragged him away into the dense brush.

Essam jumped up, panic in his voice, "*Yaba, Yaba* come back, don't leave us!! *Yaba*, come back!" But his calls were in vain, his father now gone from his sight. He turned to his sister who was trembling, her eyes pleading for comfort. "We must tell *Yumma*," he told her. "She'll know what to do." With urgency fueling him on, he grabbed her hand, and together they raced down the hill.

Running, Essam called out to his mother, "*Yumma, Yumma!*" But they were too far from home, his words lost in the broad canopy of trees. Jameela was crying, tears covering her cheeks, her three-year-old legs trying hard to keep up. She stumbled and fell, "Essam!" she reached out to her brother. He lifted her, brushing the leaves from her dress. "Please, Jameela. Don't cry," he begged. "We must hurry!"

The children had traveled the rocky dirt path from the orchard to home since the time they could walk, but now the once familiar trail seemed strange and foreboding. His fear growing with each second that passed, Essam kept his eyes to the ground. He jumped over stones, and dodged twisted branches, still holding tightly his sister's small hand.

Although he tried his best to be brave, the tears started flowing. He wiped them away, but his eyes filled again. They clouded his vision and he failed to see the large stone up ahead. He came down hard, twisting his ankle beneath him, scraping both his arms and his legs on the rough pebbled ground. Jameela followed along, toppling beside him. Terrified, she was now sobbing desperately.

"It matters not, Jameela," he pleaded with her. "It matters not. Come, please . . . hurry!" Helping her to her feet, he gave no heed to the scrapes and bruises that covered his body. His heart was pumping furiously, his lungs aching for air. Finally he rounded the last bend on the path and saw his mother working in the garden outside their home. With a gasp and a cry, he called out with all the strength he had left.

At first the distance kept her from hearing their words. Nisrina thought they were just laughing and being silly children. But they were running so fast. As they approached she realized something was terribly wrong. They were not laughing, they were crying! In fact, their screams were frantic, they were sobbing and wailing. The only words she could make out were "*Yaba*" and "the soldiers" repeated over and over.

Seized with terror, Nisrina fell to her knees as the frantic children rushed into her arms. She gathered them up and holding them tightly, pleaded with them, "Tell me, what is it that's wrong? What is it that's happened?" They could barely speak, their words coming in short bursts, captured between breathless sobs. Finally, Essam told the story of how the soldiers beat his father, dragging him away into the brush. Nisrina, horror-stricken was desperately shaking her head. But when he finished, she knew it was true, what her heart could not accept—her husband was gone. And dropping her head in the palms of her hands, she, too, began to cry.

THIRTEEN

Conscription

THE TWO OLD WOMEN heard the wailing and crying. Running to the kitchen window, they looked out across the court where they saw their pregnant sister-in-law crumpled on the ground, her two small children gathered in her arms. She was rocking back and forth, tears streaming down her face.

"God forbid, it must be the baby," Dora said, glancing at Mona.

Without another word, they grabbed their shawls and ran out the door leaving the half-washed okra sitting on the kitchen counter, the lamb meat chopped in small pieces on the wooden block. The stew would have to wait. They went running across the courtyard, past the fountain and the olive trees, their aprons flapping against their thighs as they caught the flurry of the eastern wind. They moved swiftly. Mona in the lead, Dora limping close behind, her walking stick left abandoned on the hearth. As their bare feet followed along the stone pathway, they called out to Nisrina.

"Is it the baby?" yelled Mona.

"Is it your time?" Dora called.

Nisrina did not respond. She was on bent knees, collapsed under the giant fig tree, planted at the far end of the courtyard when her husband was first born. Rocking back and forth, she could only cry as she held her children tightly. The scattered sunlight filtering through the deeply lobed leaves cast ominous shadows across her face, and the birds overhead flitted frantically from branch to branch, their screeches echoing across the valley floor.

"I see no blood," said Mona, "I'm sure the baby is fine."

But Dora knew this was not in keeping with Nisrina's calm nature. Something must be terribly amiss. Even the birds' songs were disturbed.

"*Mahrt akhouy*, wife of my brother," Dora pleaded with her, "What is it? What is distressing you so? Please, tell us. Are you in pain?"

But Nisrina could not look at her two sisters-in-law. She feared the impact the news would carry and she clasped her children even closer.

The two women stood helpless, unable to make sense of the spectacle before them.

"She's gone mad," Mona concluded.

"She is distressed," said Dora masking the harshness of her sister's tone.

Essam could bear their comments no longer. He broke from his mother's grasp. Only five years old, his innocence had been shattered by what he had seen. He yelled to his aunties, his face filled with fury, "The soldiers took my father. They've taken him away. They beat him and tied him. He is gone! They took my father! The soldiers took my father!"

He could say no more, the horror of the scene still tearing at his heart. He buried his face in his mother's chest and sobbed uncontrollably. Jameela was crying too and she wrapped her tiny arms around her brother, pressing against him, wanting it all to end.

Dora's mouth fell open. Her head suddenly unsteady.

Mona's eyes widened, her stomach twisting in a knot.

Shocked by their nephew's disclosure, the two old maids stared dumbfounded in space. They'd heard that British soldiers were rapidly advancing on the Ottoman Empire, and in desperate attempts Turkish forces were seizing Arab "volunteers" to fight in the Sultan's army. Farmers taken from their fields. They called it conscription. And now this evil force, this horrible atrocity, had found its way to their small village!

Gathering their senses, the two sisters began shouting lamentations and violent curses into the wind. First they pleaded for mercy, raising their hands to the heavens, and then furious, they viciously slapped the front of their thighs. They yelled and they screamed, the air filled with their scorn, until even the birds disappeared from the sky.

"We will kill those soldiers who took our dear brother," shrieked Mona. "*Enshallah*! God willing! You shall see."

"We will find him and bring him home," Dora finally proclaimed. "All will be well, Nisrina. Peace will be restored to our family once again! He will return. I promise you. Don't worry, *mahrt akhouy*, don't worry."

Nisrina, hearing their pledges and encouraged by their optimism, glanced up for one brief moment. But her hopes were quickly dashed. Through tear-stained eyes, she saw the two old maids exchange a look. She recognized the stilted rise of their brows, the fixed widening of their eyes, and she knew what they were thinking.

As she rose to stand before them in defiance of their thoughts, to denounce her children's words and decry the reality of this calamity, she saw the people of the village arriving. They were running towards her, yelling and screaming, wailing and crying. How news could travel so quickly was a constant mystery to all. Some say it was carried in the wind, others, that it was spoken through the trees. But the fact remained, the townspeople knew of the tragedy that had befallen the love of her life, and they were quickly gathering outside her home to lend their support, discuss the implications, and find out more.

As the villagers raced to her side, they spoke freely of the incident. The soldiers had been seen. The other young men of the village had escaped to the hills to hide between the boulders and crevices where they couldn't be found. They had tried to warn Jabran, but it was too late.

Through their words Nisrina acknowledged what her heart ached to deny. Jabran had been taken, and any declarations to the contrary were clearly futile. The whole town knew of the travesty. It had to be true. Their certainty made it undeniably so.

FOURTEEN

Hannah

LIKE HER SIBLINGS BEFORE her, Hannah was born in the same bed in which she was conceived. Greeted by the warm, sweet scent of jasmine, faithfully placed on her mother's kitchen table, she gasped her first breath as the heady aroma silently weaved its way into the tapestry of her mind.

Nisrina gave birth to her third child shortly after Jabran had been taken by the Turkish soldiers. But unlike her first two, there was no husband to wait outside her room. No anxious steps heard pacing back and forth between the marigolds and hibiscus. There'd been no father to take the tiny red-faced infant into his strong, calloused hands and whisper softly in her ear that no matter what happened, he would protect her and love her until his dying day.

And there'd been no midwife to guide her in her journey.

Sadly, Sabra Hishmeh, the old midwife of Beit el Jebel, had died earlier that spring, passing away quietly in her sleep. She'd had no children of her own, no daughters to whom she could teach her secrets. And because no one believed her death would ever occur, including Sabra herself, there'd been no one trained to take her place. So when she died, the small, remote village found themselves without a midwife and the women knew they would have to rely on each other in bearing their children.

Nisrina's child came quickly and without circumstance. It was her third pregnancy and she recognized the signs of impending birth before she opened her eyes. The bed was wet where her water had broken and she had spent the night in a restless slumber, the pains coming at well-spaced intervals. When she woke and realized her time had come, Nisrina sent Essam and Jameela to fetch their Auntie Dora. She further instructed them to stay at their grandfather's home until she called for their return.

Of the four women who lived in the Yusef compound Dora was clearly the more nurturing and Nisrina preferred to have her at her side when she gave birth. A woman of very few words, her eyes were gentle and her smile warm. And for this reason, Nisrina hoped that it indeed would be Dora who would return to assist her.

"This is a terrible time to be giving birth!"

Nisrina cringed as she heard the high-pitched voice screeching outside her bedroom window. "The early morning hours are for working in the fields, not for laying in bed . . ."

"It matters not," Dora interrupted her sister. "It matters not. It is for God to determine, not you or I. The child will come when his time is due, and the mother must abide."

"It is a sign, I tell you," Mona went on. "He will be a lazy child not adhering to his chores or minding the words of his elders. Oh, dear God, I'm sure that a birth at this early hour of the morning is a bad sign. He will be a frivolous child."

"Sister, many children come into the world at the early hours of the morn," Dora whispered. "I've heard that it's a sign of strength and fortitude. He is ready to start a new day with energy and vigor . . ."

"But it forces his mother to lie in bed when she should be outside working in her orchard," Mona interrupted, her voice getting louder and shriller. "Who will carry her load with Jabran now gone?"

Mona showed no sign of stopping her rant, despite Dora's hushings.

And then the sisters heard the screams. They rushed into the house, running directly into the bedroom. They saw Nisrina lying on the bed, her bare legs spread wide apart, her hands desperately grasping behind her knees. There was blood on the sheets and her back was arched, her head thrown back in pain.

"He's coming," she panted between breaths. "He's coming . . . now!" She paused to bear down. Her face turning red, her lips pressed tightly together.

Dora ran to the foot of the bed and yelled to Mona, "Bring some clean towels . . . quickly!"

However, the towels didn't come soon enough, for with the next push, the baby's head fell right into Dora's open palms. Her hands now covered in the fluids of birth, she held the child's tiny head.

"It's the head!" Dora cried. "Push again, Nisrina. Push again! He's almost here!"

Nisrina waited a few moments, panting—the short staccato sounds filling the room. It was a technique she'd learned from Sabra during the birth of her first two children. She was anxious for it to be over, her back was aching and her body felt sure that it would burst in two, but she knew the importance of her breath and took heed of her circumstance. She'd learned not to push without the force in her belly bearing down on her and so she waited for the next wave to overtake her. Clearing her mind, she focused on the senses in her body. When she felt the pressure once again tightening around her abdomen, she took a deep breath and pushed, giving it all the strength she could muster. And in that push, the entire body of the child emerged in one fell swoop. Nisrina felt its shoulders clapping softly against her opening, first one side and then the other. She blinked her eyes, realizing that she had closed them tightly in her concentration, and now knowing her work was done, she anxiously waited for the sound of life. She saw Dora turn the child upside down and repeatedly slap its bottom.

The baby took in a quick, deep breath and screamed at the top of her lungs.

It was music to her mother's ears.

"A girl!" Mona recoiled, covering her mouth.

"Yes, it's a girl!" Dora exclaimed. "A beautiful, healthy girl, *Enshallah*, just like her mother."

Nisrina breathed a sigh of relief. The child had a head full of thick, dark hair and was wailing lustfully. She lay back against the pillow, reaching out to take her newborn daughter in her arms. Dora placed the child on her bosom as Nisrina admired her, kissing her tenderly.

Mona's face scrunched up at their frivolous affections. The family had expected a male child. A second heir to the Yusef estate. A boy, who, along with his older brother Essam, would work the family's lands and carry on the Yusef name. But it was a girl! Someone who would leave her father's home to wed another. Such a misfortune! Such a travesty! Who would care for them in their old age? A second grandson was an assurance that all would be well. And now there was none. Such a lost opportunity!

Mona was anxious to tell the elders that her sister-in-law had disappointed them once again. That she'd had the ill fortune to give birth to a second girl. And now with no husband in sight and small hopes for his return, the prospects of Nisrina providing a second heir were gone. The Yusef family remained with only one male child to carry the family name and manage the estate. Mona knew that the elders would not be pleased. Such news must be delivered quickly. And she was just the one to do it.

She turned to leave.

"Mona!" Dora called her back. "Boil me some water. And bring more towels . . ."

Dora did not look up to see her older sister's face. She was working hard now, massaging Nisrina's abdomen, urging the placenta to expel itself. The baby was sucking hard at her mother's breast.

Nisrina watched her spirited young daughter, still covered with the white sheen of birth, and she saw before her an old soul. Her chest filled with warmth. She felt confident that this child would be strong, with a promising future.

As the girl rhythmically pressed her mouth against her mother's swollen nipple, Nisrina thought of Jabran. He would be proud, she thought to herself. Look how tightly the child wraps her hand around my finger. A smart one, indeed, destined to be positive and sure in her life. *Enshallah*, I think that I will not fear for this one as I do for the others . . . not as much anyway.

As she watched her daughter nurse, Nisrina felt the familiar pains start up again.

"I need to push again, Dora. It is time."

"Then push you will," Dora replied as she quickly took the child from its mother's arms and swaddled her in the clean cloths that Mona had brought her. She laid the baby close by her mother's side, all the while saying in a soothing voice, "That's right . . . push my sister. Push the afterbirth out. God willing it will come easily and . . ."

But Nisrina didn't wait to hear the end of Dora's words—she had already begun to bear down. And while Dora was still urging her on, the placenta plopped out from between Nisrina's legs, emerging with an explosion like a second child entering the world. Dora had quickly moved back to the foot of the bed, examining the bloody mass that was now lying on the sheets.

"Praise God!" she yelled. "It's in one piece! All will be well, Nisrina. All will be well. Well done." She was nodding and smiling.

Mona brought her sister the pot of boiling water and placed it on the ground at the foot of the bed. Silently, she went back into the kitchen and in a few moments returned with some additional clean towels draped over her arm. She laid them on the bed next to Nisrina. Without another word, or glance at the mother and child, Mona turned and walked out the door.

Nisrina had seen the disappointment in Mona's face. She saw her pursed lips and stone cold eyes and she knew what it meant. After Mona had left, she turned to Dora who was busy cleaning up the afterbirth. "I expect that the elders will be disappointed that she's a girl." Nisrina was searching her sister-in-law's face.

"Never mind what the others might think," Dora whispered. "You have a beautiful, healthy child and I dare say she looks just like you." She had cut and tied the cord that connected the child to the placenta and was now wrapping the afterbirth in a burlap cloth so that she could bury it in the yard later that day.

"Oh Dora," Nisrina said wistfully, "do you think Jabran would be happy? Do you think?" But Nisrina could not finish her thoughts, her eyes filling with tears.

"Do not worry, Nisrina," Dora soothed her. "Jabran would be very proud of you and his baby girl. He will be home soon. Do not fret, please. Don't cry, it's not good for the milk. You have to think of the baby now." She was patting her sister-in-law's shoulder and straightening the blankets, trying to comfort the new mother. "All you need to think about is this beautiful child that you and Jabran have created together. That's all. That's all . . . " she cooed in a soothing voice. "As soon as I've cleaned this up I will make you some tea. All will be well, my sister . . . rest now . . . all will be well."

Nisrina was comforted by Dora's gentle words. And as her daughter fell asleep beside her, she too closed her eyes and drifted into a restful slumber.

Dora remained close by Nisrina's side, watching over her and the baby as she tidied up around them. She hoped that the family would not come to see the child just yet. She wanted Nisrina to rest and gain back her strength. She knew that the young mother would have a lot to deal with once the others had heard that it was a female child. If her predictions were right, the family would not rush over to see them, and for now that was a good thing.

As it was, little Hannah had no trouble winning the hearts of the Yusef family. They watched the fatherless babe grow from infancy to toddlerhood, her big brown eyes and endearing smile quickly capturing their favor. And as the months passed, one by one they all came to cherish her sweet and beguiling ways.

Even the taciturn Mona could not resist Hannah's innocent charms. The child would stand before her disapproving aunt, and in mischievous defiance, challenge the old maid's somber instructions. With her tiny arms folded boldly in front of her chest and her furrowed brow hiding her deep dark eyes, Hannah was fearless, and although she tried not to show it, Mona relished the willful trait in her niece.

"She's just like her Auntie Mona!" Mona would proudly proclaim, patting her bosomless chest. "She is just like me!" And she'd hug the child tightly, tucking her close in, her long willowy arms wrapping around the little girl as she declared over and over that she would never let her go. Hannah would laugh and squeal, squirming to be free, until finally Mona would release her to play amongst the baubles and toys that covered the floor.

PART TWO

1917

What evil darkness has possessed a world once loved?
No body left untouched; no soul found justly aggrieved.
What beastly shadow has tethered its heinous will upon the
ruins of mankind,
As brothers lift up swords against brothers, and fathers raise
hands against sons?
For are we not all made brothers and sons in the righteous
eyes of our Lord?

FIFTEEN

Soldiers Now

THE WAGON JOSTLED ALONG at a horrific speed.

Jabran could smell the growing fear of men pressed up against him. Lying atop one another, they were packed onto the cart, body against body, soul against soul, until they could no longer distinguish between their own individuality and that of the group. They had become a single mass of human flesh, melting and merging in the heat of the hot desert sun.

His arms and legs firmly bound, his eyes blindfolded tight, Jabran had been traveling for what seemed like days now, all the while in a world of darkness. Sounds and smells were his only allies. The warmth of the sun's rays pressing down on his skin was his only timepiece, his one connection to the humanity that he'd so recently left behind.

A pattern had developed. At every stop the soldiers disembarked. An eternity would pass and then he'd hear the screams, the wailing and crying, the pleading. He'd hear the struggles, the beatings, and then he would wait for the inevitable, the insufferable—another living body, bound and trodden, thrown into the pile, and the wagon would take off.

Sometimes he'd hear shots being fired, followed by the sound of a man's breath leaving his body. Left for dead. Jabran couldn't help wonder—were these poor souls the pitiful or were they the blessed? Either way, he knew that they were all cursed. Both the living and the dead, caught up in a world not of their making. A brotherhood of the damned.

In the moment that he'd been taken and thrown into the back of the old, rickety wagon atop all those who'd been captured before him, Jabran realized he'd come upon the inevitable forces of fate and entered the raging gates of hell.

To ease his pain, his thoughts turned to Nisrina. His mind wandering to the vision of her eyes, her smile, her countenance. He felt the horror she would feel when she realized he was gone. He worried. He hoped that she would understand his disappearance. That she would somehow learn the truth of his fateful demise. That she would discern in her own mind that this was not of his doing. His leaving was not of his choice. It was the others. He was forced. Hopefully, she would know and endure until he could find his way back home to her. Hopefully.

"*Yullah*, everyone off!" Jabran was awakened by the soldiers' voices.

They were yelling orders and prodding the men with their rifles.

The soldiers had jumped up onto the back of the open wagon and were unloading their captives. One by one, they picked up each recruit, still bound and blindfolded, and threw them down onto the ground as if they were unloading a bag of rice at the local *souk,* a commodity for purchase or trade. No thought or concern was given to the individual, to the life that was now being held so perilously in their hands. Such was the state of their humanity.

Jabran landed with a thud onto the warm desert floor. Although night had descended upon them, the rocky soil held the warmth from the day's heat. He lay there. It was good to be free from the weight of the others. For one brief moment he was able to relax, to enjoy the firm, temperate surface of the earth beneath him.

A soldier removed the blindfold from his face. Jabran felt grateful. Thankful for the dark night and the cool air that soothed his eyes. He watched the uniformed man take out a large knife and hold it high, menacingly. His heart began to race. Had he come so far just to be slain and left in the desert to die? The soldier, unaware of Jabran's concerns and without so much as a glance into his eyes, brought the knife down; swiftly and accurately he cut the binding on his legs, the blood rushing through his ankles and back into his feet.

"*Yullah*, get up! The free ride is over! Now you walk on your own two feet. *Yullah*!" It was a Sergeant. He kicked Jabran hard, the pain searing into his thigh. "Don't expect us to carry you as your mother once did. You are a soldier now. You are part of the greater good, a warrior in the Sultan's army. Hah! You are one of the chosen ones!"

He laughed a loud, vicious laugh, hateful and crude.

Jabran tried to stand, but his legs would not hold him.

Many of the men lay motionless, dazed and weakened from the long ride. Their captors, impatient with the new recruits, were kicking them into submission, insisting that they move and move quickly. Jabran again attempted to stand. He held onto the wagon's side, his head spinning wildly, his legs weak like rubber. As the blood once again started coursing through his veins, his strength gradually returned. Finally, slowly, he got his bearings and could stand unassisted.

"*Yullah*, tonight we march, tomorrow you can rest," the Sergeant laughed again, that cruel laugh, the joke only his to understand.

And march they did. They marched all night through the desert. Towards the East, always towards the East.

Jabran, trying to assess the situation, had no idea where he was. Looking around he found the dark desert landscape unfamiliar. Having been blindfolded for so long, unaware of the number of days or nights they'd been traveling in the wagon, left him disoriented. He looked to the stars for a key to his whereabouts, but the night sky was too vast, the stars only telling him that they were traveling in an easterly direction, nothing more. And although it had only been a few days since he'd left his orchard, to him it seemed an eternity.

As the night progressed, they were given a small respite every hour: a sip of water, nothing more. If any unfortunate soul, who in his haste to moisten his parched lips, accidently spilled some of the precious liquid, it was considered his share, his loss, and for that hour he went without; there were no second chances. Jabran, observing the protocol, learned to be very careful, very deliberate in his movements. A man of measured ways, he strove to remain in control of his emotions and therefore, his body. Hopefully, sustaining some power of what was left of his destiny.

The hours marched on.

The men remained on foot, walking, walking, always moving forward, their destination unknown. The Turkish soldiers rode alongside them, sitting high atop their camels.

At the next respite, they paused, as once again, water was passed to all the men up the line. An old man named Boulos Abu Nassir waited his turn for his share of the water. He was thin and ragged and appeared very feeble. The lines in his face were deep like the wind-carved ravines of a canyon wall, his skin darkened from years of working in the fields, toughened to a leathery brown. But although his skin was tough, his body was frail and his demeanor weak. When it came his time to drink, the old man became anxious. His thirst overwhelming, he worried that he might spill the small share allotted to him. His hands began to shake and his lips trembled.

Jabran stood a short distance behind him and observed the man's anguish. It ached him to see this poor man's distress. It reminded him of the old men in his village. Men who were respected for their age and their wisdom. Men who'd worked hard, year after year, holding their heads up high. Toiling in the fields. Providing for their families. They always began as strong, young men. And as time passed, they'd finally grow old, the years stealing the strength of their youth. Eventually they'd become weak and feeble, needing assistance with the simplest of tasks.

He watched as the old man reached out for the water jug, his hands rocking back and forth, unable to steady them. He took hold of the jug and raised it to his lips. And just as he was about to take a sip, to quench his starving thirst, his shaking hands caused the water to splash over the edge and fall to the ground.

The Turkish soldiers laughed. That evil, hateful laughter.

"Next man!" the Sergeant took the water jug from the old man's hands and passed it on to the next in line. The old man, his head bent down, quietly began to weep.

When it was Jabran's turn, he took the jug from the soldier's hands. His own hands so steady and sure, he walked over to Boulos

Abu Nassir. He reached out and touched the old man's shoulder, his bones protruding from his slight frame. The old man looked up.

"*Ummo*," he called him Uncle, in respect and deference to his age, "Here, take my share. I am young and it is of no matter to me. Please drink. Nourish yourself."

"No, *ya Ummo*," the old man pushed his hands away, "I cannot take your share. It is for you. You are young and you have your whole life ahead of you. I am an old man and my days are few."

But Jabran refused. He put the water back under the man's chin, "I insist, please drink from my hands. You would honor me."

Jabran held the jug to the old man's lips. He continued to hold it, steady and calm until finally the old man acquiesced, desperately drinking his share.

"Enough!" The Sergeant was angry. "Enough! If you want to waste your nourishment on an old man such as this, then so be it. This time it is you that shall go without!"

And the water was passed to the next in line.

Onward they marched through the night, their legs and ankles growing numb as they steadied themselves on the sandy soil, a burn erupting where blisters formed on their sandaled feet.

As he walked, Jabran's thoughts returned to his village, to his home where Nisrina and his children were waiting for him, perhaps they were having dinner or working together in the garden. As the warm memories filled his mind, the terror of his ordeal diminished. He imagined the best. That Nisrina and his children had heard the news and had recovered from their distress. In his imagination, they were now living their lives in their normal routine. His brothers, most likely Jacob, would tend his orchards in his absence. His sisters, particularly Dora, would help Nisrina with the children.

He was sure that someone had seen him being taken by the soldiers and they had by now relayed the message to his family. *Enshallah*, they had seen his hands being tied behind his back and they saw the soldiers with their guns. He was sure of it. How could it not be so? There was no event that occurred in Beit el Jebel that had ever escaped the villagers' sharp scrutiny. Surely this one incident would not be the exception.

With those self-assurances entrenched in his mind, he could be confident that Nisrina knew he'd not deserted her. That he would return one day and hold her in his arms again. That she should not think for one moment that he was anything like Abu Riyadh, the butcher who one day ran off with Wafa Tabiyah, the town's hairdresser, with no word to his wife, no message of apology or explanation. Never to return or be heard from again.

Wafa Tabiyah was a garish woman, known for wearing too strong a scent. Her fragrance could be detected long before she, herself, could be seen. He remembered how she always stood in the doorway of her shop under the guise of attracting female customers, but it was evident that it was the men for whom she had the eye. She stood so brazenly, so enticingly. Even her teeth showed bright white as she smiled wide for passersby.

Even Jabran turned away more than once as she lifted her skirt to step over the threshold, her bare ankles showing for all the world to see. A gentleman at all times, there were moments when he found her somewhat alluring. Her ankles looked so white and soft, so appealing. Had she applied a balm or oil to soften them? He would never know.

One day the news came, quickly spreading through the village. Abu Riyadh was gone, and so was the hairdresser. His wife had awakened one morning to find his bed empty, the key to the butcher shop lying on the table near the kitchen door. There was no note. No words of regret. Only a key to a shop that had no butcher. And a wife that had no husband. The legs of lamb, hanging on their hooks, were left unattended, the chickens unfed in their coops. His wife was left to manage alone, and worse, to suffer the town's gossip. A scandal from which she would never recover. Such a travesty indeed.

No, no. He could not do that to Nisrina. He was sure that someone in the town must have seen him leaving, being forced at gunpoint. Someone must have told her. And then he began to think of Nisrina. His dear, sweet, gentle wife. Her ankles so soft. Her skin so alluring.

As they marched across the sand dunes, up one hill and down the other, the fatigue became unbearable. Anyone who dared to slow down was promptly prodded with a long pole. The soldiers, on their camels, drove the marching men as a spiteful farmer might herd his goats. Constant. Unrelenting.

The hour was late and they had been walking all night. They were weary beyond all measure, their exhaustion overwhelming. Jabran glanced up and through the dark night, he saw a man begin to falter. He wove back and forth, his arms loose, his body lethargic. Finally, his legs gave way and he fell to the ground. Within moments, the Sergeant was standing beside him, kicking him over and over again, hard in the ribs, screaming to him to rise up and continue the march. The man could not move. The Sergeant lifted his rifle, pointing it at the prostrated body. Again, he ordered the man to stand.

Motionless, the man remained on the ground.

Then, without hesitation, neither pause nor second thought, a shot rang out, loud and fierce. Blood sprayed all over, splattering the rifled soldier, the men, and the gritty earth. Everyone stood in horror, transfixed, as the memory of the sound faded slowly in the distance. The poor man lay dead where he'd fallen.

"The only good Arab is a dead Arab," the Turk muttered under his breath. He turned to the remaining men. "Let that be a warning!" he screamed. "He who falters shall not survive this challenge. Those of you who are strong enough to endure this night, I say to you, move on, move on, for I promise you, a richer experience awaits! One you will tell your children and your children's children. You must go on, for the sake of your countrymen, for the good of the people, for the honor of the exalted Sultan! For tonight you have an appointment with destiny! *Yullah*! *Imshee*!" The soldier was brandishing his sword up high in the air, commanding, motivating, and intimidating the men to start moving again.

However, the men were not inspired. The soldier's actions spoke louder than his words. Stunned, they slowly resumed their march across the desert, each man following in the footsteps of the one who walked before him.

As he passed the man who'd been shot, Jabran looked down to say a quiet blessing. And in that moment, he noticed that the fallen man was Boulos Abu Nassir, the same old man to whom he'd given his water.

The Sergeant, seeing this observation, sneered, "And what do you think now young farmer? It appears that your water was wasted on this old fool, was it not? For as you can see, it was clearly his destiny to die tonight. That was something of which you could have no part."

Jabran looked from the old man to the soldier and replied calmly, "In actuality, sir, it was he who was a part of my destiny, and for that I am honored."

The Turk grunted his contempt, smacked the side of his camel with his whip and rode on ahead.

Trodding along, the men continued their march, painstakingly putting one foot in front of the other. Their spirits broken, they kept their eyes straight ahead with not so much as a glance at the man beside them. If they did perchance succumb to a brief look, a fleeting glimpse, they quickly turned their heads away, focusing on the endless desert before them.

Each man knew what the other was thinking, the fear evident in all their eyes. They were well aware that the merciless shooting they had witnessed, would not be the last. That this event would repeat itself many times over before the night was through. And each man prayed to the almighty God that he would not be the next.

SIXTEEN

The Blue Fortress

AT FIRST GLANCE IT looked surreal, like a mirage.

Silhouetted against the brilliant light of the rising sun, was a city emerging on the horizon. Its black outline pressed tightly against the deep orange sky. They paused in awe, blinking through weary eyes, trying hard to ascertain the reality of what they beheld. Even the soldiers who had seen this sight many times before, hesitated to relish in its splendor.

However, the illusive moment quickly ended. The mood was broken as the soldiers, anxious to end their journey, began to herd the men forward once again.

"Welcome to Paradise," the Sergeant quipped. "*Qasr al Azraq*, the Blue Fortress, Camp of the Turkish Desert Brigade. Ahead is your new home."

"And very likely your last," a soldier muttered under his breath.

As they approached, the sun rose, diffusing the colors of the horizon. They could now see the camp clearly. It was a military enclave, a huge fortress built of stone blocks erected in the middle of the desert. Strategically placed on each corner were oblong towers serving as lookout posts. Soldiers were posted, their guns ready, watching their approach. To the South was a crystal blue lake, an oasis, with palm trees rising high around its perimeter. It was evident that the fortress had been designed in an organized fashion with the lake clearly in view. Water was the most precious commodity in the desert, a resource that meant the difference between life and death.

Surrounding the fortress were military tents that stretched for nearly half a mile creating a makeshift city. Jabran could see men, women and children busily going about their daily tasks. Animals for both food and labor were herded and designated to certain areas. Military vehicles were scattered about, as were a multitude of armaments.

They marched into town, a cadre of beaten, disheveled recruits, pushed and prodded against their will. The residents of the city took no notice. This scene, so strange to these captive Arab farmers, had been witnessed many times before, and those living within its confines had long grown numb to it.

As they entered through the massive stone doors of the fortress they could see additional tents that had been erected within its walls, an elaborate stone courtyard in the center. Jabran, along with all the other incoming men, was directed to a large tent located to the side of the entrance and there they were left. The soldiers who had brought them, disappearing into the pulse of the city.

Thankful the journey had come to an end, the tattered recruits entered the shelter breathing a collective sigh of relief. The enclosure was surprisingly large. A handful of new soldiers, fresh for the day, were standing at attention, their guns by their sides. They eyed the new recruits, sneering and muttering under their breath.

The Arabs quickly forgot the soldiers' daunting presence. Much to their delight the room was filled with two long tables covered with warm, freshly made food. The scents and aromas intoxicating. The men were instructed to eat their fill. They were not told twice. Starving and thirsty, they reached over the tables, grabbing and stuffing food into their mouths.

Jabran did not immediately join in the feasting. He sat quietly at the table, his hands folded in his lap, his head bowed. After a time he raised his head and looked slowly around the room. He observed the other men at the table and realized how very ragged and weary they were. He looked down at his own clothes and saw the dirt and the filth. The clothes that Nisrina had so carefully washed and lovingly laid out for him were now barely recognizable. He was glad that she was not there to see him in these circumstances. So worn and broken.

His eyes scanned the crowd for a familiar face, maybe someone he knew from his village or a neighboring town, but he saw none. He wondered what criteria had been used to select these men. Why had he, of all the people in his town, been the one chosen that day? He thought back to the moment when the soldiers first appeared in his fields. And he questioned what cruel plan of fate had brought them down his path and into his orchard. He had been there, alone and unarmed. It was the one day that his farmhand had chosen to go into town for supplies.

He realized how his life and the lives of all those men who sat in this room had balanced on a single arbitrary action, a solitary decision. He pondered how this unexpected turn, this tragic event, had launched him on a new and terrifying path. His plans to remain separate and distinct, apart from the masses, had clearly and unequivocally been dashed. He recognized that for the first time in his life, and despite his attempts to the contrary, he'd finally become a part of all things.

One of the soldiers noticed Jabran sitting there quietly, contemplative, not eating or joining in with the others. The soldier, unaccustomed to this behavior, approached the table and stopped opposite Jabran. "What is the matter, sir?" he taunted. "Does our food not please you? Is there something that you desire that we have not provided? Or is it that you would rather be sitting at the table of the Sultan himself?" His eyes were a steel gray, menacing and arrogant.

Although he knew Jabran was an Arab, he spoke mockingly to him in Turkish.

"Your table is beautifully set. The food is plentiful and the aromas are enticing. I am simply taking a moment to enjoy its beauty and your kind hospitality." Jabran responded perfectly in the dialect in which he'd been addressed.

"Ah, I see, a diplomat, eh? And how is it so that you speak such perfect Turkish, my friend? This is unusual for an Arab *fellaah*, such as yourself. I thought that you backward country peasants could only speak the language of the *fellaheen*."

The other soldiers all began to laugh and murmur hateful words of disdain for the Arab recruits.

"It is true. I am a farmer and the son of a farmer. I have worked in the fields and orchards most years of my life. But I was taught to read and write by my uncle, a renowned tea merchant, God rest his soul. And in my youth, I had opportunities to travel to many countries assisting him in his trade. I was very young and my mind was fresh and keen. And on those journeys, I learned the languages of other lands."

"Ah, a scholar, no less! And what, pray tell do they call you?"

"I am Jabran Yusef ibn Farooz."

Jabran gave the soldier his formal family name. He told him that he was Jabran Yusef, the son of Farooz. He did not mention that he was also known as Abu Essam, the father of Essam. He felt it better left unsaid, wanting to bring no attention to the vulnerable family that he'd been forced to leave behind. His wife left alone, his children without a father to protect them.

"Jabran Yusef? Ah, yes. Well then, young scholar, I hope you find our accommodations to your liking!" The soldier was toying with him, but Jabran remained a diplomat.

"How can I not?" He replied, respectfully bowing his head. "How, sir, can I not?"

Then he filled his plate and mindfully began to eat, for it would have been an insult not to have eaten from their table.

The soldier, unearthing no further reason to find fault, slowly backed away and returned to his post. But he continued to watch as the Arab farmer quietly and respectfully ate his meal.

The room was quiet as the new recruits observed this unlikely interlude. The other men noticed the boldness of the farmer who ate in such a measured way and spoke so fluently to his captor. But no one dared question it or speak their mind. Their spirits shattered, they were too hungry and too weary to concern themselves with these eccentricities.

SEVENTEEN

The Inspection

THE RECRUITS SLEPT TOGETHER in one large tent. Their beds consisted of simple mats thrown down in tight rows on the dirt floor. Their blankets were thin covers of roughly woven lamb's wool, the fabric coarse and abrasive. No one complained. They were glad to have their stomachs full and be able to finally put their heads down to sleep.

The sound of the trumpet blowing was the first reminder that they were in a new place. The second was the soldiers kicking their feet and screaming for them to get up.

"Stand at attention! You are in the Sultan's army now!"

They all jumped up.

A stern looking Turk, a field Commander, hands clasped behind his back, walked up and down the rows of men as he surveyed the new stock.

"This is the best they could get us?!" he shouted angrily. "Why they're nothing but a bunch of old men . . . Eh, what's this?"

He stopped in front of Jabran, looking him up and down with interested contempt. He noticed his height, his muscular arms and his trim waist.

"It appears you have labored hard in your life," the Commander said to him.

Before Jabran could respond, the soldier who had approached him in the food tent the previous day came forward and whispered something quietly into the Commander's ear.

The Commander's lips pursed, his eyes narrowed. Again, he looked the new recruit up and down. He circled around him, walking and humming quietly to himself, as if he were examining a strange and exotic creature that had crossed his path.

"Yes, well, we shall see. We shall see," the Commander said, more to himself than anyone else.

Saying nothing more, he continued down the line on his inspection of the new recruits. Any man appearing under the age of forty would get poked or prodded by the Commander, testing their strength and resiliency, while the older men were simply passed over with a contemptuous snort.

When he got to the end of the line, he turned to his Captain and yelled out, "Get them ready! I want no time wasted and no man spared. We'll need every breathing body trained, no matter how old and decrepit they are!"

Hesitating, the Commander glanced back one more time at Jabran. He whispered something to the soldier in charge, who nodded understandingly. Then, readjusting his jacket and clearing his throat, he marched out of the room.

Uniforms were handed out, shoddy, torn, and stained with blood, still reeking with the stench of death. It was evident that they'd been gathered recently from the battlefield and were now being recycled for the next group of recruits.

After changing into their uniforms, the men were ushered into an open field and their training for battle began. They were treated harshly, with no attention to station or skill. It was a foreboding reminder to every man of what was yet to come, for they'd heard stories of how the Turks collected Arab farmers from their fields. They called them recruits. They'd give them a cursory level of training, teaching them to use rifles. They built up their strength, while tearing down their resolve. And then in the end, they used them as cannon fodder. First in line on the battlefield. Never to return.

EIGHTEEN

Mariana

"JABRAN! COME QUICK—THEY'RE asking for you!"

Omar had run ahead to warn his friend.

"Who is asking for me?"

"The Lieutenant . . . quickly . . . he's coming."

Drills were complete and the men had finished their meager dinner. The food was nothing like it had been that first day. Now their rations were simple dishes of soup and bread, as most foods had to be brought in over the desert via the camel commissariat. It was the end of a long day of training and the men in the camp had chosen to relax outdoors playing cards together or telling stories by the fire. Jabran, however, had chosen to lie down by himself in the tent he shared with the other recruits. He could usually be found there or out walking by himself in the cool night air. He valued those rare moments in which he could be alone with his thoughts.

Now standing before him was Omar, a young recruit whom he'd befriended. Omar had become his closest comrade, his ally. He was a carpenter from a village not far from his own. Omar's father, also a carpenter, had been retained to carve the doors of the Orthodox Church in Beit el Jebel. It was Jabran's church. And although they had never met before this time, they shared a common history. Omar had accompanied his father on trips to Beit el Jebel, watching him at work and learning his trade. Perhaps, as young boys, their paths had crossed in the village square, or they'd seen each other in front of the church. Neither recalled, but the bond was there nevertheless, and now finding themselves in such ill-fated circumstances, they became like brothers.

"Lieutenant Soffa is asking after me? Well, he knows where to find me." Jabran defiantly lay back down, his head cradled in the palms of his hands.

Just then the flap of the tent flew open, and Lieutenant Soffa entered. Jabran jumped up and saluted, as did Omar who, curious to see what would unfold, remained standing nearby. They stood at attention, knowing that to disobey the military protocol to which they had now become accustomed, would bring regrettable retributions.

"Jabran Yusef?"

"Yes, sir!"

"Follow me and bring all your things."

"All my things?"

"Must I repeat myself?"

"No sir!"

Jabran gathered his few personal belongings and followed the Lieutenant outside and across the courtyard. They entered the Commander's quarters. This was the first time Jabran had been inside his private office and he wondered the purpose of the summons.

He looked around. It was sparse like everything else in the military enclave, but it did contain more of life's little pleasures than he had seen elsewhere in the camp. The floor was covered with a red Persian carpet and he could see an elaborate Turkish hookah in the corner of the room. The Commander's desk was a large wooden platform made from olive wood. It filled the back half of the room, stretching from one end to the other. A single wooden chair stood behind it. Atop the desk was a lantern, rolled maps and several stacks of papers held down by jagged stones.

"*Ahlan wa Sahlan*," the Commander greeted him. "Please, sit down. Make yourself comfortable." With one hand he motioned for Jabran to sit, and with the other signaled Soffa to leave.

"You honor me," Jabran replied sitting crossed legged on the carpet. Pillows were strewn about for comfort and support.

The Commander clapped his hands, and then joined him on the floor. Within seconds two shrouded women appeared. They were clad in dark gowns, covered from head to foot. Their faces were screened by veils that left only two small slits for their eyes. With them they carried several trays of food, delicious aromas escaping into the air. Jabran breathed in deeply. They reminded him of his kitchen back home, of his wife as she busied herself about, preparing meals for the family, his children playing on the floor nearby.

The two women knelt down to serve them. First, the savory dish of *zait oo zaatar*, a Mediterranean staple that included two plates: one filled with the finest of oils harvested from the olives grown in the region. The other plate contained an aromatic combination of finely ground, dried herbs including mint, marjoram, oregano and thyme. They placed them in front of the two men along with several giant loaves of freshly baked bread to be used for dipping. Then came the dessert tray of figs, dates and *baklawa*; the sweet smell of cinnamon, nuts and honey was enticing.

How privileged he felt to sit with the Commander and have these foods served to him in this most private of settings. He silently questioned the meaning of this unexpected hospitality, suspicious of the Commander's intent, his summons unsettling.

His thoughts were interrupted by the unmistakable scent of cardamom. The aroma of the cracked seed sprinkled in the Turkish coffee was detected as the smaller of the two women poured the hot liquid into a gold demitasse cup.

And then the unthinkable happened.

As she reached out to serve Jabran, the tiny cup slipped from her hand, spilling the hot brew onto his arm, his shirt and the top of his pants.

He heard a gasp from behind the veil.

She quickly grabbed a cloth and began wiping the mess.

The Commander was furious, "Mariana! You clumsy fool! Must we keep you hidden away? How dare you insult our guest this way?!"

He lifted his riding crop, and the thrashing began.

Without thinking Jabran instantly stood up positioning his body between the Commander's and the shrouded woman. He felt the angry blows of the lash in her stead.

"It is nothing, Commander," he heard himself saying. "Nothing that I wouldn't have done myself. Please. It is minor. It matters not. God is merciful."

The woman was crouched on knees, her head to the ground. Upon hearing his words, she looked up at this curious soldier who used his body to shield her, their eyes meeting briefly through the slit in her veil. Jabran saw a glimmer of green. He noticed her youth and sensed her dread. But mostly he saw a light reflecting from behind the veil. Her eyes. They were glowing—an emerald flame unlike any he'd seen before. Their brilliance shone through the split in the cloth, sending a tendril out to his soul. Shimmering shades of green, speckled by the allure of golden hues. It reminded him of the Jordan River after a storm, when the sun finally broke through the clouds, its radiance reflecting on the water's edge. So complex. So intriguing.

He couldn't look away. He yearned to push aside the screen that covered her face, to see the countenance that held such magnificent eyes, but he knew it was forbidden. He could never touch her veil.

The Commander noticed their interlude, and thinking the better of it, said nothing more. He smiled to himself and put down the whip. He clapped his hands, and as he did, the two women left the room as silently and swiftly as they'd entered. The two men finally alone.

The Commander, quite pleased with himself, brought out the large, ornate water pipe and carefully lit it. He inhaled, the water gurgling happily, a dense cloud filling the chamber. After a lengthy draw he finally exhaled, the smoke swirling above their heads and floating to the crown of the room. He offered the mouthpiece to Jabran, who also drank in its vapor. The scent was warming, the tobacco intoxicating.

After a leisure interlude of food, smoke and drink, the Commander finally spoke, "It has come to my attention that although you are a young man and a mere farmer, you are also a master of languages. Several, I am told. Is this so?"

"Yes, Commander, it is so."

"And how pray tell, did a farmer, a *fellah* such as yourself, come to be so learned?"

"There is no surprise or wonder in my response, sir. What I shall tell you is the truth about a man, who has, up until these most recent times lived a most quiet life. You see, the brother of my father, my Uncle Fareed Yusef ibn Marwan, was an educated man. He was a notable and well traveled tea merchant. And since he had no wife or children of his own, I was asked on many occasions to travel with him, to assist him in his work. Excused from working our family's orchards, I accompanied him on countless journeys. And in doing so, was exposed at an early age to the written word and to the many languages of the world. He was an excellent teacher and a good man, God rest his soul. The lessons he taught to a young and thirsty mind proved beneficial to me, for now I speak several languages."

"And even more dialects, I venture to guess?"

"It was a necessity."

"Yes. Yes." The Turkish Commander took several puffs from the water pipe as he contemplated Jabran's explanation. He squinted in the curious way that he had, studying the Arab's face, observing his reactions.

"I must say, young Jabran, I have been watching you since the day you first arrived. I find you different than the other men, not only in stature, mind you, but in quality as well. You have . . . how shall I put it? You have a depth that the other men lack."

Jabran remained silent, wondering what the Commander had in mind.

The leader waited a few moments before continuing, taking his time, allowing both men to have several additional draws on the pipe. The tobacco was of exceptional quality and they both relaxed as the smoke drifted lazily about the room.

"Jabran, let me not mince my words. I have use for a man like you. A special assignment, if you're interested. One that would be exceptional in nature, unlike any you've had before."

Jabran stayed still, his face stoic. He was picturing Nisrina standing in the groves, her hair blowing in the Mediterranean breeze. She was smiling at him, so warm and sweet. He sat quietly, peacefully, in front of the Commander, giving no sign of interest or distress. Although he heard his voice, Jabran was miles away in another time, another place.

The Commander eyed him carefully, looking for a reaction to his words. When he found none, he continued, "I need a man to serve as my special agent, a trusted companion and confidant, someone who will join me when I meet with men from other nations. I need you to be my eyes and my ears, to hear what I cannot hear and to understand what I am unable to discern, especially when these insufferable foreigners speak their own languages to one another."

"I see," Jabran was nodding, finally re-engaged in the conversation. "You are asking me to be your interpreter?"

"Yes, in a manner of speaking," the Commander hesitated, "but, shall we say, one of a clandestine nature. No one else shall know that this is your purpose. You will be made my First Lieutenant and remain at my side during all negotiations. This is a complicated war, my friend, and these are complicated times. Men of great stature, of wealth and power, they come to me from all over the world to negotiate or discuss, be it a trade in armaments or an alliance in battle, it matters not. What matters is that they speak to me with one tongue and then they turn to each other and speak another. One they know I cannot understand. These scoundrels have the audacity to do this in front of my face!"

The Commander paused a moment, not wanting his anger to rise ahead of him. He composed himself, taking another long draw on the water pipe. When he was sufficiently relaxed, he continued, "You see, now I want them to speak in front of me as they normally do, tell me what they will, and when they turn to each other to tell their filthy secrets, to speak in their native tongues as I sit before them unaware, they will not know that I will now be able to understand them, through you of course. Do you see? Hm?"

He took another puff on the hookah, a long draw in and an even slower draw out, blowing the smoke out in circles above their heads. He was clearly pleased with his plan. He enjoyed telling it, and, even more so, he enjoyed hearing it said.

He watched Jabran cautiously, "You, my dear friend, shall be my secret weapon."

The smoke swirled upward as the Commander smiled, his face belying his character.

"I would be honored to serve you," Jabran bowed his head in respect. Although the request for his services had not been put in the form of a command, he knew no choice had been offered. It was only his to accept. He forced a smile, but he felt a rush of dread. The Turkish regime was a harsh master, and he felt the weight of being so directly under their control.

"Excellent! Excellent! Then it is done. You will not regret this, trust me, life will be good for you my friend. I shall see to that. We shall get along splendidly! You'll see. Yes, yes . . . excellent!"

The Commander clapped his hands and Lieutenant Soffa reappeared. The Commander addressed Soffa, "I have just promoted Private Yusef to be my First Lieutenant. He is to be awarded due respect and all privileges of this position. Please show him his new quarters and see to it that he is made comfortable."

He turned to Jabran, "I am moving you out of the common tent and into a private one of your own. Tomorrow we'll begin your training. Tonight you relax."

He motioned to Soffa, who saluted him, and then obediently turned and saluted Jabran. The two men left the Commander to his scheming as Soffa led the First Lieutenant to his new quarters.

"I hope it's to your liking," Soffa said flatly as they entered the tent.

"It's more than I expected," Jabran replied.

"It's more than I expected, as well."

Jabran knew Soffa was not referring to the tent, but as always he refrained from the fray and chose silence as the wiser path. Soffa, too, wisely said no more and departed, leaving Jabran to settle into his new quarters.

He looked around. A dark Persian carpet, smaller and thinner than the one in the Commander's quarters, covered the dirt floor. There was a small cot tucked neatly in the corner. Next to the cot, a water jug and basin sat atop a crudely made table and a small lantern was placed at the foot of the bed.

He was delighted to have such nice quarters, a welcome change from the crowded housing in the common tent. But as he adjusted to his new surroundings, he realized the burden of this privilege. Overwhelming apprehension washed over him. He became nauseous. Holding his stomach, he vomited into the pan beside the bed. Instead of feeling pleased, Jabran felt dire remorse. He'd been selected to live better than the other men with whom he'd so painfully journeyed. And for that he felt anguish. He would now have finer quarters than they, and he knew it wasn't right. He thought of Omar and wondered how he would react when he heard the news. He was determined that it should not affect their relationship. Omar was the only real friend he'd made in the camp and he truly valued their camaraderie.

Conversely and what troubled him so, was that he felt relief to have finally obtained his solitude. He now had a place of his own where he could rest and reflect. He had space to breathe—something sorely lacking in this rugged, communal way of life.

And so his conscience battled with his emotions and his sense of fair play. How could his worth be considered any more significant than that of the other poor souls packed like animals in the common tent? And yet here lay his fate, and here he remained. But at what price?

As the sun set, he blew out the lantern and gazed out at the moon that shone brightly through the small window in the canvas. The distant orb was full and its brilliance lit the campground. He wondered if Nisrina was gazing at that same moon. He wondered what she would think of these new circumstances, and he wondered what exploitations the Commander had in store for him. Through his confusion and his endless musings, he held tight to his belief that the future would unfold as it was meant to, and that all things would happen in their due time. With those thoughts as his comfort and the vision of Nisrina for his warmth, he finally slipped off into a restless sleep.

She came to him in the night.
In a dream.
It was Nisrina, kissing his face, her lips so soft, her scent so sweet. He welcomed it. He reveled in it, not wanting to wake. Willing it to go on and on. He was floating, all pain and sorrow gone as he lilted

within a soft gray mist that balanced between two worlds, his senses now enlivened as they'd never been before. Her warm lips gently kissed his eyelids, a soft whisper of her breath—and he awoke.

His eyes opened slowly at first, fluttering, blinking, as he cleared the sleep from his mind. It was dark. He struggled to remember where he was. He must have been dreaming. Or was he?

He sensed her before he could see her.

She was beautiful. Kneeling over him in her nakedness—her skin white, her breasts full and round.

He gasped.

She placed her hand over his mouth and whispered in his ear, "Shhh, it's all right. Don't worry *habeebee*. I am here for you."

"No!" His dream had betrayed him. It was not Nisrina. It was a temptress sent by Satan to bewitch him. He broke free from her hand.

"What is this? Who are you?!" He turned away from her, "Please, cover yourself!"

He held out his blanket, wrapping it over her shoulders. He was a married man. He loved his wife. His Nisrina. He loved her with every part of his being, and he missed her. Her voice. Her skin. Her touch. It pained him to think of her now so far away.

But what pained him even more were the feelings beginning to surge through his body. A woman he did not know. A girl so young. So beautiful. He had covered her bareness and turned his face away, and yet his body stirred from the memory of her sight. He wanted to see her again, to hold her breasts in his hands, to have her. And he hated himself for that.

Who was she? Why was she here?

"Jabran, *habeebee*, my love," she nestled closer to him. "I am here for you." The words like a song. Her voice a sweet melody. Alluring. Intoxicating. A nightingale in the dark.

"Who are you?" He asked again. His eyes averted.

"I am Mariana."

"Mariana?" He turned back and looked at her. The serving girl in the Commander's tent? His gaze met hers, and he saw them again— those eyes. The shimmering green. The depths of a thousand oceans. Large, innocent, mesmerizing.

"Mariana? But where is your veil? Why have you come to me this way?"

"I am here for you, my love. I am yours." She was kissing him. Her lips soft, her breath sweet.

"Please stop." He pushed her away. "I cannot love you. I have a wife. I have children. I will not forsake them in this way. You are beautiful . . . my God, child, you are beautiful. But I cannot have you. Stop. Please. You must go."

"Shhh . . . No. It is you who must listen to me," her voice was low, desperate. "The walls . . . they have eyes, they have ears. Please, I beg of you. It is expected. It is expected of you, and it is more particularly expected of me. If you reject me, all will be lost. It will be the end of me. Of this I am certain."

"What do you mean?" he whispered back, horrified at what she was suggesting.

"It is as I have said. You must take me. You must make love to me." Her words were hot, coming in short bursts. "If you will not have me, then my purpose is gone. I will be passed from soldier to soldier as they did before, and when they are through with me, I will be killed." She was trembling. "Please, my fate is in your hands. I have a purpose now. I have a purpose . . ."

She pressed her lips to his.

She was atop him, undressing him, kissing him. She kissed his chest, whispering, pleading, begging for her life, the blanket now fallen from her shoulders, and for a moment, he allowed it.

As the world outside raged on with its righteous war—man against man, and country against country, Jabran Yusef was fighting his own private battle. A war of mind. A war of heart. His thoughts raced fast against the unleashed will of his body. In the dark, he felt the young girl's fear and it sickened him to know that such atrocities occurred. He brushed back her hair and cradled her naked body in his arms. She curled there like a newborn child while he hushed her cries with the palms of his hands.

"Mariana," he finally whispered to her. "Stay the night with me. You will be mine and I will be yours. But I pledge to you, I will not take your virtue. Not on this night or any thereafter. You see, no one need ever know. You will lie beside me and I will hold you. We will be one in spirit, our bodies untainted. The shadows will keep our secret. In this manner you will fulfill your duty, and I my pledge. Let the eyes and ears think what they might."

"Dear God!" the words spilled from her lips.

He hushed her again and pulled her closer to him, her heart beating steady against his chest. What animals are these that lie among us, he thought to himself. What heralds of Satan live deep within our midst? And he shuddered as the warmth of her body pressed soft against his.

NINETEEN

A New Reality

THE NEXT MORNING WHEN Jabran awoke Mariana was gone. He was alone in his bed with no sign of her ever being there.

Had it been a dream? Yes, it must have been a dream. Perhaps from the tobacco I smoked yesterday in the Commander's quarters. Of course, that was it, too much tobacco. And God knows what exotic variety that man served me. Yes, yes, just a dream, it must have been the tobacco.

But Jabran felt different, strangely exhilarated. *If it was only a dream, then why . . .*

Lieutenant Soffa entered, interrupting his thoughts. Jabran jumped to his feet, saluting him, but this time his form was lacking. His head was whirling. His legs were weak.

"The Commander would like to meet with you as soon as you have washed up. You will breakfast with him this morning."

"Of course. Of course. I will be there, right away. Thank you, thank you."

They saluted again and the Lieutenant departed, saying nothing more.

Jabran couldn't help but wonder, *was the Lieutenant aware of what happened last night? She'd said that the walls had eyes and ears. If so, then whose eyes and whose ears? Who knew about this? And then again, perhaps it was no one, only a dream. If Soffa knew anything at*

all, he'd shown no sign of it. Perhaps he did not know. It must have been
the tobacco. Of course, the tobacco. And yet, was that a smirk I'd seen
on Soffa's face?

"I hope you slept well," the Commander greeted him, bowing
slightly.

"Yes, thank God," he responded. "It's just that . . ."

"Good. I need you well rested. We have a long day ahead of us. I
have many things to discuss with you and I want you fully prepared
by the time our visitors arrive. You must have a grasp of all the issues.
I want you to know them from top to bottom, from side to side,
until you can recite them in your sleep. Remember, to master the
subject is to master the meeting."

The Commander was eyeing Jabran carefully, "Shall we begin?"

Jabran nodded, realizing that if the Commander knew anything
about his nighttime visitor, he had no plans to discuss it, certainly
not this morning, there were other things on his mind. And so,
Jabran wisely kept his questions to himself.

Breakfast was served by two women in black. When they entered
the room, Jabran's heart began to pound. Like the day before, their
faces were covered in modesty. Jabran wondered—was Mariana one
of them? Decorum required that he make no personal contact—and
yet he'd just spent the night with her cradled in his arms, hushing her
fears until she'd fallen asleep.

Beads of sweat formed on his brow. He watched the shadowy
figures as they moved through the tent. Neither gave any indication
of familiarity. Silently they attended to their tasks as they placed the
trays of food between the two men. They poured fresh, steaming
coffee from the brass *ibrik* into tiny Turkish cups. Jabran watched
their movements, straining to see if Mariana was among them. But
she was not. These women were larger; she was small, fitting perfectly
under his arm. His heart sank. Perhaps it had been a dream after all—a
soldier's lonely imaginings. A mysterious girl with sea-green eyes.

The Commander was speaking, but Jabran's mind wandered. It
had been a long morning and they had discussed an array of details

regarding the German delegation due in two days. Although he tried his best, his thoughts kept returning to Mariana. He knew her name, the sweet clarity of her eyes and the feel of her skin, but who exactly was she? They had exchanged few words, their voices kept low in furtive, hushed tones. But now he wondered—where had she come from? Why was she sent to his tent that night? And what sorry turn of fate had brought her to this Godforsaken city?

He hoped she might serve the afternoon coffee. He'd watch the hands that offered him his cup. Would they be the fingers that curled soft in his palms? Or would she come to him only when the moon filled the sky? And if she did, could he still resist her allure?

He gazed out the window searching for the occasional cloaked figure that passed, his eyes finally resting on the wavering heat that rose up from the desert floor, steaming vapors lilting high into the hot, dry air. She could be any one of them, he thought to himself. Any one of the fully clad women who lived out their lives secluded in shrouds, with only their eyes to reveal their essence. He remembered her eyes. The night had been dark, illuminated only by the moonlight that filtered in through the tent's small window. But they'd shone brightly in spite of the dim. Her breasts were white, round like twin moons. And there was the scent of her . . .

The Commander stopped talking. He was looking at Jabran, waiting for his response.

"Forgive me, sir, what did you say?"

"I said it will be important for you to follow as the conversation unfolds. I will be awaiting your signal, although I want nothing shown in your face. You must remain stoic at all times. Your sign to me that something has gone awry or that they are not being true to their word will be in the raising of your cup to your lips, like so . . ." and the Commander lifted the cup to his lips, his small finger extended to the side.

Jabran nodded, "I understand."

It had been a long day and the Commander was pleased with himself. Ready for the German visitors, he had a plan in place and his secret weapon fully engaged. Jabran understood the complexities of the meeting and would remain close by to overhear any scheming conversations the German's might have amongst themselves.

Although it had happened numerous times that day, the Commander never seemed irritated by Jabran's lack of focus, and interestingly enough, if Jabran had been more astute, he might have noticed the wry smile on the Commander's face each time he reengaged his attentions.

She came to him that night and every night thereafter.

He knew very little about her. Her words were few. Eventually he learned that she was Armenian. Her family had been killed by the Turkish military during a raid in her village. Her parents slaughtered ruthlessly as she watched from the dark of an old wooden shed. She was found and captured. Enslaved. Now, a servant to the soldiers. A servant and a prostitute.

"No, you are not a prostitute. I won't have that said," he insisted, stroking her hair.

"I see your kind ways and your gentle spirit, Jabran. You are a prince among men and I am fortunate to sleep by your side. I envy your wife, and for her sake, I pray for your safety."

He continued to resist the girl. His resolve strong, his thoughts wandering always to Nisrina. He wondered what his wife would think if she knew that his bed was warmed each night by an Armenian beauty. Could she understand the fragile innocence? He wasn't sure, but he knew that he could not let harm come to the young Mariana, and so each night as she lifted the flap and entered his tent he welcomed her into his bed.

TWENTY

A Somber Joy

THE MONTHS PASSED AND the Commander continued to marvel at the linguistic skills of his First Lieutenant. Besides Turkish and Arabic, Jabran was proficient in French, English and German. He performed his function for the Commander with superb precision. As a result, the Commander's reputation for fierce and shrewd negotiations grew, spreading throughout the land. His allies respected him and his enemies feared him. It remained that no one other than Jabran and the Commander knew their secret, the true power behind his force.

During this time Jabran noticed that Mariana, too, was changing. When she came to him in the night, he could see that her breasts were growing fuller and her stomach more round. He knew the signs of a woman with child. For in this regard, he'd had experience. It saddened him to think she'd been forcibly taken, and he feared for her safety as he silently wondered if she, herself, knew.

One night she came to him and he realized he could stay silent no longer.

"Mariana, are you aware of the changes to your person?

"Yes Jabran, I am aware."

"And tell me, do you know what this means?"

"Yes, I know."

"How long have you known?"

"Oh, Jabran!" she searched his face. "Can you forgive me?"

"There is nothing to forgive. It is simple. You are going to be a mother."

She turned away again, her cheeks flushed.

"But tell me, who is the father? He must be told. He must be held accountable."

"I do not know," she whispered.

"Ah, yes, I see." He drew her close. She was shivering.

"It is okay Mariana. All will be well. The eyes and ears will assume the child is mine, and I will allow them to think this. I will stay by your side. I will take care of you. Do not fear."

But Mariana was not consoled.

"What is it, child? What is it that distresses you so?"

"Oh, Jabran, my poor innocent soldier, don't you see? This is what they've been waiting for." Her breaths were coming in short heaves, her chest was aching.

"I'm sorry. I don't understand. What do you mean? This is who has been waiting for and . . . why?"

"You are meant to think that the child is yours . . . all this time . . . please let us not talk of it. Not now. If you will permit me, allow me to lie beside you one more night."

"One more night? What is this nonsense of which you speak?" He held her face in his hands and looked directly into her eyes. "Mariana, please if there is something I should know, I beg you to tell me. Please, I beseech you, talk to me."

But Mariana could not respond. She was too distraught. She snuggled in closer to his body. She could smell the warmth of his skin. It smelled like the mountain sage that grew near her home town, like the lavender and the poppies that grew wild on the side of the hills. It smelled of a thousand eternities being carried in the wind, a smell she had come to love, and it intoxicated her. But she could not speak her thoughts and he did not force her.

Her eyes lay shut as he gazed at her swollen belly. Her beauty as a maiden now surpassed by the splendor of a ripened woman. His body stirred. He wanted her. He wanted to take her and make her his. To enter her and lay claim to the child that grew in her womb.

His hands moved slowly down her abdomen, then across and around her leg.

She moved, her eyes now open.

He found her moistness and it thrilled him.

"No!" she could hardly breathe. She grabbed his hand.

"Just this once, Mariana. Please. Let me make this child my own."

"No!" She tried to turn away, but he held her tight. "Please, Jabran. Don't do this."

"But I want you."

"You know I would give myself to you without question. You know I love you like the earth loves the sea. But remember . . . Please. Remember your promise—Nisrina—your wife . . ."

The sound of her name brought him back to his senses.

"Yes . . . Nisrina," his tone was flat, his voice deflated.

"The child is yours, my love," Mariana whispered to him. "For you are the one that has held me each night. And you are the one who has shown me compassion. The seed is unknown, this is true, and the father an unholy brute. But as God is my witness, this child will carry your name. I shall call him Jabran."

Jabran closed his eyes, his head was spinning. She was right. The seed was no matter. With each night they'd spent in fear and uncertainty, an alliance had grown between them, the bonds unexpected. He did not understand it. The world he lived in no longer made sense. And yet as she lay beside him, her breath warm against his, he knew there was no choice. He would always protect her.

"If you permit me," she begged, her voice now humble, her lips trembling, "I ask only one thing."

"Anything," he answered.

"When you leave . . . When you are released from this service, I beseech you, I beg you, please take me with you. I will give you no trouble. I have cousins in the North, in Syria. I will go to them. Jabran please, please, don't leave me here."

"Of course," he said. "Yes, of course. I will take you with you."

"Do you promise? As God is our witness, do you give me your word?"

"Yes, Mariana, I swear by my mother's grave. You have my word."

They spoke no more that night, laying silently together, her face buried deep in his chest, his arms wrapped strong around her waist. But as they lay, Jabran slept restlessly, tossing and turning, while the child beside him quietly wept.

TWENTY ONE

The Commander's Final Hand

"JABRAN, AS MY FIRST Lieutenant you have been an exemplary soldier. With you by my side we have quelled the deceit of both our friends and our foes. I praise you on a job well done."

The Commander and Jabran were having their evening smoke.

"I am happy to have pleased you, Commander. It brings me great honor."

To the Commander, Jabran was a man whom he'd played and conquered—transforming a resistant recruit into a dedicated soldier. Using a woman to satisfy and subdue him. He admittedly valued the Arab's unique gift of languages and commended himself for putting it to good use. But in his mind, Jabran was merely a pawn for his grand design.

Jabran, however, saw himself a man unchanged. His resolve was to simply survive, to endure his captivity and to one day return home to his wife and family. The Commander's assumptions of his relationship with Mariana were flawed. But for her safety, he could never divulge their innocence. Especially with a child on the way. He longed for assurances that they would not be harmed, but he dared not ask the Commander. Not now, not ever.

The leader spoke again.

"Jabran, I have had some disturbing news. There are rumors that the Arabs, Bedouins mostly, are joining together in an uprising against the Empire. Word has it they've joined forces with the British and in doing so, have just taken Aqaba."

He watched for a reaction. Jabran remained unmoved. He, too, had heard the news.

The Commander continued, "And it has also been brought to my attention that the British are now planning an advance into the Holy Land, the city and villages nearby."

He paused again, carefully watching Jabran's face. This time, much to his pleasure he saw a twinge run across his brow.

"Is that not where you are from, Jabran? Weren't you discovered by our recruiters working in an orchard, a small town I believe? A village just north of Jerusalem? Is this not so?"

"Yes, it is so," Jabran took a long, slow sip from his cup, a lump forming in his throat.

"Excellent, excellent, then this will be a brilliant opportunity for you to prove your loyalty to the Sultan, to the Ottoman Empire, and to the greater good of your people."

Jabran remained silent.

The Commander waited patiently. He puffed the hookah. He sipped his coffee. He nibbled the sweets. He watched Jabran from the corner of his eye.

"Yes, I have the most interesting of assignments for you," he finally continued.

Jabran took his turn, a few puffs from the hookah, a few sips of the coffee. His eyes remained diverted. His heart beating hard. It was clear to him now: the Commander knew the details of his capture. He'd referenced his village and his orchard, and he was sure that his knowledge did not stop there. He dared wonder what this tyrant had in store for him. He'd been waiting for this moment since that first time, many months ago, when the Commander had called him into his quarters and enticed him with a promotion to First Lieutenant, with a tent of his own and a mistress to distract him from his principles. He dreaded what was yet to follow.

The Commander, on the other hand, thoroughly enjoyed this game of cat and mouse. He was now about to play his last draw, his final hand. The culmination of his plans for this enlightened *fellaah*. This ever so humble, scholarly farmer.

"I need you to enter enemy territory, a British encampment, and curry their favor. You are an Arab. They will trust you. Find out their plans, their strengths, their weaknesses. Where, when and how they'll attack. As soon as you've gathered that information, you'll report back to me. Time is of the essence. Understood?"

"Ah, I see," said Jabran. "You want me to spy on the British? Is that it?"

"Yes, that's it. Simply put. Bravo. Bravo. As usual, you get right to the point. So, what say you? Do you think this is something you can manage? And more importantly, can I trust you? I need to be able to trust you Jabran . . . that you will return. I must have your word, your unwavering loyalty. Can you give me your word?"

Jabran's eyes never left the Commander's.

"You have my word," he replied. "But, if I may ask, sir, will I be rewarded for such a dangerous mission?"

"Rewarded? Why your reward is in knowing that you defended the Ottoman Empire, the greatest kingdom that's ever ruled! That is your reward! What more could any man ask for? Your reward? Ha!"

Then he paused, slowly stroking his beard, studying Jabran, a man who had served him well; and now, for the first time, was asking a favor.

"I must say, you have been a faithful soldier, Jabran. You have honored the Sultan." He took another deep draw on the hookah, this time holding the smoke an extra long time, letting it out slowly, deliberately. Finally, he spoke again, "On further consideration, I believe you may be justified in your request. Perhaps your loyalty should not go unrewarded."

He took a few short puffs, the smoke now thick and dense in the room as he considered his options. Jabran held his tongue, he knew the Commander would never negotiate with him, the decision only his to make.

"This I will do for you Jabran. If you bring me the information I need, I will release you. I give you my word that this mission will be your last. You'll be free to return to your village. But if you fail me, if you do not return, I will hunt you down like a dog and may Allah have mercy on your soul!"

Jabran hid his elation, "I will not fail you."

The Commander nodded, "And . . . of course," he slowly began again, his eyes narrowing deviously, "there is this small matter with Mariana . . . I believe you have met our young Mariana, have you not, Jabran? Yes, I'm sure you have. Well, she, of course, will remain here with me, let us say . . . in protective custody. As long as you return, no harm will come to her."

Jabran's face went pale. "Yes, I have met Mariana. Yes, I see." He took a long draw on the hookah, pausing to inhale deeply, holding the smoke in his lungs, then exhaling slowly, thoughtfully. The entrapment was complete. There was no choice. He would have to return. Although his loyalties were first to his wife and his children, Jabran could not forget the promise he made to Mariana. He'd sworn it on his mother's grave. "Well then, sir, you have made the situation quite clear. I shall return."

"Excellent. Excellent. I'm glad that we could come to such an amicable understanding. You are a wise man Jabran," his eyes narrowed again, "a wise man, indeed. And since I know that this will be a long and arduous journey, one that should not be traveled alone, I will allow one soldier to accompany you. I leave it to you to select your man."

"I choose Omar Mahmoud."

"Then, Omar it is."

"When do we leave?"

"You leave tonight. I'll expect you back in four weeks, not a day later."

TWENTY TWO

A Messy Business

HE NEVER HAD A chance to say goodbye. They were gone before the sun could set.

It was better that way. He was sure she already knew. Her words had alluded to it. He realized now that she understood much more than she'd ever let on. He would return as the Commander had ordered, for his freedom, but that was not the only reason. He would come back to save Mariana. To take her away from this wretched life—this dreadful, ungodly hell.

By the grace of God, he'd save her, and then he'd return to his family.

Jabran and Omar rode their camels southward. Glad to be leaving the camp, they hoped the journey back across the desert would be less daunting than when they'd first arrived. They were fully stocked, carrying an ample supply of food, water, and tents. In the time they'd spent at Camp Azraq, they'd grown quite familiar with the setting. They knew that in order to avoid confrontation from warring factions, they'd need to stay out of sight. They would travel the open desert at night, and then follow close along ridgelines and outcroppings. They planned to parallel the railway, first moving southward crossing sharp to the west, until they reached their destination—the Egyptian city of Cairo where the British army was headquartered.

With the fortress out of sight, their hearts grew lighter. No longer in uniform, the two men traveled under the guise of adventurers. Young Arab farmers who'd decided to join British forces to fight the Turks and govern their destinies. Interestingly enough, there would be very little acting on their part as the pretext proved closer to their true spirits than their actual mission. Freed of the encampment, they both loathed to return. But as the Commander had so deviously planned, Jabran knew that choice was not possible.

Riding across the desert they were *shabaiyan*, two young men, on an adventure. They spoke of their families and their lives before the war. What they would do when the fighting was over, how they would work and live again—simple lives close to the earth.

Omar was surprised to learn that Jabran had a wife and three children. He had never spoken of them in the encampment except to Mariana. Jabran instinctively knew that some things were better left unsaid. Now there were no walls, just open country, and Jabran permitted himself to speak unfettered. He wondered how Nisrina had fared without him and how big his children had grown. He wondered if his third child was a boy or a girl, and how his brothers and sisters were doing.

He never spoke of Mariana to Omar. He dared not tell him that the lives of a fragile young girl and her unborn child depended on their return. Omar would not understand.

With their faces covered, they slept when the sun was high behind small makeshift tents. As the sun dropped low, they'd rise, eating a simple breakfast of dates and figs with honey, or dried salami, bread and cheese. Then they'd pack their gear and mount their camels, continuing on their journey.

As the days passed they spoke less and less. Now traveling south by moonlight along the easterly side of the railway line, they were careful to remain out of sight, for any passing train would most certainly be carrying a contingent of Turkish soldiers.

On the fifth night of their journey a flash of light lit the Western horizon, a sudden explosion shattering the tranquil landscape. The ground shook beneath them. The two men looked at each other. Exhausted, their spirits drained, they wondered what dangers lay ahead, but neither uttered a word. It was war after all, and these things were expected. Still, without an army to protect them, the dark of night thickened around them as they cautiously moved on. The farther they advanced, the higher the probability of encountering battle. They knew this, to discuss it gave them no comfort.

They continued guided only by the moon and the stars. The night gradually changing from black to a soft silvery gray as the sun rose in the East. They estimated that they were only an hour's ride from the Southern town of Ma'an where they would then head across in a westerly direction.

They decided to make camp behind a large cluster of boulders. Ragged and worn, they looked off to the distance. North of the city, in the direction of the railway line, was a large plume of smoke. It filled the air with a thick, dark cloud—the contrast against the early morning dawn, both frightening and compelling.

Their curiosity overtook their fatigue.

Omar turned to Jabran, "Shall we take a look?"

"Yes, let's get closer."

They rode their camels in the direction of the smoke. Nearing, they dismounted and walked to the edge of an open field, being careful to remain hidden behind the brush that paralleled the railway line.

They were not prepared for what they saw.

Pure devastation. The utter chaos of war's debris.

The train of the Ottoman railway had been bombed.

Ambushed, the massive locomotive carrying a convoy of Turkish soldiers had been derailed and turned on its side, the mighty giant silenced and broken. Bodies were strewn about. Some flung fifty feet. Human remains lay scattered in pieces, bloodied arms, shattered legs. If there were survivors, there was no sign of them.

They looked up at the sky. A contingent of large birds was circling overhead, their menacing presence the only sign of life.

Stillness pervaded the valley. The stench of gun powder lingered in the air.

"Perhaps we won't have to go all the way to Cairo after all, Jabran. We may find our Brits closer than we think."

"*Enshallah* we find them before they find us," Jabran replied.

"What's to worry? We're on their side now, remember?"

"Yes, let's hope they see it that way, eh? And let's hope they hold their fire long enough to find out which side we're on. We all look the same to the Europeans."

"*Iyah!*" Omar was shaking his head, "This war . . . it's a messy business, isn't it Jabran?"

"Yes, it is Omar. A messy business, indeed."

They heard a noise. A groaning, not far from where they stood. It was mournful, secluded, rising up through the early morning mist.

The two Arabs glanced at each other.

"I think it's coming from *that* over there." Omar pointed to a large mass of human flesh, crumpled and twisted on the ground nearby.

"He's still alive, come . . ."

Omar reached out and grabbed his arm. "Jabran . . . our mission, is this wise?"

"To hell with our mission! That man's alive!"

Jabran broke past Omar's grip and proceeded forward. Bending low at the waist, with his head down, he stepped out into the open field. Stealthily he approached what was left of the moaning corpse.

As he drew nearer, the cries grew louder. Jabran, with Omar now at his side, stood over the man. They saw his eyelids shudder. Jabran knelt down beside him. How could this man be alive? His face and hands were burned, he was covered from head to toe with soot and grime. Blood was everywhere, his uniform black and shredded. The stink of decay overwhelming.

"Worry not," Jabran said reassuringly, "we've come to help." Although he had no idea what he could do for him.

The man reached out and touched his shirt, "Please, help me."

He spoke English.

"British!" Jabran looked at Omar. He turned back to the soldier and spoke to him again, this time in his native tongue.

"It's alright, don't worry. We're here to help. Can you move?"

The Englishman whispered, "I've been hit . . . my leg . . . please . . . help me . . ." His eyes rolled back as he passed out.

Carefully they lifted him and carried him through the brush, back behind the mountain of boulders. The massive rocks, extending high, formed a wall sufficient to serve as protection from the sun and wind. Omar set up camp while Jabran tended to the soldier's wounds.

The man's leg was covered in blood, several pieces of shrapnel embedded in his thigh. Jabran tore open the ragged remnants of his trousers, then carefully with the tips of his fingers, pulled the pieces of twisted metal from the wounded leg. When he was done, he took out a small flask of whiskey and opened the top. Omar was watching him from the corner of his eye.

"Is that really necessary?" he asked.

"I have no choice. It needs to be sterilized. It's good that he's unconscious."

He looked up at Omar who was watching him. "Come, hold him down. Yes, that's it. Hold him tight."

Jabran poured the whiskey on the man's open wounds. The soldier screamed, his body jerking upward to escape the pain. Omar tightened his grip. The soldier fell back and passed out again.

Jabran and Omar looked at each other.

"It's done."

Jabran wrapped the leg with strips of cloth torn from his *thobe*. The white fabric quickly turning red, the bleeding slowly subsiding.

He turned his attention to the man's face and hands. Jabran thought back to a time long ago, when his son, a mere boy of two, burned his hand on the *taboon* in the center of the courtyard. Nisrina had been baking bread on the hot rocks when Essam eagerly reached in to grab a loaf. Hearing their screams, Jabran came running from the house. In an instant, he scooped Essam up, and went fast to Dora's home. She'd know what to do. He could still hear the dreadful sound that came from his young son's mouth, and see the look on his wife's face as she eyed the tiny scorched hand—the skin shriveling back against itself.

As expected, Dora didn't hesitate. Jabran stood helpless as he watched his older sister work. She put the screaming child on the kitchen table, all the while soothing him with soft words and hushing sounds. She grabbed ingredients from her shelves and made a healing salve to put on the wound. And as Jabran now played that scene back in his mind, he knew exactly what he had to do.

He made a paste of honey and olive oil from the rations they carried with them. Then, running to the edge of the brush, he found a succulent plant growing close to the ground. Recognizing its healing nature, he broke off a stem, splitting its thick fleshy leaf in two, and squeezed its gelatinous liquid into the paste. He tore strips of cloth from his *thobe* and soaked them in the mixture; then took the poultice and gingerly wrapped the soldier's wounds, being careful not to disturb the fragile layer of burnt skin. The soldier moaned, but did not wake. Jabran was thankful, it was better this way. When he finished, the soldier's breath grew more even, his pulse steady.

Jabran and Omar looked down at the British soldier. A stranger to their land, he appeared no older than they. And yet he had traveled far to risk his life to free their country. No words were said. Exhausted, the two Arabs lay down beside the injured man and closed their eyes.

Having spent most of his military service in the Commander's company smoking fine tobacco and eating well-prepared meals, Jabran had not experienced the untoward ways of combat. So, it came as quite a surprise when he opened his eyes to find the barrel of a gun pointing straight down at him. Omar was nowhere to be found, the injured soldier still in a deep sleep.

"Good morning," the voice was menacing, the uniform Turkish. Jabran's heart sunk.

"Good morning," he replied trying to ignore the rifle in his face.

"Now, why, pray tell, is an Arab sleeping in the middle of the desert beside a wrapped mummy?"

"This man is greatly injured, I was passing on my way to Ma'an. I bandaged his wounds."

"And why, *Enshallah*, are you going to Ma'an?"

"I go to seek the tea merchant there. I hear that he has excellent teas. High words have been spoken."

"High words?" The Turkish soldier's eyes narrowed. "Where are you from?"

"I am from Amman." Jabran, not wanting to draw attention to his true origins and the family he left behind, claimed to be from this Northern city.

"Tea!? Humph! You are traveling about in search of tea?! Do you not realize that there is a war taking place around you?"

"I believe this man's injuries speak to that point."

"Well, young seeker of teas, I have other plans for you. I have a wagon that could use one more passenger. I think that a big, strong, strapping Arab such as yourself would do just fine to fill that space. First, let me take care of this . . ."

The Turk pointed the rifle at the injured man. He took aim. But, before Jabran could protest, before he could raise an arm in protection of the young soldier, a shot rang out, the Turk falling fast to the ground, his rifle flying high in the air, ringing off a shot of its own.

Omar jumped down from the top of the boulders.

"It's a messy business, isn't it Jabran?" He said with a smile.

"Yes, Omar," Jabran breathed a sigh of relief. "A very messy business."

"Come, we must move quickly. I was out scouting the horizon and there is a band of Turks, over to the East, not too far from here. Recruiters. They will have heard the shots and come looking for their comrade. Let's make haste. I saw a ravine, about thirty kilometers to the West. We can take cover there and follow it westward. It's dense, thick with brush. It will be dark soon, the best time to travel."

"But, our friend here, he's too weak to travel," Jabran turned to the Brit.

"We have no choice. He'll ride with you. This rifle will be *my* companion." Omar held up the gun with which he'd killed the Turk, obviously taken from the debris at the train wreck. He continued his urging, "*Yullah!* Let's go! There's no time to waste!"

They quickly packed their gear and lay the British soldier across the front of Jabran's camel. Jabran reluctantly took the Turk's rifle. Unlike Omar who had spent his military servitude in armed battle, Jabran had never killed a man and was not looking forward to the prospect.

They mounted their animals, kicked their sides and whipped their hind quarters. "*Yullah! Yullah!*" they called out as the camels began their fastest run yet.

TWENTY THREE

The British Camp

JABRAN AND OMAR'S DECISION to take flight was a wise one, for the Turkish soldiers were not far behind. Led by Lieutenant Volkan Bey, a small contingent of soldiers was out on a reconnaissance mission. They'd left the remainder of their force behind with a wagon full of new recruits, instructing them to continue back to their military base. He knew his Commander would be pleased with the additional forces.

Volkan had heard the two gun shots fired earlier that day and wondered why his scout had not returned. Curious, he advanced his patrol to investigate.

It was now late afternoon. The sun was inching its way towards the West, the heat intense. The air still. With no breezes to diffuse it, the plume of smoke from the fallen railway continued to hover in the twilight sky covering much of the area overhead. The Lieutenant knew something was amiss. He drove his troops on.

Volkan arrived at the abandoned campsite to find his scout lying face down in a pool of blood. He dismounted his camel and walked over to him. A fiery man, tall and thin with a short trimmed mustache, Volkan stood harshly over the body. His eyes were cold like hardened steel. His brow furrowed and menacing. The man was dead, there was no doubt. His face barely recognizable, the bullet having pierced straight through his head.

Volkan did not hesitate; he kicked his comrade, once, then twice, finally turning him over with his foot. The leader turned to the ragged men who looked on in horror, his metal eyes piercing deep, his finger pointing accusatorily at the corpse, "Carelessness. Pure and simple. Let that be a lesson to you all." He looked up at the smoke-filled sky, "Now, let's go see what *that* is all about."

The Turks dismounted their camels and moved in the direction of the smoke. Arriving at the edge of the clearing, they stepped out into the open area and saw the overturned railway car.

The soldiers were stunned.

The heat of the sun had quickly taken its toll—the stench now overwhelming with decaying flesh. Bodies were sprawled about, lying in their own hardened excrements. Insects hovered, the constant buzz of their wings piercing the solitude of the arid plain. The soldiers resisted the scene, turning their heads. They weren't sure which they feared most: that which lay before them or their Lieutenant's hateful scorn.

The vultures that had previously been circling overhead were now hunched over the rotting corpses. Large and menacing, they were tearing the flesh, entrails hanging wildly from their mouths. Disregarding the Turks, they continued their feasting on the fodder of war. Former men. Husbands and sons who only days ago had names and lives, hopes and futures.

"Get their guns!" Volkan yelled.

The soldiers did not budge.

"I said, get their guns! We're not going to leave those weapons! Remember your orders, no arms left behind!"

Finally, the soldiers started to move. But instead of moving forward to get the guns, they backed away, slowly, deliberately, step-by-step towards the safety of the brush.

"Don't you understand?! What are you waiting for? Must I nurse you like children?!"

But the troops had no ears for their leader's commands. Wide-eyed and terrified, they continued their retreat, deeper and deeper into the brush until they could no longer see or be seen.

When they'd placed enough distance between themselves and the wreckage, they turned and ran.

Volkan, standing amidst the bloodshed and rubble continued barking orders. Only now they were screams and obscenities. He demanded their return. They had a duty to the Sultan. Revenge would be taken.

His shouts fell on deaf ears. There were no words invented that could have coerced those soldiers to return. No orders given that would have persuaded them to rummage through the pungent decay. Weapons indeed. They would have none of it. They fled with no intentions to return. And now, free from the horror, they mounted their camels and quickly rode off.

"You fools! Swine! You suffering ass of a donkey!" The Lieutenant was livid as he heard the camels' hooves fade fast in the distance.

The vultures sensing the shift, stopped for a moment, their carnage suspended. In unison, they turned their heads and hungrily eyed the pugnacious Lieutenant.

He was standing alone. A leader with no troops. His heated rants lost to the wind.

Volkan, observing their pause, became further infuriated. He lifted his weapon, firing multiple rounds in their direction. Some birds flew off. Some lay dead.

When sufficiently gratified, he walked forward plucking through the chaos, weapons dangling from his arms. His mood was hard, his temper assured. Fully armed, he returned to his camel muttering angrily to himself.

"As God is my witness, I will find the devils that caused this massacre. I will have my revenge."

He mounted his camel and rode towards the West in the direction of the ravine.

Omar was a jackrabbit. One moment he was there, riding alongside Jabran, and the next he was gone—darting up ahead or far to the side to scout their surroundings. Jabran was glad he'd selected Omar as his traveling companion. A truer friend he could not have had. And now he owed him his life. Omar had seemed young and inexperienced when they'd first met. But watching him these past few days, Jabran realized how much he'd changed. While Jabran was in the Commander's quarters, sitting cross-legged on plush rugs and soft pillows, eating sumptuous meals and smoking tobacco, Omar had been out training, working hard and learning maneuvers. He had gotten stronger, leaner and quick of mind. How very well suited he was for this work, seeming to come alive in the short week they'd been traveling together. Jabran was proud to call him his brother.

As they traveled through the ravine the wounded soldier remained unconscious, limply straddling the camel's neck while Jabran held him in place, periodically pausing to check his breathing. His breaths were shallow, but it was enough to satisfy Jabran—the soldier continued to live.

"Up ahead a few miles, there's a military camp, they're British!"

Omar had just returned from one of his reconnaissance trips to inform Jabran of his findings.

"This is good news," Jabran said. "Our friend here needs proper attention."

Omar tore the cloth from his white *thobe* and tied it to a tall stick. He wanted no misunderstanding—they came in peace. The two men rode on in silence, Omar holding the white flag high in the air. Each one wondering what reception lay ahead.

By the time they reached the British encampment it was dark. As they approached, they were met by two soldiers on camels of their own. The British could see that they were Arab civilians carrying a white flag.

"*Salaam alay kum*, peace to you," the Brits greeted them in Arabic.

"*Ou alay kum a salaam*, and to you, peace," Omar replied.

"Greetings to you," Jabran spoke in English.

"Ah, I see you speak the King's language. Excellent. I dare say, it makes things so much easier, don't you think?"

Jabran and Omar smiled at the two soldiers, relieved that their reception had been so civil.

"We have a wounded soldier here. One of yours I believe. We found him, barely alive, at the train wreckage just north of Ma'an. We did what we could . . . he's badly hurt."

The soldier looked at the bandaged man who limply straddled the neck of Jabran's camel. He motioned to them. "Follow me. We have a medic, he'll know what to do."

At first the camp looked deserted. It was dark and quiet, few lanterns were lit. But within minutes, the grounds were covered with British soldiers who'd heard of the two visitors. The wounded man was immediately taken to the medic's tent.

"How did you find us? We thought we'd secured a pretty private place here. Off the beaten track and all."

Speaking to them was a young Colonel. He paused apologetically to introduce himself. "I'm sorry, forgive me. I'm Colonel Billingham. I've been out in the wild far too long now and it seems I've forgotten my manners." He was a tall man, handsome, with thick blond hair, and as Jabran watched his face in the light of the lantern, he couldn't help notice the Colonel's eyes. They were clear blue like the Mediterranean Sea. It made him think of Mariana with her impish green stare. And then he thought of Nisrina.

The Colonel cleared his throat. Omar poked Jabran in his side.

Realizing the Colonel awaited his response, Jabran snapped back to the present. He responded, "I'm very pleased to meet you Colonel. I am Jabran Yusef and my friend here is Omar Mahmoud. And as far as how we found you, well, I have to give credit for that coup d'état to Omar. He's the one who provided the reconnaissance and quite frankly saved both me and our wounded guest from the bullets of a Turk. I was afraid that our luck had run out and then he appeared and . . . pow!"

He made the motion of a gun going off, "He saved our lives."

They both turned to Omar, who was smiling. The "pow" gave him a hint that Jabran was recounting the bullet he had expended on the Turkish soldier. He was proud that his story was being told, but not confident enough with his English to venture a response or enter into the discussion. He remained silent and let Jabran do the talking.

"You say you encountered a Turk? A soldier?" the Colonel asked. He was eyeing the two men carefully. He glanced at their camels and guns, the saddles and packs, all typically used by the Turkish military.

Jabran nodded, and the Colonel invited the Arabs into his tent.

"I am very interested in what you've experienced. What you saw. Please tell me, where and when. What exactly took place?"

It was clear that the Colonel wanted to know more, and Jabran, happy to curry his favor, began his tale. He took his time and went into the details of the day. He had privately rehearsed the part that pertained to their roles, who they were and why they were out adventuring through such inhospitable territory. The fact that they were young Arab adventurers from Amman wanting to join with the British and help take back their country from the Turks. He told him what they'd seen at the fallen railway. How they followed a dark plume of smoke and saw the overturned train and the damaged tracks. He spoke of the bodies and the carnage and how they heard the moans of a soldier and then had the opportunity to speak briefly with him, finding he was British. What they did to bandage his wounds and stop the bleeding.

Then he repeated in detail what happened via their encounter with the Turkish soldier. How the tyrant held them at gunpoint and threatened to kill the bandaged man and force Jabran to join their contingency, and how Omar had suddenly appeared from above and finished him off, putting a stop to the terror. He concluded with the fact that Omar had seen others approaching from the East, recruiters with a wagon. And how, because of that impending threat, they quickly took off towards the West carrying the wounded man with them, choosing to follow the protection of the thick brush that grew in the bottom of the ravine, the most logical route to travel undetected.

The Colonel nodded as Jabran spoke. He listened intently to every word, never interrupting or asking idle questions. He let him talk until he had nothing more to say, all the while watching both men carefully.

Then he asked, "Do you think there's a chance that the others, those from the Turkish contingent, may have followed you? I mean, followed you here to our camp?"

Jabran looked at Omar and repeated the question to him in Arabic. Omar responded that anything was possible, but he had kept a sharp eye on all sides and had seen no sign of it.

Jabran didn't need to translate back to the Colonel. He understood every word. In fact, he joined in on their conversation speaking perfect Arabic. He was clearly a learned man, familiar with the language and culture of the desert people.

Omar and Jabran briefly exchanged looks. They were glad that they had not spoken between themselves of the real reason they were interacting with the British forces. They had not revealed any clues that their actual purpose was to obtain information about British plans of advancement, how and when they planned to move into the Holy Land, Azraq or Damascus.

The Turks knew that if the British forces were to take Damascus, it would be disastrous. Their Commander had suspected that the British were advancing northward, especially after taking Aqaba. The bombing of the railway line pointed to that route. To be able to deliver the details back to their Commander would be crucial for a successful Turkish defense.

Jabran noted that, although he'd been kind and welcoming to them, Colonel Billingham was a perceptive man. One who could become a very good friend or a most formidable foe. And in spite of their clandestine cross-purposes, he hoped with all his heart that it would be the former.

TWENTY FOUR

Volkan

VOLKAN HAD CHOSEN THE same path through the ravine. He saw the fresh prints left by the two camels and surmised that their owners were not far ahead. He hoped they would lead him to the British. But he was both wicked and shrewd. He knew he must be careful. Hold back. Bide his time. He camped in a small cave on the north side of the canyon wall. He had very few rations. But that didn't concern him. No one would detect him there and he needed little in the way of food or water. He welcomed deprivation. He thrived on it, constantly reminding himself, *my name is Volkan, the Volcano, and my nature is my birthright. No man dare cross me!*

His plan was to lie quiet, remain underground, undetected until the time was right, and then, true to his name, like a volcano, he would erupt.

He thought of the men who'd deserted him, recruits gathered from all reaches of the earth: Arabs, Armenians and Mesopotamians. He would get his revenge on them as well. They were not worthy of the honor of the Ottoman Empire. They all disgusted him. Yes, he would seek them out, find each one and make them regret their cowardly impudence. But for now he needed to focus his attention on the British devils, their demise his prime intention. He would deal with the others later.

The next morning, Volkan ventured out of his cave. Continuing on the path, he followed the markings left by the camels. He knew it was unlikely that the others would be traveling in the heat of the day. Most traveled by night. That was their weakness. But he thrived in the heat. This was the opportune time for him to sneak up unaware, he was sure they would all be sleeping.

The sun had reached its highest point in the sky when Volkan came upon a thicket nestled far into the side of a mountain. He slowed his pace and dismounted his camel. The tracks changed at this point. More camel prints, and men on foot, it was here that they'd dismounted. The camp was close at hand. He climbed up the side of the mountain to its highest crest. When he reached the top he saw the first sentry stationed on a large boulder to the north. He looked to the east, the west, and then to the south. His eyes found four sentries, four positions. Their placement gave him the circumference of the camp. Although he could not see it hidden in the dense vegetation, he was certain that he'd ascertained the camp's location, the sentries posted above its perimeter.

And so his work began. Like a tiger stalking its prey, one by one, he approached from the rear. Quietly, stealthily, he grabbed each sentry from behind, his arm across their necks, holding them in a lock, their bodies immobile, unable to breathe. He acted before any one of them knew what had happened. A quick snap and their necks were broken.

Having cleared the way, he descended the mountain back to the ravine. Carrying a pack of explosives, he moved from tree to tree; at times he hung from branches, at others he moved on the ground. He saw the encampment. The tents were scattered about, with distinct divisions that indicated the tribal boundaries of their allies. Before him was the Arab revolt of which he had heard. A contingent of dogs that opposed the Sultan. The British in the center, the various Bedouin tribes encircling the perimeter.

Oh, the weakness of their lot, he thought to himself. *Such impudence. Such depravity.* He smiled wickedly. *And now the mighty volcano shall have his vengeance.*

Volkan's plan was impeccable. He surreptitiously planted explosives at key points around the camp.

Satisfied with his work, a job well done, he was ready to retreat. His goal was to climb to the highest point and then with gunfire, set off the explosives. He grew giddy at the thought of his shrewdness. Such cunning, such wit, he could hardly hold back the admiration he held for himself. Surely after this coup, he'd be made Captain. His Commander would not hold back that honor, not this time.

Volkan turned, he slipped into the brush, his self-aggrandized musings running wild in his mind; and then, as he was about to ascend back up the mountain, he heard a click. He froze. The sound was unmistakable.

"*Marhaba.*" A voice in his ear—an Arab. He could feel the hard, cold steel of the gun in his back. "*Mashallah*, God willing, just give me an excuse. I'd love to blow your head off."

Volkan turned white. This was quite unexpected. Not part of his plan.

"What do you want?" he asked, remaining frozen in place. He needed time. Time to assess the situation. Was this a lone interloper? Or were there others?

"What I *want* is to blow your filthy head off. But unfortunately, it doesn't matter what *I* want. I must leave that decision up to the Colonel. Now drop your guns carefully, and put your hands on your head. We'll pay him a visit."

Volkan followed his command. He dared not look at his captor. Slowly he lowered his artillery. He put his hands in the air and turned to walk back to the camp, the rifle now following him, dead center in his back.

The Colonel hearing their approach stepped out of his tent. "Well, what have we here?" Billingham saw Omar, his rifle fully cocked and pressed against the back of a Turkish soldier.

"I found him laying explosives around the camp," Omar was solid.

Billingham called to his men, who immediately came out of their tents.

"We have a prisoner. Search him and secure him. And check around, he may not be the only one out there."

He glanced again at Omar who was shirtless wearing only his pants. He noticed the bruises that covered his body, a common sight among Turkish soldiers. He'd seen it in other defectors who had joined his ranks. It never ceased to sicken him. He realized there was more to these two Arabs then they had told him. He said nothing on the subject, but turned to instruct his men to seek out and disengage the explosives that had been set.

TWENTY FIVE

Truth

THAT EVENING, COLONEL BILLINGHAM welcomed Jabran and Omar to his tent. They were to dine with him in honor of Omar's bravery. The three men shared a simple meal, then sat back and relaxed with English cigarettes and fine European whiskey. Jabran and Omar were thrilled to be sharing the evening with a British Colonel—such an unexpected end to a harrowing trek. They hoped to accomplish their mission and return to Camp Azraq without the need to travel to Cairo. To gain the Colonel's confidence was critical, and time was of the essence. The Commander had given them only four weeks to accomplish their goal. Not a day more. They'd been gone over a week now and they needed another week for their return journey. Only two weeks remained to garner the Colonel's trust and learn his battle plans.

And then there's the matter of Mariana. You've met Mariana, haven't you, Jabran? The Commander's words played back in Jabran's mind like an angry wound. Yes, he'd met Mariana. And they both knew that he would keep his commitment. He would return.

The Colonel was talking, his glass raised up, he was making a toast. He turned to Omar smiling warmly, "Let me start by saying that I was quite impressed by your diligence and courage today Omar, and on behalf of myself, the whole camp, and His Royal Majesty the

King of England, I thank and commend you wholeheartedly. You saved our lives." They lifted their glasses and toasted good health.

Omar blushed and tried not to show it, but he was very pleased with himself and grateful for the recognition. He wondered what his father would think if he could see him now. He would be proud, he was sure of it. Jabran had been right about Omar—this work suited him well, and it had not gone unnoticed.

They raised their glasses again and the Commander continued, "I am thankful that the two of you stumbled upon our modest camp. You brought back one of our injured men and for that we can never repay you. I am humbled by your valor." Again, they clicked their glasses and took a sip.

But the Colonel was not finished, he paused a moment, thoughtfully measuring the best way to approach his next comment. As a gentleman, he wanted to be sure that his guests were not offended, but more importantly, as a soldier, he needed the truth.

Finally, he began, "Let me also say that you are welcome to stay here as long as you wish. But first, I must share with you a bit about myself, and how I command. I want you both to understand the precepts by which we live."

Jabran nodded, "Of course."

"I am an honest man. One with whom frankness and integrity are, shall we say, a way of life. It is my creed, one from which I do not waver."

Omar and Jabran glanced at each other.

"And having said that, I dare say, I think this is a time for honest words."

He watched their faces as he slowly lowered his glass to the table. "You see, there is something bothering me about your presence here in my camp. It is not in what you say, for your stories are admirable, but rather in what you do not say. I suspect there is something you are not telling me."

He puffed on his cigarette, then snuffed it out, his eyes directly on them.

Jabran and Omar remained silent, looking down at their hands.

"Let me be frank," he continued, "I think that maybe you are not adventurers as you say you are, but rather defectors from the Turkish army."

,abran felt a dread rise up in his core.

"If you are defectors, that is understandable and I would gladly take you into our forces. Lord knows, we could always use good men. In fact, I have done so many times before. And if this is the case, you must realize that you have nothing to fear."

He continued to watch them. They looked back at him, not daring to catch the others' gaze for fear of what they might reveal.

"But more importantly, you understand, is that I must be able to trust you. I must know that what you say is the truth. And if I know this, then you will be my soldiers, and all my soldiers are my sons."

At these words Jabran and Omar exchanged furtive glances. Still they said nothing. Although his sentiments were compelling, Jabran did not know if he could trust the Colonel, and therefore did not waver from his original account. Omar read the caution in Jabran's eyes.

The Colonel saw their looks. "We are moving our encampment tonight, as soon as the sun sets. This location is vulnerable. If you and the Turk found us, then others will too. We'll say goodnight for now. But remember, if you have anything you'd like to say to me, my door is always open."

He smiled at his little joke, for they all knew he had no door. And for the moment, the two Arabs had no words. They thanked him for his hospitality and retired silently to their quarters.

During the night the camp was packed and moved. A well organized unit, everyone knew their function and performed it efficiently. They left, traveling through the night, the sliver of moon providing little in the way of guidance. But the soldiers were accustomed to traveling in the dark, they rode atop camels that moved easily over the rough, dry terrain, the animals stepping surefooted over stones and unseen holes, moving northward to higher ground.

Prisoners remained on foot with hands bound securely behind them. They weren't many, but the few who'd been captured were joined together in a row; one to the other, secured at the waist, with the first man's rope affixed to the back of a camel.

When they reached the top of the mountain, Colonel Billingham motioned to his men to stop and make camp. He knew they would benefit from this new location. Their ability to see out was enhanced by the altitude, and the steep rise would slow any approaching forces.

The troops reassembled their new home.

While it remained first and foremost in their minds, Jabran and Omar avoided discussing Colonel Billingham's words. When they were finally alone, Omar could hold back no longer. He looked hard at his friend.

"Why can't we defect? We'll join the British forces. Or better yet, return back to our homes, our families," Omar pleaded. "I cannot return to that miserable fortress!"

Jabran shook his head. He turned away. But Omar was not finished.

"We did not willingly join the Turkish army. We were forced at gunpoint, remember? And then we were brutally beaten—have you forgotten the atrocities?

But Jabran had not forgotten. He looked up at Omar.

"Omar, we gave our word. We told them we would return and so we must. Trust me, there is more at stake here than you can imagine. It is not just about you or me." He shook his head, "I can say no more, please accept what I say."

Omar looked in his eyes. Jabran was both his friend and the First Lieutenant in charge of this mission, and so, he said no more.

Jabran could not explain his position to Omar, but without explanation, his actions made no sense. The Colonel had been kind and fair, so graciously evenhanded. He even offered to call them his sons. What reasonable person would not come forward and be honest with a man like Billingham?

But Jabran was no longer a reasonable man. He was a creature caught in a web. He could not speak of Mariana. He'd lain beside the young girl night after night, and had held her in his arms. Who would believe his virtue? Or hers? And although he'd held her close, breathing in the warmth of her scent, he remained true to Nisrina. When he thought of his wife, his body ached with desire. He wanted to hold her. To touch her. To hear her voice in his ear. But those things were not possible. She was safe in Beit el Jebel, in the Yusef compound, while Mariana was left in an ungodly place, vulnerable and alone. She needed protection, the victim of beastly men. What if this had been his daughter? He shuddered at the thought. He knew he must keep his promise to protect her and the child within her womb.

The walls—they have eyes and ears. Jabran kept hearing Mariana's warning. No, it was best to simply stand down. Hold his position. Be patient and bide his time. He could not disclose the truth to Omar.

There were other Arabs in the British encampment. Mostly Bedouins, they came from separate and distinct desert tribes, joined together by British urging. They were given promises of an independent Arab Nation, free from the tyranny of the Ottoman Empire. They gathered, united in a mutual cause. It was time to launch an uprising, they were told. Then freedom would be theirs. Freedom to rule themselves. The British had assured them of this. And although they did not trust one another, the different tribes did share that common hope and therefore banded together to fight against Ottoman rule.

At first the tribesmen were wary of the two newcomers, questioning and discussing the implications of their presence. But the worries did not last. Word had spread of how Jabran had saved the British soldier's life, and how Omar's foresight and bravery had spared the entire company from destruction at the hands of the Turkish Lieutenant.

The two adventurers were welcomed and trusted. They became like family to the patchwork brigade, their stories repeated again and again.

TWENTY SIX

Betrayal

VOLKAN HAD BEEN SECURED in a small cage, separate from the other prisoners. Tightly bound, his hands and feet were further weighted with rusted irons. His only human contact was when food was brought to him. Slipping it through a small opening carved into the wooden slats, the sentry would check to see that he remained shackled.

It was on such an occasion that Jabran found himself in front of Lieutenant Volkan.

"Mealtime," he said as he slipped the tray of bread and soup into the opening at the base of the cage. Until this time, Jabran had no reason to interact with the devious interloper and now he paused a moment to look into the madman's eyes.

And Volkan, in turn, saw his face.

For a moment neither man could look away. There was something in Volkan's eyes that held Jabran's gaze. A menacing taunt that pulled him in. Finally, he turned to leave.

"First Lieutenant Yusef? Is that you?" The voice was familiar.

Jabran paused.

He turned back and looked again at the man in the cage.

Like a starving animal, Volkan was stuffing the bread and soup into his mouth.

"I'm sorry, do I know you?" Jabran asked.

"It *is* you! Ha! I knew it! I'd know that voice anywhere!"

"Who are you? Where are you from?" Jabran looked intently at the prisoner, his eyes narrowing in the dim light.

"They told us you had defected. Why, there's a price on your head, Lieutenant! Ha! And here you are serving slop to a prisoner of war! The great linguist, First Lieutenant Jabran Yusef! Ha! I have met the enemy and it is you!"

The prisoner had the advantage. He was loudly calling out Jabran's name and his Turkish military rank. Jabran stepped closer to the prisoner, his eyes never leaving the madman's face. He spoke softly now, "And how is it that you know my name?"

"How do I know your name?! How do I know your name?!" Volkan was laughing, the food in his mouth sputtering onto Jabran's face, foamed saliva gathering between the folds of his parched lips. He was incredulous. "Why, don't you remember me Lieutenant? I was there when they first brought you to Azraq—a stubborn farmer! I am the one that told the Commander about your silver tongue. He whisked you away from the rest of us. Do you not recognize me?" His grey eyes squinted narrowly, "It is I! Volkan!" He was pounding his chest. "From the food tent. The day you arrived! Ah!" He pointed his dirty finger through the cage, his wrists bleeding from the chains that held him. "I can see it in your face, you do remember! You refused to eat even a small bite until you had thoroughly assessed the situation. You spoke to me in perfect Turkish, the same dialect that I used with you.

"The Commander had been looking for a man like you, Jabran. And now . . . now, he curses your name! He has called all his officers to be on the lookout for you and that stinking comrade of yours—Omar." He spit on the ground. "My good man, there is a handsome price on both your heads!" His hands were moving as best they could, bound so tightly he had spilled his soup, laughing loudly, crudely showing his teeth with the half-eaten food still left in his mouth.

Jabran took a step back. He could not let Volkan reveal his identity. But to reason with him was a waste of time. This was a madman. He needed time to think. He turned and quickly walked away, hoping no one had heard the soldier's revelations.

The next day Jabran managed to be at the mess tent when the prisoners' food was ready. He volunteered to take Volkan's tray to him.

"I'll take it," he said flatly to the cook.

As he walked over to Volkan's hovel, his mind kept repeating yesterday's conversation—*defected . . . a price on his head . . . the Commander furious.* What a strange turn of events. What had he done to evoke such retribution? Had the Commander planned this all along? Or had he somehow learned of Jabran's intent to return and escape with Mariana? Impossible! He had shared those thoughts with no one. And as shrewd as the Commander was, Jabran was certain he'd not yet developed the ability to read his mind.

He knew he had to do something about Volkan. To quell his voice. But he didn't know exactly what that would be. This man was a dangerous threat. If revealed, his knowledge of their mission could prove deadly to both he and Omar, not to mention Mariana and the baby.

As he walked to the makeshift prison cell he felt a cold, piercing wind. It cut into his eyes and face, his cheekbones aching from the icy chill. He noticed clouds gathering overhead. Dark, thick billows. A storm was moving in.

Volkan was dozing, sitting upright, the space allotted kept him tightly bound. Jabran kicked the sides of the cage. Volkan woke and took the food from him.

"I see you've come again," Volkan jeered.

"You said there is a price on my head?" Jabran was firm, straight-forward. He wanted more information.

This time Volkan ate half his food before he would talk. Jabran stood there watching him, disgusted by his boorishness.

"Yes," he finally belched. "There is quite a substantial price. The Commander plans to send the military police after you. There was talk about searching your hometown and the surrounding villages. He assumed that would be your destination."

Jabran winced. He hoped that Volkan had not noticed. His thoughts turned to Nisrina. His children. *If they even dared touch one hair on their heads . . .*

"Tell me, First Lieutenant," Volkan continued, "Why here? Why did you choose to join with the British? Why not just return to your farm, your family? Has our war unleashed such a passion that you could not go home?" Volkan, dropping all pretenses, was now clearly curious.

"My affairs are of no concern to you," Jabran replied. He hated this man. This soldier who stood for all he detested. This creature who dared to stand before him and question what passions burned in his heart. His own so dark and evil. He wanted to kill him. To silence him and undo all that he had said.

"Well, they may be soon enough."

"What do you mean?"

"I understand that he is assembling a contingent . . . the Commander . . . to go to Beit el Jebel. To find you and bring you back to him. He gave orders to destroy your village. Oh, and there's one more thing . . ." Volkan motioned for Jabran to come closer, he wanted to whisper in his ear. Jabran leaned in to hear, the prisoner's voice lowered, "I hear that you have a very beautiful wife . . ."

Jabran grabbed him by the throat and began to choke him, "I'll kill you. I'll kill all of you. I swear it! If anyone goes near her, may God hear my pleas!"

Volkan was gasping for breath, Jabran unrelenting, "Now, tell me everything. Tell me what you know, or I swear to God almighty, you will not survive this day!"

Volkan still gagging motioned to Jabran that he was willing to talk. Jabran released his grip, "Speak devil!"

"It's just as I've said. The Commander formed a plan. He was talking about Beit el Jebel. He wants to set explosives, burn the village. You understand? In retribution for your desertion. You are the example of what happens to treasonous skum."

"When? When was this to happen?" Jabran's arms reached through the posts again, he grabbed him roughly by the shirt. He would have killed him on the spot, snapped his neck like a pullet, but he couldn't. He needed the information. It couldn't come fast enough.

"I don't know. I was sent out to scout for recruits, men trained in explosives. They were headed back to Azraq when I got sidetracked here." Volkan, for the first time was shivering. Perhaps it was the cold wind that had come in from the East. Perhaps it was Jabran's furor unleashed so abashedly. It didn't matter, Jabran was beyond caring.

He threw the Turk to the ground, then turned and marched off—straight to Colonel Billingham's tent. Billingham was outside. He had just returned from dinner with his men.

"We need to talk," he told the Colonel.

"Let's go inside," Billingham motioned with his head. He gave orders not to be disturbed.

Jabran sat down in one of two small wooden chairs. He took a minute to compose himself. The Colonel sat opposite him and waited patiently for Jabran to begin.

Taking a deep breath, he began, "I apologize for what I am about to tell you, for I am much ashamed. You have been good to both me and Omar. You have treated us as one of your own. As you so graciously stated—as your sons. You are a man of honor, and I come to you to say that I have dishonored you, and for this I beg your forgiveness."

Jabran was looking straight into the Colonel's eyes. He marveled at their clarity, their deep azure hue, and he wondered how God could create such magnificent eyes. *The window to a man's soul*, his mother had once told him. And if her words were true, then Billingham's soul was pure indeed.

"I see, please continue," the Colonel had been waiting for this.

"Sir, I am here to tell you that I am not what I say I am. I have been lying to you."

"Go on."

"My name is Jabran Yusef, in that I have been forthright. But it is not the full story. I am in fact, *First Lieutenant* Jabran Yusef, with the Turkish Desert Brigade. I have been sent here by my superior. I have approached you under false pretenses, with the full intent to obtain information on your plans for advancement and take that information back to my Commander."

Jabran paused, allowing the Colonel time to absorb what he'd told him. Then he continued, "I am deeply sorry. It was not my choice to deceive. I was ordered, nay, *forced* by my Commander. I was compelled to obtain the information and return with it to the

Turkish encampment. I have only three weeks left to return, or else . . ."
He looked down again, unable to finish his sentence.

"Or else what?" The Colonel leaned in.

"Or else there will be dire consequences. Believe me on this."

"Yes, of course." The Colonel sat back in his chair, his fingertips
lightly tapping his lips.

Jabran continued, "And now, I have just learned from Lieutenant
Volkan that the Commander has made a fool of me. He has double
crossed me, and is threatening my family and my village."

For one brief moment, Jabran choked-up as the horror of the
situation began to sink in. To hear it said by another was one thing. But
when he spoke the words himself, the utter dismay was overwhelming.
But this was no time for emotions. Composing himself, he looked
straight at the Colonel, "Believe me when I tell you, I am through
with the Turkish Commander and his false pretenses."

The Colonel was interested. "Tell me more. Where is this camp
located?"

"In a fortress."

"A fortress?!"

"Yes, an old fortress, hidden in the middle of the desert. It lies
to the East, beyond the western ridge. They call it *Qasr al Azraq*, the
Blue Fortress."

"*Qasr al Azraq*? I've heard tales of it. I thought it was only a
myth. Can you give me the specifics?"

"Of course. It's very old. The walls are made of black basalt,
each side approximately 80 meters in length. There are many tents
surrounding it. The camp has all the aspects of a small village.
Complete in every respect."

"Where exactly is it located?"

"By camel, I would say it is about a two day ride east of Amman.
Maybe 100 kilometers give or take."

"But that's pure desert, how can an encampment of that size
subsist there? What is their water source?"

"There is an oasis. The fortress was built adjacent to it."

"Of course. I see." The Colonel was quiet. He snuffed out the
cigarette he'd been smoking. He looked sharply at Jabran, "How do
I know I can trust you?"

"I give you my word."

"I see." The Colonel took in a deep breath.

"In fact, I'll take you there. It is a four day ride. We can leave today."

The Colonel hesitated. "I have another plan," he said. "We have a secret force. Aeroplanes. We'll attack from the air. They won't know what hit them."

Jabran's eyes widened, he was terrified by the prospect. He could only think of Mariana. He had to warn her. He needed time to reach her, get her out of there.

"Colonel, there is more," he looked down, his voice softened. He hesitated. "You see, there is a girl."

"A girl?"

"Yes, a woman now. She carries a child."

"Ah! I see. Yes, now I see." The Colonel rose from his chair. He paced back and forth. Lit another cigarette. Took a few puffs. As he inhaled, the end of the cigarette flickered and glowed, its glistening embers bright against the darkness that had now descended upon the tent.

He continued, "It's funny isn't it, Jabran? No matter how hard we try . . . to be soldiers . . . to be strong fighting men . . . to fight for our rights and our country. It's funny how in the end it comes down to the simplest of things—a woman and her child."

He looked at Jabran intently, "I'll give you one day's lead, no more. You leave tonight."

TWENTY SEVEN

A Tormented Soul

HE RODE IN QUIET desperation.

The wind from the northeast was fierce. Its frigid arms surrounding him in a bitter embrace while dark, threatening clouds gathered overhead. The smell of damp hung in the air, urging him to hasten. And hasten he did, in spite of the turbulent night that lay ahead.

Billingham had encouraged him to take along a companion. Omar had begged to be included. In fact, any one of the good men in that camp would have been honored to accompany him on his trek. But Jabran knew that he had to make it on his own. He could not explain the reason to anyone, especially not Omar. Only Billingham knew of Mariana and he'd been sworn to keep his secret.

Although it was a four-day trek, Jabran promised the Colonel that he would complete it in three. The Colonel gave him one day's lead—on the morning of the fourth day the British planes would drop their bombs. They'd arrive at daybreak and descend upon the fortress in concert with the rising sun.

Jabran had been confident that he could reach Azraq and escape with Mariana before the dawn of that fourth day. But he had not anticipated the harsh wind that pushed against him. Strong and unrelenting.

He whipped the hindquarters of his beast, kicked her sides, called out to her with urgency, and forever obedient, she moved along as best she could.

Jabran thought it wiser to avoid contact with any persons who might be searching for him. *A price on your head,* the Turk had said. And so he decided to circle around the town of Amman, knowing that the indirect route would add hours to his trek.

The shock of the Commander's betrayal was surpassed only by Jabran's resolve to save Mariana. He had to reach her before the British engagement. And before the Commander could do her harm. He saw her face in his mind, that gentle smile, those stunning eyes. He sat upright in his saddle, tall and straight, intent to make it on time.

As he rode through the night, his troubled thoughts began to quiet.

So rare the moment of silent discourse, his tranquil mind envisioned Nisrina. She stole her way in, her image resting tenderly before him. His wife. His life. So innocent and pure.

I will make it back to you, he promised her. Just a brief detour, that's all.

Clouds continued to roll in, the air electrified. Jabran shivered beneath his cloak.

And then the rain came. It fell in torrents. One moment there was a flash of lightening, the sky on fire. The next, a clap and the clouds opened. The drops were huge, blinding him.

Leaning forward, he closed his eyes and let the camel lead the way. Pressed firmly against the animal's neck, he listened to the sound of its labored breath and felt the rocking of its pacing gait against the rugged land.

Then, in that quiet repose, with the rain pounding hard on his aching back, his body moving in concert with the pace, he began to weep.

The sky gave its consent, their tears blending as one. For as the heavens wept, so now might he. He felt God's intention. His permission to cast off his suffering and cleanse his heart. He no longer knew which tears were his and which were the heavens.' He no longer cared. He kept his face down, buried deep in the wet of the camel's coat. And in that state, he humbly and quietly placed his life in the hands of the Lord.

They rode on together, man and beast. Jabran kept warm by the animal's heat. The musty smell of its soaked fur filling his nostrils. Comforting him. Giving him solace.

It did not last—the camel's foot . . . a rock, a hole . . . he wasn't sure. He heard a cry—a strange, human-like quality as she stumbled and swayed. She went down to the ground.

He urged her to continue, to rise up and complete their journey. He kicked her hard and called out to her, "*Imshee! Imshee!*" But the beast was down. She would not rise.

Jabran dismounted. He took his pack and in the cold, wet night went searching for cover. He found a small indentation, a dimple in the canyon wall. It looked as if an animal had once slept there, carving its shape into the stone with the heat of its body, and now deserted, was left for any traveler who might seek shelter. Jabran crawled in, and there he spent the night, the rain falling hard like a raging ram protecting its young.

The morning brought the sun. The air warm and still. The sky, a brilliant shade of blue. The ground, still damp from the night's downpour, cast an earthy smell over the valley. Jabran awoke as the thick, rich scent filled his nostrils. He nibbled on the dates that he'd brought with him, and drank water from his pack. With renewed determination, he went in search of his camel.

He found her where he'd left her; standing now, grazing quietly on the shrubbery that grew nearby. Relieved to see her in such good spirits, he patted her down, whispered soft, soothing words, and then mounted her.

Determined to make it to the Turkish camp before the British aeroplanes, he dug his heels into her thighs. They raced for hours in the hot sun, not stopping until they'd reached the edge of the valley where finally they paused to rest. Jabran surveyed the road ahead, gazing out towards the Eastern horizon. Searching against the glare of the desert floor he saw his next challenge—before him lay the arid plain.

The sun reached its peak in the noontime sky, the heat rising. The camel showing signs of fatigue wobbled and weaved. Her breath came in shortened spurts as she rumbled her displeasure. Against his will, Jabran stopped. Knowing it wiser to rest during daylight hours and travel in the cool night air, he dismounted and set up camp. Taking shelter in the shade of his camel he slept soundly.

When he finally woke the moon was high in the sky. Time was running short. The trek had proven more difficult than expected and he still had far to go. Angry for losing precious time, he quickly remounted his beast and rode hard, straight through the night, stopping for neither food nor water.

On the final night of his journey, Jabran feared the worst. The rocky terrain and their hurried pace had taken their toll. His clothes were covered with the dust of the desert and his pants clung to the sweat and dirt of his body. His shaggy beard covered his face; and his hair, once soft and curly, was tangled and dry. The rations he'd brought along were running low even though he ate only once a day. But he would not rest. With only a few hours before daybreak, he'd not yet reached the crest of the hill from which he could see the fortress.

The camel slowed. Jabran whipped her backside. He used all his strength to kick her, his heels digging hard into her flanks.

"*Yullah, Imshee!*" he commanded, his voice growing hoarse.

But the camel was exhausted. And with one more kick and one more call for her to move on, she swayed and went down.

Jabran dismounted. He pulled at the animal. He pleaded with her. He cursed and he screamed.

The camel turned her face away. She would have none of it.

Jabran fell to his knees and called to the heavens, "Oh, my Lord God, have mercy on me!" But the only response was the arduous wind blowing hard against the sandy soil.

He rose up, and pushing back the matted hair from his blood-stained eyes, he looked hungrily to the East. Without hesitation, he grabbed his water sac from the camel's back and began his lone march across the barren desert.

He walked on until the black of night gently faded to the soft hues of dawn.

The sun was rising.

Upward through the haze it released couriers of color as the sky slowly changed in a dazzling display. Shimmering shades of red-orange, magenta and yellow lit the horizon, but its beauty was lost on Jabran. The magnificence only delivering the most shattering of news—it was now the morning of the fourth day.

Within moments he heard a rumble. The distant sound pulsing across the soundless terrain cast an ominous ode to the brilliant sky— the hum of approaching aircraft, coming from the South. It was the British aeroplanes as Billingham had warned. They were here, and he was powerless to stop them.

He thought of Mariana. Somewhere in the camp, so unaware. Probably just rising, beginning her day's work. Cooking breakfast for the dreadful Commander who slept soundly in his soft feathered bed.

The agony of what was about to unfold tore at Jabran's soul. It was he who'd brought on this unpardonable doom; his words that initiated this merciless calamity.

Jabran Yusef, the man who'd always lived his life in quiet contemplation, who'd prided himself to walk away from the fray, shook his head in utter despair. Why had he now been cast as the heinous villain?

Then he thought of Nisrina. This was for her, he chided himself. There was no choice. He had to protect her from the insanity of the Commander. He thought of his children—his legacy, so innocent and small, a whole lifetime lay ahead for them.

And he thought of Mariana and her unborn child, the innocent babe who lay sleeping in his poor mother's womb; and the promise he'd made to her—to deliver them safely from the wretched camp.

The sound of the planes grew louder. Still out of sight, he felt the thick, dull drone in the distance. The vibration ominous and foreboding. The time had come and he had failed her. He had placed his life in the hands of the Lord and had been forsaken. His only hope was to reach Mariana and trust that by some miracle she would be out of range of the bombs' destruction. Perhaps she had risen early and had gone to fetch water. Surely they would not target the lake. He would find her there and carry her off, and together they would escape this evil city. He would double back, retrace his steps, and find his camel. By now the beast would be rested and ready to carry them back to the safety of the British camp. All would be well.

Standing at the base of the crest, he knew Azraq lay just beyond its rise.

Then he heard it. The sound of munitions exploding hard against the ground. The earth shook. One after another. He began to run, faster and faster, upward to the top of the hill. He was entranced. His eyes fixed wide. The smell of smoke permeated the air. A black mist rising high in the distance. A dark cloud forming, filling the heavens. He didn't stop to think. Putting aside his agony and thoughts of fateful outcomes, he had but one goal—to reach Mariana.

At the top of the crest he saw Azraq, remembering it as he'd seen it the first time, a reluctant recruit. The horizon aglow in its orange cast, the walls of the fortress silhouetted black against the sun's radiance. At the time, it had seemed the gates of heaven.

But now it was different. The orange glow was giving way to black smoke and dark ash. The tent city that once surrounded the castle was flattened and stripped. People were running. Animals scattered. Most lay dead. The acrid stench of burning munitions filled his nostrils. He ran, not stopping until he reached the gates of the fortress. He ran past the heat of destruction and straight towards the massive stone doors.

Using all his strength, he pushed the doors open and stepped over the threshold. What he saw was no longer the organized city he'd once known. What lay before him was disorder and ruin. Bodies were everywhere.

He had to find Mariana, but the chaos made his head spin.

He ran straight to what remained of the Commander's quarters. He picked through the broken debris and saw a leg and then an arm from beneath a shattered table, stone blocks piled atop the worn wood. He pushed the blocks aside, groaning with their weight. There lay the Commander. His eyes were closed. His body limp and battered; his breaths escaping in short bursts. He reached out and put his arm under the leader's head. He lifted him up.

"Commander, it is I. First Lieutenant Jabran Yusef."

The Commander's eyes fluttered open. Blood was trickling from his ears, his nose.

"Jabran, my friend, is it really you?" he whispered.

"Yes, Commander. I have returned. As I promised."

"I knew you would my boy. I knew you would." His breath came in gasps, his voice an undertone. "It seems that you came a bit late, though, eh? Such a pity. We would have celebrated, no?" He began to close his eyes again.

Jabran called to him, "Commander, listen to me. I must know. I heard that you had sent men out to search for me. To bring me back in disgrace. A deserter . . ."

The Commander shook his head in protest, his eyes opened wide.

Jabran continued, "That you had a price on my head and would soon burn my village and torture my family."

"What's this? No. No. Of course not." The Commander's voice grew stronger, he was upset. "Jabran, my boy, as God is my witness, I have never doubted you. You were my confidant, my friend. My First Lieutenant. We had great times."

"But Lieutenant Volkan . . . I met him west of Amman, he said . . ."

"Lieutenant Volkan is a liar and a cheat. I curse his name." The Commander tried to spit, but his mouth was too dry.

"What?" Jabran could not believe his ears.

"He and two others left our regiment some time ago. They were deserters. I later heard they joined another camp. Renegades, they were, not men of the Sultan. That man was no good. No good, I say. I tried to reason with him. I tried." The Commander shook his head again. "He was no good." He began to cough, blood now sputtering from his mouth. His strength waning.

It had not been that long ago when the Commander had been the strong one. The one with power. The predator with his prey. But fate had an interesting way of turning the tide—unexpectedly and without warning.

Jabran knew that this man, who hovered on the doorstep of eternity, was now, for the first time in his life an honest man. For as each soul reaches the heavenly gates, his spirit knows that the march is over, the game is done, and the claws of evil are finally released. Having reached that moment, the Commander was purged of his wicked ways. His spirit broken, he sought peace with his maker.

"Oh dear God," Jabran moaned. "What have I done?" He turned his head away, unable to look at the man he'd betrayed. And then he turned back to him, "and Mariana . . . Commander, where is Mariana?"

"When you left she was heartbroken. Couldn't cook a thing. Kept burning the *maftool*. I allowed her to move into your tent for comfort. She should be there. Go to her."

The Commander closed his eyes again.

Jabran bowed his head. He held the Commander's body closer to his own, his heart beating hard through his chest. He whispered, "Forgive me."

But it was too late. The Commander could no longer hear him.

Jabran rushed out, straight to where his tent once stood— remnants of a time now past. There he found Mariana. She was lying on the ground covered in debris. Her swollen belly moving up and down with each breath. She was alive. For that he was grateful. He moved the wreckage that had fallen upon her and bending down, reached out and cradled her in his arms, stroking the hair from her forehead as he'd done so many times before.

"Mariana, my friend. I've come to take you away. Come, let's go."

"Jabran?" Mariana's green eyes were searching for him.

"Yes, Mariana. It is I, Jabran. I'm here."

"Oh, Jabran! I knew you would return. And my child, is he safe?" Her hands moved to her belly.

"Yes, you are both safe. You are with me now. Come, let us go before more planes arrive."

"Jabran," Mariana grabbed his arm. "I'm frightened."

"Do not be frightened. I am here now. Can you rise up? Let me help you."

She reached out, "I cannot see you."

She was looking straight at him, her green eyes as brilliant as ever. He looked closer. She was looking directly at him, and at the same time, past him.

His heart broke into a million pieces. Those beautiful eyes. What had he done?

He would take her to the hospital. It was certain. They would repair her sight.

"Jabran, are you still there?"

"Yes, my little one."

"Hold me, Jabran. Hold me closer. Don't let me go."

He held her close and the tears began to pour down his cheeks. They fell on Mariana's face. And she knew he was weeping.

"Please. Do not weep. I am not sad," her voice was soft, calm. Her breaths came in short, uneven gasps. "Jabran," she implored, "the baby, can you save him?"

"Hush, Mariana. All will be well, do not worry."

"Don't let him die with me," she begged. "Take him from my belly and raise him as your own. Promise me."

"Mariana!"

"Promise me!"

"I promise."

"That is good. Now I can rest."

"Oh, Mariana. Please forgive me. Please . . ." He began to sob, pressing her closer to him, his face tight against her cheek, "Forgive me."

"There is nothing to forgive . . . For you see, it is I who have sinned. At first I was forced. Forced by the soldiers . . . Then, later, forced to entrap *you*. I knew what it meant. I knew what I was. And then something changed inside me. Perhaps it was the baby . . . I felt graced by God. He washed me clean." She smiled a sweet smile, her voice growing weaker, her breath more shallow.

"Please, Mariana. Do not talk. Save your strength."

"Jabran, come closer."

"I'm here Mariana."

"Jabran," her voice was barely audible now, her hands reached out, fragile and weak. They softly gripped his shirt, "the child . . . it will survive. It must survive, Jabran."

He was nodding. Blinded by his tears.

She looked up at him. Directly at him. With those green eyes. Now vacant and pure.

"Please, if I may ask one more thing, only one more . . ."

"Of course," he said.

"When you speak of me . . . in those quiet moments, when you hold him close and he asks about his mother . . . If you could find it in your heart . . . please . . . remember me with kindness."

"Oh, Mariana!" Jabran cried out, he held her closer.

They were her final words.

She drew her last breath, her eyes closed.

"NO!" He sobbed, his whole body shaking.

When his tears were spent, he rose up like a wild man, running into the middle of the camp—his eyes to the heavens, his arms outstretched—he screamed at the top of his lungs. He shook his fists at the blackened sky, the soot and the dust swirling wildly about; and he cursed the aeroplanes that flew overhead. He cursed Volkan, the evil liar—the perpetrator of folly and ill will. And he cursed the day they'd ever met.

Then he cursed himself a hundred times over for what he'd wrought. For although he'd never raised a gun against another man, it was as if he, himself, had finally pulled the trigger upon an entire city.

Again he lifted his fists in anger and rage; he opened his mouth to curse the heavens and the righteous God who allowed these things. But before he could utter another word—a sound—a whistle—and a bomb exploded.

PART THREE

1919

My heart it aches for thee oh mother.
With your life, you gave me mine.
And if, perchance, I help another.
To live,
To love,
To tenderly hold a babe in arms;
Then through these hands sweet things will come.

TWENTY EIGHT

Lamia

A LOUD RAP AT the door interrupted her dreams.

Two years had passed since Nisrina had given birth to her third child. The war was over and soldiers had long since returned to their homes, however Nisrina had yet to hear her husband's voice or experience the joy she'd seen in other women's faces as their ragged men threw down their garb and held their wives once again. And yet, despite the misgivings and whispers of the villagers, she was convinced it was only a matter of time until Jabran's return. Never doubting his homecoming, she waited faithfully for him.

And now there was banging at her door—sharp, quick movements.

She woke with a start, her heart racing. Was it Jabran? Was he hurt or injured? Had he finally come home to her? Who else would be pounding on her door at such a late hour? The sound so hard and brisk. What misguided urgency awaited her attention? Who could it be? Forgetting to throw a wrap around her shoulders, she bolted from her bed and ran to the door.

It was not Jabran. But there was no time for regrets. Before her stood a man covered in the fever of dread. His face was mottled. His eyes wild, on fire. It was Tawfiq Malawy, the husband of her childhood friend, Lamia Saleema, who was now called wife of Tawfiq; and his distress was unmistakable.

As planned, Lamia had completed her education at the girl's school in Dar el Qamar and, after living full time in the women's dormitory for four years, had returned home a confident and able young lady who could read and write. When Lamia came back to Beit el Jebel, Nisrina noticed how her friend had changed. Lamia was now worldly, mature—so different from the chubby, short-necked girl who had said her hopeful good-byes on the walkway in front of her father's farmhouse. She had left an awkward child, eager to embrace the world, and returned a beautiful woman. Even her neck had grown long and graceful, and she carried herself with such poise and stature that she reminded Nisrina of Mrs. Arden, the grand lady who had visited the Huniah farm so many years before.

When they were reunited, the two friends ran into each other's arms. It was like old times, as if they'd never been apart. Like young girls, they jumped and laughed, they squealed and danced, around and around in circles, their hands clasped together as they did years ago. They cried tears of joy and delighted in the constancy and strength of their unchanged affections.

But in as much as their friendship had not been altered by time or space, the girls themselves had changed. Lamia was now an educated woman, and Nisrina a wife and mother. And as they reacquainted, they silently recognized the two different paths their lives had taken.

Leaving her children with their Auntie Dora, Nisrina took Lamia, and together they walked up the path from Nisrina's house. Arm-in-arm, laughing and talking they wandered into the far reaches of her husband's orchards, until finally they arrived at the crest of the hill.

Nisrina noticed Lamia's clothing. She wore the modern garments of a *medineeya*, a cultured woman of the city. Looking down at her own worn, country *thobe*, painstakingly embroidered in the patterns of her village, she, for the first time, felt ashamed of her clothes. But this was a time for rejoicing and Nisrina would not allow vanity to steal her attentions. Her friend and confidant had returned from a great adventure and she wanted to hear her tales.

The two women looked out towards the west, across far-reaching miles of rural countryside. As the noise of the compound disappeared in the distance, the green hills and blue skies sung to them—a melody of times past and memories not forgotten. The gentle breeze and sweet, familiar scents of sage and narcissus, jasmine and lilies softened their senses. There, amongst the wide-spread branches of the fig trees, the two friends sat down beneath an old gnarly specimen, eagerly sharing the stories of their lives. As they gave their accounts, remembering the outrageous and the sublime, they giggled and laughed until their bellies ached.

And when their laughter was over, Nisrina inhaled deeply, finally finding the courage to speak of her husband's abduction. Lamia's eyes opened wide as she heard the sad story, and when she finished, the two girls wept in each other's arms.

They spoke of the future, of their hopes and dreams.

Nisrina declaring with certainty that Jabran would one day find his way back home to her, and he would finally meet Hannah, the daughter he'd never seen, named in honor of his mother. Her eyes moistened as she continued, predicting how he would marvel at Essam and Jameela, declaring that she had raised them well and what fine young children they had become.

As Lamia spoke of the things in her heart, Nisrina listened intently. Through the inspiring guidance at the Girl's Boarding School for Cultivation and Readiness, Lamia had developed aspirations that were no longer in keeping with those of her father or the small village to which she'd returned.

She professed that she'd never marry or give birth to a child. With absolute resolve she declared that she would be an independent woman, living free of a man's rule or financial support.

"I see no reason to be dominated by a man's will," she declared decisively to her friend as they sat and watched the sun dipping low behind the horizon. "To rise when he commands it, and to quake at his displeasure." She was shaking her head.

Pausing for a moment, she looked thoughtfully at Nisrina, searching her face for understanding, not wanting to offend her childhood companion. But her convictions were strong and she went on to speak her mind. "And I refuse to ever bear the ungodly pain of childbirth!" She was shaking her head emphatically. "No, no. I've seen how these ways have aged my mother and the women of our village. Their backs are bent and their words are measured. I want no part of it. I want to be my own woman, to work for the good of all people, to fight for the rights of our sisters and make the world a better place."

Her eyes were ablaze, her nostrils flared. Lamia had always been a girl of high spirits and strong will, but never had she witnessed such confidence or determination in her friend.

"But, my dear Lamia," she countered, "how can you wish to live a life of such loneliness? How can you expect to survive in this world without the protection of a husband at your side? Who will care for you in your old age if not your son, and your son's son?"

"Don't you see, Nisrina?" Lamia turned to face her old friend. "These are things that our elders would have us believe, but they are not true! I can think for myself! You! You, too, can think for yourself! You could learn to read and to write! You do not need a man to do it for you!

"I am able to work and care for myself without relying on another. I need not labor in the fields or slave in the kitchen as our mothers did. I seek a vocation in the classroom or perhaps the ministry—places where women are valued for their thoughts and contributions." She took Nisrina's hands and held them tightly in her own, "There is a whole world out there, Nisrina! A world waiting to be experienced, to be embraced! And I, for one, intend to live it!" Lamia beamed with such joy and enthusiasm, her cheeks were flushed and her head held high.

An unexpected chill ran down Nisrina's spine. Realizing she no longer knew the girl who sat beside her, the mother of three just nodded to the stranger—this woman who espoused such scandalous and foreign ideas, so boldly declaring her brave independence. She had expected that Lamia would return changed, able to read and write, but had not expected the shattered alteration in her friend's thinking, so very different from her own. She could not fathom how this *fellaha*, this country girl with whom she had shared a childhood of memories, could now have such grand schemes. But she respected her will and her clear-minded thoughts, and said nothing more to dispute her. Nisrina was delighted to see that in spite of these changes, Lamia's smile remained the same, large and infectious. And as Lamia clasped her hands in her own, Nisrina felt their softness, a small calloused mound where her pencil was held.

They continued to talk all through the night, stopping only when the sun reappeared in the sky. Sending a bright yellow ray up through the clouds, it reminded them that they must hurry back to their families.

In the routine of her life, Nisrina remembered Lamia's words. They played back in her mind again and again. And she continued to marvel at the change in her neighbor. What kind of school could this be that would encourage a woman to give up her dreams for a husband and children? To renounce a home filled with love and laughter? As she went about her day, cooking and cleaning and feeding her children, Nisrina feared for her friend. She worried that Lamia would never know a husband's sweet love. And it saddened her to think that she wouldn't experience the joy of a babe's suckling lips on her swollen breast, or smell the sweet, milky, scent of its freshly washed skin.

She shook her head and sighed as she bent over the large basin, her fingers rhythmically kneading the floured dough that would soon turn to bread—maybe her father, God rest his soul, had been right—maybe education was not a good thing for women after all.

As strong as her convictions were, Lamia's plans were short-lived.

News quickly spread through the village that Lamia's father had arranged her betrothal to a man who lived on the outskirts of the village. A man that Lamia felt was clearly beneath her.

Tawfiq Malawy was the town's carpenter and within the month, before anything to the contrary could be said or done, Lamia was married.

It could be agreed by all that Tawfiq Malawy was a handsome man who worked hard at his trade and attended church on a regular basis. Tall and thin, with a fine crop of hair, his features were comely, a strong hook nose and straight white teeth. When he walked through town on his way to the *souk* or a patron's home to build tables or shelves, he always strolled along with a smile on his face. His clothes were clean and his thick handlebar mustache neatly maintained. But Tawfiq was a man who could neither read nor write, and to Lamia Saleema, that was a fatal flaw.

So, rather than see the beauty in his tall stature and calm brown eyes, she saw only a laborer, a peasant who relied on his hands to earn a living—a common man to whom she, as a woman and now a wife, must remain obedient in all things.

At the time of her betrothal, Lamia wept constantly, refusing to eat.

Nisrina tried time and again to comfort her, to explain that all was not lost. She talked for hours to her—calming her, placating her. She mustered all her reasonings to convince the sophisticated bride that, despite the disappointment of her lofty goals, she could still have a good life as the wife of a village carpenter.

Lamia spoke openly to Nisrina. She confided how she'd begged her father not to force her hand in this issue. She pleaded with him to relinquish his promise to this *fellah*, for now she was a scholarly woman. And as a woman who could read and write and think for herself, what could she possibly have in common with a simple carpenter? She felt that she had come too far and worked too hard for her education to be wasted. She wanted more than anything to be able to put what she'd learned to good use. She yearned to use her knowledge to teach other young girls, or apply her skills in government work. She wanted to live in the city, help with town management, and support herself as an independent woman. She lamented that now all would be lost, for none of these things would be possible if she were the wife of a poor peasant craftsman.

Lamia's father saw things differently. Rather than have her look to the future as an enlightened woman, Josef Saleema expected his daughter to return to Beit el Jebel, to reside in his home and remain under his care until she was properly married. In his mind, her return was not just a visit. She had come back to stay.

And although he had supported the idea of schooling for his daughter, sending her off to experience life outside her village, his own world had not changed. He was still a *fellah*, a peasant farmer. It was all he knew and he expected his daughter to remain a part of it, to come back to their family, their home, their village and its simple way of life. Her father's vision was for Lamia to wed a peasant man such as himself, and be a good wife and mother. He expected her to partake in the daily tasks of village life, to serve her husband and raise his grandchildren. It was all he knew. All he would ever know. Anything else was out of the question.

When Lamia protested, father and daughter argued long into the night and for several days thereafter. Josef Saleema found himself cursing the day that he'd sent his daughter to the grand school and gave his blessings for her education. But as much as she protested, he would not falter. He demanded that she marry the man he had chosen for her, insisting that she not dishonor him, but rather take her place in village life as an obedient wife and bear her husband many children.

Lamia was given no choice. She married the uneducated carpenter as she choked back her tears.

In the early days of her marriage, Lamia suffered in both heart and mind. Each morning as she rose from her bed and looked at the man who lay sleeping beside her, she wondered what her life might have been like. And at the *taboon*, while the other women chattered away, exchanging gossip and complaining of aching backs, her thoughts would wander—carried aloft with the birds that took flight amongst the cypress and olive trees.

But as time passed, hard work washed thin her dreams. Her tasks as the wife of a carpenter were many, and they kept her hands busy from sunrise to sunset, until finally the lofty imaginings she kept close to her heart, drifted away like white, wispy clouds in a warm summer's sky. And as they vanished, so too, did her sense of loss, for she had come to love the kindly man who called her his wife and she came to value his simple views and honest ways.

As months turned into years, Lamia remained without child. With each changing moon her blood would come and she'd sadly take out the rags she kept in the basket beneath her bed. Some said it was her high and mighty ways that kept her womb barren. While other, more vicious tongues claimed that hers was a marriage without love. But those were foolish words, for anyone with eyes and ears could plainly see the gentle touch and tender words that passed between Lamia and Tawfiq.

Lamia was heartbroken. Having changed from the early days when she'd declared that she would never bear a man his child, she now feared that it was her past reticence that cursed their hopes for a family.

One day, the two women decided to prepare a pot of stew, their work made lighter by sharing the chores. Squatting around a basin filled with water, they were rinsing and cleaning long strings of lamb intestines purchased fresh from the butcher. As the waste from the entrails oozed out of the hollow tubes, dripping blood on the outer edge of the pot, Lamia's face went pale. She quickly stood up and ran into the bushes where Nisrina heard the sounds of her heaving. Lamia had always had a strong constitution and cleaning lamb intestines was something that never bothered her before. Nisrina suspected the cause, but thought it wiser to say nothing, not wanting to bring the evil eye upon her blessing.

The child took a strong hold within its mother's womb and over the next few months Nisrina watched Lamia's body change. She noticed her belly grow big and round, and observed how her steps became slower and measured. She knew that it was only a matter of time before her dear friend would join her in experiencing the joyous bliss of motherhood.

But now Tawfiq was standing at her kitchen door in the middle of the night, and he was clearly distraught.

"Nisrina!" Tawfiq called out to her, his trembling hand pressed hard against the open door, his knuckles turning white. "It's Lamia! Please, come quickly."

Nisrina grabbed her shawl and with bare feet ran out the door, Tawfiq following close behind. The town was still without a midwife, and those among them who'd experienced the painful blessings of birth were often called to assist the women who came after them. Nisrina had three children and she knew what Lamia would soon be going through. She stopped briefly as she passed Dora and Mona's home and banged on their door. Through sleepy eyes, Dora answered and saw the look on Tawfiq's face. She nodded as Nisrina asked her to watch her children while she went to Lamia.

"God be with you all!" Dora called out as Nisrina and Tawfiq disappeared into the darkness.

As she ran the four mile distance on the dirt road that separated their homes, Nisrina felt the panicked apprehension of the gentle carpenter who followed alongside her. She sensed his trepidation, and silently shared his fear. The child was not due for several more months. But when she'd seen Tawfiq standing at her door in the middle of the night, his eyes crazed in panic, the sweat dripping profusely from his brow, she understood the urgency of the matter and she prayed that all would be well. As she moved quickly in the dark, stepping over stones and dodging potholes, Nisrina feared the worst. She would find out soon enough, she thought to herself as she crossed the last fork in the road. She would find out soon enough.

Even before she reached the crest of the hill where the carpenter and his wife resided, Nisrina could hear the screams echoing through the trees. Tawfiq stopped behind a bush to vomit, his head was aching, his pulse out of control. He couldn't bear to hear his precious wife's voice in such anguish and pain. To know she was suffering made him wild with fear. He blamed himself again and again. He knew she was a learned woman when he married her. One who had wanted to remain single and work in the city, to stay childless and independent. But for him, she had changed. She'd given up her hopes and her lofty aspirations. She had lain in the large wooden bed he'd carved especially for her. She finally learned to love him, and when the time came, was proud to carry his child. And for this—for him—she now suffered.

Nisrina ran on ahead. Men were of no use at a time like this, she thought to herself. But, she too, felt a sickness deep in her stomach and hoped she could make it to the house without stopping. *It's too soon for Lamia to deliver.* The words kept repeating. *It's too soon.*

Nisrina burst through the door and saw her friend splayed out on the floor. Her swollen body was writhing and twisting. Her face wrenched in pain, unrecognizable. What had become of the Lamia she'd once known? Nisrina saw the blood that had pooled beside her and observed how it covered her gown, her legs, and the tops of her feet.

"Lamia!" Nisrina called out to her, but Lamia gave no response. She just continued to thrash and twist, to wail and scream. Curdling sounds emanated from her mouth like an animal in heat. The room had been torn to shreds as if a wild boar were unleashed within its walls. Tables were overturned and the window coverings ripped from their nail heads. Nisrina was thankful for the fire that crackled in the kitchen hearth as it warmed the house and shed some light in the dimly lit room. But even the flames from the fire were not enough. She grabbed a candle that was burning on a dresser in the far corner and brought it closer to her friend.

"Lamia! *Ya*, Lamia!" Nisrina spoke softly as she bent by her side. She stroked her hair and covered her sweat-drenched body with dry blankets from the bed.

Lamia turned to Nisrina and with shaking arms reached out, "It's too soon, Nisrina. It's too soon," she cried.

Tawfiq stood in the doorway wringing his hands and cursing his name.

"It is my fault that she suffers!" he cried out in remorse. "It is my seed that poisons and tortures her so! If I could take ten times the pain from her body, then dear God, please allow me this justice." He fell to his knees beside his suffering wife, his face in his hands, tears streaming down his cheeks.

"How long has she been like this?" Nisrina asked furrowing her brow.

"Two days now, maybe three," Tawfiq was scratching his head, "I'm not sure. She wouldn't let me call for you. She wouldn't let me call anyone. She kept saying it was too soon, far too early. But the pains kept coming. Then she got worse . . ." He began to wring his hands, pacing back and forth. He repeatedly slapped his fists against his thighs, his temples. Then cursing his name he dropped back to his knees to pray.

Nisrina was worried. Lamia's body was hot, the perspiration soaking her hair, her face and her clothing. She needed to get closer, to see what was going on between her legs.

"Tawfiq!" Nisrina called to him. "Light me another candle, please . . . light me as many as you have. And bring me clean rags . . . and boil water, quickly!"

Tawfiq rose from his knees, his whole body shaking. Glad to be given something to do, he placed a pot of water on the fire, then set about to light every candle he owned.

Nisrina placed a candle on the floor. She kneeled closer to her friend, whispering softly in her ear, her murmurings a melody being sung in the wind, faint and faraway. To Lamia it was the voice of an angel who'd come to save her. She began to calm.

As the next wave of pain enveloped her body, she struggled with all her might to follow her friend's directions, to focus on the candle that'd been placed on the floor before her. She began to moan. With fists clenched tight, her back arched higher and her head twisted from side to side.

Nisrina turned back to Tawfiq who was handing her a pile of clean rags, "Listen to me Tawfiq. Run to the villagers and tell them to come. Tell them Lamia needs help . . . that I need help! *Yullah!* Quickly! Go!"

As he ran out the door, Nisrina turned back to Lamia and spoke firmly to her, "Short breaths, Lamia. Like this . . ." and Nisrina demonstrated the short staccato breaths that Sabra Hishmeh had taught her during the birth of her own children. The breaths would help her focus her mind away from the pain, allowing her to save her energy for when the urge to push became the strongest.

Comforted by Nisrina's familiar voice and sure manner, Lamia began to relax. She mimicked Nisrina's breaths the best she could, but she was exhausted and her eyes were glazing over, staring into space. Her body still tight and thrashing about.

Nisrina gathered the candles together on the floor until their flames formed one glow. Then stooping down on her knees, she spread Lamia's thighs to examine the space between her legs, the light barely sufficient.

She gasped! Her eyes opened wide as her hands covered her mouth.

She couldn't believe what she saw in that dark shadowed room. Emerging from the opening between Lamia's legs was a small foot with five tiny toes. They were dangling outside her body as if suspended in space, the rest of the child still hidden within. As she looked closer, trying to understand the circumstances, she heard Lamia start to moan again. Softly at first, then her faltering control gave way to a howl.

"Short breaths like this . . ." Nisrina called out, panting rhythmically. "Like this . . ."

Despite the calamity before her, Nisrina held fast, focused firmly on bringing Lamia back to her breathing. She needed the poor woman to control her urge to push; and she needed to figure out what she should do next. The room grew hot as sweat formed on her brow, a panic rising up in her chest.

Her children had all been born head first. But she'd heard many stories of babies born in reverse. She knew that under these circumstances both the child and mother's health were gravely at risk. She had once witnessed Sabra turn a child while it lay deep within its mother's womb. Nisrina remembered holding the panicked woman's hand as she watched Sabra perform her magic. But this child was already emerging! It was too late for such things . . . or was it?

Oh, if only Sabra were here! She would know what to do! She'd been trained by her mother and her grandmother before her. What did Nisrina know of such things? Yes, she had given birth to three children, and although she had suffered as all women suffer, her births were uncomplicated, the first two aided by the gifted hands of a caring midwife.

As she quickly considered the situation, Nisrina recalled that she'd once seen Sabra use a knife to open wide a woman's passage, and then she'd applied poultices and rags to stop the bleeding and heal the wound. Both the woman and child had survived unfettered. She wished she had paid more attention. Did this circumstance call for this? How could she know? Who could she ask? Where were the other women of the village? And what was taking Tawfiq so long to return? He left what seemed like hours ago—they should have been here by now!

Just then Lamia let out another groan. But this time her voice was decidedly weaker. Her breathing more shallow. Nisrina began to fear for her friend's life.

I must act quickly, she thought to herself. I cannot wait for the others if I want to save my good friend.

Nisrina wondered if another position might help. She encouraged Lamia to turn over, to go onto her knees and turn her face to the floor. She found a low bench upon which her friend could rest her head and around which she could wrap her arms. She added a pillow to soften its harsh edges.

"All will be well," she kept saying to Lamia in a soothing voice. "All will be well." But her hands were shaking and her lips trembled fiercely.

As she repositioned her, Nisrina said a silent prayer to the dearly departed Sabra Hishmeh. She prayed that the old midwife would guide her in her actions and instruct her on what to do. And she prayed to God almighty that he might save the life of this child and its deserving mother.

Without further hesitation, Nisrina rose to her feet and went into the kitchen. There she found the sharpest knife with the thinnest blade and she dipped it into the boiling water. She watched the water bubble and steam around its razor edge and when she was sufficiently satisfied she went back and kneeled down beside Lamia.

She instructed her to keep her head down and continue to pant. She told her not to push just yet, not even when the strong contractions overcame her body. Lamia was too exhausted to respond, but the sound of her quiet panting told Nisrina that she'd understood her words.

Nisrina moved to the place between Lamia's legs, she took a deep breath, and holding the knife in her right hand, her left pressed firmly against the inside of Lamia's thigh, she carefully cut the thin, stretched, layer of skin that held tight the opening of life. She imagined herself cutting the delicate membrane of a chicken when preparing it for Sunday stew and was thankful to Esma who had taught her so well—to slice and remove only the outer membrane and not puncture the flesh.

With sweat now dripping into her eyes, and the smell of blood and body fluids piercing her nostrils, she completed her incision. She thanked God for her steady hand and prayed that it would soon be over. Lamia made no sound or movement and Nisrina wondered if her friend had died or passed out from exhaustion, but she could not stop to check, she needed to continue what she had started.

With the opening widened, Nisrina took her hand and reached into Lamia's womb. She felt something—the second foot, she was sure of it. Tiny toes, an arch, a heel—unmistakable. She gently wrapped her fingers around it. Lamia must have felt the hand inside her and she awakened to a great urge, she gave out a loud moan and pushed again with all her might. As she pushed, Nisrina ever so lightly held on to the child's heel, urging the babe to come forth.

The second foot came out.

Nisrina took a breath. Lamia was quiet again.

"Are you with me?" She called out to her friend. "Lamia, my Lamia . . . we are almost done. As God is my witness, I now hold both his feet in my hands."

Finally Lamia responded, it was a whisper, "Another . . ." and she began to push again.

With Nisrina's guiding touch and Lamia's final contraction, the baby completed its arrival into the light—the torso followed the legs, then the shoulders, the right, the left, and finally the head.

It was a girl!

The child instantly screamed a lusty, triumphant cry. And as Lamia heard her daughter's voice, she buried her face in the pillow and wept a new mother's tears. Tears with no name—they were sobs, they were whimpers, they were cries of awe and relief—an ecstasy matching no other in measure or scale.

Nisrina swaddled the child in a simple cotton cloth and wiped her face clean. She handed the small package to her mother. Lamia gazed into her daughter's face. The child's eyes were open and she stared at her mother, blinking and watching, content in her arms.

"So it was you!" Lamia said to her daughter as she fingered the child's delicate hands and feet. She gently touched her little ears and stroked her soft, full cheeks.

"How is it possible," she whispered sensuously, "that someone who caused me such pain and regret, now gives me such joy?"

While the mother and child reunited with sighs and yawns and tears of joy, the village women arrived. They could be heard climbing the rugged hill toward the Malawy home. They were singing and chanting their ancient songs of birth: odes of joy and light, of love and hope. As they entered the house, they gave rise to a liveliness that spread like sweet honey throughout the room, and with them they carried baskets of aromatic herbs, and jars of scented oils. They held offerings of freshly ripened fruit picked fresh from their gardens along with loaves of freshly baked breads. They brought cheese and meats, and sumptuous wines.

Delighted to hear the cries of a newborn fill the air, they circled around the mother and child to witness this miracle called life. With congratulations and multiple blessings pouring from their mouths, with songs of good health and long life rising from their lips, the women quickly went to work. One began preparing a poultice for Lamia's wounds to heal the cut and stop the bleeding, while another began to massage her stomach to encourage the afterbirth to expel itself. Lamia's neighbor, Wedad Saeed, an aged woman whose fingers were bent and stiff from the passing of years, hobbled into the kitchen to make a special tea to nourish the new mother. Some went down on hands and knees and wiped the floor clean, and others moved to replace the furniture that had gone awry. Lamia's clothes were changed and her body washed. And finally, when the smell of blood had dissipated, she was anointed with aromatic oils. As they worked they told stories and tales of what a beautiful girl her daughter would be. How she would help her mother with the chores, and one day fetch a rich dowry for her family. They predicted that because she'd entered the world with her feet planted firmly on the ground, this was a sign of good things to come.

Nisrina watched as they filled the room. Their energy and sounds heralding like a mighty wind from the heavens. She saw how gently they ministered to her friend who was now smiling and nursing her newborn child. And as her daughter lustily drew in sustenance, Lamia turned to gaze upon Nisrina, thanking her over and over again for all she'd done. She blessed her hands, her words, her thoughts—calling her sister and mother, vowing to raise her daughter in her honor.

"I will call her Rina, after you, my friend," Lamia spoke through grateful eyes.

"Rina Malawy," Nisrina repeated softly. She liked the sound it.

The women ululated and chanted their blessings—that this child from heaven would help her mother in all things womanly, and would one day grow to marry a mighty man who would take care of her and bestow upon her the gift of many grandchildren.

Whereupon Lamia turned to her friend and whispered sweetly, "She will learn to read and write and make her own choices."

With tear-filled eyes Nisrina could only nod and smile. She breathed in deeply. It was as if the darkened room had suddenly overflowed with an iridescent light. The fragrance of rose petal tea now wafting through the room enlightened her senses, while massaging oils scented with the dense, dark, essence of agarwood warmed her soul.

As she held her sister's hand Nisrina silently said a prayer of thanks to the midwife whose spirit had guided her from above, and to the almighty Lord who'd blessed them all and seen them safely through. She closed her eyes for a moment and as she did, time stood still.

All would be well, she said to herself. All would be well.

TWENTY NINE

The Time Has Come

WHEN THE TWO OLD maids walked through the open door, they found Nisrina on her hands and knees scrubbing the stone floors. She wanted her home to be clean and spotless for her husband's homecoming. And although she'd not heard from him since that tragic day, she did not let that discourage her. Nisrina had faith that Jabran would return. She wanted to be sure that when he walked through the door, she could show to him—prove to him that she'd been sure. That she never lost hope for his return.

Every day as the sun would set, she'd stroll through the orchard where he'd been taken by the soldiers. She'd climb the hills and look out over the green valleys, past the vineyards and the olive groves. She found that just being there, on the pathways where he'd worked, amongst the mighty fig trees, helped her feel closer to him. These had been his fields. His labor. His life.

She prayed three times a day, lit a candle in the church every evening, and kept her children clean, fed and close by her side. Her son Essam was now seven years old, and his sister Jameela was five. Two-year-old Hannah knew her father only from the stories the family told, and the wedding picture that sat atop the table in their sitting room.

In his absence, the little family had fallen into a comfortable routine, but as she went about her daily chores, Nisrina always kept an eye on the path leading to their home. When he arrived, she would be ready for him.

The old maids were impatient.

"Nisrina, we must talk," said Mona.

Nisrina, tired from her hard work, addressed Mona with the respect of her position, "Sister of my husband," Nisrina asked her, "What can I do for you?"

"We must talk," Mona repeated, while Dora remained quiet, glancing nervously around the room.

"Of course. Please. Come in."

But the two women had already entered of their own accord. Nisrina rose from her knees, wiping the damp hair from her forehead with the back of her hand. She motioned to them, "Sit down. Please. Let me make you some coffee."

"There is no time for coffee. The elders are waiting. Come, we must go."

Nisrina's heart began to race. She quickly looked around for her children and saw them just outside her home. They were playing a game with a stick and ball. Hannah, following after her older siblings.

"Of course," she replied. "Let me just clean up a bit."

"There is no time for that now. They are waiting."

And with that, the two unmarried sisters marched Nisrina across the courtyard and into the home of their father, Farooz.

As she walked through the arched doorway, Nisrina noticed the chill in the room. The stone walls still cold from the nighttime temperatures, the dying embers in the fireplace providing little in the way of warmth or comfort. Tiled floors were covered with intricately woven red and blue carpets from Persia, the threads worn thin from years of use.

Sunlight streaming in from the high windows surrounded the perimeter of the sitting room, and through its haze Nisrina could see the elders seated on the sofa in the center of the room, their large protruding bellies hanging uncomfortably over their sashes. All three were there: Farooz, Najeeb, and Jacob.

Each man held a string of beads which they fingered repeatedly in a nervous manner. Nisrina knew that when the elders worked their worry beads, serious matters were to be discussed. She could see the brothers' wives, Marta and May, in the kitchen. They were peeking around the corner with one eye, trying not to be seen, but staying close enough to hear what might be said.

Farooz motioned to Nisrina to take a seat on a very large, ornate chair covered in red and gold silk brocade. Its arms were covered by delicate doilies that were crocheted by his late wife Hannah, a woman Nisrina had not the pleasure to meet, but had heard highly of from her husband.

Nisrina resisted his choice of chairs. "Forgive me. My clothes. I have been working all day and they are dirty."

"No, no. Sit my child. It is fine. It is of no consequence. Please, sit and let us talk."

Farooz was motioning again for her to take the finest chair in his home. His voice was raspy and his breath uneven, a result of the many excesses he had entertained in life.

Obediently Nisrina sat on the edge of the chair, her hands folded respectfully in her lap, her nervous eyes scanning the room. She wondered why the elders had summoned her in front of the entire family, now offering her this seat of honor.

The two wives ventured out from the kitchen, quietly joining Mona and Dora in the sitting room. They sat in the far corner, facing Nisrina, their faces stippled in the shadows.

Keeping his eyes averted, Farooz leaned over and picked up the small Turkish coffee cup that was on the table before him. He held it between his thumb and forefinger, his little finger extended out to the side in the elite European fashion. He took a long, slow sip and carefully returned the cup to its fragile saucer. Nisrina noticed that they were using their finest china, the one with the gold leaf etchings, imported by the traveling merchants of Syria.

Being the eldest of the Yusef family, Farooz was the one to speak on the family's behalf. He cleared his throat and wiped his mouth carefully with his handkerchief. Then looking down at the beads being artfully manipulated in his hands, he addressed Nisrina, "My child, you know that we love you and that you are like a daughter to us."

A hum filled the room as the family nodded, murmuring sounds of agreement and support. He continued, "But it has been two years now since your husband, my son, God bless him, was taken from us by the Turks."

To which all the women, save Nisrina, let out exclamations and scourges towards the Turks, repeatedly cursing their families and their homes, their rulers and their way of life.

Farooz, allowing the emotions of the moment to calm down, took another slow sip of his coffee, inhaling loudly as the liquid passed his lips.

When he felt that the room had sufficiently quieted, he began again, "My dear Nisrina, as you well know, a substantial amount of time has passed since our dear Jabran was taken from us. The war is over, soldiers have returned to their families. And although we have heard no concrete news of his whereabouts, we have, in fact, been riddled with many rumors that speak to his demise. We have given this unhappy subject much thought and consideration. We have asked around, questioned many and submitted our inquiries . . . but all our efforts have been in vain." He shook his head, "It is deeply lamentable, but as it stands, we could come to only one possible conclusion."

Nisrina began squirming in her chair. She was wringing her hands—around and around they nervously twirled. Her mouth had gone dry, her breathing shallow.

Farooz, his gaze never wavering, watched her hands as they moved. They were small, delicate and despite her hard work, neatly maintained. He noticed how she took extra care to trim and polish the smallest nail of her left hand, the one she'd entwined with his son's at their marriage ceremony. He sniffed inward at the fragile futility.

"Please know, my dear, this is not a decision that we take lightly. However, in spite of a lack of evidence, we have no other choice but to conclude that Jabran will not be returning to us, and as a family we must now prepare to accept and mourn our loss."

A morbid stillness came over the room.

Nisrina could only gasp, her hands now covering her mouth.

His words dangled above her head, refusing to disperse. She couldn't believe what she had just heard and she quickly played it over in her mind. She was shaking her head. And as the harsh reality of his words began to sink into her brain, she tried her best to fight the tears, to remain strong, but they nevertheless began pouring down her cheeks.

Farooz waited patiently as she processed the family's position regarding the status of her missing husband. Resolute, he refused to acknowledge her reaction, the others in the room disappearing in a silent pretense, not daring to move.

He continued, "We have discussed your situation and realize that you, having been married and given birth to three children, cannot continue to live your life without a husband by your side. You are still very young, Nisrina. And as you know, these circumstances, if allowed to continue will only bring disgrace to you, and more importantly to our family."

Nisrina could not believe the words she was hearing. Her mind began to reel. At first she could only shake her head in protest and then the pleading began, she dropped to her knees and knelt before the elder who now held her fate in his hands.

"No. Please. No! He will come back, I know it. I feel it in my heart! Deep, here, within my heart and soul," her fists were pounding her chest. "God would not do this to me. To us. To our family and his children. Please, let us wait six more months. He is your son. Please do not forsake him this way!"

Distraught, Nisrina grabbed Farooz's hands and held them to her forehead in deference to his authority, hoping beyond all hope for his mercy, his understanding and compassion in this matter. The tears streaming down her face.

The three men had expected her reaction and they were not moved.

They had made up their minds.

Their son and brother was dead, of this they were certain. He was not coming back and it was time for his wife to move on. Farooz stoically continued, "There is a man in the village whose wife has recently died. You know him as Salah Abdelnour. Although I realize he is on in years, in his graciousness he has agreed to take you as his wife. To marry you. To give you a home. And to make a respectable woman of you again."

Nisrina was numb.

She knew the man of whom they spoke. He was very old and walked with a cane, bent over and staid. There had been rumors that he used to beat his wife. It was no surprise to anyone when she suddenly died. *Of all the villagers, they would choose him?!*

She couldn't move. Couldn't speak. Her eyes saw nothing.

Farooz continued, "The children however, will remain with us. They belong to the Yusef family. He will not take them and you cannot keep them."

Upon hearing this last statement, Nisrina found her senses.

"NO!" she screamed, rising to her feet. "On this one point there is no negotiation."

"I know this must be difficult for you, it is difficult for us all. But you are young, Nisrina. You will have more children. In fact, we have inquired, and he is willing and able to sire children with you."

"NO!" she replied again, her fists were clenched. "ABSOLUTELY NOT! I will never give up my children. As God is my witness, I will kill us all before I let you take them from me! I swear this on my father's grave!"

Nisrina was no longer the obedient daughter-in-law. She had become a mother scorned. Being threatened in this manner, she meant every word that she spoke, and more importantly, the elders knew it. To Nisrina, her father-in-law's intentions were only too clear. His feigned compassion—empty and hollow. He wanted her children. Her son in particular. And she was not about to let him have them.

But Farooz was a shrewd man. His tactics carefully measured. Wanting to avoid a scandal, he knew things would go much smoother if he could garner Nisrina's compliance. All his remaining children were childless. Najeeb and Jacob's wives were both clearly barren; his two daughters now old and unmarried could never sire an heir. Nisrina's children were his only legacy. And although the law was in his favor, the children belonging to the Yusef family, he could take no risks. He had to consider how his actions would appear to the villagers. After all, he was the head of a well respected family and he did not want to seem harsh or unkind to his daughter-in-law. He had a benevolent reputation to maintain.

Marta, as the wife of his eldest son, had the most to gain from the proposed arrangement. She would have first choice to Nisrina's children and she was anxious to have the matter resolved. So, in the short moment that Farooz paused, weighing and measuring his next move, Marta rose from her seat and stupidly whispered into Nisrina's ear, "If Salah Abdelnour is not your preference, perhaps we can arrange for another choice."

Nisrina's hand rose up and slapped Marta hard on her cheek, "You are so anxious to have *my* children," she screamed, "that you would sell me off to the first available suitor? Have you no compassion for my pain? Can you not understand a mother's love?"

Marta bellowed and postured, claiming false accusations. But her pleas fell on deaf ears. Her whispers had been overheard by Farooz and it was clear to him that she had provoked the confrontation.

In an attempt to bring peace to the room and calm his fretful daughter-in-law, Farooz needed a diversion. He told Marta to quiet down, and motioned for her to leave the room, "My coffee is cold," he told her. "Please, bring us all some fresh coffee. And some desserts, we need to sweeten our mouths before we continue our discussion." With the back of his hand, he wiped the two sides of his large, handlebar mustache: first to the right and then to the left. He twirled the ends tightly, thoughtfully and stroked his gray beard.

Nisrina was enraged when she saw both Marta and May scurry into the kitchen to prepare the refreshments. She heard them on the other side of the wall, whispering and wondering, while pots and plates banged and rattled.

She rose from her chair and began to pace the floor. Holding her head high she looked straight ahead. But her hands were shaking and her thoughts ran wild. Her lungs could no longer hold the air that moved around her, pain engulfing her chest. Finally, she could stand it no longer. She needed to hold her children. She longed to take them in her arms and breathe the softness of their skin. She turned to leave, the indignation of their proposal still searing through her veins.

"No, Nisrina, wait! Please sit, let's discuss this. I'm sure we can come to an amicable resolution," Farooz sounded sincere while his two sons fidgeted restlessly on the sofa beside him. Occasionally they'd sneak a glance at Nisrina. Marveling at her beauty, but concerned about her threats. Najeeb, the older and harsher of the two brothers, wanted to jump up and demand his rightful claim to her children, but instead he remained quiet, knowing better than to speak above his father's words. In deference to the old man's age and authority, both sons remained seated and morbidly silent.

Reluctantly, Nisrina returned to her chair. However, she was no longer weeping. Her brow was furrowed, her jaw clenched tight as she waited to hear Farooz's "amicable resolution."

But before he could open his mouth to speak, the smell of baked apples, oranges and dates filled the air as Marta and May entered the room carrying trays laden with warm refreshments. May's held a large, gilded bowl filled with stewed, honeyed fruits, the sweet aroma lilting alongside her yielding a soothing calm. Marta passed around a tray of coffee, the steam from the hot *ibrik* sending the allure of Turkish blends and cardamom softly across the room. The quiet gloom suddenly became filled with hushed murmurings, softened by the sounds of pouring coffee, and the clinking of fine cups and saucers.

Everyone partook, with the exception of Nisrina who sat upright in her chair, strong and alert, ready to defend her children. In her mind this was no time for self indulgence and it sickened her to see the family's lightheartedness in this matter. Her stomach turned as she observed their unfeeling extravagance and her fury filled the room, the walls pressing heavy with its rage.

Yet all eyes remained loftily averted. They quietly sipped their coffee and ate the sweetened fruits. No one dared look up, the harrowed silence pushing down like a stone upon the wheat.

Marta had quickly retreated to her darkened corner, pouting and whispering noiseless words to May. While Mona, nervously cleared her throat, staring restlessly out the window.

Jacob, bent at the waist, arms hard on his thighs, stared down at the well-worn pattern of the Persian carpet beneath his feet. Furtively working his worry beads, he remained silent, occasionally peering up and stealing sheepish glances at the others in the room. Anxiously, he wondered if the outcome of Nisrina's situation would bear an effect on him and his well-ordered life.

Even old Farooz, the stalwart patriarch of the family, was untypically quiet. Seeming at a momentary loss for words, he kept his head turned, squinting his eyes and twitching his chin in a most quizzical manner as his mind grouped and regrouped around his racing thoughts.

It was Najeeb alone, with his steel-cold gaze, who maintained a strong composure. Keeping watch from the corner of his eye, it was clear that he had something on his mind, but in deference to his father, he dared not utter a word.

Finally, when she could stand it no longer, the silence was broken by the soft voice of Dora. It was known by all that Dora could abide neither angry tones nor challenged positions. In moments of controversy, she always retreated into the backdrop where she remained, shadowy and still. And so it was especially intriguing when her voice was the one being heard under these most estranged of circumstances.

"I have a suggestion that might be satisfactory to us all," she stated.

All eyes turned to her.

"I have heard that there is a course being offered at the Catholic University . . . the one taught by the nuns in the city . . . a course that would be helpful not only to our dear sister-in-law, but also beneficial to both our family and the village."

Cups returned to their saucers. Mouths were instantly closed as bites into warmed confections ceased. The room was quiet. Had Dora, the complacent one, the one who always stayed in the background avoiding confrontation of any kind, now become the peacemaker?

"Please continue," Farooz said, sipping his coffee with a long, slow inhale, the sound of his breath filling the silence of the somber room. He was clearly intrigued by her proposal. "It would be a blessing if what you say is true. Pray tell us, what is this miracle course being offered at the nunnery?"

"It is training for becoming a midwife," she stated.

"Ahhhhhh!" Eyebrows lifted all around.

Nisrina said nothing. Still infuriated, her hands were tightly clasped, hovering just above her lap. But she was listening. She'd heard Dora's words. And her thoughts were churning.

Their village was without a midwife. Sabra Hishmeh had died over two years ago and there'd been no one to replace her. And now, whenever a child decided to come into this world, the townspeople had to rely upon each other or call for a midwife from another village. This of course, was not a practical solution that could be sustained for any reasonable period of time. Babies tended to come when they wanted, and mothers required assistance.

Their village needed a midwife. Nisrina needed an honorable occupation if she were to remain an unmarried mother. And the family would benefit both financially and socially by her well respected trade. It seemed a plausible solution; at the moment—the only solution.

Nisrina thought about the birth of her own children; they came into the world easily enough and without complications. But she also remembered the angst and fear she'd suffered when Lamia's child was born. She'd been alone, facing decisions which carried the fate of a mother and child's life. She recalled how she fretted, not knowing what to do, and how her hands had trembled so. She remembered her prayers, and how she'd finally been guided by the memory and spirit of Sabra Hishmeh. And then finally, she recalled the sacred look of love and hopefulness in Lamia's eyes as she held her newborn child in her arms for the first time.

Now they were proposing that *she* become the midwife of Beit el Jebel. Was that possible? Could she follow in Sabra Hishmeh's footsteps and learn the intricacies and mysteries of a revered midwife? She questioned her chances for success—was this something she, an uneducated farmer's wife, could achieve?

Furthermore, Nisrina was not Catholic and she wondered if the nuns would accept her at their school. Having lived a most sheltered life, her world was small. She'd never left the comfort of her village and close-knit community. She'd gone directly from her father's house into her husband's home, never venturing as far as the city or its neighboring towns, never attending a church outside her own faith. The thought of plunging into a new world was both intimidating and intoxicating. Her heart was pounding. She knew she couldn't allow them to take her children from her. That could never happen.

She realized there was no choice, she had to try.

No, she thought to herself, she must do more than try. She must succeed. Not only for her independence and self-esteem, but more importantly, for the sake of her children.

Nisrina turned to Farooz who was watching her.

"Yes," she nodded. "I will go to the nunnery and learn the art of midwifery. My children will remain mine, and I will support them with my earnings." She held her head high, her eyes never wavering from her father-in-law's hardened gaze.

"Then it is settled," he replied.

A gasp was heard from the corner where Marta and May were huddled.

Farooz turned to them, his eyes narrowed, his brow casting a shadow across his face. With pursed lips he spoke not a word, but the two women were instantly silenced.

Farooz was shrewd. If she succeeded, Nisrina would become a great asset to the Yusef family. She'd bring honor to their household while providing coins to their treasury. And if she failed, then he could justifiably and without reproach, take her children for his eldest son. Regardless of the outcome, Farooz's reputation in the village would remain untarnished. He'd be thought an elder who ruled his family in a fair minded and compassionate way.

After much discussion and negotiating it was agreed. In the following weeks the family would go into mourning for their dearly departed Jabran, and Nisrina would sadly don the black attire of the grieving widow for all the villagers to see. It was arranged that after a respectable period of time Farooz would make arrangements for her to go to the nunnery in the nearby city. He would make a generous donation to the Catholic Church, one they could not refuse despite their adversarial faiths. And there Nisrina would stay for six months while she attended the courses taught by the Sisters of Mercy.

During that time, Nisrina's children were to remain in their father's home and be raised by their Auntie Dora until her return.

Finally, it was decided that Nisrina's son Essam, dear, sweet, seven-year-old, Essam Jabran Yusef, would be declared the master of the family and the head of her household as the last remaining man of the house.

THIRTY

A New Beginning

AS ARRANGED, NISRINA ARRIVED at the Catholic school to meet with the Mother Superior at precisely ten o'clock in the morning. However, events at the nunnery did not always go as planned and the Reverend Mother found herself unexpectedly occupied. She sent word that she would not be able to greet her new student until much later in the day. A young novice named Sister Miriam was asked to give Nisrina the news.

Sister Miriam had been brought to the convent at a very young age by the wife of a wandering nomad. The woman who carried her to their doorstep arrived in cloak and veil and told the Sisters that the child's parents, who only weeks before had taken refuge in their caravan, had suddenly fallen ill and succumbed to a strange disease. She claimed she knew nothing of the child's family or her country of origin and asked that the Sisters take pity upon the young waif and raise her as their own. The Mother Superior saw the innocence in the child's eyes and the trepid fear in the woman's face. Nothing more needed to be said as she took the girl into her arms, for in her mind, their sanctuary was now her sanctuary, their home her home. She was raised by the nuns, living and growing in the midst of kindness and orderly ways; and when she came of age, she announced to the

Mother Superior that she'd chosen to follow a life of celibacy and wished to serve the Lord.

Sister Miriam was a small girl who seemed lost within the folds and layers of her flowing gown. Her skin was dark and her lips, full and sensuous. She was heedless to her unadorned beauty as she nervously greeted Nisrina with a hearty smile. Her hands remained buried in the sleeves of her robe, while she explained to Nisrina that the Mother Superior was otherwise occupied. She motioned for her to wait on a small bench in the hallway and nodded graciously as Nisrina thanked her for her hospitality. Then the young novice bowed slightly as she bid Nisrina good day, walking away mumbling to herself about lost time and schedules to keep.

Nisrina sat down on the designated bench, the only bench, and waited.

It was understandable, she thought to herself. The Mother must have many pressing issues demanding her attention. I'm sure she'll be out to greet me in no time at all.

Sitting stoically on the hard wooden bench in the foyer of the large anteroom Nisrina occupied herself by reciting hymns quietly in her mind. She tried not to think about her children or the warm comforts of the home she'd left behind, for she knew this would only make her sad and she needed a brave face and a strong demeanor for meeting the Mother Superior.

The hours passed without event. Occasionally Nisrina would shift in her seat and straighten her skirt as she gazed about the room.

It was an impressive building. Stone columns rose up two stories high, flanked by massive archways. Small windows, set high into the walls, were separated by paintings of Holy Saints and scenes from the Bible. As the sun's rays passed over them, they emitted a radiant glow that seemed to make them come alive.

There were no artificial lights, save that which illuminated from the candles lit at precise intervals down the long dark hallway—their flames casting flickering shadows on the stone, block walls.

The scent of incense filled the air as smoke weaved its way through the passageways and meeting rooms of the cathedral; and as it swathed her in its serene bouquet, Nisrina calmed, finding herself in awe of what would be her new home for the next six months.

Occasionally, a group of nuns, their heads bowed in prayer, would pass by. Unaware of the new stranger in the room, they floated along in a choreographed union, their meditative state detaching them from their worldly surroundings. Nisrina watched as the processions appeared and departed.

She continued to wait. The room was soundless, the hallway empty.

Finally, Nisrina noticed three shadowed silhouettes approaching from the far end of the passageway. As they came nearer, she saw three women shrouded in white, carrying large clay buckets, brushes and cloths. Kneeling on the hard, cold, limestone floor, they would stop at intervals, silently washing and rinsing the stones. The first woman scrubbed the blocks with a harshly scented soap, the unforgiving odor invading Nisrina's nostrils and overpowering the bouquet of the fragile incense.

She watched as the second woman, following behind the first, quickly rinsed the soap away, water sloshing from her bucket. The third, who trailed a short distance back, carefully and meticulously, dried the wet floor with a large rough cloth. As they approached, Nisrina noticed blood stained markings on their robes where their knees pressed hard, against the sharp stone blocks.

She called out to them with a cheerful, "*Sabah el kheer!*"

But the women neither responded nor looked up from their work.

She thought perhaps they had not heard her, so she called out again, "*Salaam alakum!*"

Again, no reply.

Exacting, they continued to clean and scrub, their faces pointed to the ground, their minds absorbed in their work. She watched as the second woman poured the clean water onto the stones and swished it over the blocks; the water seeping into the cracks and crevices made a hissing sound as air raced to escape the intruding liquid.

Nisrina scratched her head. There was no mistaking that she had spoken loud enough for them to hear, but not so loud as to offend. Perhaps they were deaf, she thought to herself. But they were working right in front of her feet now, their brushes scraping the floor. They were not blind, she was sure of that. How was it that they would not speak to her or at the very least, acknowledge her presence with a smile or a nod?

"They are postulants," she heard a voice from behind her say.

"They have taken a vow of silence. They cannot speak to you, or concede your existence."

Nisrina turned to see Sister Miriam standing in the doorway.

"Oh. I see. Forgive me, I did not know."

"It is of no matter," Sister Miriam responded. "You will learn."

And with that, she disappeared back into the darkness as suddenly as she had come.

The day progressed, the sun moving low in the sky. The postulants were long gone. Nisrina, her stomach beginning to rumble, found herself sitting alone in the dark. There were no further signs of Sister Miriam, and even the sight of an occasional nun passing by had ceased. Restlessly, she squirmed in her seat.

The hours pressed on and still no one came. Nisrina's head became heavy. Her eyes slowly closed. She had risen very early that morning, long before the sun had come up, and after a painful farewell to her children and Dora, she'd boarded the bus to the city. Now, as she drifted off to sleep, her dreams began to replay those bittersweet memories: her children's tears and parting kisses, Dora's brave face as she held little Hannah in her arms, and their hopeful waves of farewell as the bus departed. Nisrina stirred.

"What have we here?"

The question echoed loudly through the empty hall. Nisrina woke with a jolt.

A second voice was heard, caring, nurturing, "My child, how long have you been sitting here? Why are you not with the others?"

Nisrina struggled to remember where she was.

Standing before her were two formidable figures. The habits that surrounded their faces were crisp, white, their black gowns flowing long to the ground.

"We can't have this!" the first nun interrupted, her head held high. "Sister Angelina? We have students sleeping in the hallway? See to it immediately!" She clapped her hands, the sound sharp, decisive;

then turned and briskly walked away disappearing into the long, dark corridor.

"Yes, Mother Superior," Sister Angelina said as she watched the Mother's figure fade into the shadows.

"I was told to wait here," Nisrina explained, sitting upright.

She was rubbing her eyes, her voice cracked.

"My child, I am so sorry. You've done nothing wrong. We thought Sister Miriam had seen to your needs and helped you to settle in." She shook her head, "That girl, sometimes I just want to . . . well, never mind. Come. You must be starving. Have you had any dinner?"

Nisrina shook her head, her stomach was growling. She thought back to the postulants with their blood-stained robes and their silent voices. She wondered if they'd eaten yet. She knew this was not a good beginning and was worried of what was yet to come. But Sister Angelina's smile was warm, her voice soft and reassuring. "It is minor, nothing to worry about, come with me. We'll see if cook has anything left in the kitchen. I could use another bite myself, and I do prefer my food warmed over, the taste is so much richer, don't you think? Hm?"

She smiled sweetly and extended her hand.

Nisrina quickly gathered her belongings. Numb and stiff, she could only nod, following the Sister into the dark. They walked a short distance outside the alcove, passing several closed doors with large brass handles. Nisrina didn't have time to wonder what was behind the doors, for within minutes she could hear the sounds of the kitchen: pans and dishes clanging about, and a low, deep voice grumbling softly in the backdrop.

They approached a pair of old, wooden doors left slightly ajar, and entered through into a large, warm kitchen. The room, still lit by candlelight, was sparse and spotless. Rustic counters made of timber filled the perimeter of the room, and a large oak table sat squarely in the center. A steaming, black, metallic oven, the likes of which Nisrina had never seen, stood across from the table with barely enough distance for two people to pass. The aromas greeting her senses were a soothing mixture of exotic spices and rising yeast. At the far end, an elderly woman with enormously large arms and a soft, dark mustache was busy cleaning up. The lines in her face reflected years of hard work, her shoulders hunched from the toils of chopping, cooking and baking.

"Good evening, Sister Alodia," Angelina greeted the cook. "This is Nisrina Jabran Yusef. She is a new student in the midwifery program and will be staying with us for the next six months."

The old nun eyed Nisrina suspiciously. Through squinted eyes she stared at her handmade *thobe* and the tousled hair that crept out from beneath her rumpled scarf. She turned her face away. "Is *she* the non-Catholic?" she said to no one in particular. "I heard that we were getting an outsider! Is this what it has come to now?"

"You are right, Sister, she is not Catholic. She is of the Syrian Orthodox faith. But Mother has agreed to take her in. Besides, as you well know, it is not for you or me to question the Mother's judgment." Sister Angelina's sweet lips were now pursed.

She went on to tell Alodia the reasons why Nisrina had been sent to the convent, and as the old cook heard the sad story there was a subtle softening around her deep-set eyes. But she quickly looked away again, rubbing the back of her hand against the side of her face and gruffly motioning for Nisrina to take a seat at the table.

"I suppose she's hungry, is that it? I just finished cleaning my kitchen and now you bring me this . . . this *mongrel*?" Her eyes narrowed again as she turned her head to one side. Then, mumbling sharp words beneath her breath, she proceeded to bring out trays of food that had been neatly packed away for the day.

"Perhaps we could have some of your *war'ak inab*, hm? You do make it so deliciously, peace be to your hands," said the kindly nun, who by now, much to the cook's displeasure, had seated herself quite comfortably at the large wooden table across from Nisrina.

Alodia took pride in her stuffed grape leaves and was secretly delighted that everyone coveted an extra serving when she made them. But she only grumbled as she brought out the soft rolled leaves stuffed with spiced rice and tender lamb's meat. Placing it over the now dwindling fire in the kitchen hearth, the food crackled and sizzled in its pot as the familiar scents of steamed grape leaves, allspice, and curry filled the room.

"And I expect you want some of my *baba gunooz* as well, eh?" Her hands were on her hips.

"Oh, yes Sister. That would be delightful. If it's not too much of an inconvenience of course," a big smile spread over Sister Angelina's face, her eyes disappearing beneath her full, red cheeks.

Alodia looked sideways at Sister Angelina. She noted her widened waist and rounded belly, but just shook her head as she moved to prepare the savory dish. A baked eggplant dip, she always insisted on using the freshest *tahini*, a rich oily paste ground from the seeds of the drought tolerant sesame, a plant grown wild and harvested in the hills that bordered their city. Stirring vigorously, she added the spicy, pungent flavor of crushed garlic, the flesh on her arms swaying back and forth as she skillfully plied the thick mixture.

When she was sufficiently satisfied with its consistency, she sprinkled a soft blanket of golden paprika over the smooth blend, adding a garnish or two of freshly chopped parsley and the fragrant juice of a ripened lemon.

The scent of garlic and lemon floated through the air as she placed the dish before the two hungry women. Swallowing hard, they bowed their heads in thanks to the Lord, and then the feasting began. Nisrina and Sister Angelina delighted in every bite, eating as if they hadn't had a meal all day, while Alodia watched surreptitiously from the corners of her eyes. When they finished, they wiped their mouths and carried their emptied plates to the basin that sat atop the counter. Nisrina was impressed and a little curious at the intricate flavors and scents she'd experienced in Alodia's kitchen. Although many of the spices were familiar to her, there was an undercurrent of flavors unlike those from her village. She looked about the room. She wanted to know more about the cook's ingredients, but thought it best to wait and inquire at another time for the hour was late and the long day's journey had wearied her mind.

They thanked Alodia, giving repeated blessings to her hands for having done such fine work, while extending warm wishes for a long and healthy life. Turning to leave, they bid the old cook a pleasant good night, and walked back out into the darkened hallway. Nisrina shivered as the cold air passed through her thin shawl. By now, most of the candles were spent; and although some remained flickering, others left behind only a thin trail of white smoke, as one by one the flames burned out.

Out of hearing range, Sister Angelina whispered to Nisrina, "Sister Alodia's bark is much worse than her bite. We always eat well because of her. God bless her."

"Yes, the meal was delicious. God bless her hands."

Approaching the back door leading out to the courtyard, Nisrina paused a moment. Placing her hand on Sister Angelina's arm, she asked, "Sister, today I saw three postulants who have taken vows of silence."

Sister Angelina nodded, "We have many."

"Tell me Sister, why are they asked to do so? And for how long are they pledged?"

"They are being tested, Nisrina," she answered patiently. "If they are to be successful in the Sisterhood, they must be disciplined to give up all worldly things. The postulant period is only one year. In that year a woman discovers if she has the obedience and dedication needed to live a spiritual life."

"They cannot speak for one full year?" Her eyes were wide.

"Oh, no child. That, I'm sure would be asking too much of any soul. No, they are given an hour of 'recreation' each day. They are allowed to speak to one another and are encouraged to use their time to discuss topics related to laity—whatever is on their minds. And of course they can always speak during the Holy festivals."

"But their knees, Sister . . . they were bleeding through their gowns. Surely there is a more compassionate way."

"The Lord's way is not without strife, Nisrina. They are learning to suffer as our Savior suffered," she smiled kindly at Nisrina who was furrowing her brow. "Do not fret my child, they are content. They live in peaceful anticipation of the day they earn their veils and become holy brides of the King of Kings." She patted her hand, "There is no greater honor."

Nisrina shivered again through her shawl, but she thought it better to say no more. Sister Miriam was right, she thought to herself, she had a lot to learn about convent life.

Leaving the main building, they crossed the courtyard to enter the dormitory, a long narrow structure that housed the female residents.

Bending at the waist, Nisrina passed over the threshold and through the low, arched doorway. Walking down the hall she noticed rows of small doors spaced evenly apart. Occasionally, through a door left ajar, she'd see a nun in repose on bended knees reciting her rosary, a small candle lit on a table nearby.

Sister Angelina led Nisrina into one of the empty rooms.

"Please make yourself comfortable. It's small, but you won't want for much while you're here. We live by a very strict routine. Chapel is at five a.m. and breakfast is served promptly at six; the bells will wake you. Just follow the others. Have a good rest." And with that she walked out the door, closing it softly behind her.

Nisrina put her things down and looked around.

The room was sparse. The walls and floors were made of rough stone with a tiny window on the far wall. A small round table that stood alongside a single bed held a solitary candle. A thin dressing gown hung loosely on a hook nearby. The bed consisted of only one small mattress which sat atop a set of springs. The candle had been lit earlier in the evening and was now more than half gone. It provided just enough light for her to find her way around the room.

She was tired, but still she took the time to meticulously fold the few clothes she'd brought with her. She placed them neatly on the wooden shelves located under the window.

Nisrina kept thinking of her children as she put her things away. Would they be happy with their Auntie Dora? Had she left enough clean clothes for them to wear? She'd forgotten to tell Dora that Hannah liked her goat's milk warmed a bit before she went to sleep at night. And that Jameela preferred a candle burning while she drifted off to sleep.

They'll be fin e, she admonished herself. I mustn't worry. This will work. I know it will. It must, that's all. It simply must.

When all her preparations for the next day were completed, she climbed into bed. The springs squealed and groaned in protest. She blew out the candle and pulled a scratchy, thread-worn blanket up high over her shoulders, then closed her eyes listening to the tepid silence around her. She had heard tales of convent life—of dedication, chastity, and temperance. But now to see it up close— she was glad to be there only six months. Already she missed the sights and sounds of the Yusef compound: the mischievous braying of Abu Faraj demanding an extra stalk of carrot, the rattle of the kitchen door as it fought against the wind, and the endless clucking of hens in the western yard. She wondered if Essam would remember to milk the goat before he left for school, and whether Jameela would help Mona to carry in the grain. But then she thought of Marta and May, imagining their endless whisperings. She hoped Dora would be steadfast in her vigil over her children—strong enough to take control, careful enough to hold them close and shrewd enough to keep the likes of Najeeb or Jacob from twisting their way into her children's hearts. She was thankful that she was merely a student and could hope for the day she'd return to her family, her home, and the familiar ways of Beit el Jebel. She turned to one side and then back again to the other, the springs moaning with each fitful move. She missed her own bed.

Finally she settled in, and through the haze of sleep she saw Jabran. She saw his smile, the curious twist of his head and the sharp, clear contour of his nose. His arms reached out to touch her. She took his hands in hers and they held each other through the night.

THIRTY ONE

First Chair

THE CHAPEL BELLS RANG precisely at 4:45 a.m. The chimes could be heard echoing throughout the complex, leaving no one immune. Nisrina quickly dressed and joined the others who were streaming down the hall toward the small chapel. The nuns sat in the front rows of the sanctuary, while the lay students remained in the back. Nisrina said her prayers quietly to herself as she heard Hail Marys and rosaries whispered all around.

One hour later, they filed out of the chapel and walked soundlessly to the dining room. The Sisters formed two straight rows, their hands clasped respectfully in front of their hearts, their heads bowed in silent grace. In reverence they walked and Nisrina followed. She was intrigued by the natural rhythm of the women's stride, their steps floating gracefully above the limestone blocks and mosaic tiles that formed the floor.

As they entered the main dining hall, Nisrina was instantly seduced by the aromas emanating from the kitchen. She breathed in deeply, closing her eyes. It reminded her of her kitchen back home, and yet, somehow different. She sensed the subtleties of new and foreign spices. The smells were rich and sensuous and her mind drifted back to her small kitchen in Beit el Jebel, to her blazing fire, and her pots and pans. She imagined Essam, Jameela and Hannah playing on the floor near her hearth, and her heart began to ache as she realized that she would not see them again for a very long while.

Her eyes were wet when she opened them again, but her resolve was strong and she quickly wiped them dry, gazing about at her new surroundings. The room was spacious, the walls and floors, clean and well maintained. The arched ceiling of the dining hall was massive, as if reaching up to the heavens, with small windows at the top to reflect God's light emanating from the morning sky. A long wooden table stretched the length of the room, surrounded by chairs of varying sizes and shapes. She noticed that no two were alike. All clearly handcrafted, made of both fine and modest woods: from olive and cypress, acacia and cedar. As if each one had been carved by a separate master and offered to the nunnery without guile or regret.

Nisrina observed these things while savory scents drifted in from the kitchen and the soft glow of candlelight filled the room. And despite her sorrow in leaving her children, she realized that for the first time since her dreadful meeting with the elders, she was finally able to breathe. Strangely enough, she thought to herself, although she was not Catholic and had been raised in strict opposition to its Papal ways, the two churches at political odds with each other, she felt at peace in this darkened, holy convent. She sensed a serenity in its calm and quiet fellowship, its kitchen, and its long dining hall.

Everyone sat in silence, their heads lowered, their hands folded neatly in their laps while the food was brought in from the kitchen. Large platters were carried by young novitiates dressed in simple garb. Their heads wrapped tightly with white linen scarves, their clean cotton robes flowing softly to the ground.

In contrast to the simplicity of the servers, the plates they carried were piled high with delectable entrees and warm side dishes. There were eggs, cooked golden and moist, the smell of sautéed onions and fresh bell peppers floating lightly through the air. Bowls of *hummus,* a mashed garbanzo bean side dish mixed with garlic, lemon juice and the steadfast tahini were placed around the table. In the center of each bowl, Sister Alodia had sprinkled sweet turmeric and added a delicate green sprig of fresh parsley. There was warm bread and skewers of finely grilled lamb. At home, such meats were reserved mostly for special occasions such as the Lord's rising or a wedding celebration, and Nisrina wondered what riches this Church must contain.

Lastly, there were trays of fresh fruit and vegetables, most having been grown in the garden just outside the kitchen. Nisrina's mouth watered, as she observed the parade of food and the platters that were placed on the table. Looking up, she noticed that all heads remained bent and so she, too, did likewise, not raising her head again until the blessings had been given.

The Mother Superior was seated at the end of the table and with closed eyes and bowed head she prayed, "Let us give thanks oh Lord, for this healthful bounty for which we are blessed."

Then, silently, with raised arms she motioned to the others to partake.

Calmly and respectfully, the food was passed around. They ate in silence, and Nisrina following their lead, spoke not a word.

After a few moments, she saw Sister Alodia peering out through the kitchen door. Their eyes met, and Nisrina, happy to see a familiar face, smiled warmly at the old cook. But Sister Alodia, with tight lips and narrowed eyes, gave only a small, stilted nod as she continued her surveillance of the room. The old cook had no time for pleasantries, nor did she put up with small appetites or any displeasure of her cooking. She wanted to be sure that everyone was enjoying the meal and was eating hefty portions. But there was no worry, for everyone was hungry and ate well, their bodies and souls finely nourished.

As the meal came to an end, Nisrina felt someone tap her shoulder. It was Sister Miriam, the young novice with the dark skin who had first greeted her in the foyer the day before. She was there to take Nisrina to her classes and since time was running short, off they went.

Sister Najla was a tall, thin woman with small wire rimmed glasses and no smile. An instructor who tolerated very little in her classroom, she stood at the entryway, handing out textbooks, pencils, and papers to the students that passed through her door. She grunted what could only have been discerned as a short greeting to each person as they entered the room, meticulously surveying her new pupils for the semester.

Nisrina promptly took a seat at the front of the class.

"Nisrina," Sister Miriam motioned to her, "come sit here."

She was pointing to a chair at the back of the class.

"Thank you, no," Nisrina responded. "I am comfortable here."

"But you can see what the others are doing from this vantage. This is your first day. It will be most helpful to you." Sister Miriam was persuasive.

"Bless you, Sister, but as God is my witness, I want to sit close. I prefer it. I want to hear every word the teacher speaks. I think I can be more attentive from here."

The novice tried one more time to convince the new student to relinquish her front row seat, but Nisrina would not hear of it. Sister Miriam's eyes darted nervously about the room as she finally acquiesced to her young ward's wishes. She told her she would return in one hour when instructions were over and hurried from the room. Nisrina watched her new friend go and remembering the previous day—Miriam's quick departure and failure to return—she wondered if she would see her again before the sun had set.

Everyone was seated. Silence filled the air as Sister Najla slowly walked to the front of the room. Holding a long stick in her right hand, she took her position at the head of the class and in a terse voice addressed the students.

"*Ahlan*, welcome to my class. I am Sister Najla your instructor in the midwifery program. By the time you have finished this coursework you will be certified midwives. Until then, you are my responsibility.

"Before we begin, it is imperative that you understand that, as a midwife, you will be the guider of life—not the giver of life, for that is God's work and God's alone. Do you understand?"

The class murmured its acknowledgment.

She continued, her voice terse, "A midwife must never forget that as the guiders of life, a mother and her newborn child's welfare will depend on your competence and attention to detail, the enormity of the task unpredictable, the rewards incomprehensible. For that reason, be forewarned that, as your instructor, I shall not tolerate any slovenly ways. Your skills as a midwife will be tested anew each time you attend to an expectant mother. Therefore, to receive certification, your knowledge must be thorough, your judgment beyond reproach, and your temperament measured." She slammed her stick upon the lectern. "I expect you to sit upright in my classroom, to learn your lessons explicitly, and to speak only when you are spoken to." Her eyes perused the classroom. "Do I make myself clear?"

The students, wide-eyed and sitting upright in their chairs, nodded their assent.

"Very well, then. Now, open your books. Starting with the first chair, I'd like you to rise and read page nine out loud to the class."

Nisrina began to squirm in her chair. She worried that maybe she should not have sat so close to the front. She was in the second chair.

The girl in the first chair promptly rose to her feet. She cleared her throat and with her head held high, she very eloquently and precisely read page nine aloud to the class. The teacher was impressed, though not a muscle moved in her face.

She then turned to Nisrina, peering at her over her glasses. Her voice was sharp, "Second chair?"

Nisrina's face began to turn red. Perspiration was pouring from every pore in her body. She couldn't move.

"Second chair?!" Sister Najla's voice had gone beyond terse. She adjusted her glasses, looking straight through the lens at Nisrina. A hush was heard as heads looked up from their textbooks.

Nisrina did not move. She did not speak.

"What is your name, second chair?" Sister Najla moved in closer, her head cocked to one side like a cat surveying its prey.

"Nisrina." She mumbled quietly, her voice barely audible.

"STAND when you address your professor!"

Nisrina rose to stand. Her eyes cast downward.

"My name is Nisrina, Your Holiness."

"Firstly," the nun was circling the room, "you do not call me Your Holiness. That title is reserved only for the Mother Superior. And secondly, I shall ask you again . . . What, young lady, is your NAME?!"

She looked up, "Nisrina Jabran Yusef."

Everyone held their breath.

"Ah, I see—the *mongrel*. Now I understand."

The class began to snicker.

"SILENCE!!" the nun had lost her patience. She turned back to Nisrina, twirling around on the balls of her feet, pointing her stick at the new student in an accusatory manner.

"And now, Nisrina. Jabran. Yusef. Now that you are finally on your feet and facing the class, can you please open your book and read to us from page ten of your lesson? *If* that is not an inconvenience to you."

"I'm sorry," responded Nisrina. "But, I cannot." Her voice was low, her eyes averted.

"Forgive my ears, young lady . . . they are old," the nun said with exaggerated sarcasm. "Did you say that you *can* not? Or . . . that you *will* not?"

The steam from her eyes clouded her lens as the instructor stepped forward, her head cocked irritably to one side. She began tapping the stick in the palm of her hand—the rhythm unnerving.

"I *can* not."

"And, why not pray tell? Can you not see? Would you like to borrow my reading glasses?" She held her glasses out to Nisrina in mock generosity.

Murmurs and whispers were filtering through the classroom.

Nisrina lifted her head high and looked directly into the nun's eyes.

"I'm sorry Sister, I cannot read. I was never taught."

"*You* CAN NOT READ?!" The words spit out of her mouth one at a time.

"No, Sister, I cannot read."

"Cook was right! You *are* a mongrel . . . from outside the Church *and* an illiterate! And *still* we took you in? Go . . ." her arm pointed to the back of the class. "Sit in the back of the room until class is over. And then we shall pay a visit to the Mother Superior."

The class was all a twitter as Nisrina rose and slowly walked to the back of the room. The students were whispering behind their hands, some were laughing. Some had expressions of horror and judgment on their faces, shocked by the young woman who had the audacity to enroll in their class. Non-Catholic *and* uneducated. What nerve indeed.

Sister Miriam was worried. Upon arriving to meet Nisrina to take her to her next class, she saw her with Sister Najla being marched off campus. Something was terribly wrong. Nisrina should not have sat at the front of the class. That was usually reserved for only the best and brightest of students. Concerned and a bit curious, she followed them from the campus back to the nunnery. She kept a safe distance behind them, being careful to duck out of sight whenever necessary.

Sister Najla and Nisrina quietly sat outside the Mother Superior's office. They waited for one full hour in which time not a word was spoken between them. Nisrina, although frightened, drew on her resolve and managed to stay composed. Some might say that her strength was prideful, but she knew that she had come too far in her journey to allow failure to be her fate. Too much was depending on her success. Her family, her life, her children. She couldn't allow herself to think about her children, not now—oh dear God, not now—she needed to stay strong.

The Mother Superior heard Sister's Najla's story—the insults and accusations. The tirade and innuendos. She couldn't help but notice that it was her own judgment in electing to accept Nisrina into her school that was being criticized and put to the test. And she did not like that one bit. When Sister Najla was done, the Mother turned to Nisrina and asked, "Is it true that you cannot read or write?"

"Yes, Your Holiness," Nisrina's eyes were lowered. "I cannot."

"I'm sorry, but this was not explained to me when the arrangements were first made. You understand that this is a University, and although we are a charitable Order, a student is expected to be able to complete her coursework." The Mother pulled a file from the drawer behind her desk and began rummaging through its contents. "When your father-in-law made the inquiry, he didn't mention that . . ."

"Please, Your Holiness," Nisrina interrupted. "Allow me to speak in my defense."

Startled, the Mother stopped searching and looked up. Nisrina had seemed so shy, so reserved—she was surprised by her sudden outburst. "Yes, go on child, you are free to speak. Tell me what is on your mind."

"Your Holiness," Nisrina was wringing her hands, "I realize that I come to you an illiterate *fellaha*, a country girl whose sole world has been my small village—the green orchards and rolling hills my only template, the written word a stranger to me. My husband, God rest his soul, was able to read and write, but he did not expect it of his wife, nor did my father expect it of his daughter. Jabran was taught by his uncle and the beautiful words in his poetry books, I know only through his eyes."

The Mother was attentive as she heard Nisrina speak so eloquently. And although Sister Najla kept her sour face turned away, she, too, was listening intently.

"But my Jabran is gone. The elders have abandoned any hope for his return and now I must find a way to support my family . . . my children."

"I understand you have three children?" asked the Mother Superior.

"Yes," Nisrina's eyes softened, her voice calming, "I have three children. Essam, the man of my household is seven. Jameela is five. And Hannah, the baby, is two."

"Hannah is only two?" the Mother asked. "But hasn't Jabran been gone for over two years now?"

"Yes," replied Nisrina, her eyes turning red; she was determined not to cry. "Hannah was born shortly after Jabran was taken from me. She slept in my womb the day the soldiers came."

Sister Najla turned and looked at Nisrina. Her face still tight, she realized that indeed this woman had suffered, *but even so . . . she could not read nor write . . . how could she possibly complete such a difficult course?*

"And now I beseech you, Your Holiness, have mercy on me. Allow me this opportunity. Allow me to try. If I leave you today, my children will be taken from me. I will be forced to marry another. I cannot love another man, Your Holiness. It is impossible. Jabran was my first and my last. My only. Please. I cannot." Nisrina's hands were clasped tightly, held in prayer before her heart. She begged the Mother for understanding.

"But if you cannot read, my child," the Mother's voice was soft, compassionate, "how do you expect to be able to finish your courses? Do you not see our dilemma here?"

"Although I cannot read the course material, I will attend every class and laboratory. I am an intelligent woman and a quick study. I have given birth to three children of my own and have helped other women in the village at their time of need. I can fully understand what a woman is going through at that moment in her life. Please. Trust me. I will not let you down. Too many are depending on me. Please show me your mercy and consider that which I ask of you. I will not fail, of this I am certain."

"Please wait outside, Nisrina. I need to talk to Sister Najla alone. And then I will let you know my answer." The Mother opened the door and guided Nisrina back to the foyer. To the same bench she had sat on for twelve hours the previous day.

Nisrina sat down and waited, her heart pumping hard.

After a few moments, Sister Miriam peeked out from around the corner, "I've been listening through the garden window," she whispered. "I hope that donkey's ass, Sister Najla, gets her comeuppance. She deserves it. We are supposed to teach grace and understanding, but she hasn't an ounce to spare. Don't worry Nisrina, the Mother is a kind and fair woman, you'll see."

Nisrina managed a weak smile, but said nothing. She used all her strength to fight back the tears.

In a short while the door opened. Sister Miriam ducked back behind the corner.

Nisrina was ushered, once again, into the Mother's office. She could see the expression on Sister Najla's face and she knew that she still had a battle to fight.

The Mother Superior began, "Nisrina, I cannot make this easy for you. If what you say is true . . . that you can learn your lessons without reading the material . . . then we must give you oral tests."

Nisrina nodded.

"I see, so you understand. And you have no problem with this? You find that acceptable?"

"Yes, Your Holiness."

"In that case, no time shall be wasted. Your first test is today, right now. Would you please recite to us what you learned in class this morning?"

Nisrina felt a wave of excitement come over her. Despite the unpleasant encounter with Sister Najla, she had paid close attention in class. She felt confident. She rose up from her chair. Then, standing straight and tall, without hesitation, she accurately recited the key points of the hour's lesson. Although their faces remained unchanged, the two nuns exchanged a glance.

Sister Najla was not convinced.

"Anyone can regurgitate a lesson," she scoffed, rising from her seat. "We must know if you were able to understand—to actually comprehend what you have learned."

Pacing the floor, her hands behind her back, she began to ask Nisrina a series of complex questions about the morning's lecture.

Nisrina answered each one without error. She clearly understood all the nuances of what had been taught.

The Mother Superior was beaming, and for the first time Nisrina noticed how beautiful she was—her eyes radiated a joyful shade of azure blue, and her smile was warm like the red poppies that grew wild on the hills. She held out her hand to Nisrina, "Well done, my child. You may return to your classes. It is clear to me that you will be an honor to our program."

Nisrina thanked the Mother Superior and turned to leave.

"Oh, and Nisrina," the Mother called to her, "you have just earned the honor of sitting in the first chair." She glanced at Sister Najla whose face had turned to stone, her lips a tight line. "Welcome to our University."

THIRTY TWO

Friends and Foes

IT WAS ONE THING for Nisrina to impress the Mother Superior and quite another to gain acceptance from her classmates. The regrettable experience of her first class had established her as the mongrel of the school. The illiterate. The non-Catholic. The poor peasant from the countryside. And it was clear that the other students were not ready to forget. Especially when they heard she'd earned the honor of first chair, for there was another in the classroom who thought that seat should be hers.

"Well, Nisrina, it appears that you've impressed the Mother Superior, but let me say, you have not impressed me!"

Magda Attia was standing before Nisrina, her head held high, cold defiance in her eyes.

She was the girl who formerly sat in the first chair. And now, surrounded by her three loyal followers, Irena, Nadia and Helena, she had Nisrina cornered in the back of the classroom and wanted it known to her, as well as to the rest of the class, that she would not stand by complacently and allow this upheaval to occur. With each word ferociously spoken, Nisrina could smell the *hummus* lingering from Magda's breakfast. Cook had used a lot of garlic that morning and the smell which would normally be welcome, now caused her stomach to turn.

"I'm only following the Mother Superior's instructions. I'll gladly relinquish that seat to you. It matters not to me." Nisrina wanted no trouble.

"It's not that easy, mongrel. The Mother's word is final. But you *will* earn that chair, Nisrina. I'll guarantee you that! This shall not go forgotten."

Her cohorts sneered in support, as their leader showed her teeth.

Magda Attia came from a wealthy family. Her clothes were of the finest fabrics imported from France and she carried herself with a sense of confidence and privilege. She was younger than Nisrina and it was obvious, as it was with all the girls at the university, that she was a *medineeya*, a girl from the city. A more refined and progressive class, they encouraged their daughters to attain a higher education.

The professor's entry into the classroom signaled all the students to take their seats. Magda took the second chair next to Nisrina, her three comrades in the row behind. Nisrina, determined not to let the *medineeya* disrupt the purpose for her being there, sat upright, resolved to pay close attention to the lesson.

However, Magda had other plans. When it came time for her to read aloud, Magda turned her back to Nisrina as she read from her textbook. She kept her voice low, so much so, that Nisrina had to strain to hear her words. Irena, Nadia and Helena giggled as they saw Nisrina's distress and when it came their turn to read, they did likewise.

"You look so sad, my friend. Do you miss your children?"

It was Sister Miriam. She had noticed Nisrina sitting alone under an olive tree in the garden outside the dining hall.

"I'm afraid I've made some enemies, Sister Miriam."

"You mean Sister Najla? She's just a mean old taskmaster. Just do well in your studies and she will come to the same conclusion that the Mother and I have made . . . that you are a good person and very deserving of this opportunity. Trust me on this. Just do your best."

Sister Miriam was patting Nisrina on the back, trying to comfort her in her own sweet way.

"No, it's not Sister Najla that I'm worried about. It's the other students, my classmates. I'm afraid that my being here may have been a big mistake. I'm worried. A woman like me. I just don't fit in. I don't belong. I miss my children. Their warm breaths on my neck, their sweet smiles . . ."

"Nonsense! Listen, my child. It is not up to your classmates to determine if you should be here or not. This is in God's hands. It is for Him to decide. He has brought you to our school. Please, leave this to the Lord, you won't regret it."

Nisrina looked into Sister Miriam's eyes and studied her face. She noticed how very young she was.

She couldn't be more than eighteen, maybe nineteen years old, Nisrina thought to herself, and yet, her words and her presence are comforting to me.

It was odd to have someone younger than herself, call her 'my child' but she was glad to hear the words, feeling calmed by the Sister's expression.

"But, what can I do?" she asked her. "You see, they turn their backs to me when they read out loud to the class. And they speak so softly I cannot hear them. How shall I learn if I cannot read or hear the lessons? I will surely fall behind and then ultimately fail." Nisrina was shaking her head forlornly.

"I have an idea!" Sister Miriam jumped up from the bench. "I will read the lessons to you. I can do it every day."

"I could not ask you to do that," replied Nisrina. "I'm sure you have your own responsibilities to attend to, rather than be bothered with my problems."

"You will help me to reach my novice goals. One of my sacred intentions is teaching and this will allow me a chance to help you and meet my goals at the same time. What say you?"

"Why, I'd love it! Thank you Sister. Thank you so much."

"See, God, does have a plan. We only have to have faith."

"Yes," smiled Nisrina very relieved and pleased that they'd resolved both their problems.

As she watched Sister Miriam walk away, Nisrina couldn't help but think that she did have faith . . . faith that her husband, her dear Jabran, was alive somewhere. He had to be. She resolved to herself that she would just have to pray harder about it. Then God would surely know what was in her heart and lead him back home to her.

As an added measure, although she spoke of it to no one, on many a night when her lessons were done and her chores completed, Nisrina would wander out to the garden and look up into the night sky. There she would stand amidst the sweet scents of jasmine and lilies, searching the darkness for a star. The ever so illusive first star. When she'd see the distant silvery glimmer twinkling down on her, she would close her eyes and make a wish. A wish that her beloved Jabran would return and she could feel his loving arms wrapped tightly around her once again; a wish that he could see his children grow and flourish, especially the youngest, her dear sweet Hannah who had been sleeping in her womb when the soldiers took him from her.

Maybe one day . . . someone . . . somewhere . . . will hear me.

Whether the Heavenly Host heard her or not remained a mystery. But her wishes were being heard by at least one pair of ears, for as she stood in the garden pleading so passionately to the stars, someone was watching her from their dormitory room. And as she listened to Nisrina's deepest thoughts, Sister Alodia's heart ached. With memories long-ago buried, but not forgotten, the old nun said a quiet little prayer: a request for compassion, mercy, and most of all, hope for the sad little *fellaha*.

The months passed and Nisrina flourished. The assurances she gave to the Mother Superior on her first day in class proved to be true—although she could neither read nor write, she had certain advantages that the other students did not. She had not only given birth to three children of her own, she'd also witnessed or assisted many of the women in her village. Hospitals were an unfamiliar luxury for *fellaheen* women. Babies were born at home or in the fields, and any available woman who could, would gladly help.

As promised, Sister Miriam continued to read the lessons to Nisrina.

After classes, they would meet on the bench under the big olive tree where they'd first made their plans to study together. Alodia could see them from her kitchen window and she noticed how hard the two ladies worked. Although she tried to maintain her distance, she found herself cooking nourishing snacks for them. Each day, she'd prepare something different—sometimes it would be several soft, round loaves of freshly baked bread steaming hot from the oven. Or on a particularly warm day, she'd make a cool bowl of *tabouli*, a finely chopped salad of parsley, scallions, tomatoes and mint made especially hearty with the addition of *burghul*, loosely-ground wheat soaked overnight in water. She'd blend the mixture with the savory oil of the olive, along with the tart juice of a lemon or two.

Carrying the food out in her massive arms, she'd carefully place it on the ground alongside their feet, hesitating a moment to see their reaction. Their eyes would always open wide and they'd thank her profusely. They'd bless her hands and her heart many times over, the sincerity unquestionable. But Alodia would just grunt and rub her palms tightly against the sides of her apron, turning back once or twice before she left, to point out the freshness of her ingredients.

"Finish every bite now, you hear?" she'd growl to them as she walked away. "The Lord's food is not to be wasted!"

Checking back periodically she'd ask if they wanted more. They'd raise up their hands in protest and shake their heads no, thanking her again and again.

And so, as their bodies were nourished, so were their minds. Sister Miriam would read out loud and Nisrina would listen—as Alodia hovered quietly nearby.

The readings, coupled with her calm, attentive manner in class, allowed Nisrina to excel in her studies. Even Sister Najla, although she'd never declare it so, had come to depend on Nisrina to have the right answers. And she couldn't help notice how Nisrina took time to help her classmates, assisting some of the slower students in their studies. Through her kindness and friendly manner, Nisrina had gained the respect and friendship of the other students—with the exception of four.

Magda Attia was the daughter of Nabih Attia, the owner of Attia Hotels, small prestigious inns found scattered along the Mediterranean coast. A successful man, he wielded both power and influence in the region, but his success came at a cost. With little time for family life, he'd arranged for his only daughter to attend the Catholic

University, assuring her education while protecting her virtue. He was known throughout the region as a ruthless opponent, his misdeeds tempered by generous contributions to the Church. Her three comrades Irena, Nadia, and Helena were more than just friends to Magda—they were her cousins, the daughters of her father's brothers. Three men who very gratefully worked for their brother in positions they'd otherwise have found unattainable.

So, although the honor of first chair meant nothing to Irena, Nadia, and Helena, it came as no surprise that the three sheep never questioned their shepherd's harsh biddings. Loyally, they continued their ill-will towards their cousin's rival. And at every turn, they made sure that she knew it.

Younger than Nisrina, they found ways to make her life at the university untenable. If they passed her in the halls, they would shove her into the other students and make it appear that she was clumsy. Other times they would come from behind and pull her head scarf off, making her appear an immodest woman. If they could, they would sit near her at lunch and glare until her stomach turned and she could not eat her food. Nisrina wanted no trouble and would always apologize for any mishaps that might occur, never pointing a finger at the real culprits.

In time, she became all the wiser, making it her business to know where Magda and her cousins were at any given time of the day. She studied their habits and patterns and made certain to avoid them whenever possible.

Nisrina's ever growing friendship with Sister Miriam helped to sustain her. That alliance, coupled with the knowledge that she had only three months left in the midwifery program, soon to be reunited with her children, was all she needed. The worst was over, she told herself again and again. She would succeed . . . *Enshallah,* God willing.

THIRTY THREE

Convent Life

NISRINA LEARNED THAT LIFE in the convent followed a strict and orderly manner, an air of submission present in all their tasks. When she questioned the rigorousness of the cloistered life, she was told that the women were there of their own free will, and that the postulants and novices were being socially and spiritually prepared for holy matrimony with the Lord.

Postulants were the lowly of the low, their days spent in silent service. They were the voiceless figures who kept the grounds spotless, washed the priests' clothes, and served them their meals. They could be found emptying bed pans long after the candles had burned their last glow, or crawling in the rafters to clear decaying mouse remnants from a well-sprung trap.

Their time in "obedience" might take them to the well to fetch water for the kitchen, or to the laundry where they washed and ironed the community's clothes. Using a heavy flat iron heated over a fire, they'd press tightly the robes and holy garments of the priests and nuns.

As it had for decades, the Chapter of Faults took place every Friday afternoon. It was there that postulants assembled to publicly confess their faults and receive penance from a superior. However, the girls lived in a sheltered cocoon of piety, separate from the outside world and its wicked devices, and as such, had little to confess. As they stood in line to face their superior, they were inclined to create a fault. They'd tell a tale of wicked thoughts or reckless indiscretions so that they could gain forgiveness and finally take their seat.

Any mail received was opened and read. They were allowed to write home to their families once every two weeks, which was also read by their superior before being posted.

Novices were a step removed. No longer vowed to silence, they sang in the choir, their voices raised in traditional Gregorian chants, and they tended the monastery's vegetable and flower gardens growing food for all to share. They observed legislated time in classes of their own, learning the order's regulations and governing charter, which they were expected to take to memory. They studied the bible and their faith as dictated by Rome, and they raised their voices in prayer at dailies in the chapel. Recreation time allowed them to move about the sanctuary grounds, walking in quiet conversation or prayerful contemplation. On rainy or cold wintery days when outdoor leisure was not a viable option, they spent their time in the community room where they darned the priests' socks and knitted woolen shawls for the Sisters.

The Sisters, led by the Mother Superior, were the teachers, the cooks, and managers of the organization. A teaching convent dedicated to merciful education for women, they watched over the flock and assured that life in their community functioned towards its sacred grand purpose—to serve the Lord, and the priests who carried out His holy work.

As kindly as the Sisters treated her, Nisrina could not reconcile the agony and isolation she observed in her midst. She questioned them over and over again: Was suffering a requirement to serve the Lord? She could see the pain in the postulants' stilted gazes as they worked on bended knees, the sharp edges of the limestone blocks slicing their flesh, their bloodied hands and gowns a witness to their agony. She thought of her own two daughters and shivered at the thought that they might ever share such an arduous fate. Her heart ached for them, and yet she knew she had no recourse, no power to affect a change in this matter. These things were of the Church and she had always been taught to accept a higher wisdom.

It was on just such an occasion, when her thoughts wrestled with these solicitous matters, that Nisrina encountered postulant Mary. The hour was late, the community long retired, when she was wakened by the sound of weeping outside her bedroom window.

Nisrina rose from her bed, wrapped herself in her warmest shawl, and ventured out. As she rounded the corner of the dormitory, she found the form of a girl wrapped in a tattered blanket, her head in her hands, her shoulders moving gently to the rhythm of her tears. The night was cool, a gentle breeze danced across her face catching her hair and cooling her brow. Nisrina could smell the sweet fragrance of jasmine, the blooms releasing their scent when the world was dark.

"Pray tell, what matters of consequence bring you out on such a night?" she asked the weeping child.

"I . . . I'm sorry Sister," the postulant responded, her voice forlorn.

"No, please, forgive me," Nisrina interrupted. "I am not a Sister. I'm merely a guest in this home . . . a student at the university. Please, call me Nisrina."

"Oh! Lord forgive me!" the postulant covered her mouth. Nisrina saw the terror in the young girl's eyes as she sealed her lips and shook her head, remembering that she was not allowed to speak, her vow of silence extending even into the night.

"Fear not," Nisrina assured her. "Surely, even the Lord understands the human frailty of his bride-to-be. He is a merciful God. Does this not seem reasonable?"

Nisrina reached out to the girl, removing her hand from her mouth.

"Take heed," she continued, "all is not dire, for it will give you something to confess at your Chapter of Faults."

The girl smiled, her eyes softening.

"Yes, that's much better. What is your name?"

"Mary," she whispered wiping the tears from her cheeks.

"Mary," Nisrina nodded. "Tell me, what troubles you so?"

"I cannot find the words," Mary stammered.

"Is it your family? Do you miss them?"

Mary nodded.

"I miss mine too. I miss my son Essam, and my daughters, Jameela and Hannah."

"I am frightened," Mary said.

"Pray tell, of what?"

"I don't think I am worthy of this life. I haven't the strength . . ." She hid her face in her hands.

Nisrina lifted her head and looked into the young girl's eyes. She saw the hopeful innocence that blanketed her.

"Was this life something you chose for yourself?" she asked her.

"Yes," Mary nodded. "I had a dream, a vision. He came to me and took my hand . . . and I knew then . . . I knew that I wanted to serve Him. At the time I was certain. But now . . . now I am no longer sure." She shook her head, "I'm not worthy . . . I am so very, very weary."

Nisrina saw the bloodied cuts in the young girl's hands, the darkened circles that surrounded her eyes.

"Come with me," she said, leading her back through the dormitory.

She took her across the courtyard and into the kitchen, and there she washed her wounds. She applied ointment to the open sores and wrapped her hands in clean, dry cloths. She reached in a basket and gave the girl a round loaf of bread, then took down a jug and poured water for her to drink.

"Take this . . . eat and drink," she told her. "I am a mother and I know a child's pain. You need rest and nourishment if you are to be readied for your Lord. Your heart is pure and your mind is strong. If it is your desire to follow this path, you will succeed. I'm sure of it. I will keep you in my prayers."

Mary nodded and thanked Nisrina. She kissed her hands and blessed her over and over for her kindness. Nisrina gently placed her lips on the young girl's forehead, and whispered to her, "All will be well. Don't worry sweet Mary, all will be well. But you must go now, get some sleep. It will be morning soon."

The two women departed company, each returning to their own quarters for the night.

In the shadows, Alodia made not a sound as she watched and listened. Nothing happened in her kitchen without her knowledge, and this night's interlude was no exception.

THIRTY FOUR

Understanding

NISRINA WAS CHOSEN TO assist with the first childbirth of the session, her fellow classmates observing from the far corner of the room. The hospital had become somewhat familiar to her, although its sparse, antiseptic rooms contrasted sharply with the simple bedrooms of her village.

The woman had been in labor for twenty-four hours, her screams now coming at regular intervals, her opening fully dilated. The doctor was bent over her, warning her not to push. When he heard the students ushered in, he shook his head, reluctantly moving to one side.

Nisrina stepped forward to examine her.

She could see that her strength was waning, her progress at a standstill. She wondered why the doctor had waited so long to call her in, but immediately put her thoughts aside to attend to the struggling mother. Feeling her stomach, Nisrina noticed that the child had not descended properly. The head was at the top of the womb. If the mother were to push, the baby's legs would come out first.

Memories of Lamia flooded back to her. A grave risk had been taken that day and it was only by the grace of God that Lamia's daughter was born healthy and strong. She couldn't allow this mother to suffer as Lamia had suffered, nor would she let the risk to the child's life go unheeded. This time it was early enough to rotate the unborn babe.

Knowing that birth in the reverse position could easily compromise the infant's airway, Nisrina turned to the attending physician, "The child is breech, why haven't you turned him?"

"Don't be ridiculous! You can't move the baby while it's still inside the mother! We have given him time to turn naturally and he has not done so. I have no choice but to operate."

"The mother is too weak!" Nisrina countered, she did not trust the surgeon's knife.

"I realize the mother is fragile, but it's a risk I'm willing to take. I'm sure we can at least save the baby." He crossed his arms in front of his chest. He would not defer to this young girl who stood before him. He was an experienced surgeon, he knew better.

"No, I've seen it done. The midwife from our village had great success. I'm sure I can do it. I've watched her many times." Although not entirely true, Nisrina felt compelled to convince the physician of her knowledge in the matter. Resolute, she felt this was the surest way to save both mother and child, no other alternatives acceptable.

"Nisrina, there is a lesson for you here, my child," Sister Najla, who was watching the events unfold, stepped forward placing her hand on Nisrina's shoulder. "You must understand that there are some things that are simply not in our control. They are God's will. He has put the baby upside-down inside his mother and now the outcome is for God to determine, not you."

"No! The mother is too frail to endure an operation. Her face is pale, her pulse weak. And to allow the baby to come out with his feet first is far too dangerous, he may not get enough air. He might die or risk being *habeel*, brain damaged, for the rest of his life. I will not let that happen." Nisrina's words were passionate, but she retained her composure.

The doctor lost his patience. He pushed the high-handed student out of his way, but Nisrina stood her ground, resisting his shoves, her elbows held tight at her waist. She could hear the other students tittering behind her.

"No doctor, wait!" It was the birthing mother. She was weak and in a great deal of pain, but she was awake and had heard their conversation. "I don't want my baby to die or be born *habeel*. I trust this woman." She turned to face them. Nisrina saw the agonizing plea in her eyes.

She was panting now, holding back. She reached out and took Nisrina's hand in her own, needing to touch her, to draw strength from her. She wanted to express herself before the next painful contraction. "The *fellaheen* . . . they sometimes know things that we do not. Please, let her try. I insist . . ." her words were interrupted by another piercing scream.

There was no time left, if Nisrina was going to save the baby without jeopardizing the mother's life, she needed to act quickly. The doctor reluctantly succumbed to the mother's wishes and stepped aside. He motioned to Nisrina to continue. She placed her hands on the swollen abdomen, carefully feeling the form and outline of the baby's body, and then she closed her eyes.

Nisrina's hands worked furiously. The woman was moaning, then screaming as the apprentice manipulated her belly. Unnerved, the doctor moved to intercede. He did not want to lose both the mother and the child. But something in Sister Najla caused her to step forward again. She put out her arm and this time she held the doctor back. They exchanged glances. The look on Sister Najla's face was clear. The doctor stepped aside.

Nisrina neither saw nor heard what was going on around her. Her eyes still closed, she continued to manipulate the unborn child while the mother cried out in agony.

It was as if the Holy Spirit himself had taken over Nisrina's body, or perhaps it was the spirit of Sabra Hishmeh. Her hands seemed to float above the woman's abdomen and yet they touched her skin and pressed against the child's form, sometimes lightly, sometimes firmly, she massaged and kneaded with strength and grace.

Finally, after what seemed an eternity, she stopped and pulled back. Sweat was covering her brow, her hair was matted against her head, her clothes soaking wet. She opened her eyes and looked at the mother who was now almost passed out from pain and exhaustion.

She brought her face very close to the birthing mother's and spoke calmly and firmly to her, "I need you to find all the strength you have now, it is time for you to push out your baby."

The doctor again moved forward, and again Sister Najla held him back.

"Let the student complete her exam." Sister Najla was firm.

The doctor shrugged, a bit miffed at such an intrusion into his operating room. But nevertheless, he was somewhat in awe of what he was witnessing. This *fellaha*, this young girl from the village, had taken over. But he held back with his comments. He knew that repositioning the child in-utero may, in and of itself, have damaged its brain. Then he would speak up. But not now. He was a patient man. He felt sure that no one would be able to find fault with *his* actions. He'd done his best to bring sensibility to the situation. In the end, he would have the last word and claim that he tried to stop this debacle. But for now, he would wait.

Nisrina had bonded with the woman. Together they developed a rhythm of pushing and breathing as the contractions waxed and waned. The woman's strength continued to fade, but Nisrina would not let up. At the peak of the next contraction she yelled, "PUSH!"

And the woman pushed and screamed.

"Don't scream. Please. Use your energy to push out your child, don't waste it in the sound of your voice."

Nisrina was clearly in charge.

"Again, now PUSH!"

And finally, on the next push, the child's head popped out.

"I see the head," she called to the mother. "You're almost done, one more push!"

The woman pushed again and the child was born.

Everyone gasped. It was blue. Not breathing.

The doctor puffed up. His head held high, his chest inflated. Now he could claim his superiority. The country girl had killed the child. A boy, no less. The family would be outraged and he could now point his finger at this non-Catholic student working in a Catholic hospital. This illiterate *fellaha* with her unorthodox ways. She would be sent back to the village where she belonged, and in disgrace. Now he would have his day.

But Nisrina remained unaware of his thoughts. Her focus was on the health and well-being of the child. Without a moment's hesitation, she turned the baby upside down and slapped his bottom.

No breath.

She slapped again. Still nothing.

She put her finger in his mouth and pulled out a rope of thick, stringy mucus. She massaged his chest. And then she did what none of them had seen before. She put her mouth over the child's nose and mouth and breathed her breath directly into the child.

Had she gone mad?

She quickly turned him over and once again solidly slapped his bottom with her open hand. The child took in a breath and started to scream. Everyone in the room gasped and cried out with him. There were tears of joy as everyone reached out and hugged the person next to them, followed by exclamations of praise and thanks to God.

Nisrina, finally seeing color in the baby's body, handed the child to its mother. She turned to the doctor, "We must stop the bleeding, or we will lose her." The doctor nodded and came to help. They now worked together on the mother. The room was quiet as the students and teacher watched Nisrina. No one dared breathe a word or move a muscle. She was massaging the woman's abdomen while the doctor, watching her actions from the corner of his eye, tended to the after-birth and monitored the mother's vital signs.

Sister Najla took the baby from the mother's weakened arms and wrapped him in a soft, warm blanket. She gazed at the sweet little face peeking out at her.

Surely this is a miracle. The work of God, she thought to herself. And Nisrina . . . hmm, maybe the Mother was right, she is an exceptional child. No, it appears that she is not a child after all, she is a woman. A woman who has clearly been touched by the hand of God . . . it's unfortunate that she isn't a Catholic.

Word had spread of Nisrina's success in the delivery room. The baby was fine. A healthy seven pound boy whom the family named Nishat, meaning liveliness or energy. The mother was doing remarkably well, and she and her new son had returned to their beautiful home to be pampered and cared for by servants and nannies. The birth of her son had bestowed the highest honor given to any woman, and with her new role in life she was now called *Oum* Nishat, the mother of Nishat. Her parents, a wealthy couple who lived in a large home overlooking the city, offered to pay Nisrina for saving the life of their grandson. However, as a student she was not allowed to accept payment for her services. So, after much negotiations and closed-door discussions, the family finally acquiesced, and as an alternative gesture, made a large donation to the university.

Everyone was pleased.

Everyone, that is, except Magda Attia.

THIRTY FIVE

Figures in the Night

"NISRINA, IT'S LATE."

It was not the first time the senior nurse had observed how hard Nisrina worked with the new mothers.

The nurse continued, "Why don't you let me finish with Mrs. Abboud? You've been at it for six hours now. You need your rest. A new day will be here before you know it."

"Let me try once more. She's having trouble nursing the baby. I think we may be successful this time. Just a few more minutes, please. Then I'll go home."

Nisrina saw that Mrs. Abboud had been near tears more than once in the last twenty four hours. She was a tiny woman with small breasts and short nipples. The baby was having a hard time latching on to her. If she could not successfully feed the child it would be given to a wet nurse for its nutrition. Mrs. Abboud would be shamed. Her husband disgraced. A mother who could not feed her own child? What would the people think? Already the relatives were streaming in to give their blessings and well wishes. They had noticed that the child wasn't eating. Mrs. Abboud saw their silent, disapproving looks. She could hear the whispers in the hallway. It had already begun.

"Good evening, Mrs. Abboud." Nisrina came into the room smiling and carrying a cup of hot tea, the steam from the cup slowly drifting up into the softly lit room. Even Mrs. Abboud in her distressed state could not help but notice the warm inviting aroma that preceded the tea. It was a unique smell, one she did not recognize.

"I've brought you a special tea that will make you feel better. It's used by the women in my village and it work wonders at times like these . . ."

"What is it?" Mrs. Abboud was now sitting up, anxious for anything that might assist her.

"It's made with an ancient herb grown in the hills of Mesopotamia. I bought it from the vendor in the *souk* this afternoon. It will relax your nipples and allow the milk to flow, trust me. This way your son can have a nice dinner before he settles in for the night. Shall we try it? Hm?" Her voice was cheerful, soothing.

"*Shukran,*" Mrs. Abboud thanked Nisrina and took the hot cup from her hands. At this point she was willing to try anything to save her family from disgrace.

She sipped the tea.

"*Saalem adaykee!*" She blessed her hands. "This is delicious!"

Mrs. Abboud sipped the tea slowly until it was gone. Setting the empty cup aside, she lay back against the pillows which had been propped up at the head of her bed. For the first time since she had passed through the large, double doors of the hospital building, she was able to let go. She closed her eyes, her breath slowing to a steady, rhythmic pace; and then, within a few short minutes she felt a strange tingling in her breasts. She opened her eyes and looked at the child sleeping quietly in the small bed beside her.

"I think it is time to feed my son," she said.

Nisrina handed her the child. Mrs. Abboud opened her gown and Nisrina reached out to touch her nipples. "Permit me to help, please."

Mrs. Abboud nodded.

Nisrina began to massage the mother's nipples. In a few moments she saw a light fluid begin to drain from them. She helped Mrs. Abboud position the baby at her breast and with her fingers, deftly popped the now full and protruding nipple into the baby's mouth. He began to suckle.

"*Ya Allah*! He's eating!" Mrs. Abboud was elated. "It's wonderful! Such a sensation! Thank you, Nisrina. Thank you!" Tears of joy appeared in her eyes.

Seeing the suckling child gaze up at his mother warmed Nisrina's heart. She thought of her own children, remembering their births and how she held them in her arms, so tiny and frail. She recalled her own concerns when she first put them to her breast and how they looked up into her eyes, suckling with murmurs of delight. She smiled to herself. Her work here was done. She softly whispered to Mrs. Abboud, "You are a good mother, *Oum* Khalil. Enjoy your son." Then she quietly left the room with the satisfaction of knowing that the mother and child had found each other.

There was a special lightness in her step as Nisrina walked across the schoolyard on her way back to the dormitory, her arms loaded with packages of herbs and teas that she'd bought at the local *souk*. Although it was quite late and the campus now deserted, she gave it no thought. She was experiencing the bliss of midwifery. It suited her well. What began as a frightening endeavor was now her calling. She was filled with joy, her thoughts racing between the last few months and the future. She practiced the stories she'd tell upon returning to the village. She imagined her children's bright eyes, and could feel their arms wrapped lovingly around her. She would be returning with a sense of pride and self-sufficiency. She would be a midwife. A *dayah*.

She was still smiling to herself as she rounded the corner and entered a dimly lit alleyway that led back to the nunnery. However, her smile faded as she peered down the road. Several figures were lurking up ahead. She reminded herself that the laws were very strict in her country and she need not worry. People felt safe in their homes and on the streets. Doors remained unlocked at all hours. And if a perpetrator should act against another citizen or their property, they would be harshly dealt with. If an item was stolen, the thief would be apprehended and the offending hand would be swiftly cut off.

Nevertheless, she was curious as to who would be out at such a late hour. And why they were standing there, clustered together.

It was too dark to see who they were, and the moon, a mere grimace in the sky, offered no assistance. She drew nearer and could tell by their clothing that it was a small group of women. But they were not moving—neither forward nor back. They remained huddled in the far corner, their silhouettes casting an ominous shadow against the stone walls of the adjacent building. Anxious to get home, she continued but cautiously slowed her pace. The shadows up ahead ever so slightly shifted their positions.

Nisrina was now painfully aware of the sound of her steps echoing in the alleyway. They seemed to get louder and louder, contrasting with the deafening silence of the night. She heard her heart thumping loudly in her chest, but again reminded herself that this was a safe city and they were merely women who were lost or in need of assistance. She was a *dayah*, after all, and her duty was to serve others.

She moved on. Within moments the figures were before her.

There was no turning back.

Nisrina, mustering all her courage was about to speak to them, to call out a traditional welcome and ask if she could be of assistance, but her words were given no chance as she found herself face to face with two glaring eyes peering out from under a shroud. With an animal-like quality, the gaze emitted a yellow glow, the reflection of a light that streamed down from a nearby building. It was unworldly, and yet, strangely familiar. Those eyes. That stare. A shiver ran down her spine. She stopped—her feet frozen to the ground, her heart racing.

Standing before her in the dark alleyway, late at night without another living soul around was Magda Attia and her cruel little entourage of mindless sheep.

They circled around her.

"*Marhaba.*" Nisrina's voice cracked as she gave her greeting.

"*Marhaba.*" It was Magda's voice, of that she was certain, but it was not the voice she applied in class or the tone she'd use in the dining room. This voice was different. It seemed to resonate from a dark place deep within her throat, like an animal growling, ready to attack, and Nisrina was only too aware that she was now her prey.

"Magda? Is all well? What brings you out so late at night?" Nisrina tried to sustain a state of normalcy.

"You Nisrina. You have brought me out on this evening."

"Me?"

"Yes . . . you." It was that animal voice again.

"I'm sorry. I don't understand."

"She doesn't understand," Magda repeated turning to the others. "Well, maybe I can help you understand, Nisrina."

Her face was close to Nisrina's. Too close. It was the second day in class all over again. Only this time there were no teachers around to intercede. No one to walk up and disperse the interlopers.

"You, my dear, Nisrina," she continued, her finger now poking into the *dayah's* chest, "you are an illiterate *fellaha*. A mongrel, not of The Church. You don't belong here. And yet you seem to have fooled everyone around you . . . everyone that is, except me!" Magda was spitting out her words through tightly clenched teeth. Her accomplices murmured their agreement, making sure that Nisrina knew they were not fooled either.

"I'm sorry if I have caused you any inconvenience. Please forgive me. I want no trouble. I will be gone soon and then it will be over."

"Yes . . . you will be gone soon. That is certain . . . there is no place for you here." Magda began circling around her, inspecting the young woman's face, her headscarf and her simple, handmade *thobe*. She observed the packages that Nisrina held in her hands and wondered what this illiterate student had purchased at the souk. "Nisrina . . . do you understand so little about this world, about this city? Do you think that you can come to us from your village and enter the University without the slightest of consequences . . . without penalty or cost? You come here not knowing how to read or write. You do not even possess the lessons of our faith or know how to recite our prayers."

Nisrina's eyes were wide. She was trembling. What could she do or say to make Magda understand? How could she help her realize that she meant no harm? She wanted a chance to learn, and then return home. She would never see her again. She meant no injury toward her or her friends.

Magda continued, "Do you think you can just walk in and take over as first chair, *my chair*, with so little effort? Do you think this action against me is justified? Hm?"

She pushed against Nisrina's shoulder. Just a small shove, but it unsteadied her. She stumbled back.

Magda did not pause, "Do you think that you're the first woman to lose a husband? Many women have lost their husbands in the war, many men have not returned to their wives and families, but I have seen no others arrive on the doorstep of our church and ask for undue consideration. How does your loss warrant such privilege? Tell me Nisrina, what is so special about your Jabran?" Her voice was cruel, unyielding.

Nisrina had heard enough. It was one thing to endure insults and innuendos against her religion and her lack of education, against her background and upbringing, but to speak disrespectfully of the memory of her husband, her dear sweet Jabran, the gentlest, kindest man she had ever known, was more than she could tolerate.

"I may be poor," she said to Magda, "but I can assure you that what I have, I have earned through my own hard work. And do not speak to me of my husband. His name and his memory are sacred! They are not to be sullied by your spiteful lips!"

Nisrina dropped her packages, her fists were clenched, her face inches from Magda's. Months of silence, of taunts and insults were over. She was ready for the fight.

But before she could speak another word, Magda's fist was pummeling deep into Nisrina's stomach. She tried to catch her breath, to regain her position and contend with her foe. But she was on bended knees, given no chance to rise up. What seemed like a hundred hands were striking her body, the four girls slapping her from every direction. She put her arms up over her head and prayed that it would soon be over.

Suddenly, a searing pain erupted in Nisrina's left ear. She felt the warm blood trickling down her cheek and across her face. Through the stars now dancing before her eyes, Nisrina saw the jagged crack in the stone floor. It grew larger as her head fell fast to the ground, smacking firm against the hard, cold pavement.

Everything went black.

She was spared the memory of the kicks and taunts that followed—the charges into her stomach, her groin, and her legs. She never heard the girls' cruel laughter as they congratulated one another and ran off like restless thieves into the night.

Nor did Nisrina feel the two large arms that several hours later, scooped her up and ever so carefully, ever so tenderly, carried her back to the safety and sanctity of the old stone nunnery.

THIRTY SIX

Alodia

WHEN NISRINA HAD FAILED to return to the dormitory, her room empty and her bed unslept in, Sister Miriam had gone directly to Sister Alodia for assistance. Together, they alerted the Mother Superior who instructed a full search of the campus.

But it was Sister Alodia who found her.

The Sister feared the worst. In the moment her eyes beheld the bloody body sprawled on the stone walkway, her soul shattered and her heart grew despondent. She felt this undoing to be no fault but her own.

How could she have treated this young woman with such ill will upon her arrival? She chastised herself for having labeled the girl a mongrel. What right had she to instigate such a flagrant degradation? Was this girl who came so humble and bruised, any different than the girl she once was—a heartbroken child arriving in the dead of night on the steps of the Convent of the Sisters of Mercy, her only possessions the clothes on her back, her heart shattered and shamed?

In her unleashed grief, Alodia's memories came flooding back like the mighty waters of the River Nile. They were vivid, precise, as if only yesterday. A soul in need of compassion. A love forever lost.

From the time she was a very young girl, Margarit Louseres Bedrosian always knew she would become a nun. It was a rite of passage that her parents had raised her to expect and a calling that she herself had accepted with grace and humility. Her family lived in a small Armenian village located in the rural countryside, deep within the Turkish-ruled Ottoman Empire. There they lived and farmed the land, a simple life, close to the earth and steeped deeply within their faith—the Armenian Church.

So it came as quite a surprise to Margarit when she found herself, at the young age of fourteen, standing beneath the mulberry tree in her father's northern pasture passionately kissing her long time neighbor and friend, Aram Arcopian, her fingers moving through his thick, black hair, her labored breath coming in measured heaves.

It had started as only a mild flirtation on his part, or so it seemed. He was teasing her for carrying her father's sickle on her hip as only a man would do. And indeed, she had no difficulty lifting the heavy tool, for she'd been blessed with large, strong arms, something that she'd often been teased about, and for this, felt overly self-conscious. But nevertheless, her female pride had gotten the best of her and she'd thrown the tool down alongside the dusty dirt road and stood there with fists clenched at her hips as she snarled angrily in his direction.

"I can lift like a man and I can fight like a man! So, you, Aram Arcopian, had better take heed of that fact!"

"No, it is you, Margarit," he replied tauntingly, "who had better take heed of the fact that you are a woman! And to do a woman's work is a gift from God. A gift of immeasurable riches . . ."

"And what exactly is it that you would have this woman do?" Margarit interrupted, her face flushed by his impertinence. She had not yet thought of herself as a woman, only a young girl destined to cook in her mother's kitchen and work hard on her father's farm until the joyful day when she would willingly give herself to the Church like her older sibling, Sister Mary Esther had done, dedicating her life in service to the Lord.

Aram was well aware of Margarit's plans, for she spoke of nothing else and he knew that he would not, or could not accept her decision to wed the Church. The fact of the matter was that he wanted her as his wife, and had wished this quietly to himself since they were young children playing together in the fields and climbing the rocky hills that surrounded their village. He loved to watch her wrinkle her nose when she was angry or upset, and he chuckled at the lively tempo with which she chanted her hymns. He always warmed at her dinner table, her breads and pastries like none other in their village. And although he could never find the words to ask her, he felt that she loved him too.

"I would have you wed me!" he finally blurted out, much to his own surprise.

"Wed you?!" she retaliated.

"Yes. And is that so terrible?" He puffed up his chest and took in a deep breath, turning directly to face her. "You must know how I feel about you Margarit."

His voice had softened, his tone alluring.

Margarit quickly turned her head away from him. The boldness of his disclosure disturbing to her. It was contrary to all that she had been taught, all that she had come to expect of her life. A life that had been pre-planned, pre-destined since she was a mere child tugging at her mother's dusty skirt; and now his reckless proposal was quite intolerable, his words piercing straight through her, stabbing her chest.

But he did not allow her turned stance and seeming indifference to deter him. He had waited too long for this encounter. The time was now at hand. Her days as a free woman were short-lived and he knew that she would soon be moving to a convent to learn the ways of the Sisterhood and take her vows of obedience and servitude.

He moved closer to her. Slowly, as if he were gliding through air, his feet hovering silently above the earth. She could feel his warm breath on her cheek, as his eyes began to frantically search her face for signs of reciprocity.

He was convinced that she loved him as much as he loved her.

If only she would look at me, he was thinking to himself. If only her eyes would gaze into mine. Then I would know for sure.

As if reading his mind and knowing his thoughts, Margarit continued to look away, not wanting her face to belie her long-held position of fidelity to the Church.

But he had come too far now. For him, there was no turning back. He had spoken his heart. He must know her response. He reached out to her and took her arms in his strong hands, his fingers wrapping easily around her well-formed biceps. As large as her arms were, his hands were larger and he had no trouble holding her firmly, pulling her closer to him.

Margarit felt the soft Mediterranean breeze that was drifting through the olive trees. She could hear the rustle of the leaves and the chirping of the crickets. Her senses were enlivened as her heart began to race. He drew her nearer, her legs becoming weak and her back soft. She could no longer think through the cloud of unleashed emotions, fearful by the very nearness of him. With her world spinning out of control, she could not find the words to protest his behavior. For the first time in her life, Margarit began to feel. The sensations were unfamiliar, they puzzled and confused her. She felt vulnerable in front of her childhood friend, her solid armor splintering like fragile glass, fragments in a storm.

As he held her tightly, she tried to push him away. Her hands were on his chest, her face turned to the side.

"Look into my eyes, Margarit," he was saying to her. "Look into my eyes and tell me that you don't love me as deeply as I love you."

Margarit was emboldened by his challenge. She would look directly into this foolish boy's eyes and speak the words he'd defied her to say. She would tell him that she didn't love him, for she loved God with all her heart and all her thoughts. She had no trouble with that dispute. Bravely, she turned her head back to face the brazen young lad who knew nothing of what constituted true love and devotion, certainly not the kind of love she felt for her Lord. She looked straight into his lovelorn face. But as she did she felt a change—soft scatterings like snowflakes from the sky. She saw the light brown color of his eyes and the tiny green and golden specks that danced there. She watched as they glistened in the reflection of the noonday light. As hard as she tried, she could not break her gaze. For Margarit was seeing the likeness of her own love in his face.

As their eyes locked, she could not speak the words he had challenged her to say. Aram saw her hesitation and he pulled her closer still. He was breathing heavily now and his breaths both frightened and enlivened her.

Margarit could not tell if she had pushed her mouth to his or if he'd been the one to touch her lips first. She could no longer think for herself. Nor did she want to. At first it was soft, slow, barely a whisper of a kiss. She could only feel. And as she surrendered to her senses, her body filled with warmth like the evening kettle on her mother's hearth. She felt the glorious vibration of love as it lifted her off the ground and twirled her through the air, high above the branches of the olive trees, the almond orchard and over the mighty cypress. It surged into her finger tips, her chest, traveling down her jellied spine. The unleashed passion magnificent. She wanted to crawl inside of him, to become one with him, and she yearned to have him crawl inside of her. He felt her fervor and pressed his lips hard against hers, his mouth engulfing her mouth. As he did, she did not resist. She could not refuse him. She found her lips pressing even tighter, surrendering all she was to the young Arcopian boy.

In that moment of surrender, Margarit realized that her life had forever changed. How could she give her body and soul to God now? She had already given her heart to Aram Arcopian, and she felt neither shame nor regret.

Margarit's father and mother were not pleased.

When their daughter came to them, with eyes wide and cheeks flushed, they saw the change in her. Only moments earlier they'd seen the young Arcopian boy walking away, up the path towards his home, as Margarit floated in through the old wooden gate. Her parents glanced at one another, a merging of minds. And hence, were not surprised when Margarit, who had always been honest and direct, told them straightaway of her undying love for Aram and how she could no longer honor her pledge to the Church.

Salem Bedrosian understood the delicate implications. He had watched the two young people since they were first born. Their mothers were neighbors and close friends who shared chores, outdoor ovens and food from the fields. When the two women gave birth within three days of each other, they naturally raised their children together. And so, as their mothers worked and visited side-by-side, the children did likewise. The babies were placed on the same blanket together where they were fed and changed, sometimes even nursing from the same breast when one of their mothers was taken ill or was too busy to stop and feed them. As toddlers, the two youths had walked for the first time holding on to each other's hands, taking their first steps in concert with their mothers' urgings, and laughing together their first laughs.

Looking back, Salem Bedrosian realized it was no surprise that it should one day come to this. He had been given all the warning signs, but had refused to acknowledge them. They were only friends, he kept telling himself over the years, no, actually they were more than friends, they were like siblings. Would a sister marry her brother? Unheard of! Furthermore, he was comforted in the fact that everyone knew that Margarit had been promised to the Church as her older sister had been. He owed it to the Church, everyone knew that. For it was the kindly priests who had kept his family fed during times of famine. And it was they who sheltered them after the great fire devoured his home. No one knew better than Salem Bedrosian that his wife and children would have starved if not for the undying compassion of the Armenian priests. And in turn he had promised them both his daughters—to serve the Church for all their days. So now, when his sweet, young Margarit came to him, her lips still red and inflamed where she'd pressed them hard against the boy next door, he knew that he had to carefully handle the matter.

"Margarit," her father began, his voice well-paced. "Margarit," he repeated. "I can understand that you have had a flight of fancy for young Aram. It is not uncommon. He has a comely stature, and you are becoming a woman. These things are not unheard of."

Margarit's mother nodded wisely, but she knew it was best to remain silent and let her husband take charge.

"My dear, sweet Margarit," he continued, his hand resting lightly on the top of his young daughter's head. "As you well know, our family would have died many times had it not been for the compassion and charity of the Church. We owe them our lives and our never-ending gratitude. They have seen us through the starvation of the famine, and the homelessness of the fire. They held you when you cried and fed you when you hungered. You are surely as much a child of theirs as you are my own."

Margarit's eyes were tearing up. She was shaking her head. She knew what her father was saying. She'd heard it before, but not now, she thought to herself. She could not bear to hear it said now. Things had changed. Could he not see that? Could he not feel her suffering? Her love?

"Margarit," he repeated her name. "It is not only a matter of divine fate, but also a matter of honor. I cannot allow you to disgrace our family by refusing to take the veil for which you've been promised. There simply is no recourse. The decision is made."

Margarit was sobbing now. Inconsolable. Her face buried in her hands. She knew there'd be no changing his mind. She realized that behind his amiable manner was a man for whom the church meant all, his kindness tempered. For most fathers would have taken the rod to their daughters by now. She also knew that despite his gentle way, the harsh decision would never be altered.

"But father, I love him!" the words spilled from her mouth.

"I'm sorry daughter."

"How can I tell him?" she cried. "How will I find the voice?"

"I will tell him." It was a statement made, not for discussion.

"No, father. No, please . . ."

But it was no use. Her father had already wrapped his cloak around his shoulders, positioning the small fez hat upon his head. Stoically, he walked out the door as poor Margarit collapsed to the floor.

That was the final time that Margarit spoke of her love for Aram.

The next day, she learned that he'd been sent away. She knew not where and dared not ask. Rumors from the villagers spoke of his being sent to The Silent Brotherhood, an isolated monastery in the hills to the north, to serve out his life. Others claimed he was sent to America to work in the cloth business with distant relatives. But it mattered not where he had gone, for to Margarit, the love of her life was as good as dead.

Three days after Aram was sent away, Margarit, too, left her childhood home to fulfill her destiny with the Church. However, word of her illicit behavior had spread throughout their small village and the priests of her childhood would no longer have her. They rebuked her and turned her away. Her parents were humiliated. They could no longer keep the daughter who had brought their family such shame; and the Church would not take her.

Inquiries were made and journeys taken, while the shunned young woman lived in the barn outside her family's home.

Finally arrangements were made for her to attend a Catholic convent far away in the land of all things Holy—a church that would turn away no soul, no matter how foul their stench. There she would take the vows of a new faith and become a new woman. Chaste once again, she'd become one of their own.

Margarit said her final goodbyes to her mother and father who stood on the side of the road, holding tightly each other's arms. Whispering words she refused to hear, they bade farewell to the daughter they could not know. Through tear-filled eyes they watched, in a waveless parting, as she rode away on a mule-drawn cart, knowing they would never see their child again.

Margarit arrived at the small teaching convent in the City of Jerusalem where, giving up all earthly things, she entered the strict ways of the Sisterhood. She shed her clothing and her undergarments and donned the scratchy, woolen cloths and habit of the postulant. Her clothes, her scarves, and the thin golden bracelet that once belonged to her mother were placed in a trunk and sold to the shopkeepers for charitable use.

There, amongst the starkness that she now called her home, she lived a chaste and unforgiving life, her first year spent in atoned silence; her meals shared without a spoken word. Each Friday she assembled with the other postulants for the Chapter of Faults where she publicly confessed her indiscretions, receiving a weekly penance from the Mother Superior. Her mail was intercepted, read and discarded, never knowing if a soul had reached out to her.

And thus Margarit Bedrosian persevered until her heart was pure once again.

When she was deemed ready, she took her final vows and chose for herself a new name—Alodia, meaning riches. For through the Church's teachings, she finally realized that her life was rich in her unwavering love and dedication to the Lord.

THIRTY SEVEN

Renewed Hope

THE SMELL OF CHICKEN boiling in aromatic spices of cinnamon, ginger, and curry was the first of Nisrina's senses to announce that she had rejoined the world of the living, followed promptly by the sounds of pans clattering and a soft, melodic hymn being hummed nearby.

As Sister Alodia prepared dinner for the women of the convent, she kept a careful eye on the beaten and battered girl who lay motionless in the corner of the room. The old cook had insisted a small cot be placed inside her kitchen as she worked. In that way she could watch for any signs or stirrings from the sleeping woman, her once pretty face now swollen and blue.

The familiar smells and sounds were soothing to Nisrina and she allowed them to comfort her. She did not remember the confrontation with Magda Attia. The slaps, the punches and kicks, endured only three short days ago, were buried deep in her memory. For now, she only knew that she was in a warm, comfortable place. She was not alone. And her mind would let her go no further.

The hours passed as Nisrina slowly came to her senses. Finally, her eyes opened. And, with the almost imperceptible sound of her lashes separating, Sister Alodia turned her head and saw her young student come back to life. She dropped her ladle into its pot and rushed to Nisrina's side.

"Praise be to *Allah*," she cried out as she knelt down beside her.

Nisrina softly smiled up at her, and seeing that tender little smile, Sister Alodia began to weep. It was the first time that the old nun had wept in many years. In her training she'd been taught to be stoic in the face of adversity and to always put her faith in the hands of the Lord. But her capacity to endure had finally reached its threshold. Perhaps it was her advancing age that weakened her resolve, or the similarity of a young girl's heartache that moved her so. But whatever the cause, years of emotions that had been bottled up came rushing out. The memories and pain that had been disallowed and disavowed poured to the surface. She clasped her hands to her chest as her heart once again ached for the love of a boy who'd been abruptly taken from her, and she sobbed at the thought of a lifetime lost.

She was unashamed as she knelt down and wept at the bedside of this young girl. This non-Catholic child whom God had so justly put in her care. Alodia knew that it was no coincidence that she was the one to find Nisrina. It was no accident that her arms were the vehicles that so carefully carried her back to safety. Back into the light and sanctity of the nunnery. It was evident to her that God had led her to that dark corner in the alleyway. His intentions clear. He had placed this ward in her compassionate charge. And now it was Alodia's task to nurture, comfort and protect this girl, as she had once longed it be done for her.

Watching the old nun bent and weeping, Nisrina reached out and gently placed her hand atop Alodia's bowed head.

"Sister, why do you weep so?"

"I weep for my soul, child."

"I'm sorry Sister, I don't understand." Nisrina's voice was weak.

"I weep from relief, knowing that you are back with us. I weep for mercy, that my sins be forgiven. And I weep for joy, in the knowledge that God in his compassionate grace has given us both a second chance."

Nisrina was tired. She heard the old nun's words but they did not make sense to her. She did not understand. Her memory of the beating lay suspended in the recesses of her mind. She only knew that there was warmth coming from the kitchen fire, and the fragrant scents from the old cook's bosom, aromas from years of cooking and baking and spicing and herbing seeped deeply into her core and they comforted her. And with nothing more than a whisper and a smile she closed her eyes again and drifted back into a sound sleep.

PART FOUR

1920

I leave you now. I cannot stay.
But know that I will always love you.
One day I pray you'll understand.
My flesh departs, my soul remains.
And though our hands no longer meet,
You'll touch me always in my heart.

THIRTY EIGHT

And Home Again

"QUICKLY, NISRINA, THE CEREMONY is about to start!"

"I'm coming, Sister Miriam. I'm just having trouble tying my scarf."

The two girls had just finished dressing and were now running across the campus trying to get to the graduation ceremony on time. Nisrina was graduating first in her class and had been asked to give a speech at the commencement. She had been practicing all week with the help and encouragement of Sisters Miriam and Alodia. Since her mishap, Sister Alodia had taken full responsibility for Nisrina, watching over her like a mother hen. Nisrina only too pleased to receive her caring attentions.

It had been over a month since the unfortunate encounter with Magda Attia and her staunch coterie. However, the assailants were never publically named as Nisrina refused to identify her attackers, who mysteriously enough, were called back home a few short days following the incident. Pulled out of school, the four students were returned to their families on the questionable pretense of pending marriage proposals and flourishing courtships. By the time Nisrina had fully recovered, the girls were gone from the school and her forgiving nature saw no purpose in exposing them to the strict laws of the land. The thought of seeing her classmates suffer beatings or imprisonment was not something she cared to initiate. She chose to forgive and forget, the secret hers to keep.

With the love and support of the Sisters she had healed body and soul, save one remaining consequence of her beating. The final blow delivered by Magda had left Nisrina deaf in her left ear, requiring her to turn her head in the direction of a speaker. It gave her an affected tendency to tilt her head to one side, making her seem inquisitive or thoughtful.

"Fellow students, teachers, and blessed Sisters of Mercy . . . I stand before you today, your humble servant. I came to you six short months ago unable to read or write, my life shattered, my children left behind. And together, we have learned, we have grown, we have risen high, above all expectations; and now we stand united as sisters, as *dayahs*, women with honor, hope and a bright future. Your support and teachings have become my salvation and I will be forever grateful. As I look out at all the familiar faces, I know that each one of you will go forward, reaching out to your communities. And using the knowledge and skills that we have gained here, make the world a better place . . . for women, for children, and for our families. We are part of a greater good. We are watched over by a higher power. And in His mercy, we have been blessed by our creator, our Lord, *Allah el Akbar,* God is Great."

The crowd roared. Nisrina paused, waiting for them to quiet. Finally she continued, "And although I leave here today, I do not leave alone, for I take a part of each of you with me. I take you in my heart, in my mind, and in my soul. God be with you."

She did not expect the standing ovation. The crowd was cheering. They were clapping and smiling. She represented all women and the hope for a new future. Nisrina, standing at the lectern, smiled back at them, but in her mind she had already left this place. She was thinking of the upcoming reunion with her children, her home, and her village.

Although she shared it with no living soul, she continued to hold a constant and never ending hope that her beloved Jabran was still alive. Somewhere. Out there. One day waiting to come home to her. And in that hope she found sustenance.

She stepped from the bus, the driver carelessly watching her descent, hastily closing the doors behind her. A squeak, a groan and he drove away, the departing breeze blowing powdery ashes in moon-shaped swirls around her feet. Nisrina stood there, satchel in hand, her eyes shielded while the dirt and debris settled back to the earth. The bus' disappearance left a vacuum where emptiness took hold. The air was still. No sounds could be heard except the faint cry of a bird off in the distance.

Nisrina had forgotten the quiet tranquility that made up the fabric of country life. For the past six months she'd become accustomed to classrooms and schedules and lessons to be learned. Outside the walls of the convent lay the never-ending movement of the city, its singular pulse thundering unguarded through the narrowed cobblestone streets—merchants in the *souk* calling out, their wares unsurpassed; the yellows, oranges, reds and greens of the vegetable stands; and butchers with storefronts of freshly cut lamb. There were shoppers pausing at carts of dried fruits or imported silk scarves, their wrangling voices lifting high in the air; the donkeys' clamoring hooves against hardened stone roads; and melodic calls to prayers from tall minarets.

But now, as she stood alone on the solitary dirt road that led into town, the calm of the countryside came back to her. A world that moved unhurried. Its pace, measured by the hues of the hillsides and the scent of the breeze. Where white wispy clouds acted as sentinels drifting in a silent show of slow motion. Here, there were no distant calls to prayer. No towering minarets or giant cathedrals reaching up to take her breath away. Beit el Jebel was a rural village where people spent their days under the sky's broad canopy. Working from dawn till dusk, families were spread out, tucked away amongst the grains of the fields and the fruits of the orchards. The sounds of the village were soft and gentle. And the only calls to worship were heard on Sunday when the clang of church bells rang out.

Nisrina put her satchel down and looked around. She took in a deep breath. The rich, fragrant scents of sage and wildflowers slowed her pulse. She heard the whisper of the wind through the trees, and the sound of a bird's wings flying somewhere overhead. It all came back to her. This was her life. This was her world. It was good to be home.

As reality took hold, Nisrina realized that something was missing. This was the Beit el Jebel bus stop; there was no doubt about that. It was the only one that came anywhere near her town, located off the main road on the south end of the village. But no one was there. No one had come to greet her. Where were her children with loving smiles and excited hugs? No sisters-in-law with stories to tell and ears to listen. Nor elders finally delivering solicitous nods.

There was only quiet.

Nisrina wondered . . . had they not received her letter? The note written for her by Sister Miriam telling them the news of her graduation, the honor of being chosen first in her class, and her arrival time and day? She knew it had been sent. She had walked with Sister Miriam into town to post it. Surely they must have received it by now. Perhaps they mistook the arrival date.

There had to be an explanation. There had to be. But still, a foreboding overtook her senses.

Nisrina bent down and picked up her satchel. For the first time she noticed its tattered edges and marred surface. The tapestry faded and dirty. It had been lent to her by Lamia. Together they had packed it, six long months ago. They had placed it on the bed in her bedroom, and with mixed emotions filled it with the few belongings and necessities that she owned. Nisrina knew that although it was sparse in content it held many hopes. Lamia had told her that it would bring her good fortune as it had been a gift to her on the day she departed for school. Nisrina had smiled gratefully, assuring Lamia that the bag would serve her well, and it had.

Now, having returned a *dayah*, she stood alone at the bus stop, her destiny waiting.

She turned towards town and silently began her solitary walk home.

As she approached the center of town, Nisrina noticed the black shrouds that covered the windows and doors of the village. The streets were empty. Someone had died. It was clear now why her family had not greeted her at the bus stop. Her thoughts were no longer of herself. A loved one had been lost. The town was in mourning. Nisrina knew what she had to do. As the town's people had shared in her joys and sorrows, she must now put aside her happiness to share in their grief. But the question remained—whose loss? She pulled a long, black scarf from her bag, wrapped it around her head and shoulders and hurried towards the center of town.

As she approached the town square she could see the funeral procession not far ahead. Falling into place at the back of the crowd, her face partially covered by her shroud, Nisrina wondered who it was that had passed. Which family from their small village was suffering the angst of loss? Within moments Nisrina felt a hand on her left shoulder, she turned, it was Fareeda Sumara, the woman who ran the seamstress shop in the village.

"Nisrina, my child, you do not belong back here. You must move up to the front with your family."

Nisrina's face went pale. Her head turned far to the left straining to hear from her good ear. "I don't understand." It was all she could muster.

"You have not heard? Forgive me, of course not, you must have just returned!" Fareeda noticed the suitcase in her hand. "Forgive me. It's Farooz. It was his heart. He was harvesting the figs, the ones from Jabran's orchard. He fell to the ground. Gone in an instant. Thank God, he didn't suffer. It's been two days now. Forgive me. I am so sorry for your loss. God be with you."

Nisrina's legs became weak, her knees buckling under her. She had only heard part of the words as she turned her right ear to Fareeda's voice. Fareeda thought she didn't understand as the affectation gave Nisrina a curious look. And no one in the village was aware of Nisrina's mishap or her diminished ability to hear.

"It's your father-in-law, Nisrina. It's Farooz, he's dead," she repeated firmly.

And with that Fareeda grabbed Nisrina's arm and led her to the front of the funeral procession where she placed her in line with the others. She saw her children walking beside their aunties. She let out an unexpected cry and they turned to see her.

"*Yumma, yumma,*" they called, running to her.

"Oh my darlings . . ."

Dropping her satchel, she held out her hands as they fell into her arms. She hugged them, devouring the feel of their bodies and the scent of their skin. Tears poured down her face as she showered them with kisses—on their hair, their foreheads, their cheeks and eyes. With tiny sounds of joy escaping from her lips, she hugged them again and again, savoring the softness of their flesh and relishing in their joy.

The crowd of mourners, with faces pale and eyes of sorrow, silently stopped the procession. They turned their heads to observe the homecoming. Not a word was spoken, not a whisper hushed. Behind their shrouds of black, the Yusef women, Dora and Mona, Marta and May wore wistful smiles and shed bittersweet tears as they watched the children reuniting with their mother. Najeeb and Jacob, both carrying their father's casket, saw how mother and children embraced each other. Jacob shed a tear as he saw his nieces and nephew take hold of their mother's arms, refusing to let go. But Najeeb, now the eldest member and new head of the Yusef family, mustered neither a tear nor a smile. His lips were terse as he watched the sentimental reunion, and through glaring eyes he noticed the change in Nisrina. A change of which, she herself was unaware. She'd left Beit el Jebel a frightened girl, unsure and shy, and had returned a confident woman, a *dayah*. The Nisrina who stood just steps away had a newfound maturity. She was self-assured and poised—and the sight of it incensed him. He remained silent, and after a moment, the crowd turned back to complete their escort to the cemetery.

Nisrina could see that her children had grown taller in the six months since she'd seen them. Her heart swelled with pride, but she knew that she must maintain her composure in respect for her family's loss. Dutifully, she marched on with the others, keeping her eyes straight ahead, all the while aching to stop and hold her little ones in her arms again. She glanced at her sisters-in-law, their faces covered, their heads bent down, and she ached for them.

It was known to all that Farooz had been the patriarch who held their family together, and it was an undeniable fact that he would be dearly missed. She watched her brothers-in-law carrying the casket of their deceased father through the quiet streets of Beit el Jebel, and silently said a prayer.

THIRTY NINE

Najeeb

THE WIFE OF FAROOZ had died many years before him; thusly, as he passed into the great beyond, there was no widow to suffer the loss. And although the village people showed their respect for the mourning family by forgiving them their debts and helping them to tend their orchards, behind closed doors it was being whispered that the patriarch's reputation for women and wine had at last taken its toll. With windows closed and shutters drawn, hushed voices proclaimed in the night that the self indulged patriarch had finally gotten his due and it was high time he answered to his dearly departed wife, a sweet woman who had not deserved his philandering ways. But there were others who insisted it was a man's prerogative to enjoy the sensuous pleasures of the flesh. After all, he was a man and not beholding to any woman's scrutiny. They maintained that it is the woman who must know her place, while a man is free to enjoy his liberties.

As the eldest son, Najeeb was now the new head of the Yusef family. Although short in height, he was considered a large man, his girth looming portentously over the members of his family. Najeeb resembled his father in appearance, his nose was large with a crooked hook, his eyes dark, deep set, and buried under a thick, heavy brow.

And like his father, Najeeb partook in the excesses of life—women, drink, and smoke his regular companions. But unlike his father, who regularly practiced the ways of civil diplomacy, Najeeb's manner was crude and abrupt. A cruel master who demanded unreasonable deference from all he encountered, he extended no regard to decency or proper social behavior.

So it came as no surprise that when the father died, the family suffered more than just the loss of the old patriarch—they also suffered a new repression under the rule of the son. And living in a small village as they did, with lives interconnected in every way, there were few events that could be easily concealed. Consequently, at the end of each day, when darkness had descended upon the town, the people of Beit el Jebel turned away their faces and spoke in quiet whispers to one another, lamenting the unfortunate fate of a once proud and honorable family.

"What is this?" Najeeb abruptly threw the cloths on the floor. "Do you expect me to pay for these unworthy fabrics? How dare you come into my home and insult my wife in this manner?!"

"But, *Ya Ummo*, these are the finest cloths from Damascus. I chose them myself!"

The cloth merchant was shaking. He had dreaded his meeting with Najeeb, as the elder's reputation for severity and bad-temper had now spread well beyond the boundaries of Beit el Jebel. And even though he called him, *Ummo*, a title of respect and deference, the high regard was not reciprocated.

"Then you are a fool! A donkey's ass!" Najeeb continued. "Why my young servant could select better than this! Must I send a child with you to do your work? *Imshee, Yullah*! Be gone from my home! You are no longer welcome here!"

Najeeb's face turned red, his arms waving wildly as insults hurled from his mouth. Rising from his seat, he raised his arm, about to thrash the merchant who sat trembling before him, and just as his hand was about to descend, he saw a young girl standing outside his home. She was minding a complacent donkey, her eyes cast downward, her face hidden by the shadows of a pomegranate tree. But as the setting sun shone down upon her honey-colored *thobe* it cast an outline of her form and the vision aroused him. Her hair, modestly covered with a scarf, defied its delicate cloaking, the breeze blowing small wisps out onto her shoulders. Its color was golden brown and when she moved, the errant strands shimmered and glistened in the bright sun.

"Hm. Pray tell me, is that your animal resting under my pomegranate tree?" Najeeb's eyes were squinting against the light.

"Yes, sir, he is a good animal and spares my back from a heavy load," the merchant responded.

"And the girl that stands there with him, holding his reins . . . she is a comely lass, who, I dare say, might serve my favor. Is that your servant girl?"

"Why, no, sir!" the merchant jumped up, the hair bristling on the back of his neck. "That young lady is my daughter! And I demand the respect she is due! My servant indeed!"

The merchant's temples were throbbing as he stood to leave. His only child, she was his pride and joy. He saw the bestial look in Najeeb's eyes and he regretted the day that he'd agreed to come to the Yusef compound. He deplored the impoverished circumstances that required him to degrade himself in this manner. He'd always been a respected merchant who traveled through many countries to sell his wares. But the war had taken its toll on many of the smaller villages, his patrons choosing to make do with what little they had, the wealthier of them journeying to nearby cities to purchase their cloths.

"That is too bad," Najeeb offered. "For she truly tempts my passions." He began to twirl his mustache, a chortling noise emerging from a place deep in his throat.

The merchant trembled. He'd heard the stories of the elder Yusef's wicked mind and he felt it wiser to confront him no further; his only choice was to depart and to do so with haste.

He ran out the door. Neither bidding Najeeb farewell, nor stopping to retrieve the beautiful cloths he'd brought with him. Left strewn on the floor, he willingly sacrificed them to save his daughter's honor.

Once outside, he motioned to the unsuspecting girl, and grabbing the donkey's reins they hurriedly ran from the Yusef compound.

Najeeb laughed crudely as he watched the two of them flee. Then he stopped, his eyes narrowing as he twirled his mustache, first to the right and then the left. He would find them later, he thought to himself. There was only one road into and out of the village. The sun would soon disappear behind the mountain, they couldn't go far. No doubt they'd be camped alongside the road sleeping under the stars, and then he would have his way—later the young maiden would thank him.

Deliciously tucking those thoughts to the side of his mind, Najeeb strutted back and forth on the sitting room floor, his protruding stomach leading the way, his large hips bringing in the rear. He rocked on his heels at every turn looking down at the beautiful cloths he'd garnered, congratulating himself on the well-run transaction. He smiled wickedly. He'd gotten a better price than even he'd expected. Yes, a very good price indeed.

"Marta! Get in here, *Yullah*!" Najeeb yelled to his wife.

"Yes, my husband, how may I serve you?"

"What does a man have to do for a cup of coffee in his own home!? Is this the way you reward my indulgence?"

"Forgive me, my love. It is done, it is done," she replied.

"And there," he gestured to the owing cloths still strewn on the sitting room floor, "There are the fabrics for the dresses you have been hounding me about. Get them out of my sight! It's about time you took more care in your appearance."

"Yes, my love. They are beautiful. God bless your generosity. Thank you. Thank you."

Marta went down on her knees and gathered the rolls from the floor. They were beautifully textured, exotic fabrics ranging in a variety of rich, jewel-toned colors, made from the finest of silks, linens, and Egyptian cottons. She marveled at their beauty and was honored that she'd been treated to such extravagance.

"Wait!" he grabbed her arm, his fingers leaving marks on her skin. "This cloth here . . ." He pointed to a fabric, a cerulean shade of blue, its vibrant color interlaced delicately with soft golden threads. "I want you to make a dress for Nisrina with that cloth. I think the color will suit her skin well . . ."

Marta stared up at her husband.

On more than one occasion she'd noticed how Najeeb had watched Nisrina on her way to the chicken shed. How when she lifted the hem of her *thobe* and stepped lightly over the muddied threshold her bare heels would catch the early morn's light. She observed how, when this happened, her husband's thoughts went astray, not hearing her words. And she became aware of his eyes lighting up when the young widow delivered the eggs to their door. She knew her husband to be a man of strong needs, and as his wife, she serviced him well. But now, to choose the most lively of cloths for Nisrina? And expect her, the wife of the eldest, to stitch them for her? The blood boiled beneath her skin. Then her eyes caught his glare.

Moving as quickly as she could, taking care not to rumple the fabrics, she ran out of the room, readied to prepare a pot of hot coffee for her generous husband.

FORTY

The Tyrant and the British Colonel

IT WAS NOT UNCOMMON for Nisrina to be called out in the middle of the night, leaving her children to assist a woman in labor. Farms were spread throughout the mountainside, and the trek to reach an expectant mother, at times proved daunting. If she could, Nisrina would often ride her husband's donkey, Abu Faraj, to the home of a mother in need, the animal's sure-footed gait safely manipulating the tangled twists and turns of the steep mountain paths. If the donkey had labored particularly hard that day, she would simply take off on foot. Grabbing her bag, she'd run, her chest heaving, her bare feet sparing no pain. She'd often travel for miles before she'd reach a young mother laboring with child. At times it might be hours or possibly days before Nisrina could complete her work and return home. And if she was called to go to another village, she might not see her family for a week or more.

Dora watched over the children in Nisrina's absence. They'd become accustomed to her even-handed ways, and felt nurtured by her hearty, well-seasoned cooking. She'd often gather them around her and tell stories. Her tales always included a lesson that taught them honesty and kindness towards others. They'd laugh out loud as their old auntie imitated the sounds of animals, and they'd shudder, wide-eyed as she'd feign a monster's evil moan. But no matter the feast and no matter the tale, upon hearing Nisrina's footsteps, Essam, Jameela and Hannah would fly from the comfort of the old maid's bosom and run out to greet their mother. They'd jump into her arms, and one-by-one she'd twirl them around.

The months passed and word spread of Nisrina's hard work and forthright manner; her talents, now being discussed not only in the village of Beit el Jebel, but also in neighboring towns. The people spoke of her skill in assisting young women, and her name appeared in favor on expectant mothers' lips. The new *dayah* soon became known as *Oum el Loulad*, the Mother to All Children. But despite the admiration and recognition that preceded her, Nisrina remained humble and loving, and in her humility she was beautiful.

As things would have it, her beauty did not go unnoticed.

More than a year had passed since Nisrina had formally mourned the loss of her husband. And now, many men in the village began to make inquiries after her. As custom dictated, the subject of matrimony was transacted with the family elder. Men would come to visit. They'd bring their fathers and uncles and have closed-door discussions with Najeeb. Nisrina unaware of their proposals.

"She's a beautiful woman," one man would say.

"Surely she must be available now," another would insist.

But Najeeb repeatedly discouraged the suitors.

"No, she is not ready for marriage. Enough time has not passed," he would argue. If he were particularly agitated by the admirer, he'd say, "She is devoted to her children and will never leave their sides, especially not for the likes of you!" Then he'd throw them out of his house as he had done to the cloth merchant.

Interestingly enough, although these matters were never discussed with Nisrina, Najeeb's refusals were in line with her feelings. Nisrina remained convinced that Jabran was still alive and would return to her one day, and as she had told the family the first time re-marriage was proposed to her, she would never leave her children to take her place beside another man.

Najeeb was aware of her feelings. But they were not the reason he deflected her suitors.

It was time for the date festival, and the Yusef family had joined the rest of the village for a walk into town. Merchants from neighboring towns would be there to sell their wares and the anticipation was infectious. Games and toys were set up for the children with prizes to be won. The women of the Yusef family had worked many hours to make items to sell at the booths, and together Nisrina and Marta had sewn beautiful clothes for the children to wear.

Dora brought jars of pickled olives, the fruit picked from her father's orchard. She had the gift of knowing the exact combinations of spices and herbs needed to create the most delectable flavors. She never measured her ingredients and preferred to vary them from jar to jar, no two ever the same. In some, she'd use a combination of crushed coriander seeds and fresh garlic, while others were infused with rosemary and peppercorns. One of her favorite techniques was to add the foliage of the hardy fennel plant. Its wispy leaves, combined with slices of oranges and lemons, could be seen floating at the jar's edge. The fragrant plants releasing a citrusy anise flavor that infused the tender meat of the olive.

May brought her specialty dessert, *knefe*, made with shredded phyllo dough and ricotta cheese, the pastry first baked to a golden crisp, then drenched in sweet, orange blossom honey.

Along with the clothes she'd made for Essam, Jameela and Hannah, Marta made special aprons and shawls to sell to the women of the village.

Mona prepared a giant pot of *maftool ou jaja*, a practical dish known for its knack to feed many. The scent of couscous, garbanzo beans and boiled chicken enhanced with onions, turmeric and allspice encircled the air as they walked along.

It was a beautiful day, none more perfect could be imagined. The sun shone brightly in the sky and the wind blew gently from the west, carrying with it a fresh breeze. The children, dressed in their new clothes with their hair combed smartly in place and their faces scrubbed clean, ran ahead laughing and poking one another. As they ran, they played a game, using sticks to propel a ball forward, each one taking turns. Even little Hannah carried a stick of her own now.

On the path into town they passed the home of a young British Colonel who'd taken up residence in their village. A specialist in

Middle Eastern affairs, he'd served in combat during the war and was now stationed in Beit el Jebel as part of the British occupation. He and his wife, Katherine, sat on their front porch smiling and watching the townspeople walk by. Katherine, well into her first pregnancy, cradled her swollen belly against her opened palms; it was clear that a new British subject would soon be joining their household. Although he would be the first British citizen born into their village, many of the townspeople suspected he would not be the last.

The end of the war had brought British military rule to the Holy Land. Soldiers stationed throughout the region provided protection from rebel Turks, assuring peace, while encouraging colonial civilization. The villagers, relieved to be acquitted from the harsh law of the Ottoman Empire, found the change refreshing, but realized that one oppression had merely been replaced by another. And although they had no conflict with the British people, finding them a refreshing distraction, they were well aware that they were still not free to rule themselves. They viewed the new leadership with a cautious resolve, choosing to live their lives within the boundaries of tightly knit tradition—close to the land and their faith.

As the Yusef family neared the Colonel's home, the children's ball, having been kicked ahead, took that particular opportunity to acquire a mind of its own. As fate would have it, the ball rolled to the left and stopped on the walk directly in front of the porch where the Colonel sat. Hannah, only four years old, ran after it squealing and laughing, her arms outstretched in childish pursuit.

Nisrina froze, as did the entire Yusef family. They held their breaths, not sure of the Colonel's reaction to the young interloper. Hannah, unaware of any social improprieties, entered the yard, running up to the porch to retrieve her ball.

The Colonel rose from his chair and descended the steps of his porch. Reaching down, he picked up the ball and quietly walked over to Hannah who was now standing still, watching the tall, fair-skinned man in the strange uniform. Transfixed, she stared at his auburn-colored beard. Her mouth agape, her eyes wide open. The Colonel, smiling broadly, reached out to hand the ball to her.

Mesmerized, Hannah made no attempt to take it.

"Here you go, little one. Here is your ball."

Surprisingly, he spoke perfect Arabic, but Hannah remained stilted. She'd never seen such a man before and wasn't sure what to make of him.

"It's ok. I won't bite," he said smiling.

Hannah's eyes grew wider at the prospect of his bite. This was something that hadn't occurred to her and for him to have proposed it in such a cavalier manner only added to her guarded curiosity.

Nisrina ran to retrieve Hannah, lifting her up in her arms.

She stopped and smiled shyly at the young Colonel, momentarily held by his eyes. They were blue, crystal clear like the shimmering waters of the Mediterranean Sea, the sun's reflection glistening off its surface. She had seen eyes like that only one time before in her life. It was at the nunnery, in the face of the Mother Superior.

As she gazed at him, he likewise was distracted by her. He couldn't help notice her simple beauty and it gave him pause.

Again he held out the ball.

"*Shukran,*" Nisrina thanked the Colonel and took the ball from his hands, the tips of their fingers accidently touching. Nisrina blushed. The Colonel looked away.

His wife, enjoying Hannah's misadventure, rose from her seat to join in the merriment, her hand supporting her belly as she moved cautiously down the steps. Nisrina's trained eye noticed that she was not long for delivery.

"I can see that your child is coming soon," she said to the Colonel's wife.

A collective gasp was heard from the crowd that had gathered nearby.

In her professional curiosity Nisrina had forgotten her place. She had brazenly spoken to both the Colonel and his wife without any formal introduction or male intermediary.

Najeeb was infuriated by her unthinking, emboldened actions. And furthermore, he did not like the way the young soldier was smiling at Nisrina. He stepped in, putting his enormous body between her and the Colonel. "Forgive my unseemly sister-in-law. She is a midwife, and in her earnest, has forgotten her manners." As he spoke, he roughly pushed Nisrina back behind his torso with the palms of his hands. His bulbous frame all but hiding her.

Katherine, not impressed by what she'd just witnessed, came forward. Casually brushing Najeeb aside, she walked directly up to Nisrina, her hand held out in greeting. She felt it was time to introduce a new etiquette to the region.

"Good day to you, my dear. I am Katherine Billingham. And this British subject who has just intercepted your daughter's ball is my husband, Colonel Billingham. Fondly known at home as Billie." She laughed, her teeth showing. Her Arabic was not as precise as her husband's, and she sometimes resorted to a mixture of half-chosen words. Colonel Billingham smiled at his wife, a twinkle in his eyes. She was a pretty woman, tall and thin. Her blond hair, uncovered, hung loose to her shoulders.

Nisrina took Katherine's hand in her own, the two women locking gazes.

"I can see that your time is near," Nisrina repeated to her.

"Yes, it is. I'm glad to know that there is a midwife in the village. I believe I've heard of you. *El dayah* of Beit el Jebel, or should I say *Oum el Loulad*, yes? Your praises have been highly sung by Doctor Noltey at the hospital in Jerusalem." She patted her stomach. "That's where this little one is going to be born."

"Then you will be in good hands," replied Nisrina.

Colonel Billingham came forward, putting his arm around his wife. He held her close.

"And what do they call you?" he asked Nisrina.

"I am Nisrina Yusef, *Oum* Essam." Nisrina held her head high.

"It is good to meet you *Oum* Essam." He smiled again, looking directly into Nisrina's eyes. Perhaps he looked a moment too long. Nisrina blushed and lowered her gaze.

Najeeb was pacing back and forth. "We must go now," he muttered coarsely, this time grabbing Nisrina roughly by the arm and leading her back to his family who waited on the path behind them. They, along with the crowd that had gathered, were transfixed on the unusual interaction that had just unfolded. So unlikely was this cross of social discourse, that no one had been able to move or speak, the implications yet to be determined.

The Colonel and his wife had not been in their village long, and with the exception of a handful of merchants and the local magistrate, no one had experienced the guise of any social interaction with the foreigners. And now, for Nisrina to have so cavalierly made the formal acquaintance of them both? Why, it was the likes of nothing they'd seen before. The Yusef family knew that the gossip and innuendos would soon begin, and they dreaded it. For to live in a small village was to live under scrutiny, a thousand eyes upon their souls.

As Najeeb and Nisrina returned to the group, the family shifted nervously to the side, their voices hushed, their eyes averted. Only after he'd positioned her safely in the center of the Yusef women did they quietly resume their journey into town, trying their best to proceed as if nothing irregular had just occurred.

However, pretend as they might, in that short interlude a curious crowd had collected and the whispering begun: *An unmarried woman speaking directly to a British soldier? A Colonel, no less? And the manner in which it was done—openly on the streets of Beit el Jebel! Matters of such delicacy? Unheard of!*

FORTY ONE

Judgment Day

NAJEEB AND JACOB WERE behind closed doors locked in serious discussion.

Marta knocked. Her hands were shaking. She was allowed to come into the room for the sole purpose of delivering refreshments to the two elders. Her role had been made clear from the start—she was only there to serve them.

"Enter," Najeeb called brusquely.

Marta slowly opened the door, its creaks and groans seeming louder than ever. In her arms she carried a tray filled with whiskey, two empty glasses, and an assortment of meats, olives and bread; the pungent smell of lamb kabobs wafted in with her. With eyes cast downward, she entered and placed the tray on the table before the two men.

Najeeb and Jacob watched Marta as she moved about the room, their lips pressed tight, their eyes inflamed. Unbeknownst to her, they were discussing the implications of her sister-in-law's behavior pertaining to the British Colonel and his pregnant wife. However, in her presence all conversation had stopped. They watched as she bent down with her delivery and they continued to eye her until she had left the room, closing the large wooden door behind her with a solid thud.

It was evident that Nisrina's conversation with the British Colonel the previous week had caused quite a stir in their village. More than one eyebrow had been raised. More than one story told. It was now widely known that the widowed wife of Jabran Yusef had stepped outside of accepted protocol. It did not shed favorably upon her and even more so, it did not shed favorably upon the Yusef family. In a small village such as Beit el Jebel, the whispers and looks of the villagers carried much weight. People were quick to judge and quick to blame. And as expected, the people were talking.

"But she is a midwife," Jacob, the milder of the two brothers reasoned once Marta had left the room. Aware of his brother's vicious temper and his unholy ways, Jacob spoke in Nisrina's defense. He was now gravely concerned for his sister-in-law.

"It matters not," Najeeb was firm. "The fact remains that she behaved like a common whore with no suggestion of proper upbringing or concerns for our family's reputation." He was pointing his finger upward in a gesture of familial supremacy. "This, my brother, is what comes from educating women and sending them off to universities. I'm telling you, I knew that she'd be trouble. I knew it from the day that Jabran first decided to marry her.

"Oh, what a choice he made! Our youngest brother who mother pampered so thoughtlessly . . . our foolish brother with his head in the clouds . . . with his books and his poetry and his mastery of languages. His travels with our uncle to lands far and wide . . . such opportunities that boy was given! Such exposure to the world! When all along he should have been here at home, working and toiling in the fields with the rest of us.

"And the greatest injustice of this calamity . . ." Najeeb's face grew redder, "the greatest injustice of all was that it was *he* who was blessed with children to carry the Yusef name. Not you or I! Oh, the inequity! The cruel twist of fate! The only legacy to our family and it was given to him!"

Najeeb was pacing back and forth, rocking on his heels, twirling his moustache. "His selection was marred, his decision flawed . . . I say to you, that woman is no good. And now he is gone and *she* remains for us to suffer. Such a burden. Such a burden."

He was shaking his head. "She has sullied our reputation. She's embarrassed our family. No, Jacob. There is no other alternative. I am convinced. This cannot go unpunished."

Jacob's mouth hung open. He had to think of something to stop his brother's ranting. It was vital that he bring reason into the conversation. Persuade Najeeb to let it pass. The people were quick to judge, yes, that was true, but they were also quick to forget. It was not as if Najeeb, himself, had lived without indiscretions. The villagers had, on many occasions, lifted an eyebrow at his crude behavior. But he was blind to that. How could he convince his brother to forgive Nisrina and move on?

Najeeb paused to light his cigar.

Jacob watched as his brother's mouth puffed and inhaled, the flame flickering with each breath. He watched those bitter lips engulf and surround the fat roll of tobacco, sucking and licking, his crooked teeth yellowed and stained. The smoke rose up, its acrid scent filling the room.

This was the moment, he thought to himself. He would have to speak now if there was any hope at all for reigning in his brother's temper.

Jacob took a deep breath and in a soft, calm voice, began, "And yet, through her work as a midwife she brings a handsome income to the family treasury. I should hate to see the loss of those finances."

"She's a liability." Najeeb was getting red again, smoke encircling his face.

"Najeeb, my brother, you are the eldest in our family and your word is law. But before you make a decision you may regret, please take note. Consider her children. They are so very young. Who will raise them? This is not for us. Our wives are not accustomed to such little ones, with their tears and soiled faces. Too many years have passed. Our women are no longer young, and they have no patience for childish demands. And Dora and Mona . . . they are far too aged. Why, just yesterday I saw Mona defecating in the garden. She said she was feeding the onions! This is not normal behavior, my brother. And she gets progressively worse with each passing year. God knows what she'll do next."

Najeeb would hear none of it, "Mona is our sister and the blood in her veins is pure. It is Yusef blood. Until she marries, she remains a part of this family and is beyond reproach. Nisrina is not. Her blood is from the Huniah family and quite frankly, in my mind, its purity has always been in question.

"Stop and think . . . her husband is dead and yet she remains in our compound, eating our food while we tend her orchard. Where is the virtue? She carries our name and retains control of the only children in the Yusef household, the heirs to our land. Can you say this is just? Must I remind you brother, that it's only by the grace and generosity of our good family that she has been allowed to stay? And now this! Now she has brought shame to us all!" He was shaking his head, "She has no rights in these circumstances. No say in the matter."

"But, she is loved by so many. What will the townspeople think? What will they say if you cast her out so callously? There will be grave talk, I tell you . . . much worse than a mere indiscretion with a British Colonel. And more importantly, dear brother, what will the women of our village do without their midwife? I shudder to think . . ."

"They'll do what they've always done." Najeeb rose from his seat, his hands clasped tightly behind his back. "Women have managed for ages without the services of a *dayah*. They will continue to do as the generations before them have done: have their children in the fields, the way God intended it to be."

He began to pace back and forth, pausing occasionally to rock on his heels—something he was known to do when agitated or aroused. He stopped and stared out the window towards the western horizon. Deep in thought, his eyes locked to the distance, moving only to twirl the ends of his mustache or puff on his fetid cigar. His face had turned to stone. "My decision is final," Najeeb asserted. "I will handle Nisrina."

Unbeknownst to the elders, Mona was gardening just outside the eastern window of Najeeb's private sitting room. Bent down where the two men could not see her, she toiled with her small-handled hoe. Working quietly, she listened to their conversation. She'd sensed that the elders were up to no good when she'd heard them order Marta to stay out of the room. She knew Najeeb was not pleased with the whispers and chattering of the village gossips, and she was concerned. Of all the people in the village, Mona in particular, knew the extent of her brother's rage and vile temper.

Although most people had long since forgotten, Mona had once been a pretty young girl. Her mother used to say that the sun came up just to see her daughter smile, and the flowers bloomed by the mere touch of her hands. But one day, in the early Spring, Mona lost her smile. Her father blamed it on her change into womanhood and turned his face away. Her mother lamented the daughter she no longer knew, but buried her sadness and did nothing to help her.

And now, as she worked beneath the window, Mona recalled the fleeting memories of her youth. Her mind wandering back to when the sun's warmth on her cheeks was a good thing, and the bird's song rang like music to her ears. As she cleared the wild grasses that crept between the irises and lilies, she listened to Najeeb's heralding words about Nisrina, and the sound of his voice sent a shiver up her spine.

FORTY TWO

Final Words

IT WAS EARLY MORNING and the Yusef compound was quiet, save for the sound of rustling leaves as the wind blew through the courtyard. Taking Abu Faraj and the children with them, the family had gone on an overnight trek to visit the *souk* in a neighboring village. They planned to stop along the way and spend the night with relatives they'd not seen for many months. Only Nisrina remained at home, she'd been asked to stay and prepare a meal for their return.

Unaware that the elders had recently concluded a private discussion, with her as the main topic, she willingly agreed, appreciating the two days she'd have to herself.

Nisrina was in the kitchen singing softly. She found comfort in working near her open window, feeling the temperate breeze on her face and listening to the rhythm of nature's song. She was making *imjadara*, a lentil stew made with rice and sautéed onions. She'd just finished washing and draining the rice and lentils, being sure to pick any loose stones that may have been left in the mix. Then she sprinkled the wet legumes with a generous amount of freshly ground cinnamon she'd recently purchased at the local *souk*, the spicy, sweet aroma filling the air.

While she worked, she smiled to herself as she recalled how she'd argued with Sameer Malouf the spice merchant, insisting that she wanted only his freshest cinnamon. She was careful to ask that he select it from the bags he'd brought back from Cairo. Mr. Malouf tried in vain to convince her to buy from his older collection, the ones he'd purchased months earlier. But Nisrina knew that they were of a lesser quality, lacking in both color and taste. She was adamant—maintaining that only the fresher, Egyptian spice would do. The merchant and midwife argued and bartered, until finally she convinced him to sell her the newest stock. She was able to reach such a bargain that she purchased a bit extra to share with her sisters-in-law.

When she finished preparing the rice and lentils, she turned to the arduous chore of chopping onions. This was her least favorite task, for their sharp scent and cutting fumes burned her eyes and made them tear. Grown in the garden outside her kitchen, they were large and yellow, rich in flavor. And today, as always, when she tangled with the heady vegetable, her eyes burned, forcing her to stop and wipe away the sting.

"Your family has been gone only a few minutes and already you're whimpering and crying like a newborn babe?"

It was Najeeb's voice.

Startled, Nisrina jumped, turning to face him, she wondered how long he'd been standing there.

"Forgive me, my husband's brother. I thought I was alone. Did you not go visiting with the others?"

"Obviously I did not go, for I am here with you. Am I not?"

He sniffed in a pinch of tobacco that he held between his two fingers, "Although if anyone could be in two places at once, I suppose it would be me."

His tenor was menacing as he stood in the doorway.

Nisrina stared with mild curiosity. He rocked back and forth, a forced smile spread across his face. She wondered why he had remained behind, but didn't dare ask.

Turning away, an icy chill ran through her. As usual, his manner was brusque, his eyes lewd. Not wanting to prolong or encourage his stay in her kitchen, she kept her back to him as she finished her meal preparations.

However, Najeeb did not leave. And although she could not see him, her eyes fixed wholly on her work, she could feel him standing there.

He remained behind her, unmoving. Watching as she chopped the onions for the lentil stew.

She could hear the sound of his breath; it was getting harder and faster. The hairs began to rise up on her arms, a shiver down her spine. But still, she did not turn around.

She dared not turn around.

As the moments passed, so overbearing was his presence, she struggled for air, her heart racing.

Then, darkness veiled the room—she felt him closer.

His putrid breath was on her neck as he came closer still.

"*Habeebti*," he whispered in her ear. "Where are your manners? Surely you would not deprive *me*, a humble guest in your kitchen, of enjoying a cup of your delicious coffee? Made so sweet by the mere touch of your hands, hm?"

She froze.

He had used the familiar term '*habeebti*' to her, meaning '*my love*'.

She knew only too well that these words were used solely for the most intimate relationships, those between husband and wife, or parent and child. To treat her with such disrespect was unheard of. And he was standing so close. She feared that he would notice her hands which had now begun to tremble. She prayed that he would take a step back, away from her, to a proper place of decorum.

But Najeeb did not retreat; he remained, tormenting her mercilessly with his hot breath and his poorly chosen words.

Pressed up against the chopping block, Nisrina realized that she could no longer move, neither forward or back. Nor could she turn around as Najeeb had now positioned himself far too close and he showed no sign of moving his large, rotund body.

This was not right. His conduct clearly out of order. But what had she done to elicit such behavior? What was on his mind? What were his intentions?

She wondered if she had encouraged him in some way, or was this a misunderstanding? Something that would pass. Be forgotten. Never spoken of again.

But the word was unmistakable—*habeebti*. No, something was clearly amiss. She did not like it, not one little bit. She was unsure of what to say. But one thing was certain, she needed to move away and move away quickly.

She could not breathe.

Instinctively, she shifted her body along the sideboard in an attempt to put some distance between them. She tried to have her movements appear normal, her motions casual, but inside, she felt desperate. She stretched out her arm, reaching for the tomatoes that sat in the wire basket under the window. Her reach failed, toppling the basket, the tomatoes falling swiftly to the floor.

Shaken, she realized that her only option was to maintain a semblance of respectability. Mustering her courage she turned around and faced her tormentor, "Forgive me, my husband's brother. You are correct. Where are my manners? Here let me put a pot of coffee on the stove for you." She tried to free herself from his proximity, but her attempts were thwarted.

"Nisrina," Najeeb was sneering, "don't you think it's time you stopped calling me 'my husband's brother'? If you'll recall . . . your husband . . . your loving Jabran, is dead . . . gone. He is no longer with us . . . and you, my love, are now alone. You have no husband."

He ever so gently touched the tip of his mustache, "And I, my dear, sweet Nisrina, am without my brother. We have already mourned. So, please, let us drop these foolish pretenses, eh?" He reached out and put his arms around her, she turned away, his mouth pressed hard against her ear.

"Nisrina, we are alone. No one will know. I want to hear you say my name as I have said yours . . . Say it to me now. Say Najeeb."

His breath was hot.

She struggled against him.

"You push me away?" He chided her mercilessly. "You push *me* away and yet you gaze into the eyes of the British Colonel? Yes, I saw you," he was grinning fiendishly as he spit out his next words, his saliva spraying in her face. "I saw the lust in your eyes, Nisrina. I saw the loving glances that the two of you exchanged."

Nisrina's face was filled with horror; she shook her head in denial, "No. No," she cried. "That is not true. I love only Jabran. Only Jabran . . ."

"And you think you can turn away from me?" he went on, "I think not dear Nisrina, I think not . . ."

She cried out, trying to push him away from her. But Najeeb was engulfed by hunger, her resistance tantalizing. His eyes rolled back in his head, he no longer heard her pleading words or the sounds of her disgust.

"Let me satisfy the desire in you," he kept saying, "I am the elder . . . you are a Yusef woman . . . trust me . . . yes, yes, my brother would want it this way. It shall be me that satisfies you now . . . it shall be me."

He grabbed her by the hips and pulled her closer. She could feel the hardness of his manhood against her. She shivered with revulsion. Her stomach sickened, she began to gag.

But before she could move a single muscle, before she could think another thought, she felt his mouth searching her face. Like an animal, he panted—rapidly, heavily, hovering over her. She could feel his hot, vile breath on her eyes, her cheeks, and encircling her mouth. He found her lips and holding her tightly to his body, he began to kiss her. First softly, tenderly, as if there were feelings between them. But as she continued to struggle, to push him away, he pressed his lips down hard against hers. She tried to turn her head, to escape his filthy mouth and probing tongue, but he was too strong for her. He held her tightly, determined now to have his way. Grabbing both her arms, he pushed her to the ground, her head striking hard against the rough stone floor. Then raising her skirt high above her head, her face buried under the cloth of her garments, he brutally forced himself upon her.

When he had finished, he stood over her and straightened his clothes. He looked down at her with contempt. She was lying on the ground in a curled heap. That is how we train our women, he thought to himself. Now we'll see if the Colonel will have her. I'd venture not.

He opened his mouth and spat on her.

Lying on the kitchen floor, Nisrina struggled to understand what had happened, to make sense of the vicious attack. But her mind was devoid of any thought or reason. She could not comprehend her brother-in-law's harsh accusations or his vile retribution. She wept wretched tears of shame and loathing. First for Najeeb. Then for herself.

His spatter landed on her arms and in her hair; she could not turn to face him or move to wipe it off. Her head was pounding, her vision blurred. Her body ached all over. She could not focus— neither vision nor mind. She remained turned from the sight of her assailant, her cheek laying flat against the cold stone floor. Her tears covering her face.

Najeeb turned to leave, his conquest complete, his vengeance satisfied, but before he crossed the threshold of Nisrina's kitchen, he paused one last time and looked back at her. His face was hard, his eyes like steel as he watched the woman who dared to resist his advances. Seeing her lying there weeping, curled up like a small round ball, he twirled his mustache mindlessly, rocking back and forth on his heels.

Finally, he spoke to her through clenched teeth, his voice like ice, "Nisrina, you are not worthy of wife or mother. You are nothing more than a common whore and it's high time that the good people of the village knew this. You have one hour to pack your things and leave this house. Your home is now my home. Your children, my children."

And with those words he spat again, then turned to leave.

As the eldest son of the Yusef family, Najeeb had lived a privileged life. But rather learn from his privilege and social opportunities, paying forward the kindness and deference always shown to him, he had become arrogant and cruel—what some would call a monster; others—a bad seed.

But regardless of the reason, the fact remained that Najeeb had made many enemies and many mistakes in his lifetime. But of all the mistakes, his greatest by far was the one he'd made that day—it was the last words that came out of his mouth, the final statement he'd made to Nisrina on his way out the door . . . "Your children are my children."

And so, with his back turned to leave, the knife that formerly lay idle on the kitchen counter, the one that just minutes earlier had been slicing through aromatic onions meant to flavor his dinner, now found itself plunged deeply between his shoulder blades, piercing succinctly and directly into the left ventricle of his beating heart.

Najeeb, his face horridly contorted, his arms outstretched, reached for the life that was slipping away. He fell to the ground, frozen. Unable to move, unable to breathe, he was frozen by death in the same violent manner he'd lived out his life.

FORTY THREE

After the Fall

TIME WAS A STRANGER.

Nisrina rose from the ground covered in the splattered blood of her tormentor. She didn't know how long she'd been passed out. She didn't care. Passively, she looked down at her brother-in-law and saw the knife protruding from his back. She noticed the look of horror on his face, and observed the blood and bodily fluids now spread on the floor.

She felt nothing. All senses had left her.

Entering a time and place unfamiliar, she moved outside herself, silently observing as she looked about the room.

Seeing him lying in her doorway, she knew what she needed to do. With surprising calm, she stoically pulled the knife from his back and walked to the basin. Carefully and meticulously she washed the bloodied knife. She was thankful that she'd gone to the well that morning and had an ample supply of water to use. She rinsed the basin, watching as the red blood swirled, mixing arrantly with the fresh, clear water. Finally thinned and dissipated, she poured it out, the basin clean once again.

She reached for a towel that hung on a hook near a large jar of olives. They were the olives harvested from the Yusef orchards. The ones that she and Dora had prepared together. She remembered how they had sliced them open, one by one. A slow process that took all her patience, but she never complained. The two women had worked together, side-by-side, listening to the sounds of the bubbling water from the courtyard fountain as they sliced and talked. Dora taught her how to hold the small sharp knife and cut a half circle into each olive. She explained how the crack in the fruit provided an opening for the bitterness to escape. And when each olive had been sufficiently split, they soaked and rinsed them in salted water. Over and over again they rinsed them, until Dora was sure that the bitterness was gone. Then they filled the large jars with brine and olive oil and sealed them tightly. Dora had included fresh garlic and tender young leaves from the anise plants that grew wild on the hills outside their compound. They'd lend an added touch of flavor, she told her. Nisrina recalled how the two of them had fun laughing and gossiping, cutting and rinsing. It seemed a lifetime ago, a faint memory now.

Perhaps a false memory, never happening at all.

But the olives were there. A testament of their lives. Proof of what once had been.

She observed the jars lined up so orderly and neat on the open shelf, and she saw the olives packed tightly within. They had turned out tender and tasty, a validation of what she could no longer be part.

Nisrina dried the knife and carefully placed it back in its drawer, then hung the towel on its hook. Standing in the middle of her kitchen, she looked around, surveying the scene.

Najeeb still lay in the doorway where he'd landed. His large body blocking the entrance. A pool of red surrounding his frame. Nisrina appreciated that there was a second entrance to the kitchen, it would come in handy at a time like this.

She removed her blood-stained apron. It fell to the floor. Pulling her thin linen dress up over her head, its delicate red embroidery blending subtly with splatters of blood, she dropped it soundlessly atop the crumpled apron. Then she reached for her shawl, throwing it too, onto the pile of clothes. Without another thought, she gathered them up, tossing them fearlessly into the fire. The flames flared up, warming her face, devouring the cloth.

And then turning in her nakedness, she left the room to prepare her bath, leaving Najeeb, the eldest son of the Yusef family, the elder and head of the compound lying strewn and alone on the kitchen floor with the dead look of horror still etched on his face, his mustache inexplicably trimmed to a short stub.

FORTY FOUR

A Scandal

BY THE TIME THE Yusef family had returned to their compound it was late at night and Nisrina was gone. Needless to say, the unspeakable shock at finding Najeeb lying dead in the doorway of her kitchen soaked in a pool of blood caused quite an uproar in the tightknit family. The children, their eyes averted, were taken to their aunties' home with promises of sweets and special treats. Marta, after much wailing and weeping, was heavily sedated and immediately put to bed. However, even in her drugged state she could not keep her mind from wandering. She worried about the implications of this change in status—what effect would her widowhood have on her standing in the Yusef household?

Jacob, always a more reasonable man than his older brother, and now the last remaining elder of the family, was horrified. He had no choice but to call in the town's Chief Magistrate to investigate. However, his dread of the Magistrate's involvement in private family matters was exceeded only by his fear of the townspeople's whispers that were sure to follow.

How will my family ever survive such a scandal? He thought to himself. This horrific event pales in comparison to Nisrina's illicit behavior with the British Colonel and his wife. What's a man to do? He pondered it over and over again. What's a man to do?

As the hours passed, the family realized that Nisrina was nowhere to be found, her disappearance giving grounds for much speculation. Was she the architect of this dreadful offense or yet another victim? Had she fled in guilt or was she abducted by the evil perpetrators? Perhaps she, innocently enough, was away on a call, assisting a mother giving birth, knowing nothing of the atrocity lying cold and decaying on her kitchen floor. The fact remained that no one knew and no one dared to venture a guess. Only Jacob was aware of the conversation that Najeeb had planned to have with Nisrina and he chose firm nondisclosure of that fact as the wiser path.

What's more, it was well known that Najeeb had made many enemies over the years. And throughout the region there were a number of husbands and fathers who had, on more than one occasion, been heard to vow their deadly revenge against him. It was entirely possible that this was an act of passion's final retribution. Yes, entirely possible.

"We have no choice," the Magistrate was nervously saying, a just-lit cigarette dangling loosely between his two fingers.

"But surely, this is something you can handle yourself," Jacob responded. He was getting progressively worried, agitated, as he paced back and forth on the kitchen floor, staying as far from the body as he could manage. His head continually turned away from the sight of his brother lying there dead on the floor. Soaked in his own fluids.

The Magistrate watched him pace. He knew there was no alternative, but wondered if Jacob would listen to reason, "No, my friend, I tell you, I have no choice. Things have changed. I haven't the autonomy I once had. The occupation you see . . . the British . . . things are different now. No. I must inform the Colonel. My hands are tied. No, no. There is no other choice."

The Magistrate was inhaling hard on his cigarette between each sentence, each thought, as if the cigarette alone held the oxygen he needed for his sustenance. Smoke was filling the room with every exhale. And mixed with the smell of the now decaying body, the air was becoming quite putrid.

Years ago, in an overwhelming victory, Abdullah ibn Abdullah had been elected the youngest Magistrate in the town's history. This came as a surprise to no one for he was a man much revered. Some say it was because of his trim, handsome looks and the sweet, eloquent manner in which he spoke. While others declared it was simply because Beit el Jebel had no crime and so it mattered not who the Chief Magistrate was. If they had to elect someone, he might as well be a pleasant fellow.

But Abdullah ibn Abdullah was a man for whom time had not been kind. He was no longer young and admittedly had put on more than just a few pounds. Furthermore, and much to his dismay, as the years had passed, along with them went his hair. His head, which at one time housed a thick, black, curly mane, was now bare, and all that remained was a rim of gray fuzz encircling its perimeter. Like other men in the village, he sported a wide mustache in the hope that the additional hair would distract from what he lacked on top. But regardless of his changed appearance, the townspeople all admired the man and continued, year after year, to reelect him to the honorable Office of Chief Magistrate.

In spite of their support, Abdullah ibn Abdullah increasingly became an anxious man. Uncomfortable in the post-war environment, he became prone to bouts of excessive perspiration further aggravated by increasing consternation. As a result, although he remained in his official capacity, he tended to dress lightly and could often be found out of his official uniform, walking the unpaved streets of Beit el Jebel, and courting the villagers in the local cafes with warm words and wishes for good health.

But today's circumstance was unprecedented—nothing could be worse.

Jacob pleaded, "*Ya Ummo*, have you considered the implications of such an action? What will the townspeople say? Oh, dear God. The talk . . . the talk! How will my family ever survive such a scandal?"

The Magistrate shook his head, "Let's not dance around this, shall we? The facts are clear. We have a dead body, obviously stabbed. Your sister-in-law is missing, nowhere to be found. And look around you, there is no sign of struggle or theft. Unusual circumstances to say the least!"

He paused, blowing out a long trail of smoke. It found its way upward, rising high, up to the ceiling, swirling softly against the dim light cast by the kitchen lantern.

"My dear friend," he continued, "despite your fears to the contrary, I think you must accept the plain fact of the matter . . . the scandal has already occurred."

He wiped the perspiration that was forming on his head, his handkerchief ready for just such an occasion: large, clean, and white. "Now we must find a way to deal with it. Trust me. I have no other choice."

Extinguishing his cigarette in the ashtray perched precariously on the edge of the counter, he motioned to his Junior Officer. It was time to run and fetch the British Colonel. And although he knew there was no other alternative, he dreaded the Colonel's reaction at being raised from his bed at such a late hour.

He stepped outside and looked up to the heavens as if to find an answer to this outrageous dilemma. Clouds had covered the moon, the night sky growing darker.

It looked like rain.

He lit another cigarette.

Precisely ten minutes had passed since the police officer had been sent to summon Colonel Billingham. And now, there he stood. There in Nisrina's garden, dressed immaculately in his British uniform, his hair combed neatly in place, his shoes polished clean. The only sign that he had been recently awakened from slumber was a slight drowsiness around the perimeter of his eyes.

However, the Colonel, upon seeing the sight of Najeeb lying in the doorway, quickly woke up. Any fatigue that accompanied him promptly vanishing.

"I say!" said the Colonel. "It certainly does look like we have quite the situation here."

Standing tall, strong, as if at attention, his hands clasped tightly behind his back, he turned to Abdullah, "What are the details, Chief?"

"This is how we found him, Your Lordship. The family had returned from two days out of town, gone to a neighboring village, visiting relatives and such. When they returned, late this evening . . . well, ah, here it is before you . . . you can see for yourself!" He motioned towards the corpse with both his hands in a dramatic flurry.

"I see. Hm. You say the entire family was gone? No one remained in the compound?"

"Well, actually, er, well, to be exact Your Lordship . . . Nisrina, ah, or rather *Oum* Essam, ah, that is Najeeb's sister-in-law, well, um, well, she stayed behind . . . you know, to cook . . . for the family."

"And where is she now? What does she have to say? What is her take on this?"

"Well, er, actually . . . well," the Magistrate began wiping his head again with his handkerchief, the sweat now rolling profusely over his forehead and into his eyes, the circle of wet under his arms increasing in diameter.

"Well, you see, Your Lordship . . . *Oum* Essam is not . . . Well, actually, what I mean to say is . . . she's not . . . ah . . . She's not at home. Not at this time, you see . . . no, no, she's not at home."

"Not at home? Why it's a rather late hour, I'd say," the Colonel looked at his watch. "Hm. Well then, if she's not at home, then, where is she?"

"She's not here . . . not here," the Magistrate was shaking his head vigorously now, as if this would help the Colonel understand the situation, which he, himself, did not understand at all. "Uh, you see, she is a dayah, a midwife, you know and . . ."

"Oh, yes! Of course! The midwife. I see, I see. Yes, I remember her. I remember her well. We met on the street, why just the other day. Lovely girl. Yes. Just lovely." The Colonel smiled remembering his meeting with Nisrina. "But, where is she now? Off assisting some poor woman giving birth, I dare say?"

"Yes, yes, that's possible, that's certainly possible," replied the Magistrate, he was wringing his hands. Beads of sweat blistering all over his head. "But, actually, the truth of the matter is . . . you see, sir, the truth is . . . ah . . . that actually . . . well, quite frankly . . . we're not sure. We're not sure where she is and well, ah . . ."

Jacob could stand his babbling no longer. In a high pitched tone, his arms waving about, he interrupted, "The truth is, Colonel, that we don't know where she is. We don't know if she's off on call as *dayah,* or if she has any knowledge of this . . . this atrocity! Nor do we know if she has been abducted for that matter! The truth is we just don't know!" He was pacing again. "But *she,* sir, is not the problem. The problem is lying here before you. The problem is my brother, who is now dead! He's been lying there in a pool of his own blood for God knows how long and it's past time to get him out of here. He must be prepared for a proper burial. For God's sake, please sir, have some decency! We are all suffering! My God, we are suffering!"

And with that he broke down in tears, his head buried in his hands.

"Of course, of course. I've seen enough." The Colonel turned to the Magistrate, "Please call the mortician and have them take this poor man away. Prepare him for his loved ones. Let's clean up this mess and give this family some dignity. It's late. We'll meet again tomorrow. Yes, I say, we'll discuss this further in the morning. Don't you think? When we're fresh, eh?"

"Of course, of course," The Magistrate parroted the Colonel. He motioned to his officers to remove the body and instructed them to clean up the blood stained floor. "*Shukran* Colonel, thank you, thank you. I'm sorry to have had to call you in at such a late hour. It's just that I wasn't sure. Things are so different now, you know . . ."

"No worry, my friend. No worry. These are difficult circumstances at best. You did the right thing in calling me. Rest assured. Now let's all get a good night's sleep. Shall we? Things will be clearer in the morning. We'll deal with this then."

The Colonel turned to Jacob with his outstretched hand, his heels clicked together, his back straight and tall, "My condolences to you and your family, sir. We will get to the bottom of this, I promise you. But for now, let's all get a good night's sleep, shall we?"

Jacob, numb from the day's events, could only nod. He knew that sleep was not something that would come easily. Certainly not tonight.

FORTY FIVE

I Leave You Now

NISRINA KNEW SHE WOULDN'T need much.

She packed a small bag, one she could easily manage. It included nourishment for her journey: dried figs, hard cheese, and a round loaf of bread. She also packed the jewelry given to her when she was betrothed—her twenty-four-karat gold bangle-bracelets, fourteen in all, given to her by her husband's family. Gold jewelry gifted to a woman on her wedding day was hers to keep until the day she died. Meant to sustain her should her marriage end, it would keep her from starving or being forced to sleep on the streets. She felt no remorse in taking them.

There was her gold locket, the one worn by her mother. The outside held a blue stone set at its center. The blue served as an amulet to ward off the evil eye. However to Nisrina, its true value lay within—a picture of her mother on one side and her husband on the other.

Finally, she took her wedding band, small diamonds set in twenty-four-karat gold. Many had thought the stones too small, their sharp words hurtful. Tiny chips they called them. But in Nisrina's eyes they were beautiful, delicately arranged in a thin circle around her finger. She loved how they reflected the light on a warm summer's day. Jabran told her that he captured the stars from the heavens for her to hold in her hands. The stars. She sighed. They could see what she could not. They held the answers she so desperately sought. But did it matter anymore?

Nisrina knew she could no longer remain a member of the Yusef family. Najeeb's breach violated both her body and soul. If her husband found his way home to her, she could never face him, the shame too great. She was changed. Dirtied. No longer his virtuous woman. No longer his wife. In her ungodliness, she could not call him husband. Nor could she claim his children as her own. For their sake, to spare them the pain of an unchaste mother, she had to go.

On that one count Najeeb had won. His glories, however, would be enjoyed in the raging fires of hell, not in the Yusef compound. Unable to force his iniquitous will against the loving people she once called family, her children could now live in peace. And in this knowledge Nisrina found comfort.

As she looked over her things she decided to include some photographs. Her favorite was the one taken on the day of her wedding. She smiled briefly. Jabran looked so handsome, standing there tall and proud in his golden *thobe,* and she looked so young.

She shook her head and carefully returned it to the table.

Instead she took a picture of her three children, choosing the one that had been taken after the Easter holiday when the roving photographer, Rahmed Ahmoodi, had come to town. She remembered how excited they all were. Dressed in their finest clothes and standing so still, they bravely posed for the picture. Essam wore his little fez hat, and she'd put ribbons in Jameela and Hannah's hair. Even Mona and Dora had agreed to join in. And now, holding the photograph carefully, her fingers lightly traced the outlines of her children's faces as she etched the memory into her mind.

She knew she'd never see them again. But felt certain that Dora, although quite on in years, would be kind and diligent, raising them as her own. Under Dora's care, Essam, Jameela and Hannah would live with love and compassion, the virtues she valued the most.

Walking slowly through the house, Nisrina surveyed her home. It felt empty. All that remained were memories of a time she could not hold. As she passed through each room she tidied up where needed, straightening pillows and smoothing linens. She noticed the wash yet to be done. It would have to wait. She would have to let it go as she was letting go of so many things.

She laid out her children's night clothes in anticipation of their return. She wanted to be sure they would sleep in warm clean clothes their first night without her. For Jameela, she selected the nightgown with the soft crocheted flowers decorating the lapel. Dora had crocheted them by hand for her, designed to match the flowers that grew each spring outside her bedroom window.

For Hannah, she chose the floral print pajama, the cloth had been purchased especially for her from the merchant who'd come in from Syria. *"A special cloth, just for you,"* he said smiling at the little girl who clung shyly to her mother's skirt. Hannah always won the hearts of the nomadic merchants. Having journeyed so far from their homes, and longing to see their families, they saw the likeness of their own children in her sweet smile and soft round cheeks.

Nisrina held up a blue-striped nightshirt for Essam. Caressing it tenderly between her fingertips, her heart skipped a beat. He would be strong, he must be. He was the man of the family now. Her little man. She took in a deep breath and lovingly touched the linen cloth to her face. Feeling the softness of the folds, she breathed in its scent, the smell of olive-oil soap lingered there, and her eyes moistened. Her son loved her handmade soaps, and knowing it would please his senses, she always added an extra branch of freshly picked lavender to the blend, the ripened blooms full and soft, falling like purple scatterings into the creamy white mixture. Would Dora remember to add that special touch?

She carefully laid his shirt on the bed, smoothing the creases, fingering the cloth.

When all was in order, she looked around one last time. Hesitating, she went back to the night table and again picked up the wedding picture, and this time without thinking or glancing at the photo, she stuffed it in her bag.

As the moon hid behind the passing clouds, Nisrina quietly boarded the bus.

She'd been walking for miles, moving as if in a trance along the back streets and deserted pathways outside the village. When she found herself back on the main road, she hailed an old bus that rambled by. She had dressed in modest attire, her face hidden from view; and clad as she was, no one dared look upon her or interrupt her solitude. The bus ride was long and dusty. It jostled about, moving slowly over rocky dirt roads. Every bump and pothole jarringly harsh.

Nisrina sat quietly. Her mind closed to all thoughts. Finally she closed her eyes, succumbing to a restless sleep.

She stepped off the bus. The hour was late and the streets quiet. Unlike the first time she arrived in the Holy City, the alleys and byways were now familiar. Although gone for the night, the smells from the vendors' carts still lingered in the air taunting her memories. She looked across at the distant landscape: the Wailing Wall, the golden Dome of the Rock, its brilliant curvature reflected in the star-lit sky, the soaring minarets, and the multitude of Christian crosses perched high atop glorious spires were familiar and warming. The sight gave her calm, and her lungs filled with air.

She knew the route without thinking, the sound of her footsteps on the empty, cobbled roads urging her on. Making her way through the narrow streets, she walked at a steady pace past the sleeping market and the shopkeepers' doors. She saw shadows move slowly behind the baker's windows, the glass clouded over from the steam of the ovens, the smell of freshly baked bread warming the air. In the distance, she heard the wail of a hungry child, as its mother moved quickly to quiet his tears.

Rounding the last corner, she passed the charitable hospital where she'd completed her test in midwifery. Then she walked through the alleyway towards the convent. Her heart raced when she saw the small glass windows atop the tall stone building, the spire and the cross. Nothing had changed. She was touched by its surety. The first time she entered its cloistered walls seemed so very long ago, she was innocent and trusting. And now—such shame.

The rusted, iron gate protested as she passed through it. She followed the narrow path that ran along the old stone wall. Then she made her way by the small chapel where the Sisters gathered for their morning prayers, the scent of incense drifting out to greet her. Finally she came upon the long columnar building that housed the sleeping nuns. Making the sign of the cross, she bent down and stepped through the low-rising doorway into the old musty corridor, the smell of half-burned candles mixed with frankincense and myrrh filled her nostrils. She'd forgotten how all encompassing the fragrance was in these close quarters—thick and dense. She breathed it in, its warm bouquet soothing her mind. With soft steps, she moved down the hall and within minutes found herself at the small wooden door that she knew so well.

She paused a moment before knocking. Her head was aching and her heart, which moments ago had been calmed by the familiar scents of the convent, now beat wildly within her chest. She had no choice. There was nowhere else to go. She took a deep breath and ever so softly, ever so gently, tapped on the old familiar surface.

There was no response.

She looked down the dark hallway. The small doors that lined its perimeter were closed. All was quiet. She knew the hour was late. That the Sisters had long said their prayers and laid down their heads. She feared terribly that any noise she might make, any creak, or untoward sound would wake them and they would come flowing out of their quarters. She wanted to see only one nun. She wanted to wake no other.

She knocked again, this time louder, firmer.

"Who's there?" the familiar voice finally called out, clearly perturbed and yet somewhat uncertain as to who would be knocking at such a late hour.

"It is I, Sister . . . it is Nisrina. I have returned."

Alodia jumped from her bed, forsaking her shawl or any thoughts of cover or modesty. She flung open the door. Standing before her in the dark was Nisrina. No words were spoken. Nisrina removed the cover from her face and Sister Alodia looked into her eyes. She saw all she needed to know. Purple bruises had blossomed on her neck and her cheeks. Her lips were swollen and her face was red. Alodia wrapped her arms around Nisrina and guided her into the room.

Surrendering to her warmth, Nisrina followed the old cook's lead. As she entered the familiar space, the walls became her sanctuary and her legs gave way beneath her. Crumpled at the old nun's feet, she buried her face in her hands, her chest heaved, and she began to sob.

She cried all through the night, her body shaking, her head aching, while the nun sat patiently by her side. Alodia asked no questions, she just held her. Occasionally she'd sooth her with gentle pats and soft whispers, "It matters not," she would softly say. "It matters not."

When all her tears were spent, Nisrina became still. Her eyes were swollen shut and her body weak and limp. Alodia lay her down between the covers of her small bed, gently tucking her in and pulling the thin cotton sheet and the old, woolen blanket up over her shoulders.

In no time at all, Nisrina was asleep.

Alodia walked over to the cabinet in the corner of her room and took out another blanket. It was an extra one that she kept hidden away for those especially long winter nights when her bones would ache and her teeth would chatter. The old cook carried the blanket and quietly lay down on the stone floor alongside the bed. And there she remained.

The next morning found the cook's kitchen in a state of flurry. Alodia had given orders that she was not to be disturbed, and furthermore, would not be available for her usual duties that day. The novice nuns were called in to take over her responsibilities in the kitchen.

Most of the meals had been prepared the day before and to a trained eye, very little needed to be done. However, the novices were not experienced in this capacity—a fault of Sister Alodia's. She had always been hesitant, if not downright resistant, to allowing anyone access to her kitchen and thus had not planned for the occasion in which she might not be able to do her job. Steadfast and reliable, it never occurred to her or anyone else that she might at some time need assistance in her duties.

And so the day began.

While Nisrina slept, Sister Alodia slipped out to meet with the Mother Superior. The Mother assured the old cook that she would be given full autonomy over Nisrina's welfare and promised to keep the knowledge of her presence confidential until they learned more of her circumstances. It remained a mystery to them why Nisrina had returned in the middle of the night, battered and frightened. But they knew of her fine character and her strong resolve, and more importantly, they loved her very much. So for now, her secrets were hers to keep as she slumbered in the old cook's bed.

FORTY SIX

Case Closed

MARTA SLEPT SOUNDLY, STILL sedated from the night before.

Jacob and May lay huddled in their bed, whispering.

The Magistrate, having had the most harrowing of nights since first taking office, remained sound asleep snoring, an empty pint of whiskey on the floor by his bedside.

The only household stirring was that of the two old maids. For it was there that the children of Nisrina had spent the night. Essam, eight years old, was astute enough to know that something terrible had happened the night before. But more importantly, he wondered what effect this mysterious event might have had on his mother.

"Where is my mother?" Essam asked Dora as she prepared his breakfast.

Ever since his father had been abducted by the Turkish soldiers, Essam, far too old for his years, had taken upon himself the welfare of the women in his family.

Dora stopped stirring the eggs and looked up.

"Your mother wasn't home last night, *habeebee*, but maybe she will be there this morning."

"Yes, I know that she wasn't there last night Auntie Dora, that's why we slept at your house. But I'm asking you, where is she?"

"I think," said Dora thoughtfully, "that maybe she went on a call to deliver a baby."

"Oh." He thought for a moment, watching Hannah pull hard on the cat's tail. "But you don't know for sure?"

"No, I don't know for sure. We were gone all day, remember? And when we came home, she was not there."

"But Uncle Najeeb was there, wasn't he?"

"Yes, *habeebee*, Uncle Najeeb was there."

"Auntie Dora?"

"Yes, my love?"

"Why was he lying on the floor? Auntie Dora . . . I saw blood. Did he fall and hurt himself?"

"Yes, Essam. I think Uncle Najeeb did fall down and hurt himself."

"Is he better, now?"

"Oh, so many questions, for such a young lad!" Dora was not sure how much to tell the boy. His sisters were on the floor, playing with the cat. She was glad they were occupied, hoping they weren't listening.

"Is he better, now?" Essam was determined.

Dora took a deep breath, put down the spoon and walked over to Essam. She lifted him high up onto the counter, and holding his cheeks lovingly in her hands, she looked straight into his eyes.

"I think he is not in pain, Essam. But he will no longer be living in our compound."

"Why is that?"

"Well, *habeebee*, your Uncle Najeeb has gone to . . ." she hesitated before she could say the next word, " . . .heaven."

"Is he dead?"

"Yes, Essam, Uncle Najeeb has died. He is dead and is now in heaven with the angels."

"Like my father?"

"Yes, Essam, like your father."

"Did the Turkish soldiers hurt him? The way they hurt my father?"

"No. I think he got hurt when he fell down."

"I want to go home and see my mother."

Jameela and Hannah both looked up. It was obvious they wanted to see her too.

"Ok, we'll go after breakfast. We'll go over there and check—see if she's home. But eat first, finish your breakfast. For all we know, she may have had a long hard night and is now sound asleep in her bed."

"No! I want to see her now!" Essam yelled, jumping off the counter.

He ran out the door.

Jameela and Hannah, forgetting their tryst with the cat, did not want to be left out. They dropped the string and ball they'd been using to taunt the poor feline and scurried after Essam. Their brother was going home to see their mother. They wanted to go too.

Dora, seeing the children run out the door, quickly grabbed her cane and ran out after them.

Nisrina's house was just a short distance from Dora and Mona's home. Essam stayed in the lead as they ran through the center of the courtyard. He followed the landscaped pathways, past the large stone fountain, the fruit and the olive trees.

Mona, working in her garden, looked up as she saw the entourage racing toward Nisrina's home. Not quite herself anymore, Mona just shook her head with a low, "tsk-tsk" and continued digging in the flower bed, pulling weeds and turning the soil.

Essam flung open the door and burst into the house, "*Yumma, yumma!*" he called out to her.

There was no response. The house was quiet.

He ran from room to room, his sisters following close behind.

"*Yumma, yumma!!*" they shouted in unison.

No one was there.

Jameela and Hannah did not quite understand what was happening, but they felt Essam's distress, and so worried too.

An ominous gloom pervaded the rooms. An emptiness foreshadowing their fears. Not finding their mother, the little girls began to whimper, and then to cry.

"*Yumma, yumma!!* Where are you?!" They called again, through tear-stained faces.

Dora scooped the two girls up in her arms, trying at the same time to keep Essam calm.

"All will be well," she kept telling them, "Do not worry. All will be well."

"Where is she?!" Essam demanded. What secret was she keeping from him?

But as it was, Dora was hiding nothing. The truth remained a mystery to them all.

She had no answers.

"Essam, *habeebee*, I am telling you the truth. I don't know where she is. This is the honest truth. As God is my witness. But, please, listen to me. Now, stop and think . . . your mother . . . she is a resourceful woman, is this not so?"

Essam nodded, looking down. He could not bear to look in his auntie's eyes for fear of crying.

"She is an intelligent woman, am I not right?"

Essam nodded again. Dora sat next to him.

"Then she will return to us soon. I am sure of that." She put the two girls on the sofa beside her and turned to face Essam. Taking both his hands in hers, she spoke calmly, "Hear me out, *habeebee* . . . please . . . How many times has she had to leave us in the middle of the night to help some poor woman who is giving birth? Many times! Many times she is gone for days. Remember when poor Mrs. Kateefa had her twins? Why, your mother was gone for two weeks to the next village! She was working and helping to make the poor woman comfortable. She saved her life! And the twins' lives too! And you should see those boys now. Why, they're growing like weeds!"

Her chatter was working, Essam was calming down. "Am I right, do you remember?" He was nodding reluctantly, his eyes still to the ground. "Yes? You see . . . I'm sure she's fine. And remember, no matter where she is, or what she is doing, she will find her way back home to us. Trust me on this . . . she loves you very much. She will return."

"The way my father did?" He looked back up at her.

Dora's face fell, her skin turning white. The child understood far too much. She tried not to cry. She held him tight.

But Essam did not want comforting. He wanted his mother. He lashed out, hitting Dora with his fists as hard as he could, screaming at her, crying, "I want my mother, I want my mother, bring her back, please, bring her back!" He was sobbing now. All of Dora's logic and reasonings forgotten.

She took him in her arms, and she too began to weep. "I know, my little man, I know," she cooed softly between her tears. "I want her back too."

Jameela and Hannah climbed into her lap, Essam at her side. She held them close while they wept for their missing mother. Finally, Dora said to them, "Come children, let's go back to my house and wait for your mother there. We'll see what Auntie Mona is doing in the garden. Let's hope that she hasn't scared the cat again with her crazy antics! There's no telling what that silly Mona will do!"

The children, relieved to have something else to think about, started to laugh, half-hearted giggles escaping their mouths. They too, over the years couldn't help but notice the ever increasing oddities of their peculiar Auntie Mona, and the way she tormented the poor cat. They nodded and rose to leave, their snuffling noses filled with the thick remains of fallen tears.

As they were leaving, Dora turned and noticed the night clothes that Nisrina laid out on the beds and without a word she gathered them up and took them with her, wondering to herself what Nisrina had in mind before she left her home.

A short while later, Dora, having settled the children at her house with a large plate of fruit, slipped quietly away. She headed back to Nisrina's, not sure what she hoped to find.

The house was quiet.

As she walked through the rooms, she saw the laundry yet to be washed, and she noticed the pillows neatly arranged. The bed linens were smoothed tightly against the bed, not a wrinkle in place. Reluctantly, she entered the kitchen, the memory of last night's horror unsteadying. She looked about carefully, noticing the onions left out on the counter, partly chopped, partly whole. Although clearly in the process of being cut, no knife was visible. The tomatoes were toppled, their basket turned on its side, some having splattered, bright red clumps smeared on the floor.

She turned to the hearth and noticed a small shred of fabric hanging over the edge. She moved nearer, adjusting her eyeglasses, leaning forward for a closer look. Then ever so carefully, she reached out and pulled the fragment of cloth from the fireplace. She held it up. She was certain. It had to be—she recognized the fabric from Nisrina's cotton dress, the one she'd worn yesterday when they'd left for the market. Dora took the unspent piece and rolled it up into a tight ball. She put it in her pocket, wiping the ashes from her fingers onto her apron, and then quickly she turned and hurried home.

As the townspeople began to stir from their slumber, so did the village whispers. Wedad Salem, the mortician's wife, was known for having a wagging tongue and she could hardly wait for the sun to rise. *You'd never believe what was found in the Yusef compound . . . in the widow's home, no less . . . on the floor. No! Worse yet . . . in the doorway of her kitchen . . . It was the dead body of her husband's brother . . . Yes! Najeeb! Najeeb Yusef was found stabbed to death in Nisrina's kitchen! He was just like his father, philandering and such. It's no wonder. And Nisrina seems to be missing. Does anyone know of an expectant mother whose time was due? No . . . No talk of women in labor, not at this time, no, nothing has been heard.*

Abdullah ibn Abdullah woke to the sound of someone banging on his door.

"Your Excellency, your Excellency!" a voice called out.

His head ached from the night before.

"Your Excellency, the British Colonel is calling for you. Please sir, are you there?"

"Yes, you fool, I am here. Where else would I be at this hour?" The Chief Magistrate was clearly perturbed.

"But your Excellency, it is almost noon!" The young police officer was trying hard not to be critical of his employer, but the British Colonel was waiting, and, well, that certainly was a matter worth addressing.

"Almost noon? The British Colonel? Why didn't you wake me sooner, you donkey's ass?! What does he want? Oh, my God! Yesterday . . . Najeeb . . . oh, my God, I remember now."

"Sir, the British Colonel is waiting for you. He wants to discuss the . . . incident."

"Eh? Yes, of course, of course. Tell him I'll be right there. I'll be at his office immediately, right away, right away . . . oh dear God, where are my pants?"

The British Colonel and the Chief Magistrate met Jacob at Nisrina's house shortly after noon. Together the three men and their officers investigated the home for any clues or evidence that would shed light on the perpetrator. To the men, everything looked in its proper place. In fact, although not entirely surprised, they were quite impressed by Nisrina's immaculate housekeeping. It momentarily crossed Jacob's mind that it would have been nice if his wife were as tidy a housekeeper as Nisrina. Such flawless habits. A model wife.

In their inspection, the men saw no sign of a struggle. They found no weapon. In fact, other than their memory of the dead body that had previously lay in the doorway, the floor now wiped clean by the Magistrate's men, there was nothing that indicated that anything out of the ordinary had ever taken place.

Oddly enough, even the partially chopped onions that Dora had seen earlier in the morning, and which the men had failed to notice the night before, were now gone and the counter wiped clean. The tomato basket that had been toppled was righted and the tomatoes that had been on the floor were gone. No evidence that would link anyone to the crime could be found.

"I take it the midwife is still away?" the Colonel asked.

"Yes," responded Jacob, who was much calmer this morning. "If a child is coming in another village, she might be gone for days."

"Right. Well, I'm just glad that she didn't have to witness this unfortunate event."

Jacob, struggling to put the previous discussions with Najeeb out of his mind, nodded to the Colonel, then excused himself and stepped outside. He needed to clear his head, to breathe some fresh air.

He had not lied to the Colonel. He simply did not disclose all of the information. And what he did say was true. If a child was about to be born in another village, Nisrina could, indeed, be gone for days.

He saw no reason to disclose the fact that he was unaware of any pending births in the neighboring towns. For who was he to provide this potentially misguided information? And as for Najeeb's ill-cast intentions to deal with Nisrina, well, his memory was not what it used to be. No, no, it was not entirely clear what Najeeb's intentions were. In fact, Najeeb had only been slightly concerned with Nisrina's behavior, just mentioned it in passing. Or more precisely, now that he recalled, there was no mention of it at all, just a look, nothing that warranted any discussion and certainly no action. That was the way it was, as his memory served him. He was sure of that. Besides, Nisrina was a gentle soul, not in any way capable of such violence. Everybody knew that.

Jacob continued to fight the other thoughts that were creeping their way to the forefront of his mind—that the Yusef family would be better off without Najeeb, and that he, Jacob Yusef, was the better man to lead the family.

With Jacob out of the room, the Magistrate took the opportunity to confide in the Colonel. He got close to his ear, a cigarette in one hand, his handkerchief in the other.

"It can be said," the Magistrate whispered softly, beads of sweat beginning to form on his forehead, "And no offense to the departed, God rest his soul . . . but, it can be said that Najeeb had many . . . well, shall we say . . . many adversaries. May he rest in peace and God bless his eternal soul . . . but, it could be said that he was not always, well . . . not always a virtuous man."

The Magistrate began to wipe his brow and the top of his head.

"A bit of a brute, eh?" replied the Colonel. He remembered his recent encounter with Najeeb on the street in front of his house.

"Yes, yes, well put, a bit of a brute," whispered the Magistrate. "And, furthermore, with all due respect," he continued, "I would be remiss in not saying that there are many men out there, in villages far reaching . . . *many men* . . . with wives and daughters, you understand? With wives and daughters . . . for whom his demise would be . . . shall we say . . . a welcomed relief?"

The sweat was now dripping profusely. The Magistrate, trying to keep up with the flow, opened his handkerchief wide, the largest portion covering his entire face. He managed to keep one eye uncovered, watching the Colonel, wondering if he had overstepped the well established bounds of British propriety.

"Ah, yes. I see." The Colonel was thoughtful. He stared out the kitchen window to the small garden just outside the house, and then his gaze went out to the fields beyond. To the green rolling hills and the carefully planted orchards.

The minutes passed as Billingham reflected on the war that had just been fought against the Turks and the Germans, with their ever so "holy" empires. A war of country against country and man against man. Principles held against principles lost, until the fusion of disparate ideologies unleashed a violence of unprecedented magnitude. He still harbored the horror of seeing his comrades blown to dust in the flash of an eye. A mere moment. Now they were beside him and then they were gone. They were men, good men. Men with families, and men with children. Men who had kissed their wives and girlfriends good-bye at the station, promising to return with flowers in their hands, and kisses on their lips. And then, they were made into soldiers, never to return.

Of those who did come back, many had lost their limbs, an arm or a leg, a bullet in the spine. Inoperable, they'd tell them. Cannot walk. No longer whole. And the worst of the calamities were the soldiers who on the surface had kept their bodies fully intact for all the world to see, but had irrevocably lost their nerves. Unable to cope or live in a civilized society.

He shuddered. The horrors of war.

He heard the Magistrate cough and shuffle, his mind returning to the Yusef compound—to the situation of Najeeb on the kitchen floor, and the philandering ways of a country farmer, and to the glittering stars of the parliamentary sky; and he knew that this was a man whose only result was to suffer the consequences of his own doings. The Colonel, well knowing that it was inconsistent with the assessment of the prior government, found himself to be quite resolute.

He turned to the Magistrate and took off his gloves, "Mr. Abdullah, I think this concludes our investigation. The way I see it, this is an unsolvable crime with no evidence, no leads, and any number of unknown potential perpetrators. A crime of passion and revenge, I'd say. Best put to rest."

The Magistrate's eyes opened wide.

The Colonel continued, "I will make my report and I advise you, sir, to do the same. We are finished here. Case closed."

"Yes, yes, I agree, case closed, case closed," the Magistrate mumbled, only too happy to have finished with this unpleasant business. And now he could not be faulted in any way, for it was the British Colonel who had made the final decision. After all, they were an occupied territory now. The British were in charge of these things, not he, a mere town magistrate.

"I say, let's inform his poor brother, and get back to the art of living, shall we?" said the Colonel.

He led the Magistrate out into the garden where they delicately explained their conclusions with Jacob. Working together they stated their position and tried to communicate it in a calm and reasonable way.

Jacob's reaction was one of outrage.

"How can you take so lightly the violent demise of my dearly departed brother?! Has no one taken into consideration the consequences of this heinous crime? Have you not measured the magnitude of this calamity? Can you not see the tremendous loss that we are suffering here? What about his wife? His livelihood? Where sir, is the justice? We cannot allow these atrocities to continue. We must seek revenge against the perpetrators. I tell you . . . as God is my witness, our family must be vindicated!"

Jacob was ranting and raving. He was pacing and posturing, he knew that anything less would be considered negligent. He was, after all, the grieving brother and new elder of the family. It was his job to assure that this violent tragedy did not go unresolved. That all measures had been taken, all avenues exhausted. He further knew that the power of his words and his astute resolve would quickly find their way to the villagers' ears.

The Colonel, although familiar with the ways of the desert peoples, having studied the language and cultural mores of the group quite extensively, was still unaccustomed to such emotional outbursts in his presence and upon his person. And desiring immensely to keep this investigation under his control, gave one and only one response to Jacob. It was spoken through British teeth.

"My dear Mr. Yusef," the Colonel began, "I can understand your grief. However, I do believe that it comes as no surprise to you that your brother's reputation and indiscretions have long preceded him. Even I, living in this village for but a short time, have witnessed his displays of public immorality.

"And, as you well know, your brother's life was filled with many opportunities of the earthly kind, with no thought of consequence or significance. I say to you sir, that in consideration of the manner in which he conducted his life, and in consideration of the effect it had on the lives of those around him, it is amazing that he has lived this long."

Jacob looked away, the truth painful to face.

But the Colonel did not heed his discomfort. He continued, "Furthermore, it appears to me that concerns of the *impact* of his actions should have been coursing through his veins and brains long before he chose to make this the pathway of his life.

"In my capacity here, I've tried to approach this genuinely. Was he an honorable man? Could he have avoided the final consequence that occurred upon his person? And finally, in light of such a calamitous life, and the lack of even a shred of evidence as to the how and why of this tragedy, is there truly any reasonable recourse that we could pursue in this matter?

"These, sir, are the questions which not only you, but your entire household should ask in distinct earnest before anyone dare cast the first stone. I say to you once again Mr. Yusef, and it is my final time in saying such . . . this case is closed."

Jacob knew that he had pushed the British Colonel as far as he dared. And although he would never publicly admit it, he knew the Colonel was correct in his words. He, too, was secretly relieved to put this messy business behind him. But more importantly, he could now face the townspeople and be exonerated from their malicious gossip. *"Case closed."* That's what he would tell them. *"Case closed. We shall discuss it no further."* He knew that although some unpleasant days remained ahead, the family would survive this distasteful incident and once again be able to hold their heads high in the community.

And although this was no time to show it, he had a renewed hope for the future.

And so, the Magistrate returned to his office and the Colonel to his wife.

The new, and now only, remaining elder of the Yusef family, Jacob Yusef, went to his family to comfort them and start the painful mourning process. Marta would be given special consideration as the newly bereaved widow. He would treat her with kindness and understanding. Both she and Nisrina would be allowed to remain in their homes. Nisrina could raise her children as she saw fit without fear of malice or prejudice. They would forever be protected by the family name. This would be a time for healing and a time for revitalization. A new era in the Yusef family. Jacob was only too happy to be the head of this, now, kind and loving family. He'd had enough of the many years of tyranny spent under his father and his brother's rule.

However, as he walked back through the courtyard, one thought continued to plague him. It was Nisrina. In the back of his mind, he continued to wonder—*where, in fact, had she gone?*

FORTY SEVEN

Redemption

IN THE LIGHT OF day Sister Alodia could better see the swelling and bruises on Nisrina's face. They covered her mouth, her cheeks and her neck. She saw dried blood on the back of her head where she'd fallen on the stone floor. A loquat-sized bump now raised on that spot. These inflictions were different than the time she'd found her lying in the alley behind the nunnery. Alodia knew these markings were made by large, strong hands. She'd seen this before on women seeking sanctuary, and she knew what it meant.

Nisrina slept all the next day and into the following night. Remaining in Sister Alodia's bed, her sleep alternated between periods of deep slumber and fitful murmurings. The cook realized that healing would take time and called Sister Miriam in to assist. It pained the young novice to see her old friend in such a state. Her eyes moistened as she nodded her understanding. This was her calling. She would do what was needed. Together, the two nuns took turns staying by Nisrina's bedside—sitting, watching and praying—she was never left alone.

Alodia borrowed a fragrant, healing incense from the church vestibule and burned it in a corner of the bedroom. She knew that the sweet scent would help soothe Nisrina as she slept. She ordered a second bed to be brought into the small room where she lay down, her eyes open, listening to Nisrina's staggered breaths. But as darkness descended and the hours passed, Alodia's eyes eventually closed as she, too, gave way to a restless slumber.

The mood around the kitchen was quite solemn. Leaving most of the work to the more talented of the novices, Sister Alodia occasioned short, unexpected visits to the cookery. She would drop in throughout the day, checking on their work and giving them instructions. The novices were, with no uncertainty, completely and totally intimidated by the old cook. But they respected her immensely and were honored to assist in her time of need. And although she said nothing, Alodia found an unexpected comfort in having the young nuns busying about in her kitchen. Their youthful enthusiasm was contagious, and she wondered why she had not employed their skills sooner.

"Sister Alodia! Sister Alodia! It's Nisrina, she's stirring. She's asking for you! Come quickly!!" Sister Miriam was breathless as she ran into the kitchen to fetch the old cook.

"Glory be to God!" Sister Alodia dropped her scrub brush, "The one moment I step out of the room, and she decides to wake? But never mind, never mind, she's awake now, that's all that matters . . . and she was asking for *me* you say?"

"Yes, Sister, those were the only words that came out of her mouth. I ran for you immediately."

"Fine, fine," the old nun repeated as she breathlessly ran back to her room, her large bosoms swinging back and forth, her steps echoing in the quiet hallway.

Upon reaching the doorway, she turned to Sister Miriam, "Listen to me carefully . . . I want you to bring us some hot tea and a plate of *kurshellas*, the anise biscottis I just made. I left them cooling by the kitchen window. Leave the tray outside the door. Do you understand? Just leave it on the floor. Do not disturb us under any circumstances. Is that clear?"

"Yes, sister," the young nun nodded. She knew better than to argue or ask any questions at a time like this. She was relieved that

Sister Alodia was there to take charge, to give instructions, and make things right again. She was trying her best to focus on the directions she'd been given, while passionately holding back her tears.

"*Hamdallah a salaam*, Nisrina, *Ahlaan, Ahlaan!*" the old nun greeted Nisrina with a big smile and blessings for her recovery, for her wakefulness. But her attempt at cheerfulness was not reciprocated.

"Sister Alodia," was all Nisrina could say. She was trembling, her eyes cast downward, the memories of her ordeal still fresh in her mind.

"Never you mind, my child. Never you mind. Everything is going to be all right now. You are here at the church and here you shall remain for as long as you wish. This is your sanctuary. There is nothing to worry about. You are safe now. And as God is my witness, He shall heal all your wounds."

"But Sister . . . I have . . . I have . . ." and once again Nisrina began to weep.

"No. You have shed enough tears my child. No more tears now. God will prevail. You are safe . . . you are safe." Her arms around Nisrina, she began to pat her, to soothe her.

"Sister Alodia," Nisrina looked intently into her old friend's face, her voice lowered, barely audible she whispered, "Sister Alodia, I have sinned. I didn't want to, but I did. I bathed afterwards, but I still feel . . . well, I mean, oh Sister, I still feel so dirty. Can I ever be forgiven?" Nisrina was shaking her head, "I must be forgiven. Is there no hope?"

Alodia spoke, her voice soft, assuring, "Nisrina, you have not sinned. It is clear. The sin was against you, my child. There is a difference. You must understand this. You will understand, it just takes time . . . it just takes time." She held Nisrina's face gently in her hands and looked into her eyes, "You see my child, the sin was not only against you, it was also against God and He shall triumph." She wrapped her arms around her, "Fear not my child, for there is nothing you have done wrong . . ."

Nisrina interrupted her, "Sister, I need to bathe again. I need to bathe here, in the church, in sanctuary. I need to have confession, I need to confess my sins and be forgiven."

"You shall my child. There is plenty of time." The old nun thought for a moment, she remembered the Mother's words. That she was given full autonomy over the girl. She nodded to herself. "Let's prepare the bath. I will bathe you in God's forgiveness."

"Stay with me Sister. Stay with me. I want no others in the room."

"Of course, child, of course."

The old cook prepared the bath. She took out the large tub. She brought in boiled water and poured it in the vessel filling it half way. Then she took out a small decanter of Holy Water—water taken from the well at the Church of the Holy Sepulcher and blessed by the Priests.

"But I am not Catholic, Sister, how shall God forgive me? I am Syrian Orthodox." Nisrina was aware that the two Churches followed somewhat different paths.

"Worry not, for with the help of God, I will give you blessings from both churches, the Catholic and the Orthodox, you will be doubly blessed. Fear not, God is greater than any one church. He is all forgiving."

She sprinkled the Holy Water into the vessel and began to chant, "By this Holy Water and by Your Precious Blood, wash away all our sins, O Lord.

"This bath is blessed by the sprinkling of this Holy Water, in the name of the Father, and of the Son, and of the Holy Spirit, from now and forever and unto ages of ages, Amen."

Then she turned to Nisrina, who, having shed her clothes, stood naked before her. The old cook felt the earth shudder. Nisrina's body was covered with dark bruises. It was clear she'd been violated, and the nun's heart ached. The anger, the repulsion—she wanted to scream, but instead she casually shifted her gaze to gather composure. Holding the side of the tub, she prayed for strength and mercy. Remaining stoic, she turned back to Nisrina and began the cleansing of the fragile young woman.

She helped Nisrina step into the vessel, all the while whispering prayers and soothing words. She took out a clean washcloth and a new bar of soap and very calmly began to bathe her. She washed her head, carefully cleaning the hardened blood, now caked in her hair.

She washed her face and softly soaped her arms, her breasts and her stomach. And then she washed her legs and her feet.

"Here too," Nisrina pointed to her womanly parts, and the old nun nodded.

She ever so gently washed her where she had been violated and in so doing, repeated multiple blessings and prayers for the sins that had been committed against her.

Soon, the warm water, the Holy Blessings, and the soothing touch of the old nun's hands began to comfort her. Nisrina relaxed.

When she felt sufficiently cleansed, Alodia took her softest towel and wrapped it around Nisrina's battered body. She gave her clean, warm clothes to wear and then together they sat and quietly sipped the hot tea left outside the door.

Unable to eat, Nisrina declined the *kurshellas* that the old cook had made fresh for her that morning. To which Alodia muttered softly, "It matters not, it matters not."

After a while, Nisrina spoke, "I want to confess my sins now."

"Shall I call for Father Joseph?" Alodia asked, "Or shall I call in a priest from the Orthodox Church?"

"No! No priest!" Nisrina was adamant, "Only you Sister. I will speak only to you. No one else, no others, please!"

"I see. Then, so be it. Let us begin . . . Please, whenever you're ready."

And Nisrina began her tale while Sister Alodia listened.

She told about her family going to the next village, and how she was asked to stay behind to cook the meal. She told about chopping the onions and Najeeb appearing in her doorway. She told about his breath on her neck and his uninvited caresses, his inappropriate words of endearment and her shock in hearing them. How she reached for the tomatoes, how he persisted. How she struggled to push him away, but he held her tighter. She told about his kisses and his probing tongue—the pressing, the thrusting, the pain. How she found herself on the floor crying, feeling ashamed and small as he spat upon her. And then she told of the words she'd heard him say. The words he dared to speak to her, which he never should have uttered—that he would take her children from her and raise them as his own. As she repeated it, reliving the horror, her shattered soul cried out, tears streaming down her face.

She told the old nun about how, when she rose to undress, to wash the sin from her body, she saw him lying there, dead in her doorway, the doorway to her kitchen, with blood all around him and body fluids everywhere and . . . and a knife in his back. How she wasn't sure if she was the one who had put it there. She couldn't remember, but she feared the worst. And she begged for forgiveness if it had been her hands that had taken his life.

As she said this, she looked down at her open palms. Were these the hands of a murderer? She knew not. She only knew that he was dead, and she was glad for it. And she asked the Lord's forgiveness for any joy in that fact. For as her heart struggled with the terror of it all, she was comforted to know that he would never have her children.

She had endured such shame, she knew she could no longer stay as Jabran's widow or be a respectable mother to his children. And, *Enshallah*, if Jabran, whom she loved with all her heart, should ever find his way home again—oh, the shame of it! She could never face him, not now, not after what Najeeb had done to her. She knew of nowhere else to go, she found herself on the bus, and then finally, knocking quietly at Alodia's door.

The nun said not a word. She nodded and patted Nisrina's arm. She rose up and went to a tall cabinet in the corner of her room. There she opened the top two doors. They creaked languidly, as if to say that they too, understood the gravity of the occasion. Alodia reached in and took out the lone bottle of wine. It was a fine wine given to her by the Mother Superior, one that she had been saving for its highest purpose. And without hesitation, she opened the bottle, threw away the cork and proceeded to say blessings over the wine.

She poured two glasses. Then, reaching out she took the first glass and cradled it in both her hands, she held it out to Nisrina and said, "Here drink, for this is my blood which I give unto you for the remission of sins."

Nisrina took the wine and sipped it slowly. Alodia took the other glass and said the prayer again.

As the hours passed, their moods lightened. They had finished the wine. Nisrina had been cleansed and forgiven. And now the smell of freshly baked food was drifting in from under the door. Alodia peeked out and saw a tray filled with delectable dishes that had been left outside. She made a mental note to thank Sister Miriam for her initiative and good judgment and carried the tray into the room.

The two women sat on their beds and ate and talked through the day and into the night.

They agreed that Nisrina would stay for an unspecified period of time. She would assist Sister Alodia in her kitchen and learn the art of cookery. She had been absolved of any transgressions and her sins were washed away. Repentance for any wrongdoings that she may have committed would be in lay service at the nunnery.

The sorrow she felt in giving up her children still tore at her heart, the hole unhealed; but she knew that she could not face them. And yet she felt blessed, for she'd been forgiven. In Sister Alodia, she had a new family. Her only request to the old cook was the promise that she not be required to chop onions, to which Sister Alodia wholeheartedly agreed.

FORTY EIGHT

And From These Seeds

NISRINA HAD FOUND A home in Sister Alodia's kitchen.

The Sister was a magnificent cook and took the time to teach Nisrina all her culinary secrets. And Nisrina, a cook in her own right, learned fast, her skills quickly improving. But more importantly she found comfort and healing in her work, a sense of purpose and place that diminished the aching void left by the loss of her children.

In the convent she had all the necessary components needed for her recovery. As she rose each morning, greeted by a stream of warm sun shining through her window and the cheerful sound of birds singing in the garden, she sustained a renewed hope. A fresh new day.

Her life in the convent was structured, orderly, and she was surrounded by kind and gentle souls who loved her dearly. She knew she was accepted in spite of her past regressions. Never scorned nor tempted. Never judged nor criticized. She was given free rein on all her decisions. That is, except those pertaining to cooking. For Alodia ran a very efficient kitchen.

Each meal had to be ready on time and made with the freshest of ingredients. Many mouths depended on the food prepared in the cook's kitchen. And Alodia's reputation for excellence was unsurpassed. She was of Armenian descent, and her cooking reflected the palate of her culture, a region and people who lived far north of

Beit el Jebel. Through her tutelage, Nisrina learned the delicate art of blending herbs and spices, some she had never before encountered, obtained by the old nun from the traveling spice merchants that frequented the *souk*. She was fascinated by Alodia's combining techniques, how she created the most delectable of tastes and aromas, all essential in the preparation of food.

Recipes were passed down by watching and listening. Nothing was written. No measurements taken. The old cook used neither cups nor spoons to calculate the quantities. She relied strictly on her instincts. How it felt, looked or smelled.

As it turned out, the scents, sounds, touch and feel of the kitchen was just the prescription Nisrina needed to repair her broken soul. And Sister Alodia was the perfect teacher.

There was the baking of bread: flour, yeast, oil, and water. A dash of salt. That's all. The secret was in the kneading. First she would make the sign of the cross in the soft, loose flour. And then into the holy marking she'd pour a mixture of water and yeast. Then a palm full of olive oil. The sensuous liquid slipping through her open fingers. A blessing would be said. And she'd cross herself—head, heart, shoulder, shoulder.

And the mixing and kneading would begin.

It felt good.

To blend and crush and slap the dough.

First with fingers, then with palms, followed by fists.

Squeeze, press, punch.

"Not too much, mind you, or the bread will be tough. That's it. Just right."

Although Nisrina had made bread many times, Alodia's ways were refined, blessed. She baked from the heart, her strong arms gentle with the mixture.

The dough had to rise twice before baking.

The first time as a whole.

They'd cover it and wait until it had doubled in size. When sufficiently puffed, they divided the large soft mass into smaller balls of uncooked dough, and together they pressed them, one by one into round flat loaves.

They lined up the loaves neatly on the open counter and covered them again with clean, dry cloths to keep them warm. They waited until the individual loaves rose again.

"It's like life," Sister Alodia would say, as they worked in the warm kitchen. "First the child is raised with his mother until he is ready to be on his own.

"And then they are separated and he continues to grow. Richer, fuller—he develops his own unique traits and characteristics. And when he is ready to be baked, the warmth of the oven envelops him, and he changes yet again. The heat is like God's love. The breath of His Holy Spirit.

"As the dough is transformed, the loaf takes on its final form and consistency. Ah, here . . ." She held up the hot, delicately browned loaves of bread, fresh from the oven. "No two are ever the same. But each is delicious unto itself."

She broke open the round loaf, the steam escaping, rising up and out, dispersing its warmth into the room. They poured rich, clarified butter into the open pocket, and taking a break from the day's work, sat down around the kitchen table and ate to their hearts' content.

Nisrina had learned much while at the nunnery. She and the kind Sisters who worked in the kitchen had shared many warm moments together—talking, learning and laughing. And as the days passed, the memory of her dreadful nightmare weakened its heinous grip.

She knew that she could no longer claim to be the young woman who had once lived a quiet life in Beit el Jebel. She had met evil and it had changed her forever. But in this place and amongst these people she had found salvation and was reborn into a world of understanding, love and tolerance.

However, in spite of the time that passed and the wounds that healed, her heart remained heavy. She missed her children. She missed the feel of their soft skin and the sound of their sweet voices. She missed her husband. His smile, his calm sense of assuredness. She missed her home, her vocation, her identity of self. For although she was safe and happy in her days spent at the nunnery, secure and warm in Sister Alodia's kitchen, Nisrina missed her life. And she wanted it back.

FORTY NINE

The Ultimate Test

ONE MORNING, EARLY, THE Mother Superior called Nisrina into her office. Ushering her into the warm, familiar space, she closed the door behind her. She asked Nisrina to take the chair opposite the desk that sat in the middle of the room. Nisrina recalled the first time she had been brought into the Mother's office. It was her first day of school and she'd been determined to prove that she could finish the midwifery program despite her inability to read or write. The Mother's kind way and even-handed manner had given Nisrina courage to speak her mind and fight for herself. She was forever grateful. But things were different now. So much had happened.

The Reverend Mother took the empty chair next to Nisrina. She bowed her head into the broad cup of her palms. Her thin angular fingers forming a perfect bowl upon which to rest her cheeks. Perhaps she was saying a prayer or collecting her thoughts. Nisrina sat quietly, respectfully waiting as the round metal clock on the desk marked off its seconds like a nomadic shepherd counting his flock.

Wearily, the Mother lifted her head and looked straight into Nisrina's eyes, her own clouded heavy with worry, "Nisrina, a woman has come to us seeking sanctuary. She has been badly beaten by her husband and brutally raped by members of his family." The Reverend

Mother took in a deep breath, her hands were shaking as she reached out to Nisrina. "My child, she needs your help."

Nisrina held her breath as the meaning of those words sifted through her brain. The Reverend Mother was describing a woman maliciously mistreated by her family, an ordeal so close to her own. How could she face the travesty that ripped at her heart; and then again, how could she not? The Lord had presented to her the ultimate test—to face her own wretchedness in another person's misery. She had no choice.

"Of course," she whispered. "I can go to her now."

She took off her apron, silently following the Mother to a room at the far end of the corridor. Crossing the threshold, she noticed the east facing window was covered with a cloth shielding the bed from the light that threatened to enter. A lone candle flickered in the corner, casting a soft shadow on the wall. She could hear the birds outside. They were chirping excitedly, most likely building a nest in the mulberry tree by the window. Or perchance they were raising their voices in vexation to the dreadfulness that now lay before her. But how could they possibly know?

Nisrina drew in her breath. Through the dim haze she saw a figure lying beneath a plain cotton sheet. She approached, casting a glance at the woman's face. It was swollen and bruised, her eyes mere slits, unable to see. Matted and shorn, patches of dried blood covered her hair. She lay there silent, a ghost in an unforgiving womb. No sound or movement. No tears.

Frozen by the sight, the earth stopped its spinning. The weight of the stone walls closing fast on the room. Despairing memories took hold as Nisrina's feet attached themselves hard to the ground, her arms disconnected from their sockets. What madness had taken over the world? What cruelty engaged? Nisrina looked up at the Mother. She could not speak, her eyes pleading to the Reverend nun. *How does God allow this to happen?* The Reverend Mother reached out and gently touched Nisrina's shoulder, her blue eyes were clear, full of compassion.

"God does not prevent suffering," she said as if hearing Nisrina's thoughts. "But He provides comfort when man brings suffering to others."

Nisrina found her strength in the Reverend Mother's face, in her words and in her loving touch. "What is her name?" she asked softly, her eyes returning to the poor soul that lay motionless before her.

"Her name is Magda," the Reverend Mother said.

A stillness clung to the air like autumn leaves refusing to fall. The birds outside ceased their eager song, Nisrina harbored in a haze of memories. She could not think beyond that name.

She looked up at the Mother's face. Searching her eyes for answers, for more information. Trying desperately to catch the breath she so urgently needed. Yet somehow she knew the answer to her question.

"Yes, Nisrina," the Mother spoke again, "It is Magda Attia. Her name is Magda Musa now. Things have not gone well."

"But . . ."

"I know child, I know. However, it is not for us to question. In the end, righteousness will prevail, as it is written. All in accordance with God's plan . . . and His plan is perfect."

Nisrina nodded, with a lingering look back at Magda.

"I will leave her in your care." The Holy Nun departed.

Nisrina slowly approached the bed. She got closer, looking hard at the woman lying there so still. She tried to find a semblance of the young girl she'd once known. The brazen girl who attended classes wearing the finest of fabrics, and read her lessons with impeccable precision. The girl who had tormented her, and was suddenly called away for marriage and a life of privilege. Now unrecognizable.

Nisrina bent down at her bedside, and on her knees she silently said a prayer. She asked for strength. To do the right thing. And to be an instrument of God's plan. And finally she asked that the Lord heal this sad, broken woman as He had once healed her.

She rose up and instinctively knew what to do. She turned and walked to the back of the small room and began to prepare a bath. She brought in warm water and filled the tub. She undressed Magda, all the while speaking softly, soothing words of comfort. She lifted her up. Her body was light, so small. And she carried her over to the large metal tub. She placed her into the warm water, and she bathed Magda the way that Sister Alodia had bathed her.

Magda gave no resistance, unaware of Nisrina's presence.

Not knowing that her former nemesis was now cleansing her of her wretchedness.

Nisrina sat with Magda day and night. Her work in the kitchen was over. A new calling now lay before her. To heal the agony of this poor broken woman. Nisrina prayed at her bedside while she slept. And during her short bouts of wakefulness, she encouraged the young woman to sip her tea. As the days passed, the swelling in her face began to subside. The girl's eyes beginning to clear. First just a haze of light could be seen through them, then outlines—a nurse, a room. All the while she heard a soft, soothing voice that comforted her.

"Your voice is familiar to me," it was the first words she spoke.

Nisrina looked up from her work. She had been making hot tea for Magda and not wanting to distress her, avoided discussion of who she was. She continued to keep her voice low. To soothe her, comfort her. Magda drank the tea and finally was lulled back to sleep.

Waking, Magda looked directly at the woman in the room. Her vision now greatly improved.

"Nisrina? Is that you?"

"Yes, Magda. It is I."

"Awgh," she turned her head away.

"No, Magda. Please, do not distress yourself. It matters not."

"How can you say that? Look at me . . ." her voice was weak. "Of all people, I never thought I would see *you* again. And now . . . like this . . . Your voice, it sounded familiar, but I wasn't sure. I couldn't remember. Until now. Seeing your face. *Enshallah.* Oh dear God, please have mercy on me. Please have mercy. I can't bear it." Magda turned her face away.

"Magda, please, I'm here to help you."

"You can't help me Nisrina. It's too late."

"It's never too late Magda. Please. Allow me."

"I'm so ashamed. You have no idea." Magda could not look at her.

"You think I don't understand?" Nisrina's voice was cold. Void of emotion.

Magda turned to look at her. "I *know* that you don't understand, Nisrina. How could you? How *could* you? You can't imagine. The horror, the shame, what they did . . ."

"You're wrong, Magda. I *do* know. I do understand." And now it was Nisrina who turned her face away. She turned and looked at the cold stone wall. She stood there and stared at the cracks and crevices of the old building. The mortar aged and yellowed, beginning to chip and crumble. She could not look back at Magda.

"Nisrina?" Magda reached out to touch her.

"Yes, Magda. You are not alone in your misery. I too have been shamed." Tears began to well up in her eyes. "That's why I'm here . . . at the nunnery . . . instead of with my children."

"Oh, Nisrina! I'm so sorry."

Nisrina turned back to her. As their eyes met, they saw into each other's souls. Joined in their knowledge of what it was to suffer the worst aggravation against their person. And in that moment, in the humiliation and hurt that they shared, they became sisters. For what was felt by one was also felt by the other.

Nisrina moved to place her arms around Magda's shoulders. She was hesitant at first, moving slowly. She sat on the bed next to Magda, her arms now fully encircling her. Magda did not resist, nor did she pull away. She dropped her head onto Nisrina's shoulder, surrendering her will. They sat in silence for what seemed an eternity. Neither girl moving nor pulling away. Finally, Magda took in a deep breath, and then another, and another. Until her inhales were no longer breaths, but sighs, then tears, then sobs. Magda's body shook as her soul released its dispiriting anguish.

Finally Magda pulled away, looking at Nisrina,

"You were the one . . . here . . . the one that bathed me, weren't you?"

"Yes, Magda. I did. As Sister Alodia did for me."

"Thank you, Nisrina. And after all I did to you . . . Oh my friend, can you ever forgive me?"

"It is done," Nisrina nodded. Unthinking, she reached up and touched her left ear, its muffled silence still a part of her life.

"Nisrina?"

"Yes, Magda?"

"Do you know why . . . why he beat me?"

"No, Magda, I do not."

"I could not give him children."

"Oh, Magda, I'm so sorry."

"And that's not the worst."

Nisrina sat on the chair beside the bed as Magda continued, her words coming now in short bursts, "You see, it was during one of his beatings . . . he'd lost his temper and I was . . . I didn't know . . . I swear by all that is holy, Nisrina . . . I did not know . . ." she was shaking her head.

"What didn't you know?" Nisrina asked.

"I . . . I was with child . . . we didn't know . . . I couldn't tell . . . it was too early . . . and then I bled and the doctor said . . ."

She couldn't finish, she began to sob, her face buried in her hands.

There was a soft knock on the door. It was Sister Alodia. She had come in with a bottle of wine and Nisrina rose to leave. She knew that Sister Alodia would listen to Magda's confession as she had done for her. Magda was Catholic, but she, too, had refused to speak with a priest.

"No, Nisrina, please stay." It was Magda. "I want to confess to you too. I owe you that. I need your complete forgiveness."

Nisrina glanced at Alodia, who nodded her approval, then sat back down on the small chair beside Magda's bed.

Magda took a deep breath and began. She confessed to Sister Alodia that it was she who'd instigated the crime against Nisrina that dark night in the alleyway. She was the one who'd led the beating and had struck the final blow. She told her how her envy had been great and how she wanted her gone from the school so that she could reclaim the honor of first chair. She had lashed out in anger. She was cruel and knew now it was wrong. She asked for their forgiveness.

Nisrina nodded. It pained her to hear it replayed.

Magda continued, "And, Sister Alodia I ask for the Church's forgiveness, too. I beg for God's mercy. I am so ashamed of what I've done. I hope it's not too late." She looked down at her trembling hands.

"It's never too late," said Alodia. She hesitated a moment and then thinking it best, she explained further, "Magda, my child . . . we knew. You see, it was the Reverend Mother that called for your parents to come and take you home. We found your scarf. It was lying near Nisrina in the alleyway. Under the circumstances the Mother felt it best for you to move on."

Magda wrung her hands.

Alodia continued, "And although it broke our hearts to see Nisrina suffer the way she did, we bear no ill will towards you. We've always kept you in our prayers."

Magda nodded. The nuns had been fair. They'd shown her mercy at a time when she deserved none. They could have called the Magistrate and her punishment would have been severe. And yet, she couldn't help but wonder. If she had not returned home. If she had not married. She shook her head. That time had already passed. She'd made her choices and suffered the consequences. She looked at the two kindly women who sat patiently across from her. Their faces were soft. Their hearts were pure. And she was thankful for their presence. Outside, the birds were chirping. They sang unabashedly in spite of her sorrow. There was no way they could fathom her pain. And she found them no fault. They sang because they had to. They were proof that despite her hardship, life continues. And that gave her consolation.

Alodia and Nisrina waited patiently as Magda collected her thoughts and garnered the strength to tell her story, and then, finally, in a very soft voice she began, "After being sent home, I knew that my parents were angry. But they never spoke of it. Instead they told me there was good news. I had a suitor, someone who had asked for my hand in marriage, an *itulab* had taken place while I was in school. And they had consented to my marrying him. My opinion was never sought. It was decided by the elders.

"His name was Saleem Musa. He was from a wealthy family and he paid my parents a handsome dowry. It was all arranged."

Magda looked down again, her voice now barely a whisper, "He bought me."

She looked back up, "At first I didn't mind. I was young and he was very handsome. He was kind and gentle. He wanted children.

And, *Enshallah,* I did too. I tried to give him children. I swear. But every month the blood would come and he would demand to see it. He would scream. He'd lose his temper and beat me. I no longer knew the man I'd married."

Her voice was quivering. She took in a deep breath, determined to go on.

"This last time . . . when I saw blood, I thought it was my monthly bleeding. He saw it, and as usual became enraged." She shook her head earnestly, "It wasn't until *afterward . . .* when I was in the hospital . . . the doctor told me I'd lost my child." She buried her face in her hands. She was weeping.

Nisrina and Alodia looked at each other.

"He blamed me for it. He said I should have known. He said that I was not a woman if I could not tell that I had a child growing inside me. He said I was a she-devil. And that I'd been sent by Satan to torment him."

Her voice broke. She could barely go on, she looked at them wide-eyed, determined to continue, "First he beat me. And *then* he punished me . . ." Her voice dropped to a low whisper, "he sent in his two brothers . . ." She gasped, covering her mouth.

Alodia raised her hand for her to stop, but Magda just shook her head. "They came to me in the dark . . . one at a time . . . I couldn't move. It . . . it lasted all night."

And then she began to sob uncontrollably. The memory too fresh, too ghastly.

"Oh dear God, please forgive me . . ." she pleaded through her tears. "I am so ashamed."

Nisrina got up and hugged the poor woman. She held her tightly until her sobs slowly diminished. Finally Sister Alodia motioned for Nisrina to leave. And kissing Magda on the forehead, she obediently left the room. Then, Sister Alodia called in the priest who gave Magda Holy Communion.

FIFTY

Friends at Last

THE FORMER ENEMIES WERE now inseparable. They would spend hours cooking together, Nisrina teaching Magda many of Alodia's favorite recipes. And in so doing, they discovered Magda's special affinity for baking pastries and in that endeavor had found her calling.

They laughed when Alodia spilled rice all over her freshly mopped floor and teased her mercilessly about it. But Alodia didn't mind. She was glad the two women finally found comfort in their friendship. Sister Miriam, walking in a few moments later, slipped on the uncooked rice. Alodia clucked softly to herself. But hiding her mirth, she stood there with hands on hips and scolded them, "Enough you two! I could use some help here, *yullah*, sweep up this mess!"

They gardened together. Pulling weeds and planting vegetables to be used in the kitchen. They planted tomatoes and onions and zucchini in neat rows. Digging small trenches alongside each row that would be used to hold the water to nourish each plant. Magda was amazed at how much Nisrina knew. The two worked side by side and as the days passed, their hands darkened and roughened from the soil and the sun.

Magda had always lived in the city. Coming from a wealthy family she was surrounded by servants and cooks. She had no idea how to prepare a good meal or manage a prosperous garden. She watched with childlike wonder as the zucchini vines grew long and sinewy, sending curving tendrils out through the garden. She was amazed to see their beautiful white blooms open with the sun, and watched the bees flitting from one to the other. When it was time, the blooms dried and withered and in their place there'd appear a small green ball. She watched it grow bit by bit, longer and fuller. Its shape changing with each new day. Until finally she recognized it as the vegetable served at her table.

Magda learned just the right time to pick the zucchini, not too small and not too big. Medium sized were best, tender and sweet. A few were always left to grow very large. Their seeds to be harvested for the next season's plantings.

Together, Nisrina and Magda harvested the crop, carrying the vegetables in their aprons. Nisrina taught Magda how to core the zucchini for *koosa mehshee*. Then they would stuff the hollowed shells with seasoned rice and lamb. No parts were wasted. They'd cook the sweet insides of the plant, sautéing them in olive oil with onions, spices and herbs.

They also picked fruit from the trees that grew outside the kitchen. There were persimmons and nectarines, loquats and oranges. They'd fill their baskets and running breathlessly back, take them into the kitchen where they were cleaned and served at the next meal.

Alodia was pleased. The Reverend Mother was thankful. Nisrina and Magda were no longer the two downtrodden women that had first come to them.

As the weeks passed, Nisrina noticed that Magda was becoming very tired. She'd lag behind when they'd run to bring in their baskets of fruit. And she'd yawn often during the day when they were working in the garden. Sometimes stopping to rest in the shade of the olive trees. Sometimes falling asleep and not waking until the bells for dinner chimed in the tower.

Nisrina asked her friend whether she was sleeping well at night and Magda always replied that she was. But Nisrina felt otherwise. She became increasingly worried, and finally thought she should mention it to Sister Alodia.

"Sister, have you noticed a weariness in Magda lately? She seeks rest quite often. Why just today I found her asleep under the olive trees."

Alodia listened to Nisrina's concerns, nodding her head as she kneaded the bread dough with her powerful arms. But the old cook just smiled, telling her not to worry. "Everything will be fine, Nisrina. All will go according to God's plan." Nisrina listened to the old cook's voice and like a hand brushing gently over velvet, it soothed her worries. But when the next day came, and Nisrina saw Magda drowsing off during breakfast, her uncertainties returned. Magda's unexplained fatigue continued to be a mystery that no one seemed willing to discuss.

As truth would have it, there was a reason for Magda's fatigue. For unbeknownst to Nisrina, in the evening hours after everyone had gone to sleep and the candles in the hallway had burned to stubs, Magda would quietly open her bedroom door and tiptoe out. She'd walk to the main building and straight over to the Reverend Mother's office. There she would knock quietly upon her door until the Mother's voice instructed her to enter. She would go inside, silently closing the door behind her.

FIFTY ONE

Commitment

MAGDA APPROACHED THE ENTRANCE of Sister Alodia's kitchen, pausing at the threshold, afraid to enter. It was late in the afternoon and the evening meal was being prepared. Nisrina was busy kneading dough for the next day's bread. Some of the novices were cutting vegetables, while others were washing, sautéing and stirring. There was still much to do in preparation for dinner. Sister Alodia went from one to the other supervising their work. She wondered to herself how she'd ever been able to manage everything on her own. But she was getting older now and things were changing. It was nice to have the young women around to help. The kitchen was so much livelier.

Nisrina felt a presence in the doorway and looked up. At first it was only a glance, then immediately she looked again. Standing before her was Magda, only not the Magda she knew. In place of her simple cotton dress, Magda was attired in the habit of a postulant.

Nisrina's mouth fell open.

"Magda!"

"Good afternoon," said Magda, a nervous smile forming on her lips.

Nisrina covered the bread dough. They stepped outside.

"Magda . . . what is this? Are you . . .?"

"Yes, Nisrina. I wanted to surprise you."

"But, when? How? I don't understand."

"I have been receiving instructions from the Reverend Mother. In the evenings after everyone has gone to bed. That is why I've been so tired," she began to giggle. Then her face grew serious, "Oh, Nisrina . . . I . . . I've decided to join the Sisterhood. I hope you don't mind, I didn't think you would." She looked at her friend who stood before her: her eyes wide open, her mouth agape.

Gathering her composure, Nisrina responded, "Of course not, Magda." She gave her friend a hug. "It's just that *you . . . this . . .* it's so unexpected, it took me by surprise, that's all. I think I need to sit down."

They sat on the bench beneath the olive tree.

"It took *me* by surprise, too! But now it all makes sense. I've happily made my decision. I wanted to tell you myself, while I still could. You see, tomorrow I take my vows of silence."

"Oh, Magda!" Nisrina hugged her again. "Such news! You are sure then?"

"Yes, Nisrina. I am sure. All this time, all that has happened to me . . . this is where God was leading me, right back to the nunnery."

"Then I am truly happy for you," Nisrina smiled warmly.

The two girls sat side by side on the bench across from the vegetable garden. Lost in their thoughts, they watched a rabbit who had ventured out in the cool afternoon air. Sitting up on his hindquarters, his whiskers twitching nervously, he contemplated his next move. Normally, Nisrina and Magda would have jumped in fast pursuit, shooing him away, protecting their precious crop. But today they languished, allowing him to stay.

Finally, Nisrina spoke, "I must say that I'm a bit envious of you right now, Magda."

Magda looked surprised.

"It's wonderful; you know your own mind. You have purpose and direction. You know what it is that you want." Nisrina's voice lowered, she looked down, "It's settled for you."

"Nisrina, what will you do?"

"I've been giving it much thought," she replied, "and I know that I cannot stay here forever."

"I think it's time for you to go home, Nisrina. It's time for you to return to your family."

"Oh, do you think I can? Do you think I ever can?" She looked hopefully at her friend, wondering if this new postulant held the answers to her dilemma.

"Of course you can, Nisrina. Your family loves you and they need you. You have done nothing wrong. Yes, I am sure of it. It is time for you to return."

"But I never explained to you . . . about what happened, I mean, things are so unclear . . ."

"Whatever happened is in the past. It is not for me to know. It is for God's eyes only. For Him to know. For I am sure that you are pure in His eyes. He led me to you in order that I might be healed. You have been the hand of God, Nisrina. And I will be forever grateful to you."

"And you have helped me, Magda."

She looked at her quizzically. "How could I possibly have helped you?"

"You taught me that our shame was not of our making. It was the others who did us wrong. Hearing your story, your ordeal, I was able to learn much from you . . . about my own experience, I mean. It reminds me of something Jabran told me once. Looking back, it was fortuitous, although neither one of us knew it at the time.

"It was when the ladies of the village would gossip . . . about me, about our family. They would say hurtful things, as people often do. And he said to me . . . . 'Nisrina, you must never let the opinions of others affect the opinion you have of yourself.' And I can see now how very wise he was with those words.

"But to go back home . . . is it possible? I don't know. So much has happened. So many questions remain unanswered . . . I'm just not sure. But one thing is certain. I miss my children."

Magda gave her a hug. "Go to them Nisrina. I beg of you. Nothing could be so bad as to separate a mother from her children."

"Nothing?" asked Nisrina wistfully.

"No, nothing," Magda responded.

Just then, Sister Miriam burst through the doors, and ran out to the garden where the two women were sitting. She was breathless.

"Nisrina, there's a visitor. Someone's come asking for you. She's waiting in the foyer. Come quickly!"

As she entered the foyer, Nisrina saw the small figure standing there. The old woman was leaning on her cane and gazing up at the beautiful paintings on the wall in much the same way as Nisrina had on her first day at the nunnery. And although she could only see the back of the woman, she knew her figure and recognized her stance. She called out to her.

"Dora!"

Dora turned around.

"Nisrina!"

They ran to each other and embraced. Their tears flowed, neither wanting to let go.

"I've missed you so!"

"And I, you."

Sister Miriam, watching from the hallway, slipped back into the darkness, leaving the two women to themselves. And the Mother, who had been standing in her doorway, did likewise.

"How did you find me?"

"It was the Magistrate. He was in the city one day and saw you shopping at the market. He was too nervous to approach you, and instead followed you back here."

Dora's eyes looked to the right, averting Nisrina's gaze. Nisrina too looked away as Dora continued, "He stopped in and spoke with the Mother Superior. She advised him that you were on God's mission. The Magistrate came home and told us." She looked back at Nisrina, "We knew you would come home when you were done with His work."

"And the children? Dora, how are my children?"

"That's why I'm here, Nisrina. Please, sit down, we must talk." She led her to the wooden bench that sat against the wall.

"What is it?" Panic came into Nisrina's voice. "Tell me, Dora, are they well?"

"Nisrina, listen to me, it's not good . . . it's the epidemic. The influenza. It has come to Beit el Jebel, to the Yusef compound. And the children are sick. They are very sick. They need you."

"Oh, dear God! I must go to them! Have you called the doctor?" Nisrina was tugging on Dora's gown with both her hands, she needed to know.

"Nisrina, things have been difficult lately. We have very little money you see, especially since . . . since . . . Well, you see, Jacob tries to work in your orchard part of the time and he sells what he can. But it's just too much for him. And Essam, he's such a little man now, he works alongside his uncle, but you must understand, Jacob has his own home and his own fields to tend. He can't do everything."

"Did you call a doctor?" Nisrina repeated firmly.

Dora looked down, "No, Nisrina. Too many people are sick. He can't see everyone. He only sees those who can pay him."

Nisrina ran to the Reverend Mother's office and banged loudly on her door. The Mother opened it and Nisrina, in a panic, explained her story.

"Rest assured," the Mother said. "We'll have a doctor from the hospital come to your home. Don't worry. I will take care of it. They will not refuse me. You go to your children now, be quick. He'll be there before you know it."

Nisrina thanked the Mother. Then she did the unthinkable. She embraced her tightly with both her arms. She grabbed her and held her, pressing her cheeks against the Mother's chest and she thanked her over and over again until finally the Mother, smiling to herself, told her to go, her children needed her.

Nisrina and Dora turned and ran out the door. An old man from the village sat in a cart waiting for them. Dora had hired him to drive his cart to the city to pick up Nisrina. His own donkey was lame, and so Dora offered him the use of one from the Yusef compound.

Nisrina instantly recognized the animal hitched to the front of the cart. "Abu Faraj!" she called out, delighted to see her old friend. She ran up to him and nuzzled his big nose, kissing him over and over again. He seemed to recognize his mistress, as he gave out a loud "Hee-Ahh!"

"Hurry Nisrina, we must go." Dora was already in the cart, sitting atop a layer of hay.

Nisrina did not stop to pack her things or say goodbye. She jumped into the back of the cart still wearing the apron that she'd put on earlier that day. It was covered with remnants of the flour and oil she'd been using to make the bread. And as they drove away, tumbled and tossed, Nisrina noticed the distinctive, yet comforting smell of yeast that lingered about her.

But her thoughts quickly turned to her children. They were ill and they needed her. The decision had finally been made. She was going home.

FIFTY TWO

A Mother's Touch

"GO FASTER!" NISRINA WAS banging on the back of the driver's seat.

"*Enshallah*! I'm going as fast as this beast will take me!" He called back to her.

And he was. Abu Faraj seemed to sense the urgency of the situation. A faithful animal, he traveled as fast as he could, which was quite unexpected for a beast of his age. The road was unpaved, and with the ruts and the rocks and the diminishing light, it had become quite a haphazard ride.

"God forbid, if I don't get there on time, I will never forgive myself," Nisrina kept muttering.

Dora patted her hand, "There, there, *Enshallah*, it will be alright. You'll see. We'll get there on time, *Enshallah*. God willing."

But on all other counts, Dora remained silent.

It was dark when they arrived.

"We're here." The old man was shouting, trying to wake them.

The two women jumped up, realizing their ride had ended.

Nisrina could not believe her eyes. She was finally home.

"I cannot pay you," Dora's voice was firm as Nisrina ran into the house. "However, I will give you our goat. She is old, but still gives milk. A great addition to your household."

"What choice do I have?" The driver was too tired to argue. "I will take her."

He had gone a long distance and now his reward was paltry—an old goat. Dora was a village woman, so straightforward, so respectable, he'd not wanted to insult her by asking for money upfront. For now, the goat would do. It would give his grandchildren some much needed milk and eventually he'd sell her at market or slaughter her for meat. Dora brought him the nanny goat and he tied it to the back of the cart. He'd return the donkey tomorrow. He wiped his brow with the back of his hand and drove away. Dora left to join the others in the house, she would explain Jacob's missing goat to him later—much later.

The children were sick indeed. Their fevers high, they lay restless in their beds. Essam recognized his mother, but only for a moment as he went in and out of delirium thinking it a dream. He dreamt she was an angel from heaven who had come to care for him. He even saw a halo encircling her head.

Nisrina, seeing the sad state of affairs, quickly went to work. She went from bed to bed sponging her children with cool cloths soaked in rosewater. She bent over Essam and kissed his forehead. He was on fire. He opened his eyes for a moment and looked up at her. She spoke softly to him, "Hello *habeebee*. It's okay. *Yumma* is here now. You must get better, hm?" All the while she was stroking his hair, dampened by the fever. She saw him smile, a tiny crooked smile, almost imperceptible. Perhaps she'd imagined it. She heard him whisper, "*Yumma*," and then closed his eyes. He drifted off.

Jameela was pale. She had always been the hardy one. But now she looked weak, fragile. Nisrina pulled back her blankets to cool her fever, and then when she started to shake, she put them back. Always speaking sweetly to her, tenderly soothing her and patting her hand. Nisrina didn't know if Jameela could hear her or not, but, she continued to comfort her with motherly words and a gentle touch.

She then moved to where Hannah lay. Hannah was asleep, but restless—moaning quietly to herself. Nisrina could hear her murmurings and it broke her heart. Beset with worry, she climbed into her youngest child's bed and lifted her up, cradling her gently in her arms. So tiny and frail. She rocked her back and forth and sang softly to her until the little one settled back into a deeper sleep. Then Nisrina put her down and lightly placed the covers over her.

She continued going from one child to the next. Comforting and attending to each of them. All the while praying quietly to herself. Asking God for His mercy. Begging Him to spare her children. To heal them and make them whole again. She knew no other way. She'd left them and now they suffered.

"Has the priest come?" Nisrina wanted to know.

"Yes," replied Dora. "He was here this morning and brought Holy Water. He prayed over them, burned incense and gave them blessings, touching each one of their foreheads. He said he would return again tomorrow." Dora bit her lip, trying not to cry. She needed to be strong for this little family.

"Thank you," Nisrina said. She appreciated that Dora had at least been able to get the priest to come and attend to her children. His presence was always reassuring and she felt comforted in knowing he'd been there.

Before long, the doctor arrived. He came directly from the hospital as the Reverend Mother had promised. Nisrina ran to the door to greet him and led him to the children's room. He quickly attended to each child, checking their pulse, their hearts and their lungs. He looked very grave as he gave Nisrina the medicine, instructing her to administer it throughout the night.

"There's no way to know for sure." He was brutally honest. "But, hopefully, they will get better. Children are resilient. *Enshallah* this will be the worst night and if all goes well, their fevers will break by dawn. We shall see."

For one brief moment Nisrina felt her resolve begin to fail. And then, as if by miracle, she felt the Reverend Mother's touch on her shoulder as she had so many times in the nunnery. She saw those crystal blue eyes, so constant and pure, and she sensed the matron's enduring presence.

She regained her composure and thanked the doctor for coming, for attending to her children, and she took the medicine from his hands. The hour was late, and Jacob offered him a room for the night. Tired and worn, the doctor gladly accepted. After such a hard day, he did not relish the idea of the long journey back to the city. Nisrina was relieved that he would be so close should anything go wrong.

While the little ones slept, Nisrina thanked Jacob's wife, May, for watching the children in Dora's absence. It was May that left her home to care for them while Dora was gone to retrieve her.

"Of course, wife of my husband's brother, they are like my own," she replied sincerely. May knew that at her age, her chances of having children had past and like all members of the Yusef family, she had become very close to Nisrina's. She felt honored to finally be needed.

They had all heard terrible stories about the influenza epidemic. People all over the world were dying. No country had been spared. The disease, indiscriminate, gave no preference to race, creed, or color. And when it struck, it was known to strike fast and mercilessly.

Being a small isolated village, the townspeople thought that they would be spared this horrible disease. There'd been no cases reported in their town or in those neighboring. And the talk was that the numbers of sick and dying had begun to diminish; the worst was over, they'd been told. But now, here, at the end of this worldwide epidemic, when people in other lands had begun to breathe sweet sighs of relief, this dreadful disease had reached out its ugly claw and grabbed hold of the people of Beit el Jebel.

They'd heard that it usually spared the very young and the very old, striking hardest the young adults. And so the townspeople were shocked when the children of the Yusef family grew ill. Not to mention the others in the village who now suffered its rage.

"It's God's wrath!" Mona could be heard screaming from the kitchen. "The evil that's befallen this family. It's His wrath, I tell you! We'll all suffer for those who have sinned against Him!"

The townspeople had become accustomed to Mona's ramblings. Her mind continuing to deteriorate with her advancing age. No longer the stalwart woman she'd once been, her conversations were now limited to loud and sudden outbursts, spilling forth all matter of thought that passed through her head. But Nisrina had been away and was not aware of the extent of her sister-in-law's condition. Vulnerable to her words, her own perceptions ran wild. God's wrath had certainly been a possibility in her mind. The seers always spoke of the sins of the father—and of the mother. She thought of Najeeb lying bloody on the threshold and began to wring her hands.

The doctor had completed his examinations and was ready to retire for the night, and so Jacob and May, along with Mona, returned to their homes. Dora agreed to stay with Nisrina.

As they said their goodnights, they comforted each other agreeing that they'd done all things possible for the children. And being people of strong faith, they further acknowledged that any outcome which followed was now in the hands of the Lord. They would pray for His grace and His mercy. And they knew that the outcome was His and His alone to determine, for only He had the power to heal them.

In spite of their words, their well wishes and their faith, there remained an unspoken and unresolved issue. A heavy silence that pervaded the air and clouded the matter. For in the heat of the crisis, no one had dared to comment on the fact that Nisrina had been gone for so long. No one in the family had raised the issue or asked the question as to the why of her extended leave. And more importantly, no one had mentioned that when they'd returned from the *souk* that night so long ago, they found Najeeb lying dead in the narrow doorway of her kitchen.

At the present, they were only concerned with the health and well being of Nisrina's children. And, although no one would venture to say it out loud, they were all quite relieved to have such an overriding matter to command their attention.

Nisrina couldn't sleep. Dora, who elected to stay the night with her, begged her to lie down to rest awhile. She offered to watch the children and wake her if there were any changes in their condition. Nisrina would not consider it. She sat upright in the big chair in the corner of the room, her eyes wide open, her mind alert, listening to the steady breathing of her ailing children. But as the hours passed, the rhythmic sound began to lull her and eventually, even a worried mother could not resist the temptations of the night's call to slumber.

As the dawn broke, it found everyone in the Yusef family sleeping soundly. Even the little ones who just hours before lay struggling with labored breaths, slumbered peacefully. Their fevers had broken. God's mercy prevailed.

Nisrina and Dora were the first to wake and they silently tiptoed from bed to bed, feeling the children's foreheads and smiling to one another. They were nodding and quietly making the sign of the cross over each child. God be blessed. All was well.

FIFTY THREE

Secrets

MARTA CAME BURSTING THROUGH the door into Nisrina's house. She had not been there the night before, still harboring dubious thoughts of Nisrina's role in her husband's death. She had elected to remain at home nursing a sudden headache. Ignoring Nisrina's presence, she looked directly at Dora, "Dora, come quickly, it's Mona . . . she has the fever! *Enshallah*, I went to visit her. To bring her some *zait oo zaatar*." Marta was wringing her hands nervously, "the oil and herbs were fresh, the mint picked from my garden just this morning. They were fresh, I swear to God . . . and there she was, lying in her bed, hot and sweating . . . the fever's taken her mind . . . she keeps calling out . . ." Marta hesitated a moment, finally turning to face Nisrina, her face cold, her heart hard. "She keeps calling Nisrina's name . . . I don't know why . . . it is you she needs, Dora . . . you are the sister, come quickly, please!"

The three women rushed back across the courtyard to Mona's home, to her bedside.

They saw the elder sibling lying there as Marta had described. She was tossing and turning, her head was hot, her face flushed. The sheets were wet from the dampness of the fever.

Dora placed cold cloths on her sister's forehead to calm and cool her, while Nisrina and Marta changed her bedding. They did all they could to make her comfortable, but secretly they feared the worst.

The doctor stopped by to examine Mona before returning to the hospital. He gave the same advice he had given for the children, only this time he warned the family that Mona's prognosis was nowhere near as hopeful.

"You must remember that she is not a young woman," he stated. "Her constitution is frail and her lungs are quite congested. I'm sorry." He shook his head, "Hers will be a more trying battle." He put away his instruments, "Try to keep her comfortable."

Nisrina, Dora and Marta remained the day by Mona's side. Each insisting that they be the one to stay. Each encouraging the other two to leave, maintaining that they could manage alone. But it was clear, if Mona, in her fever, was to speak her deathbed wisdoms, they wanted to hear the words for themselves.

They reached an agreement—they would all stay. Each one standing sentry in a separate corner of the room, their arms crossed resolutely in front of their chests. They waited and watched, praying that the elderly Mona would soon regain her senses, hoping her fever would break. Lost in their own thoughts, they secretly wondered where the troubled mind of their sister lay.

Mona slept restlessly as she went in and out of delirium.

Finally she settled down. They noticed a calm in her breathing. It became even, without struggle or tension, and then she opened her eyes.

But she could not see them.

Mona was murmuring to herself. The only word they could discern was Nisrina's name. She repeated it again and again.

Simultaneously, the three women brought in chairs, pulling them up close, adjacent to the bed. They leaned forward. They sat and watched. Listening as Mona restlessly thrashed about, wrestling with the devil that tormented her.

And then they heard another name pass her fevered lips.

There was no question. It was clear and concise—"Najeeb."

The three women looked at each other.

Dora quickly averted her eyes, her thoughts raced back to the night Najeeb died. She relived the vision of him lying on the kitchen floor, the tomatoes splattered on the ground, and the burnt remnants of Nisrina's dress in the kitchen fireplace. Inadvertently, she rubbed her temples with her fingertips, her head was aching.

Nisrina's stomach turned inside out, she swallowed hard. It was the first time she'd heard her brother-in-law's name since that fateful night. And now its sound pierced her soul. Her mind froze, her eyes opened wide.

Marta's face went pale, her lips pursed tightly together. What was the secret that linked her husband to the missing midwife? She could not bear to look at Nisrina, and kept her face turned away.

Hovering on the cusp between the living and the dead, Mona called out again . . .

"Najeeb!" she was hollering now, "No Najeeb! No! What will mother say? Najeeb, No! You don't understand . . ."

The three women sat upright in their chairs. They looked at each other, their eyes and mouths opened wide.

Then Mona stopped. She closed her eyes—slipping into a deep sleep. A sleep of memories and days long past.

Mona was her mother's second child and her first daughter. And as such, she could always be found at her side, helping, learning, and listening. Born with a joy for life, she often lifted the wife of Farooz from her doldrums, and served as a loyal companion to her in all things womanly. As the years passed, the mother watched her spirited young daughter grow. She noticed her body begin to change as it took the shape of a woman's form, and she knew that her daughter's time to wed was not far off.

Mona, too, was aware that things were changing inside her. She turned crimson when her brothers would gaze upon her body, finally requesting that her mother allow her to use the privacy curtain when she needed to dress or bathe. She felt her breasts growing beneath her *thobe,* and sensed feelings in her body that amazed and confused her. When her mother sent her to town to purchase fruits and grains for the family dinner, the thoughts that raced through her brain overwhelmed her. Her heart would flutter and her hands would tremble, for she knew that she would see the young boy who sold figs and grapes from his tattered old fruit cart.

In her dream-filled delirium, Mona could still see his face.

He was strong and handsome and wore a belt of braided gold threads around his waist. She knew he would be there, for he came to market on the fifth day of each week, carrying the figs and grapes grown ripe on his father's farm. His father was an old man and had lost much of his sight. He could no longer make the arduous trek down the mountainside into town and so he relied on his son, Isa, to sell his crop. And every fifth day when Mona was sent into town by her mother, having been instructed to buy the freshest and most succulent of fruits, she would boldly go up to the young boy's cart and ask the handsome lad if his fruits were in fact the freshest and ripest of all those in Beit el Jebel. And he would smile at her and wink his eye, declaring that no others could match the sweet flavor of his produce.

"And how is it that your grapes are so much sweeter than the carts I've passed already?" Mona asked him tauntingly.

"I must admit, they were not sweet when I arrived into town this morning," he replied. "But just the sight of your lovely face has caused them to sugar and ripen. Your radiance has warmed them as surely as it has warmed my heart."

He smiled fearlessly at her, a twinkle in his eye.

Young Isa Huniah had been watching Mona for many months now. He'd seen how she was growing into a woman and her visage played often in his mind.

Mona blushed at his emboldened manner, but unlike so many of the girls in her village, her qualities were strong. She liked this man and imagined herself in his home, working in his kitchen and sleeping in his bed.

He handed her a ripened fig, large and purple, its skin was thick and the honeyed syrup was oozing from its stem.

"Please, taste the sweetness that I have for you," he implored. "Put this to your lips and know that what I give you is only a taste of what is yet to come."

Mona was moved by his flirtations. She blushed, but took the fig from his hands, her eyes never leaving his, and she bit into the fruit which indeed was sweet.

She smiled at him.

"Come," he said. "Let me show you what else I have for you."

He took her hand in his and led her away. She followed him down a dirt path, behind the row of small block buildings where the farmers sold their wares, then off into the wide green pasture filled with tall grasses. They were on the outskirts of town, but she didn't care. So captivated was she by his charms, she could not turn back. So sure was she of her feelings for him, she merely closed her eyes and let him lead her. She breathed in, smelling the sweet fragrant scent of the jasmine blossoms, her heart aching with delight.

In the pasture, under the shelter of an old oak tree, Mona lay down with young Isa Huniah. She could feel the sparrows fluttering in the tall branches overhead. Their songs ringing out the joy she could not express. She saw the clouds up high in the heavens, the white, billowy canopy diffusing the sun that warmed her face. She heard his breath, coming stronger and stronger beside her. Then he turned to her. She could not count the seconds before their lips touched and their passions flared. His heart was her heart, and his breath her breath. She'd never known such happiness. So handsome, he was. So bold and sure of himself.

They heard a twig snap nearby.

Suddenly two large hands reached down as if from heaven above. They grabbed Isa and lifted him high into the air. He was carried up like a pebble from the creek, and tossed back down amongst the grasses. The air expelled hard from his lungs.

"How dare you compromise my sister's reputation and dishonor the Yusef name?!"

Najeeb's voice shattered the calm. "By what authority do you take her into the fields and poison her with your words and your lurid kisses?"

Mona scrambled to her feet. Trembling, she adjusted her skirt and brushed the leaves and grasses from her hair. Backing away from Najeeb's fury, she pressed herself against the tree's roughened trunk. She'd always known her brother to be a boy of extreme temper, but had never seen his face grow quite so red, his breath quite so furious. Najeeb reached back his arm and brought it forward with the force of a breeding ram. He punched Isa hard, his fist landing squarely in the boy's stomach; the first blow quickly followed by another and then another. His fists did not cease their rampage until young Isa Huniah, humiliated and bruised, ran crying into the hills.

But Najeeb was not done; his rage yet unquenched. He turned to his sister who stood frozen under the massive tree. She'd been begging Najeeb to stop, to have mercy on her beloved, her pleas still ringing in his ears.

"So this is how you'd have it, my sister? Is this how you see yourself in the world? A woman unwed, who'd lie in the grasses with a foolish young farmer? Is that what you so desperately want? If so, then by all means, let me accommodate you . . . after all, I am your brother!"

Najeeb brazenly lifted his gown, and with a hideous smirk, revealed his readiness.

Mona was mortified. She had never seen the likes of such a thing, the donkeys and goats in her father's farmyard having more modesty than he. In disgust, she turned her face away, a harsh, guttural sound escaping her throat.

Najeeb only laughed, his voice evil and lewd. He jeered her for her timidity, saliva spewing from his mouth, "Where is your shame-lessness now, my dear Mona?" he goaded her. "Where is that passion I witnessed just moments ago?"

He took her by the arms and forced her body close to him, his hot breath all over her face. "Here, I will teach you what folly such passion can render . . . Now you will come to me! I will show you what it is that a man does to a woman!"

He threw her head back and forced her to lie on the ground. Then, lifting her *thobe* high above her head, he entered her. She screamed and cried and begged for his mercy, but he kept on, unrelenting and fierce. He was young and his heat was strong; he continued the brutal ravaging for what, to her, felt an eternity. When he finished, he walked away saying callously, "If you ever breathe a word of this to anyone, I will kill you myself."

Mona never told a living soul and even the young boy, Isa Huniah, knew not of her fate. She began to walk with her eyes cast downward, never returning to the marketplace, insisting that Dora alone be sent, always maintaining that she preferred the sanctity of her garden, and proclaiming that its care and tending was her gift to God.

As the years passed, Mona found that she could no longer look at another man, nor could she imagine sharing their beds or tending their homes. She put away the promising thoughts of hopeful young women and instead turned her sorrow to bitterness and her pain to contempt. She could love no person and no thing. She no longer remembered a time when she wore a smile upon her face or a pretty ribbon in her hair. Her mother and father never understood or imagined the horror, and eventually they accepted the fact that she was a woman who would live in their compound until her dying day.

Mona was stirring, saying things only she could understand. Dora, Marta, and Nisrina exchanged furtive glances, wondering if her chatter could be interpreted with any certainty. However, they asked no questions. No one daring to discern her words. No one wishing to break the momentum. When she'd speak, they'd lean forward in their chairs. Listening intently. Trying not to breathe. Straining to hear every syllable.

And as she began again, her voice barely audible, the three women leaned closer still, their chairs now pushed up as far as they could, "Najeeb . . . No! Please . . . I love Isa!! I love Isa Huniah!! We were to be wed!! Why did you beat him? You've scared him away!"

She continued to cry—softly, quietly, as she slowly fell back to sleep.

Nisrina covered her mouth in horror. Mona had called out her father's name—Isa Huniah. She'd said she loved him and that they were to be wed!!

Many times she'd heard the villagers' whispers, with their veiled stories of her father's clouded past. How his untoward behavior had caused a young girl's demise, darkening both his future and that of the woman he finally chose to wed. But she never believed them, assuming the tales were merely products of wagging tongues. And she certainly never dreamed that it was Mona with whom he had once cavorted, or that it was Najeeb who'd given him the beating. No wonder he'd been so pleased to betroth her to the Yusef family!

And her mother—her father's true love—is this why she was destined to die so young? Was her life sacrificed in retribution for her husband's ill-doings? A cold shiver ran up her spine.

Then the memory of her own experience with the evil Najeeb played through her thoughts. The other women knew nothing about what happened to her in the kitchen. It was not so long ago, but nothing had been mentioned since her return. No questions were asked, and she was grateful for that. She wondered what they had thought when they found Najeeb lying in her doorway. He was dead, she was sure of it, or so she thought. Her mind began to race— perhaps he wasn't. Why had no one mentioned it? Perhaps he had survived and would walk into the room at any moment to check on Mona. Say hello to his wife.

Her hands began to shake. No, he was dead. She was sure of it. But where were the questions? Somehow she knew they would never come. There were more pressing matters at hand, what with the epidemic and all.

Nisrina kept her eyes cast down, unable to face her sisters-in-law.

Mona stirred again, her face now twisting in horror, "No stop! No one will want me if you . . . please, stop, please, no!" She was shaking her head, writhing back and forth, weeping uncontrollably, "Najeeb, how could you? Shame. Shame. Now I will never marry."

Dora cried out, turning her face away. She could stand it no more. She realized that her sister, the tall one, the one who'd always been so strong, so direct, facing each crisis head-on, had all along been suffering a secret too horrid to share. And, in these fragile moments she was freeing herself from the awful memories. There was no denying the meaning of her sister's words, and Dora could not bear it.

She struggled with the recollections of their youth. Had there been any signs? Could she have stopped it? She faulted herself, thinking that she had not been there for her sister. But she was younger than Mona. She was the plain one. Always in the shadows. Dora grew accustomed to anonymity. She'd had no way of knowing. Poor Mona. All this time. No one knew.

She looked away, the horror unbearable.

Marta could not believe her ears. Poor Marta. She had always wanted children. To have a family of her own. To dress them up and take them with her to church. She was an excellent seamstress. She would have sewn clothes for them. She would have laid down her heart for them. But she remained childless. Married to a brute who had defiled his sister.

All these years she'd known of her husband's philandering ways and she had always turned the other cheek, suffering the looks and whispers of the villagers. But the implications of Mona's words were beyond the scope of her imaginings. Horrified by the possibilities of what else lay untold, she buried her face in her hands. She could not fathom it. What other crimes had gone unpunished? What other sins had been committed? She peeked over at Nisrina and saw the way she was clenching her fists tightly in her lap. Her knuckles so white.

And like the other two women, Marta remained silent, her eyes covered in shame.

Mona stirred again. She sat straight up. This time her voice was loud, her eyes wide open, but she looked into a world far beyond the room of her little house, a world that the others could not see. She yelled out, "No! Not Nisrina. I won't let it happen again. No! Not her. You beast, this is the last time. Yes, it is the knife. I have it. No, I won't let this happen. Not again. No Najeeb. No. I'm telling you, this is the last time. Awgh!" She fell back against the pillow, and began to whisper, "There . . . it is done. I stopped him Nisrina, it's alright now. You can get up. It's over. I promise you, it won't happen again. It won't happen again." She began to whimper, closing her eyes, slipping back to sleep.

All three women silently looked at each other. Their eyes wide open.

Their poor Mona, no wonder she'd gone mad.

Nisrina looked at Dora, her face was wet.

Marta could stand it no longer. She hid her face from the shame of it all. From her husband's filth and sordid degradations.

Mona's eyes never opened again.

FIFTY FOUR

The Colonel's Visit

THE FUNERAL WAS A quiet one.

Mona Yusef was laid to rest, and her secrets buried with her.

The villagers knew nothing of Mona's confessions. They asked no questions and cast no aspersions. And the three women, who did know, never spoke of it—neither amongst themselves or to anyone else. Dora, Nisrina, and Marta believed that the living should not be burdened with the painful musings of the dead. They moved on, always keeping Mona in their prayers. Together with Jacob and May, they raised the children and grew their crops. Pickling, canning and cooking delicious foods, while Nisrina continued to help new life come into the world.

The villagers accepted Nisrina's reappearance as nothing out of the ordinary. She was a mother who'd returned from midwifery school to be with her children. They were happy to see her, and delighted to have a *dayah* in their village again.

It was the epidemic that had shaken their core. Its fury ran rampant, leaving no family untouched. Its aftermath forever altering the shape and attitudes of those left behind. Women who previously told tales and whispered and judged, no longer had the will to ask questions or raise an unforgiving brow. Unaware, a subtle yielding had occurred. Like a nursling that flexed with a mother's sweet caress, a fragile softening had entered their village, and, at long last, the days of whispering and speculation finally came to an end.

Nisrina heard a knock.

Wiping her hands on her apron she rushed to open the door. Standing before her was Colonel Billingham. Nisrina had heard that he was visiting the homes in the Yusef compound to pay his respects for Mona's passing. He had already called on Jacob and May, and they advised her that he might knock on her door as well.

"*Salaam a rahsik,*" the Colonel greeted her with sympathy, his hat held neatly in his hand.

Nisrina had seen him many times in the marketplace. He was always meticulously groomed, standing tall in his uniform, his back erect and his thick blond hair combed carefully in place. Their eyes would meet, and he would nod, but she always turned away, not daring to acknowledge him or look back in his direction. And now, here he stood before her. She could not forget the scandalous gossip that occurred the last time they spoke, or her brother-in-law's vengeance that followed that event. But things were different now, she thought to herself. The villagers had changed. Or had they?

"*Shukran,*" she thanked him. Her voice trembling, her eyes shifting to one side.

"*Oum* Essam, I've come to pay my respects," he said. His voice was deep and his manner sober. "Please accept my condolences for the loss of your dear sister-in-law."

His crystal blue eyes darted about the space that separated them, alternating between her soft face and his well-polished boots.

"*Shukran,*" she thanked him again. "Can I offer you a cup of coffee?" Her question was mechanical, expected. To ask less would have been a grave insult to the guest who stood at her door.

"I don't wish to trouble you."

"No, of course not," she responded. "It is no trouble. You are welcome anytime, come in, come in."

Her cheeks grew warm, and her hands went cold. She repeatedly dried them on her apron although they were no longer wet. Jacob was away in the fields. Essam and Jameela had not yet returned home from school, and Hannah lay napping in the bedroom nearby. If only

Dora was there, or Marta or May, but they weren't. They'd gone to visit Farida, the seamstress. Together, the four women were making a quilt for a young neighbor's wedding.

She managed a smile, and graciously motioned the Colonel to sit on her sofa. He politely obliged, his fingers tracing the well-fashioned Italian brocade. He noticed the small tears and fine creases that covered the cloth and how the crocheted napkins had been used to shelter its arms. Nisrina excused herself and disappeared behind the walls of her kitchen. He watched her go and listened as she filled the *ibrik* and stoked the fire. The wind outside was biting, and she knew that the warmth of hot coffee would comfort her guest. If the weather had been warm, she might have forgone the dark, steaming brew and instead served a pitcher of tea or cold lemonade. She'd have sugared it with just a finger of honey, adding rosewater and the chill of sweet peppermint leaves. But for today, the coffee would suit them well.

The Colonel sat back, perusing his surroundings. He'd been inside her house only one time before. Shifting in his seat, he recalled the night he'd been summoned there by the Magistrate's men. He remembered the shock of seeing her brother-in-law's body lying dead on the floor. Not a sight for a woman's eyes, he was relieved that she'd not been there to see it.

Crossing and uncrossing his legs, he became aware of the feel of her home. Her kind words of welcome had lightened the air, and he breathed it in. The smell of coffee and spices filled the room. It warmed the space around him and he wondered what culinary delights had been born within these walls. The diffused light that filtered through the gauze-covered windows shimmered and danced against the tall block walls and limestone floor casting a calm across the room. He marveled at the soft handmade rug beneath his feet, the brilliant colors and pictorial scenes so familiar in Middle Eastern homes. As he studied the intricate pattern of the loom, he noticed how sections had faded and thinned where thousands of footsteps had tread, and he reached down and touched the history of its weave.

He settled into the soft cushions and smiled inwardly. Although he typically dreaded these visits on behalf of His Majesty, on this one occasion, he was pleased that he'd come.

He was impressed by the efficiency of the room. He could see that everything had its purpose, and that each piece, from the upright mahogany cabinet that sat tall in the corner, to the tightly knit throw folded neatly on the back of the cushions, was meticulously placed. He could hear Nisrina in the kitchen as she prepared the coffee. She was humming a sweet tune to herself. And he noted that it was as lovely as she.

He stood up and walked slowly around the room, stopping at a table with several framed pictures. He held the first portrait. Nisrina was seated to the left of the photo, surrounded in full by her family. Essam stood in the center. Dressed in a suit, he wore a small fez hat tilted smartly to one side. The Colonel couldn't help but notice how the camera had captured a subtle melancholy in the boy's eyes, and it saddened him to think that one so young should feel the weight of a household on his shoulders.

The family had been dressed in their finest clothes, as each one sat still, gazing into the camera's eye. He mused over the fact that the portrait had not quite captured Nisrina's beauty or her calm, pleasant way. The toe of a silk shoe peeked out beneath the hem of her skirt, and the Colonel found this amusing as he'd never seen her wear shoes upon her feet. Like all the women of the village, she walked the dirt paths barefoot, carrying her shoes in her hands to use when entering the church or a neighbor's new home.

He reached for the next picture. It was Nisrina standing in traditional wedding garb, her hand resting on the shoulder of a man seated beside her. They were cloaked in the solemnity of a couple about to take their final vows. Their faces stiff, no trace of a smile. The joy of their marriage had been obscured by the gravity of the occasion, and the intrusion of the photographer's lens. The Colonel was about to return the picture to the well-polished table, but curious, he held back, taking one more look. He wanted to study the face of the man that had captured this good woman's heart.

He looked closely at the picture. He saw the strength of character in the young groom's face, the seriousness with which he entered into this most holy of unions. He hesitated again, unable to replace the photo. There was something familiar that caused him pause.

Had he seen this man before? He wasn't sure. But something in his expression, his eyes. They looked vaguely familiar.

As Nisrina came into the room, the Colonel looked up. She was carrying a tray of coffee with a small plate of *graibeh*, Arabic butter cookies. The custom in her village dictated that visitors be offered refreshments. Visits of condolences were typically limited to coffee and cigarettes. However, for the Colonel's special appearance she made an exception. She smiled at him as she served the cookies, and in that moment his lost memories spilled forth. Almost dropping the picture, he caught himself, carefully returning it to the table. Nisrina saw this, but said nothing.

They sat down and chatted about the pleasantries of village life, the weather and the children. The Colonel spoke of his wife and daughter who returned to England during the epidemic, and how he looked forward to seeing them again. Nisrina smiled and nodded, pouring him another cup of coffee.

The Colonel grew impatient. He kept running his fingers through his hair and clearing his throat. Memories of the war and the men who'd crossed his path kept flitting through his mind. He sipped his coffee again and again, but his curiosity had bettered him. He needed to know more about the man who sat in the picture alongside Nisrina.

"Nisrina," he began, "I was looking at the pictures of your family. I hope you don't mind."

"Of course not," she replied. "They are there to enjoy. Fond memories, I must say."

"Of course," he replied. "I'm sure they are."

He sipped his coffee and nibbled the cookies. The soft buttery texture melted in his mouth. Alodia's recipe.

"These are magnificent," he said. "*Salaam adaykee*, you are an excellent cook."

"Thank you," she responded. "I learned from a very good teacher during my stay at the nunnery." And then she hesitated as she realized that it was a topic she held close. She did not mean to open that door, and certainly not with a British Colonel.

"Yes," he replied, "You were there for some time, if I recall. I suppose it was all part of your training. As a midwife, I mean."

"Yes," she answered, her eyes cast downward. "It was part of my learning experience."

"Ah, yes. I see. I see. I must confess, I've heard of your reputation. As a midwife, of course." He was beginning to get flustered, angry with himself. He was a Colonel after all. He couldn't let this small woman rattle him so, no matter how dark and beautiful her eyes. But more so, he needed to keep his wits about him, he needed to ask her about the man she called her husband. He cleared his throat again and put down his cup.

"Thank you," she replied, her cheeks turning red. "I am dedicated to my trade."

"Well, you're doing an excellent job," he enjoined. "Or so I hear, of course." He shifted in his seat. "But I must say, my wife was disappointed that you were not available during the birth of our daughter. On that one point I must chastise your absence." He smiled.

Looking up, she saw his blue eyes twinkling back at her and she smiled too.

"I would have enjoyed getting to know her better. And your daughter? They are doing well I hope?"

"Yes, yes! Fine as a fiddle, both of them. I do miss them though. But I have a duty to perform, and here I shall stay until they send me home." Again he cleared his throat. His palms were sweating.

"I'm sure that you will be glad to get home again. I hope it's not too long in coming." Nisrina realized that her statement could offend and she hoped it did not sound rude to her visitor.

The Colonel also heard the slight suggestion. *Of course,* he thought to himself, *I've overstayed my visit. I should go now.* And yet he didn't want to leave.

He rose, hesitatingly.

"I really must be going," he said. "I stayed longer than I'd planned."

"You are always a welcome visitor in my home," she replied politely.

The Colonel straightened his coat, walking towards the door. He stopped and turned back to face her. Nisrina was standing there calmly, she was half his size. He hesitated to speak what was on his mind. But he knew that if she were his wife and things had not gone well on the battlefield, he would want her to know. If it were he whose fate had taken a turn for the worst, he would want someone to go to his home and tell his dear Katherine. Allow her to grieve, to move on with her life. It was the right thing to do. He was sure of it. But could he do it? Could he be the one to break this good woman's heart? Perhaps he was wrong. Perhaps it was just a similarity of eyes and nose that taunted him so. And yet the furrow of the brow, the placement of the chin—the likeness uncanny.

Finally, he asked her, "Nisrina, the man in the photograph . . ." He pointed to the table that displayed her family photos. "Tell me . . . that man is your husband?"

"Yes," Nisrina replied smiling sadly. "That's our wedding photo. Such a long time ago." She sighed as the story unfolded. "We'd been married for what now seems such a short time; I carried Hannah in my womb. And then the war came to our orchard. We never thought the soldiers would come to Beit el Jebel, but he was captured. Taken . . . so unexpected . . . one day he was my husband, working in his fields and the next he was gone, conscripted by the Turks, fighting for the Ottoman Empire."

She shook her head as she relived the memory.

"I never got to say good-bye," she was wringing her hands, "but I believe that one day . . ."

She stopped a moment, her eyes focused hard, "No. I'm sure. I *know* that one day, he'll return to me."

She blushed as she held out her left hand for the Colonel to see, "Look, I keep this red polish on my one fingernail. This is the finger entwined with his during our marriage ceremony. I keep this nail brightly polished, so that when he returns he'll know that I've been waiting for him. That I am expecting him." She paused for a moment, "My undying hope."

The blood drained from Colonel Billingham's cheeks. "I see," was all he could say.

He studied her face carefully. Now he was not so certain. The bloodshed he saw during the war, the bombs exploding, and the scent of smoldering human flesh forever defiling his memory. He now thought it wiser not to mention the soldiers who lay on the battlefield so bloodied and torn, or tell of the man whose white, ashened face resembled the handsome groom in her wedding picture. So many were left behind. It was impossible to carry them all.

The fragmented memories ravaged his mind, as a welling moisture formed on his brow.

He argued with himself. Who was he to destroy the hopes of a loving woman?

Still on her threshold, he shuffled a bit, passing his cap from one hand to the other. Not knowing whether to stay or to go. Whether to speak his mind or remain silent.

Then finally, he made his decision, "Well, I really must be going now."

He began to leave, but stopped one more time and turned back to face her.

"Tell me, Nisrina, what was your husband's name?"

"It's Jabran," she said proudly. "Jabran Yusef."

"Ah! Yes." The Colonel fidgeted with his cap again.

Nisrina saw the sadness in his eyes; she cocked her head to one side. She heard a sigh escape from his mouth, long and drawn, as if his naked breath could release the wretchedness of his memories.

The Colonel said no more. He placed his cap squarely upon his head, nodded, and with polite thank-you's and wishes for good health, he walked out the door.

PART FIVE

1921

A jar of olives, a water jug, the use of ovens for breaking bread. My skills as dayah have been a blessing, Enshallah, it keeps my family fed.

When their time is near, new mothers call. I leave my home and run to them.

Holding their legs, I urge them on. My hands inspired by the Lord.

When there is doubt, a troubled birth, a child resistant to this world—I reach right in and bring him forth. The touch of God still guiding me.

His love is boundless, He gives me hope and takes my troubles out to sea.

And if the tide perchance comes back, I know in time He'll set me free.

FIFTY FIVE

An Old Goat

NISRINA'S DAYS WERE FILLED with midwifery and the raising of three children. She was thankful that she lived in the family compound, knowing that she could rely on in-laws for support. Her callings to assist in new births were constant now. It seemed she no sooner returned from the bedside of one woman than to be called out to another—the new babies born in Beit el Jebel coming at a rate of a hundred each year.

Essam, who had learned to read and write at the Friends Boys School, kept a birth log for his mother in a lined-paper notebook where he recorded the information she recited to him.

On the day Nisrina brought the notebook home, she carefully instructed her son to draw four columns on each of the lined sheets with a heading at the top for each column. Writing from right to left, the first column was designated for the father's name. In the second column he was to enter the name of the newborn child. While the third was reserved for the compensation she received for her services. Lastly, in the fourth column, he'd enter the child's date of birth.

Essam was always happy to add another name to the growing list of newborns in their community. It meant that his family would eat well, and still have funds to pay for their schooling. As the man of the house, he made it his business to keep an eye on their finances. A *mil* was a penny's worth, a *kirsh* equal to ten pennies; to receive payments in *jenahs* was fortunate indeed, for each *jenah* was worth a dollar.

However, Beit el Jebel was a poor village and not everyone could afford to pay the *mil*, *kirsh*, or *jenah*, which were the coinage of their land. Many times Nisrina returned from days spent at a new mother's bedside with not even a single *mil* in her purse. He'd watch her as she'd walk into the kitchen, her brow covered in sweat and her feet swollen from the long walk home. With tired, aching hands she'd give him a sideways glance and place a jar of olive oil, two pounds of oranges, or possibly an empty water jug on the table. And when she did, the young boy would pace the floor.

Today, as she passed through the gate, she stopped to tie an old nanny goat to the broken fence post. Its legs were shaky and what little hair was left on its body was mottled and thin. The ancient udder hanging low between its legs was shriveled and gray, not likely to give enough milk to feed a sparrow.

"It matters not," his mother said as she saw his worried face. "Each family pays me what they can. Am I to deny a woman in her time of need? It is unthinkable!" She clucked and tutted softly under her breath as she busied herself in the kitchen.

Essam furrowed his brow and curled his mouth, "But that goat is worse than nothing itself!" he cried. "Now we must house her and feed her, and she'll give us naught in return. It would have been better if you'd left empty handed!"

Nisrina shook her finger in front of her face, "You have much to learn my son . . . that goat meant everything to the family who gave it. It was all they had, and I honored them by accepting it."

She reminded him, "It was not long ago when we had neither a *mil* nor a *kirsh* to our name. We had nothing!" Taking the nail of her thumb to her mouth, she clicked it loudly against her front tooth, "Nothing! When your father did not return from the war, your *sido*, God rest his soul, provided the money to pay for my schooling. If the good Sisters at the convent had not agreed to take me in and teach me the trade of a *dayah,* we'd be on the streets today!" She patted her chest with her open palm, her eyebrows raised high, *"Enshallah*, it is God's will . . . remember this always my dear Essam, and never forget that we, too, are *fellaheen*. Be proud of that fact and gratefully accept what each family can give."

She held his head between the palms of her hands and kissed his forehead tenderly. "God will provide," she assured him. "God will provide."

Essam nodded. But still, he worried. He noticed the lines that had begun to form on her face. And he could see that she moved slower than in years past.

"It's important that you rest, *yumma*," he told her. Here, let me make the tea for you."

"No, Essam," she shooed him away. "Making tea is a woman's work. You finish your studies and do well in school. That alone will make me proud."

FIFTY SIX

The Hand of God

"HANNAH! COME AWAY FROM the cistern! Come away!"
Nisrina ran to pull her daughter back.

On her way to Dora's house bringing a basketful of carrots picked fresh from her garden, she found Hannah wandering on the eastern side of the compound. The four-year-old was playing near the two cisterns, shallow holes that stored runoff from the surrounding hills. The family kept them to make *sheed*, a mixture of lime and water that they used to whitewash and seal the limestone blocks of their homes.

Hannah laughed and ran off. She thought it was a game. The *sheed* had turned milky white and she wanted to put her fingers in it. Swoosh it around. See it swirl. She'd seen the *shagaal*, the workmen, pouring a powdery substance into the hole and when they mixed it with the water, her eyes went wide. The clear liquid had turned to the color of goat's milk. She loved to stand and watch them fill their buckets, and she followed alongside as they hauled the sloshing mixture to each home in the courtyard. When they dipped their brushes, she'd stare at the gooey whitewash oozing between the bristles. She wanted to help the men paint the limestone blocks of her aunties' homes, but they'd always shoo her away, threatening to smear her with the sticky substance, turning her face a bright white like *wahad bekhawif*, the frightful boogeyman in her Auntie Dora's bedtime stories. Hannah would run away squealing and screaming, not sure if the toothless old men would actually carry out their scary threats.

It was a warm, cloudless morning as Nisrina and young Hannah walked home from Lamia Malawy's house. Not a breeze stirred in the air and even the mourning doves had taken shelter in the cool awnings of the thick, dense brush that bordered the road.

The two women would often meet together in the early hours of the day while Essam and Jameela were in school. They'd work in the kitchen preparing meals for their families while they chatted away, sipping tall glasses of limeade, dappled lightly with fresh green sprigs of the peppermint's leaves. As the two mothers talked and worked, Hannah and Rina would play freely together in the yard nearby at games—twirling the dried seed of a well-devoured apricot or chasing a ball with a stick.

But today, Nisrina felt she had spent too much time at Lamia's house and was anxious to be home. She promised Marta and May that she'd show them how to bake *haigagan anoush*, an Armenian cookie made with fresh butter and carefully browned flour that Sister Alodia had taught her to make. Carrying her *tunjara* of *meklubah*, a large pot of freshly made cauliflower stew, in one hand and holding Hannah's little palm in the other, they finally caught sight of the Yusef compound.

Before they could pass through the wrought iron gates of their courtyard, Hannah broke loose from her mother's grip and ran ahead. She'd spotted the workmen in the distance and it reminded her of the cistern filled with *sheed*, the milky white liquid that beckoned her so.

She ran to the east side of the compound.

Nisrina, balancing the large pot of stew under her arm, called after her, "Hannah, come back this minute!"

But Hannah would have no part of her pleas. She ran full ahead laughing and squealing, her curly brown hair bobbing up and down as she looked over her shoulder at her scolding mother. Then with a running plunge and a childish shriek she jumped directly into the caustic mixture of lime and water.

Nisrina screamed, dropping the pot of *meklubah* in the dirt.

Frantically she ran towards her child. Hannah's little brown curls now the only thing showing above the surface.

Before Nisrina could reach her, she saw a cloaked figure, an arm, a hand—it reached out and grabbed her daughter's hair and pulled her out of the cloudy pool. Hannah was gasping; her eyes shut tight, her arms thrashing about. Nisrina was screaming, calling out her child's name, running towards the strange figure that was now dunking her daughter in the adjacent cistern of clear water, rinsing her face, her eyes, and her shivering body.

Nisrina grabbed Hannah from the man's arms, tearing off the tainted clothing. She again dunked Hannah in the clean water and finished washing the murky substance from her little body. She took her shawl and wrapped it around the drenched child until finally Hannah caught her breath and let out a healthy cry of terror. Her mother held her tightly, drying her, desperately searching her face, her torso and her limbs for any sign of damaged or burnt skin.

Hannah continued to bellow as Nisrina examined every inch of her. Miraculously her skin was intact, no burns were found. Her eyes too seemed unharmed.

"Hannah, look at me! Can you see my face, Hannah? Can you see me?"

Whimpering, Hannah looked at her mother and nodded.

They sat on the ground holding each other tightly, the young girl's face buried in her mother's arms. Finally, as Hannah's tears faded and her trembling ceased, Nisrina pressed her daughter out in front of her. "Never . . ." she scolded her. "Never again! Do you hear me? Do you understand?"

Hannah was nodding, her lower lip trembling, her eyes opened wide.

Nisrina took her daughter in her arms again and held her close, whispering, "*Enshallah, Enshallah*, never again . . . never again."

FIFTY SEVEN

Armenian Cooking

NISRINA TURNED TO THANK the man who saved her daughter's life. She wanted to express her gratitude for his quick actions and calm mind, to ask his name and tell him that she was forever indebted to his kindness. But when she looked up, she realized they were alone with the tangled branches of the mulberry tree that stood guard overhead, the bright sun filtering soft through its leaves. The workmen were still occupied on the far side of the courtyard behind Marta's house. When asked, they shook their heads. They'd not heard her screams or Hannah's cries, unaware that the frightening event had occurred. And they witnessed no cloaked figures anywhere near the compound.

Nisrina left Hannah with Marta and May. She told them the story of the sheed and the strange cloaked figure who saved her daughter and then disappeared. She gave them strict warnings to watch Hannah carefully and keep her near until she returned. Nisrina was bound for the church. She needed to light an extra candle.

On her way home, Nisrina passed the Armenian Chapel. Like her own church, it was constructed of large limestone blocks piled atop each other in alternating rows. Ten wide steps led up to an enormous entryway that belied the modest size of the structure. At the top of the steps was an elongated arch that surrounded two wooden doors leading into the chapel. She stood at the foot of the stairs, pausing, her thoughts in the past. There'd been something hauntingly familiar about the cloaked man who just saved her daughter's life, and until this moment she'd not been able to unravel the mystery that plagued her. Now standing in front of the Armenian house of worship, she realized what it was that stood out so peculiarly in her mind: it was the black robe and pointed hood. Now she remembered. It was the distinctive robe of the Armenian monks.

While in Jerusalem, she'd seen the monks in the Armenian Quarter, walking in the garden behind the great cathedral. She watched them as they filed along in unified procession within the walls of their sanctuary. She was certain. The man who saved her Hannah—he wore the robe of the Armenian brotherhood. Hesitating outside the small chapel, she pondered what her next move should be. Then boldly and calmly, with the grace of an indebted mother, she walked up the stone steps that led to the massive church doors.

Once inside, Nisrina asked to speak to the monk that saved her daughter's life.

The priest shook his head. He told her that their church was small. No monks resided there. She must have been mistaken. He walked her to the door and bade her farewell. Blessing her and wishing her luck in finding the cloaked figure that pulled her child from harm's way.

Noticing neither the fragrant sage nor the blossoming anemones that bordered the pathway, Nisrina walked back along the dusty dirt road. In the style of the *fellaheen*, she carried her shoes in her hands, her toughened feet warmed by the hard, packed dirt. Stopping briefly to remove a pebble from her foot, she leaned against a tall tamarisk tree, its wide canopy providing a respite from the temperate sun. As she stood there wiping her brow, she heard a soft crackle in the bushes behind her. The rustling sound and swaying branches told her it was too large to be a bird or hyena. It must be a man or a woman keeping from her sight. Her heart raced, a strange quiver running up her spine; she knew not if it was fear or frustration.

"Who is there?" she finally called out, trying to see through the dense vegetation.

No one responded.

"Are you hurt?" she heard her voice say. "Are you in need?"

She could hear their breathing and feel their eyes.

"I am a *dayah*," she said bravely. "*Enshallah*, please speak or show yourself to me. Perhaps I can help."

The bushes rustled again. This time louder, stronger. Just steps away from where she stood.

The first thing she saw was the black cape and the pointed hood.

His face was hidden deep within the folds of his cloth. There was a large gold cross hanging from his neck and it shimmered brilliantly in the sun's reflection.

"It is you!" she gasped.

"I'm sorry," the man responded. "I did not mean to frighten you." His voice was old.

"No, of course not. *Enshallah*. I believe you are the man who saved my daughter's life."

"Ah, the little girl who jumped into the cistern." He sounded forlorn.

"Yes. That was my daughter, Hannah."

"Children . . ." he sighed. "A gift from Allah. She was very brave."

"And very foolish."

"Yes. Tell me, is she doing well now?"

"Yes. Thank God. Thank God. She is doing well. It is a miracle that she was not burned. The lime can be very caustic."

"Yes. I know. I was passing by and saw her running. She was spirited. I had a feeling . . . I'm just glad I was there."

"You were sent by God."

He nodded.

"Please," Nisrina continued. "Allow me to thank you properly. Please come to my home. Be my guest. I will cook for you a delicious meal."

He hesitated and took a step backward. He looked down at his feet, shifting from one foot to the other. She wondered if he wished they would take him away from her.

Finally he responded, "Tomorrow . . . I must make myself presentable. I will come tomorrow."

"Then tomorrow it is. Come for dinner, you can meet my children."

The old monk nodded, and without another word, disappeared through the shrubbery.

Nisrina watched as the trees and bushes engulfed him, his pointed hood blending seamlessly beneath the branches. She recalled what the Armenian priest had told her . . . there were no monks at the church in Beit el Jebel. If that was so, then to what church did he belong? Perhaps he had come from Jerusalem or maybe lands afar. Perhaps from the northernmost hills of Armenia, or the remote and ancient isles that bordered the Turkish Empire. Perhaps.

Father Sarkis handed the monk the envelope. It was yellowed and worn. The corners tattered from years of neglect. The look in the High Priest's eyes had lost the sternness that had defined their lives. They were sad now, clouded over. It was evident that the old cleric had finally released his hold on the weary monk. His wordless gaze saying—*It is time, Brother. I can keep you here no longer.* But his mouth, buried beneath a cloak of order and divisiveness, never moved; only his face spoke with its hardened lines and crevices.

Brother Arcopian understood. No sounds were necessary, no explanations required. The two of them had survived in this manner—never able to communicate. Never seeing eye to eye on any matter, be it theological or secular.

Arcopian took the envelope from the High Priest's hands. Its edges were stained and creased. How long had it been hidden in the stone walls of the monastery? How many years had he kept this secret from him? An electric current ran through his hands, reaching up into his arms and past the throbbing ache in his chest. His fingers struggled as he desperately tried to pry it open, his yellowed nails picking at the seams.

The note inside was thin, transparent. He held his breath—he recognized the slender strokes. It was from her. The message clear.

Years of doubt and regretful suffering were finally over. He knew now what he must do. There was no doubt. He would find her.

All the next day Nisrina cooked.

She made stuffed grape leaves and eggplant stew. She employed the finest and freshest herbs from her garden: coriander and thyme, cumin and tarragon. The rich, aromatic ones she'd learned to use at the convent. She even climbed to her tallest shelf and brought down the jars of special herbs that Alodia had given her: *aveluk* in her salad and lentil soup, and *jingyal* on her bread. In her desserts she was sure to include *mahlab*, the powdered pit of the black cherry, and fresh orange blossom water. She drew on Alodia's special recipes, trying to remember everything she'd been taught. She mixed and blended until the entire courtyard smelled of heaven itself.

Nisrina invited the Yusef family to celebrate her daughter's well being and meet the holy man who'd saved her life. Jacob and May, Marta and Dora and the three children anxiously stood in a line inside the gate and watched as the old monk approached the compound.

"It smells delicious," he was smiling, his cloak now pushed back upon his shoulders.

Nisrina saw his face for the first time. His hair was thin and gray and his shoulders stooped. She noticed that his nose was bent to one side as if he'd had an altercation in his younger days and the resulting curvature now blended softly into a set of high cheekbones. His skin was light, as if he'd rarely seen the sun; and yet, his face was deeply lined with the hardships of many years. As she gazed into his eyes she noticed how very light they were—brown, with gold and green specks that reflected the light. And she felt both the goodness and sadness in his being as she bent down and reverently kissed the ring on his left hand.

The family welcomed him into Nisrina's home with endless questions and vivacious chatter. As the head of the clan, Jacob postured and posed. He told the monk of his departed father and the thriving orchards they'd once had. How the war and the influenza had taken their toll on the family and the village, and how now he worked hard to keep the farm profitable. His voice was larger than usual as he repeatedly sipped his wine, and with the drink his manners seemed to have slipped away.

Marta and May brought out tray after tray of food and set them before the monk. The aromatic scents caught the old man's attentions, his eyebrow rising just a bit. The two women nodded and smiled big as if they, themselves, had prepared the dishes. Chattering and questioning, they asked if he preferred one dish over the other . . . what his tastes were . . . where his preferences lay?

As usual, Dora silently stood back in the corner of the room and watched the goings on—her quiet nature always her point of comfort.

Essam, Jameela and Hannah ran about the room, their voices raised as they argued over who would sit closest to their visitor. Pushing and shoving, they more than once bumped his arm, or jostled his leg.

A man used to solitude and repose, the old monk's breath started coming in short heaves. Nisrina noticed his shaking hands and his quivering voice as he politely tried to respond to the series of questions.

She could stand it no longer. Jumping up from her chair and placing herself between her guest and her boisterous family, she quickly broke in, "Allow me to show you my garden."

Extending her hand, she led him out to the solitude of the courtyard.

Looking back, she motioned to the others to remain in the house.

With wide eyes they watched as she escorted the honored guest out the door. They knew wiser than to argue with her lifted palm.

"Give him the space to think!" she whispered back to them once the monk had been safely out the door.

The sun had not yet set. It was that magical time between dusk and darkness when the air was cool and the moisture from the sea began its silent creep up the peaceful mountain. The shadows had all but disappeared, which awakened the crickets that had already begun their serenade. They looked up as a few birds flitted between the tall branches of the palm and the cypress trees, and the bubbling water from the fountain sang a steady, rhythmic lullaby.

"Your garden is beautiful," he told her.

"*Shukran*," she thanked him.

She pointed out the various vegetables that were growing there. The carrots, zucchini, tomatoes, and onions. She showed him the fruit trees: lemons, oranges, figs and loquat.

"Ah, I see you also have a healthy apricot tree," he pointed to the far corner.

"Yes," she laughed. "It has two personalities. Each year it alternates between one and the other. This year it gave us large, luscious fruits, but very few in number. They were gone before we could tire of them. The year past, there were so many we could not finish them, but they were small, tiny . . . one bite and *foosh* they were gone!"

He smiled. "I too, had a tree like that . . . as a young boy, at my family's farm." His voice softened, his head moving from side to side, "Like a woman, they are . . . like a woman."

Nisrina looked up at him. Such an unusual comment to hear from a man of the cloth.

"Tell me, Father, what do they call you?" she asked him.

He smiled a half-smile, a sorry look of memories clouding his face. "No. Not father . . . Brother. Please, call me Brother Aram."

"Of course. I see. Brother. Brother Aram."

Hannah wandered out towards them. She was hungry and wanted her mother to come in and share the meal.

"Perhaps we should go in now," he suggested.

"Are you ready? They mean well. They're so excited. So pleased to have such an honored guest. Especially the one who saved our dear Hannah's life."

She lifted Hannah into her arms.

"Yes. I understand. Of course. Of course. It is fine."

Back inside, Nisrina introduced the mysterious monk to her family. Calmed and collected, finally remembering their manners, they one by one, bowed their heads and kissed the old man's ring. He raised his hand and blessed each of them. Then he blessed the food that had been set upon the table, and he thanked them for their kindness.

After the meal was through and conversation had waned, Nisrina put the children to bed. Jacob and May rose to leave. They thanked the monk for his company and told him that he was always welcome in their home. Marta and Dora also departed with thanks and kind words to the stranger.

Nisrina invited the holy man to stay a while longer, have another cup of coffee and perhaps more of the cookies she'd made.

He accepted.

"I'd love to sit a while longer," he told her. "Your home reminds me so much of my youth. My family. My farm."

Nisrina brewed a fresh pot of *kahweh Arabiyah*, she brought out a tray of the special cookies she'd made.

The monk sipped the coffee, savoring the subtle taste of cardamom. He took a bite of the cookie. Breathing in, he sighed, his head beginning to spin. The flavors were subtle, but he was sure of it. They were so familiar. They'd been there all through dinner. From the first moment that he approached the courtyard he could smell them. He could taste them. How had she, a *fellaha* from Beit el Jebel, learned to cook in this manner?

"*Salaam adaykee*," he blessed her hands. "Tell me, Nisrina, where did you learn to prepare such delicious meals? Your foods, all of them: the soup, the bread, these cookies . . . they are not of this region, but rather have the flavors and textures of my country. Of my youth. How is it that I come to your home, so far from where I grew, my mother and father long passed and my memories all but buried." He shook his head and smiled. "I am an old man, but tonight I feel young again."

"Thank you for your compliments," she responded.

She was happy to have pleased him, but happier still to have someone with whom she could share the story of how she learned to cook. Nisrina never spoke of Najeeb and the sorry morning that he'd entered her kitchen. The memory was too horrid, the violence too harsh.

To the outside world she had returned to the convent to extend her education in midwifery, to become a better dayah. Only the Sisters of Mercy knew that she needed sanctuary and healing, and she'd found it in Sister Alodia's kitchen.

And now, as she sat with this aged monk and saw the gentle kindness in his eyes, the suffering that surrounded his smile, she felt safe. He was an Armenian monk, clearly with secrets of his own. She'd stopped by the Armenian Church in town, the priest there had no knowledge of his presence. Although she'd mentioned it to no one, she was quite certain that this holy man was living in the mountains, alone and secluded. It was not just the manner in which they met, but more in his appearance, his demeanor. She could tell by the grass and straw that still clung to his gown. And the way he rapidly stuffed the food into his mouth, like a starving rabbit who'd had little nourishment for a very long while. It reminded her of Jabran when he'd been gone for days, sleeping overnight in his orchard, staying close by his trees to combat a frost or to keep the hyenas at bay.

"When my husband was taken by the soldiers," she began, "I was left with two children and one still growing in my belly." She patted her stomach and tilted her head to one side, "He has yet to return, but I wait for him each day. I know that one day God will send him back to me.

"Although I am Syrian Orthodox, I was sent to the Catholic convent in Jerusalem to learn the art of the *dayah*. I needed this skill to support my family and our village needed a midwife. I stayed for six long months, away from my children . . . unable to see them, touch them, or hold them in my arms.

"When I returned I was a *dayah* . . . respected and honored. I was able to support my children . . . taking no other husband, nor forsaking my own."

The monk nodded. There was more to this woman than he had realized. He was interested. His half-eaten cookie resting in the palms of his hands.

"But a member of my family . . ." her heart was racing now, her voice quivering. She clasped her hands in front of her heart.

"He was the elder . . . He envied me my children . . ." Her throat closed up, she could not go on.

"It is in the past," the monk replied calmly. He could not bear her distress and he found no joy in her story. "You seem to have a good life now. Am I correct in this assessment?"

"Yes, Brother. It is true. But before that could happen, I returned to the convent . . . for sanctuary . . . for healing."

"And at this convent, you found your healing?"

"Yes," she nodded. "I learned much from the Sisters. I learned that the sin committed against me was not mine to bear. The sin was with he who sinned, and it is now between him and God . . . May the Lord rest his soul."

"Yes, may he find peace," the old monk said.

He watched her intently—her kind face and her sure manner. Despite her difficulties she'd found redemption. If only he could be so fortunate.

"And the cooking?" he prompted her.

"Yes, the cooking . . . it was taught to me by an old nun. She was my savior, my mother, my sister, my friend. She was the cook at the convent. She taught me everything I know today."

"It was a Catholic convent, you say?"

"Yes, Brother. Catholic."

"The one in Jerusalem?"

"Yes, Brother." Now Nisrina was curious. What was this man seeking from her? Why had he stayed and questioned her so?

The monk's eyes began darting back and forth in their sockets. Nisrina noticed that it was he, now, whose breathing was labored.

"Tell me Nisrina . . . what is the name of the Sister who taught you to cook so well?"

"Her name, Brother? Why her name was Alodia. Sister Alodia."

"Alodia?" He stopped for a moment. "Yes, of course. She would take a new name when she took the veil . . ." he was saying this to himself. Softly. Thoughtfully. His eyes far away. "Alodia? That means riches, does it not?"

"Yes, Brother. I believe it does."

Seared into his brain, he remembered the words he'd spoken so long ago.

"No, it is you, Margarit," he replied tauntingly to her, "It is you who had better take heed of the fact that you are a woman! And to do a woman's work is a gift from God. A gift of immeasurable riches . . ."

He was certain now. The foods, the aromas, the small child in the cistern . . . it was all from God. He was leading him back to his beloved . . . back to Margarit.

All the years in the monastery had been good training for Brother Aram. The beatings and isolations, the years of silent meditation and remorseful prayers . . . they were nothing compared to the turmoil that now raced through his body. But he kept his composure in front of Nisrina.

Calmly he looked at her, "Can you take me there? Will you come with me to meet this cook who prepares a meal as my mother once did? I must meet her."

Although he spoke with an even tone, his voice quiet—his hands were gripping her arms. She knew she couldn't refuse him, nor could she find the words to ask him why.

She nodded, "We can leave tomorrow."

FIFTY EIGHT

Aram and Margarit

BROTHER ARAM AND NISRINA arrived at the convent unexpected.

The halls were empty and the candles unlit. A dark hush encased the sanctuary.

Respectfully Nisrina and Brother Aram first stopped at the Mother Superior's office. Nisrina knocked at her door, but there was no answer. A shadow passed in the unlit hall. It was a young novice that Nisrina did not recognize.

"Forgive me," she approached her, "I'm here to see the Reverend Mother . . . can you tell me her whereabouts?"

With red eyes and wet cheeks the novice nodded, "She is in the chapel. I will fetch her for you."

Nisrina looked at Brother Aram. "Something is wrong here. I feel it," she whispered. She was tempted to go directly to the kitchen to see Alodia, but something held her back. She waited for the novice to return.

It was the Mother Superior who appeared in the hallway.

"Nisrina!" Her voice was desperate.

Like the young novice who'd gone to fetch her, the Mother's eyes, too, were swollen and red. Nisrina had never seen the Superior in such a state. She'd clearly been weeping, her face so sad, so melancholy. What had happened? What could be wrong? Nisrina's heart began to race. The convent was more than just a school or a sanctuary to her. With their loving counsel and caring hearts, the Sisters had reached out to her in her time of need. This place with its sacred walls had become much more. It had become her home—the Sisters, her family. What was this terrible calamity that could cause even the strongest of their flock to weep?

"What is it?" Nisrina asked the senior nun. Not even the clear, blue color of her eyes could hide the Mother's sorrow.

"It is Alodia," the Mother whispered. It was barely audible, a hoarse, unfamiliar voice.

"Alodia?"

"Yes . . . come quickly."

Brother Aram had been silently standing back, observing, waiting. But now as he saw the Reverend Mother's face and heard the grave voice that whispered his beloved's name, he felt the earth move, his body turning inside out. "What? What is wrong with this nun you call Alodia?" his voice was shrill, unbridled and harsh.

"God grant her grace," the Mother Superior said softly. "She is dying."

The Mother looked at the man in the cloak. She could not see his face and wondered who this monk was that Nisrina had brought with her. She wondered what interest he held in their old Alodia and why his voice had cracked at the sound of her name.

She knew Alodia's story. The tale of her youth. She'd accepted her when the other churches turned her away and she remembered the sorrow that the young Margarit had carried in her heart for so very long. The Mother Superior stared at his clothes. Like Nisrina, she recognized the dark cape and pointed hood. An Armenian monk, but not one that she knew, for his voice was strange and his dialect foreign.

"Let me take you to her," she said to him. There was an urgency in her voice. Both Nisrina and Aram heard it.

"You have visitors," the Mother Superior said softly, leading Nisrina and Brother Aram into the room where Alodia lay.

She'd been resting. Her breathing labored, her skin a pallid white. She opened her eyes. They blinked for a moment, trying to clear the haze of her slumber.

"Nisrina! You've come . . ." Her voice was low, barely audible.

"Yes, sister. I am here." Nisrina knelt by the old cook's bedside. She kissed the thin, parchment skin on her weathered hands. Alodia seemed so much older than Nisrina remembered. But the student had no trouble recalling the times that the old cook had cared so tenderly for her. First from the maliciousness of her classmates' envy, and then from her brother-in-law's cruel brutality.

"I am pleased," she whispered back to her. "Somehow I knew you would come."

Nisrina tried to speak, but she had no voice. She wanted to tell Alodia everything that was in her heart. She wanted to say that the old cook was more than a teacher to her. She was the mother she'd never known. She was her sister, her auntie, her confidant and friend. But when she opened her mouth, no words came out, only a sound, unearthly and crude. She buried her face in the old cook's bosom and once again felt the warmth of her soul. And as the roar of emotions clouded her ears, she heard herself crying.

The old nun looked down at her and smiled. She remembered the time she knelt by Nisrina's bedside and begged her forgiveness. She'd vowed to care for the child until her dying day. And now she knew that time had come.

The old cook placed her hand atop her student's head. This time it was she who asked, "Child, why do you weep so?"

"I weep because I love you."

"Please, don't cry. I am happy. My life was filled with riches . . . and love."

Nisrina looked up at her friend. She saw tenderness around those old, ancient eyes. Paradise had come to her doorstep and its serenity lay before her like a tranquil sea. It was reflected in the soft curvature of her brow and the gentle flicker of her wrinkled lids.

Nisrina could see that no amount of protest would change the outcome, for heaven itself had opened its doors and was standing at the threshold.

But Brother Aram could bear it no longer.

Hearing Alodia's words, he stepped forward, removing the hood that covered his face.

Their eyes met, and in that moment the years vanished.

"Hello Margarit," the voice was the same. Alodia heard it as she'd carried it in her memory. A sound that had echoed through her mind time and time again, never fading, never forgotten. Many nights she'd lain awake, secretly worrying that she'd lost the memory of his tone or mistook his hearty tempo. But no. It was just as she'd imagined. He was standing before her. He was saying her name.

Her eyes searched his face. His thick black hair had thinned and grayed, and his straight, strong nose was bent now, turned softly awry—but she saw only the boy that she once loved. To her, he had not changed one bit. The same brown eyes—soft and alluring. She could see the fire that burned within them. And in the moment that her eyes met his, her suffering vanished.

"Aram . . ." She reached out her arms; no longer strong, they were thin and shaking.

"Margarit . . ." He whispered her name and took hold of her hands, kneeling down alongside her bed.

"So many years, Aram. So many years."

"Yes. Margarit. But not a single day passed that I did not hold you in my thoughts."

"And you in mine, dear Aram."

"Life . . . has it been good?"

"Yes," she nodded, her voice a whisper, "*Enshallah*, the Lord has given me strength to endure . . . and a family here in the Church."

"And the name that you took . . . Alodia. It means riches . . ." He smiled hopefully.

"Yes, they were your words, Aram . . . your words. I carried them with me."

"Our love, Margarit . . . it was not a sin."

"Not a sin . . ." she repeated, her eyes smiling up at him, "It was a gift from God. I've never thought differently."

"And now . . . now He has brought me back to you . . ." he paused, his head falling forward, his forehead resting softly on his clasped hands, "if only . . ." his voice broke, his eyes filling with tears. It frightened him, he could not see her.

"Have no regrets, my Aram. He smiles upon us even now."

Aram put his head down upon her bed and smelled the richness of her being. She placed her aged hands once more through his fine, wispy hair. It felt like home.

Through her eyes he was just as beautiful as the day she'd last seen him—saying adieu in her father's fields, promising to stand firm against their parents' wishes. To meet again the next day and marry. A lifetime had passed since then, but it seemed like only yesterday.

"This is not good-bye . . ." she told him, her breath labored, fighting to form the words, "but merely farewell. We shall meet again, in the loving grace of God."

The blanket where he laid his head was soaked; he could only nod. He reached over and lightly touched her cheek. She smiled back at him, placing her hand upon his. Then he leaned in and gently, tenderly, kissed her thin, parched lips.

Margarit sighed. Aram had found her.

She closed her eyes.

And as she did, she breathed no more.

PART SIX

1933

The years have passed, my hair is gray, and now my child is full with child.

My baby girl, my tiny one, you're soon to be a mother now.

I cannot bear the wait, and yet, the time is not for me to say.

When God does give, I will give thanks, my breath I hold until that day.

FIFTY NINE

Min'Allah (From God)

IT WAS THE DARK clouds that prompted Nisrina to go into town early that day. The storm was expected just before noon and she had several stops to make. Jameela insisted that she come along, her swollen belly "about to burst," as she so colorfully argued with her mother. She needed the walk she insisted, she needed to smell the air and fill her lungs. It wouldn't be long before she would be confined to the walls of the compound and her newly-gained, motherly duties.

Jameela, nineteen years old, had been married for two years now; her husband, a traveling merchant was away selling goods to neighboring towns. He dealt in the sale of miscellaneous items—peddling pots and pans, jugs and utensils. When he had nothing left to sell, he'd purchase new items from the town he was in. Buying from local artisans, shopkeepers, and makers of wares, he'd fill his empty wagon and carry off his treasures. Traveling through rugged terrain with his donkey and cart, he'd cross the plains and climb the hills. He'd pass through valleys and course his way over rivers, stopping here and there to barter and trade. As he reached each new town he'd lay out his merchandise, hoping to make an ample profit from the local villagers. Often gone for months, he'd circuit the countryside until finally, he'd find his way home again.

For the most part, Jameela accepted his absence. She'd known he was a traveling merchant when she first agreed to marry him. Her mother and brother had warned her that her life would be a lonely one with a husband on the road. But her family's soft warnings were no match for his sweet words and charming gazes. She eagerly married the merchant and soon grew accustomed to a widow's way of life.

But this time it was different. She begged him not to go. She feared he wouldn't return in time to see his first born son come into the world.

A man of little patience, he reminded her that she had her mother by her side, and what better mother than *el dayah* Nisrina, *Oum el Loulad*? Besides, he asked her, how could she expect him to feed and clothe his family if he had no coins in his well-worn purse?

Nisrina kept careful watch over her daughter. She noticed the baby had dropped earlier that week. She could see that it was now nestled deep in the birth canal. Aware of the curvature in her daughter's back and the increasingly slow, wide-stepped waddle in her walk, she kept the girl close by her side. She knew that her grandchild was not long in coming and she worried for her daughter. She had guided hundreds of babies into the world, but this one was different. It was special, unique—her first grandchild.

As the two women stood chatting with the villagers, their packages in hand and their cloaks wrapped tightly around their shoulders, Nisrina saw the slightest movement in Jameela's face. To anyone else it would have been imperceptible. But Nisrina knew her daughter. She knew every curve in her full round face and all the tiny little creases in her forehead. She could see the slightest twitch that invaded her eyes or encircled her mouth. And now, in that moment as they stood beside the well, chatting with *Oum* Samir and *Oum* Fuad, she was certain that she'd seen a subtle change in her daughter's demeanor. She was about to interrupt the moment and ask Jameela how she fared—was she tired or hungry? Should they stop and buy some nourishment before heading back home? But before she could say a word, she saw the rush of water fall forth between Jameela's legs. It soaked her *thobe*, both front and back, and she knew her time had come.

"*Yumma!*" Jameela called out in alarm. Jameela had been waiting for the sign. Her mother had warned her to expect it. She'd explained to her over and over that when her water released, then soon after, the contractions would start. But this was Jameela's first child and she was embarrassed.

Nisrina looked into her daughter's eyes and calmly told her, "It is time."

It was moments like these that she missed Jabran the most—his warm smile and mischievous wink. She wanted to hear him say that all would be well, and to touch her fingers lovingly as only he could do. But he was not there, and she knew she would have to carry on.

The past nine months had not been without incident. Early on, Jameela had bled. It was unexpected. "These things happen," she told the young mother, "and sometimes, *Enshallah*, God intervenes." The baby might survive, she assured her. It was just a little blood, a spot or two. But each day she'd walk to the church and burn a candle at the altar. She'd give thanks for their blessings and pray that the child would grow healthy and strong.

Jameela's womb indeed did grow, the child's heartbeat steady and strong. Her queasy sickness lasted only through the third month, the fourth with hardly a symptom at all. She became strong and robust, with an appetite that marveled even the greatest of cooks. She spent her days smiling and laughing, her face glowing and sweet. And all who saw her said that motherhood suited her well, and they blessed her again and again from the curse of the evil eye.

But Nisrina was a mother with a mother's heart and a mother's worry. Her days were spent pacing and fretting for she loved her daughter so.

"The pains?" she asked Jameela. "Do you feel any pain?"

"No," Jameela answered, her voice shaking. "I feel fine, *yumma*. Just very wet. I'm embarrassed." She tried to take her shawl and cover her skirt.

"That is no matter," her mother assured her. "Keep your shawl around your shoulders, you must stay warm." Looking up at the clouds, now a dark, murky gray, she furrowed her brow, "We must get you home. Are you able to walk?"

"I think I can."

Jameela's steps were slow, and Nisrina wondered if instead, she should have her daughter ride on the back of Abu Faraj. They could go faster and farther before the storm should release its fury. Wisely, she'd brought the donkey with them to carry their packages, never imagining that it would be Jameela who would challenge him at the end of their day.

Together the three women, Nisrina, *Oum* Samir and *Oum* Fuad helped Jameela onto the donkey's back. The poor girl moaned and groaned as they carefully heaved her up.

The sky was now darker and the wind piercingly cold. Nisrina feared the worst. The walk would be a difficult one, the road, rocky and uneven. Quickly they said their goodbyes and started home. Sure-footed and calm, Abu Faraj moved at a comfortable pace, carrying his delicate burden, his master guiding his reins.

As they walked, Nisrina kept watch, taking notice of the slightest grimace or moan. Her children had come quickly and she was concerned that Jameela might do likewise.

Suddenly, the clouds opened up and a thunderous bolt shot out from across the sky. Within seconds, large drops of rain began pelting down upon them. Nisrina removed her cloak and put it over her daughter's head. She struggled to keep the donkey on the far side of the path beneath the trees' broad canopies. But Jameela was shaking, her mother unsure as to whether it was from fear or the cold wind that pushed against them.

Nisrina hurried the donkey's pace as Jameela rested against the animal's wet musty mane. "It matters not," her mother kept repeating, "We'll be home soon . . . *Enshallah* . . . God is with us. Do not worry."

Despite the shelter of the trees, within minutes they were soaked, with half the distance still to travel.

"Ahhhhh!" Jameela grabbed her belly as a gripping pain seared through her abdomen. "*Yumma*, please . . . stop! I can't go on."

She slid off the donkey. Nisrina helping her down.

"I'm sorry, I can't . . . Ahhhhh!"

Another pain gripped her. She doubled over, falling to her knees.

Nisrina searched for a place of respite, the dirt around their feet now turning thick and muddy, the downpour saturating the earth. She spied a large, old fig tree with enormous branches and full round leaves. Underneath was a dry, soft area, untouched by the pummeling rain. Quickly she grabbed the thick woolen blanket from the donkey's back and carefully laid it down on the ground beneath the tree. Then taking Jameela by the arm, she urged her onto the blanket.

Uncertainty shot through Nisrina's heart, the memory of her own birth torturing her still. She, too, had been born beneath a fig tree; and tragically, it had not fared well for her mother.

But she was a *dayah*, she reminded herself. This was a luxury her poor mother did not have. And even still, would it have made any difference? Nisrina, no longer the child who blindly mourned her mother's fate, could not curse the circumstance that led poor Sabra Hishmeh away that day. She knew now that there were certain conditions a *dayah* could not reverse. Even if Sabra Hishmeh had been by their side, their destiny would have remained unaltered. No one could have saved her mother's life.

Then she cursed the wicked *Shataan*, the Devil himself, for such tragedy and folly; and she told him that he would have neither her daughter nor her grandchild. She praised God and with all her might asked that his hand be the guiding force in her family's destiny.

"Ahhhhh!" Jameela yelled again and spread her legs wide. "*Hullah, yumma, hullah!* It is coming!"

Nisrina was on her hands and knees, her face between her daughter's thighs. She was urging and directing. No longer a mother or grandmother—she was a *dayah*, carrying out her trade.

"Wait, Jameela! Don't bear down until you feel the pain again!" she yelled to her. "When it comes, then push. Push *habeebti*, with all your strength!" She could see the head crowning and she knew it would be any moment now.

The raindrops continued to pepper the earth as the two women huddled safely under the tree's wide canopy. Nisrina spoke soothingly to her daughter. She sang to her of joy and motherhood, and she told her what a fine child she would soon hold in her arms. She chanted a gentle lullaby, and for a moment she imagined her mother by her side—smiling and laughing, holding out her hands.

So this is how it is, she thought—once again we meet under a mighty fig.

"Again, *yumma*, *hullah*! Ahhhhh!" Jameela was bearing down.

Nisrina held out her arms, the child emerging, "Push!" she shouted.

Jameela pressed down hard, and the child was born.

"It's a boy!"

His lusty cries echoed from the walls of the valley and high across the mountainside. Jameela took him in her arms and kissed her son a thousand times. It was a love she'd never known. He squirmed and grunted; his fists held tight and his eyes opened wide, searching for the one he'd call mother. She offered him her breast and without hesitation he opened his mouth and latched on. Mother and daughter were laughing now, ecstatic, delighted. Nisrina told her what a fine, handsome son she had, and how very proud her husband would be when he returned. Jameela nodded, holding the child close.

"The pains, they are coming again *yumma*!"

"Push as you did before," she told her. "Be strong, push hard."

This was the moment Nisrina dreaded. It was the time, many years ago, when her mother's body gave forth a torn placenta, ripping her insides and tearing her away from her daughter's love.

The afterbirth came. It was intact.

Nisrina gave thanks. She knew now that her mother's fate would not be that of her daughter's.

She thanked God for His mercy, and she thanked her mother, whose spirit she still felt near.

"Look *yumma*, the rain has stopped!"

Nisrina stood up and saw that the storm had passed. A few lingering clouds remained overhead as the sun warmed the earth. She gasped, one hand to her mouth, the other pointing upward to the skies.

Jameela followed the direction of her mother's finger—in the sky she saw not one, but two beautiful arcs of light shimmering overhead: red, orange, yellow, blue, the likes of which she'd never seen before.

The two women praised God for His blessings, and Nisrina quietly thanked her mother for the wondrous sign.

At home, Nisrina instructed Essam to enter his nephew's birth in her midwifery log.

"What shall I put in the column for payment?" he asked his mother with his father's playful wink.

"*Min'Allah*," she told him. From God.

PART SEVEN

1934 – 1937

They say I am my mother's child; my smile and eyes like hers.
But strength is how I know her best; her love I am assured.
A widowed midwife's tireless hands bring life into the world.
As life renews, so it forgives, and thus she has endured.
Within her heart she carries him, a man I'll never know.
I cannot hear his silent voice; and yet I love him so.
His touch remains aloof to me. His wisdoms merely whispers,
And still I hear him through his books, his photographs and sisters.
And so I wonder where he's gone, my father young and strong.
But now I am my mother's child, for that's where I belong.

SIXTY

Itulab

"HANNAH, I NEED YOU to go to the *souk* for me, quickly get your things."

"But, *yumma*, Rina and I will take our last exam tomorrow. We are to meet and study at her home. The scholarship, you know . . ."

"I'm not worried about that right now, Hannah. You'll do fine, you always do. And Rina Malawy, God bless her, always tests at the top of her class. Right now I need you to go to the market for me, come now, quickly, *yullah*."

"Very well," sighed Hannah. She knew she could not argue with her mother for long. Her sister Jameela had recently moved with her husband and son to Damascus, and Hannah knew her mother missed them very much.

"What shall I buy?" she asked, thoughtlessly fingering the jasmine blooms that sat vased in the center of the table. Hannah had grown accustomed to the scent of jasmine in the kitchen, her father's first gift to her mother.

"Let's see . . . I need tomatoes and rice and . . . and zucchini. Here . . . take these coins, and go quickly, please . . . Oh, and stop at the butcher. Ask him to cut me some fresh pieces of lamb. I want them cut small, very small . . . for stuffing."

"But *yumma*! Small pieces? The butcher is so slow!"

"Never you mind, that is what I need. Wait . . . here . . ." she grabbed the books that Hannah had been studying, "take your books with you. There's no reason why Rina can't join you. I'm sure Lamia will not mind. You can sit in the butcher's shop and study together while he cuts the meat. But remember, don't make him rush or he will cut the pieces too large, tell him to take his time. *Yullah*, go!" she began to shove her daughter out the door, then she pulled her back in again. "Wait! I also want you to stop at the seamstress. She needs to do a fitting for your graduation dress. She's been waiting for days now, she's expecting you, don't forget . . . now, go!" and this time she shoved her out the door.

Hannah and Rina had grown up side-by-side as their mothers before them had done. Although Rina had been born two years after Hannah, she had come into the world feet first, which gave rise to predictions of sure footing and a strong nature. And as it was, the prophecies of the village women came true. Rina was an exceptional child, a bright girl who showed promise at an early age. Recognizing her abilities, the Quaker teachers advanced her first one grade, and then another. Lamia was proud of her daughter who finished her studies with such high honors. Rina hoped to one day be a teacher, while Hannah favored the nursing profession. As daughters of *fellaheen*, they both knew they must work hard at their lessons for the scholarships needed to continue their education.

The Quakers had built a Friends Girls School on the outskirts of Beit el Jebel. And when their classes were done, the two girls would leave the one-story stone building and wind their way through the hills and vineyards. They'd travel on foot past their homes and their mothers' well-tended gardens. Then climbing the rise that overlooked the Yusef compound, they'd settle on a grassy knoll amongst the rocks and wild flowers of the old fig orchard; and there, with the earth as their carpet, they'd open their books and study their lessons until the sun would set. Hannah had a propensity for poetry and took every opportunity to read her father's books or write verses of her own. Today, however, instead of reading or writing under the soft canopy of the giant fig trees, the two girls would be studying for their exams in the narrow entrance to the butcher's shop.

Shortly after Hannah left to meet Rina, a black sedan drove past the gates into the Yusef compound. The car pulled to a stop near Nisrina's garden and out stepped Mr. and Mrs. Badeer and their son George. Along with them was Salim Badeer, George's uncle and the elder of their family. The Badeers were wealthy people from a neighboring village. Their son was a young doctor who had a successful medical practice in Beirut, Lebanon. A handsome lad, he walked with the confidence of an educated man. His dark eyes were set deep within a chiseled face. And his nose, although a bit large, was straight and well-formed.

Nisrina had hurriedly dressed in her newest *thobe* and was brushing her hair when she heard the car arrive. Just in time, she thought to herself, running out to greet them.

Moments later, across the courtyard, plodded Jacob Yusef. The years had caught up with him and he walked much slower and stepped more carefully than he had in days past. Some time back, Jacob had made the painful decision to let Jabran's orchard go fallow. With Nisrina's responsibilities as midwife she was unable to maintain it, and Essam, choosing not to follow in the ways of a farmer, had taken the job as the new Chief Magistrate, Abdullah ibn Abdullah declining to run again. Jacob, who'd kept the orchard thriving for so many years, was reluctantly forced to let it go. He now spent his energies managing the family's expansive olive groves.

Jacob had seen the car arriving from the view of his bedroom window and as the elder of the Yusef family, he felt it his duty to meet and greet Nisrina's special guests. Nearing the house, he hiked his pants up over his belly and tucked in his shirt. He walked straight over to the Badeers, his hand proudly outstretched, smiling big for all the world to see.

"*Ahlan, Ahlan*," he welcomed them, his head bobbing up and down.

And then from around the back of the house, a third man approached.

It was Essam, the head of the household.

Nisrina proudly watched her son as he strode over to greet their guests. He was dressed in his Magistrate's uniform. She marveled at how much he looked like his father. The mirror image, she thought to herself.

When she saw him from afar, with his head held erect and his steps so confident, her heart skipped a beat. Then she remembered it was not Jabran, and she was not a young woman. She looked at her son and held a vision in her mind as she drifted back to a time now lost. A love which came lightly like a delicate butterfly sipping nectar from a fragrant blossom, then fluttering its wings it was gone.

"*Ahlan wa Sahlan*, welcome. Come in, Come in." Nisrina could hardly contain herself as she led her guests into her home.

Everyone sat down in the living room. Nisrina had been cleaning and tidying all day, her home was spotless. She put coffee on to boil and brought out a beautiful tray of homemade *baklawa*. She made it with the finest of butters and the freshest of nuts. The honeyed syrup dripping warm as it melted over the baked phyllo dough and crushed pistachios. Although Hannah had been told otherwise, in actuality, they'd been made special for today's visitors.

Nisrina poured the coffee as everyone took bites of the sweets, marveling at her culinary skills and blessing her hands.

After the pleasantries were over and everyone had sipped their coffee and comforted their stomachs, the room grew quiet. Jacob, having grown far too large for his chair, began fidgeting uncomfortably. He had not brought his worry beads, as his wife had thought them in poor taste for the occasion and advised against it. Nisrina sat up straight in her chair, repeatedly smoothing the wrinkles in her skirt.

Essam cleared his throat.

As was appropriate in these circumstances, the eldest member of the Badeer family was the first to speak, "It has come to our attention that your daughter, Hannah, has come of age and will soon be graduating from the Friends School."

The Yusef family all nodded and murmured words of agreement.

George Badeer, the young doctor, began to squirm nervously in his chair. He took a sip of his coffee.

The eldest Badeer continued, "And, as it is such that your daughter is a fine young woman, honorable in every way, coming from a most respectable family and raised by her older brother, Essam and her charming mother, *dayah* Nisrina, the midwife known throughout the land as *Oum el Loulad,* the Mother of all Children . . ."

There were murmurs of agreement from all around as Nisrina blushed and Essam sat taller in his chair.

The elder continued, "And, as it is such that I have a nephew who is older in age, and well educated and established in the medical profession as a fine young doctor . . ."

And everyone in the room smiled big and turned to George, who blushed as they murmured words of praise for his grand accomplishments.

"As it is such, my nephew has come to that time in his life when he wishes to take himself a bride, and establish himself in a home with a family of his own.

"So, therefore, on behalf of my nephew, and the entire Badeer family, I would like to *itulab,* ask for, your daughter Hannah's hand in marriage to the honorable Doctor George Badeer."

Everyone let out a sigh of relief. It was as if a very solemn cloud had just been lifted from the room and now they were all free to breathe again.

Essam, as Hannah's older brother and the male, head of their household, was the appropriate one to respond. He straightened his tie and pulled down on his sleeves, sitting very tall in his chair. After clearing his throat, he solemnly responded, "The Yusef family is proud to have you in our home today. And we are equally proud to have been asked by your esteemed and well respected family for my sister's hand in marriage. It is truly an honor for such an accomplished young man such as Doctor George Badeer to show an interest in our young Hannah."

The Badeer family all smiled proudly and bowed their heads slightly to one side, modestly acknowledging their agreement with his words.

"And, as George is a doctor living and practicing in Beirut, and Hannah has applied for a scholarship to the University of Beirut's nursing program, this arrangement would be of great benefit to them both."

They all smiled widely, knowing that this was an added advantage to the agreement.

Essam continued, "We are in favor of their betrothal in every respect . . ."

Unable to contain their excitement, the Badeer family began giving exclamations of joy and well wishes. But Essam, held up his hand to indicate that there was more to be said. The room returned to silent respectfulness.

"But before I give you my final answer, I must first confer with Hannah and obtain her consent."

There was a gasp in the room. It came from the Badeer's side.

They had been cautioned that this might happen. Doctor Badeer had been forewarned of the possibility, and thusly had time to consider his position. The young doctor had privately instructed the members of his family, that should this delay occur, it would be of no concern to him. It did not matter. From the time they were very young, he'd been captivated by Hannah's countenance. He'd seen her in the Orthodox Church each time their family visited Beit el Jebel, and their paths had crossed many times at the local bazaars. He'd had occasion to speak to her and he knew her smile and the mischievous twinkle in her eyes. Yes, long ago she'd cast her spell upon him. His mind was made up. He wanted her to share his life.

But before George could respond, the eldest member of the Badeer family, George's uncle, spoke out. His voice was terse, his words unmeasured, "And since when is the daughter of a good Arab family allowed to decide something of this magnitude for herself? Given the parameters of her upbringing, what kind of wife will she make for my nephew? This is unacceptable. It is clearly not a choice for her to make. It is for the elders to decide. We do not put a decision like this in the hands and thoughts of a young inexperienced girl." He was standing now, jangling the keys in his pocket, pacing back and forth threatening to walk out the door. "No, we shall not wait. As the eldest member of the Badeer family, I demand an answer right here, right now!" His forefinger pointed to the heavens.

This time the gasp came from the Yusef side of the room.

"No! Stop!" It was George who finally rose to speak. "With all due respect to my Uncle, to whom I give thanks for accompanying us on this solemn occasion, this is my marriage, my *itulab*. And I must say that I truly love your sister and your daughter," he turned respectfully to Essam and Nisrina. "And I am glad that you raised her to think for herself. These are new times and we are an open-minded family." He looked at his parents. "And I am an open-minded man. I guarantee you that I will not only support her extended education, and her ability to make her own decisions, but I will also love her with all my heart for the rest of my life." Resolutely, he sat down again. "I am willing to wait for her answer."

He turned to his uncle and his parents, and the look on his face told them that they had better not say a word to the contrary.

Finally, the father of the young doctor cleared his throat, "My son has spoken. This is his decision. He loves your Hannah, and if he is willing to wait for an answer, then *Enshallah*, so am I. And so is Mrs. Badeer." He looked at his wife, with a similar look that his son had just given him. His wife sat there expressionless. She gave no response. A good wife, she deferred to her husband in all matters.

"Then it is settled," the young doctor said. "We will wait for her decision."

"Thank you for your understanding. We will let you know her answer as soon as we can, and *Enshallah*, God willing, it is a joyful one." Essam was shaking hands all around.

As he rose to leave, the eldest Badeer shook hands with the Yusef family, but his face was pressed tight, his eyes puffed and bulging. Things had not gone as he'd expected. He finished his pleasantries and quickly walked back to the car.

As they were leaving, the young doctor turned to Nisrina and whispered in her ear, "I really do love your daughter, *Oum* Essam. Please . . . I hope she says yes."

Nisrina nodded, "I hope she does too George, for I already love you as my son." She kissed him on both his cheeks. And watched and waved as they drove away.

It was beginning to get dark outside. Jacob went home to his wife, thinking that this was a matter best discussed between mother and daughter. And he knew that May was sitting at home waiting anxiously to hear the details of what had occurred in Nisrina's living room.

Meanwhile, Nisrina and Essam walked arm in arm back into the house to wait for Hannah's return.

"Hannah, would you come into the kitchen please?"

Hannah knew something was amiss. She had been sent out on a fool's list of errands with the pretense of much urgency, when in fact, in her absence her mother had been entertaining visitors. She could see the half-eaten desserts still sitting on the sideboard. And there remained coffee cups, recently used, unwashed in the kitchen sink.

"What is it mother?"

"Hannah, my love, sit down. We need to talk."

SIXTY ONE

A Part of All Things (Beirut, Lebanon)

THE PATIENT IN ROOM 43 had refused his meal again.

The head nurse had been called in to speak with him, but it was to no avail. Hospital administrators had been alerted and the news was spreading quickly. It would not be good if a patient under their care should die from lack of nutrition. Not only would it damage the hospital's reputation, it would also be very difficult to explain to their Board of Directors.

Nevertheless the problem remained. He would not eat and they could not force him. The two parties were at a standstill.

"Does he have any family?" Hannah asked softly, standing outside the doorway to his room. Although still a student, she was dressed in a nurse's uniform, her trainee's apron crisply pressed, her cap fitting neatly atop her short cropped hair.

"As far as we know, he has no family and no one to speak on his behalf," said the head nurse. "At this rate, I'm afraid it won't be long." Her eyes glazed over. Lucine Haleeba had seen this before. Although it had been nineteen years, maybe twenty, since she'd first donned the nurse's uniform, her memories were still vivid. The war had ended and the years had passed, but those who survived, soldiers who'd fought bravely against the enemies' sword, carried with them many unhealed wounds. With battered bodies and lacerated limbs they struggled to return to their former lives, only to find that they could no longer work their farms or care for their families. Their psyches were damaged beyond repair as they struggled with the horrors they'd endured. And so the half-souls continued to stream back to the hospital, seeking medical attention, and hope for a better future. For some, death was their only salvation.

"Perhaps I could read to him," Hannah offered.

"I'm not sure that would help," she replied sadly. "But, it's good of you to offer and *Enshallah,* I don't think it would hurt."

And so it began.

"Mr. Suleman, Mr. Suleman," Hannah lightly touched his shoulder. "You're dreaming . . . You're dreaming Mr. Suleman."

Mashallah, he thought to himself, his heart thundering against his chest. It's her again. He reached up to his forehead and with a cold, clammy hand wiped the moisture from his brow.

Mr. Suleman would not open his eyes when Hannah entered the room. He kept them shut, his frozen face turned away. She could see the back of his neck, the form of his spine protruding through the darkened, leathered skin. His profile revealed a man with strong cheekbones and a narrow nose, turned slightly upward. The dark, thick stubble from his refusal to shave could not hide the hollow, sunken caverns of his cheeks. His lips were dry and taut. He never spoke.

Hannah wondered what visions he saw while he slept. Always struggling. Tossing and churning. Mumbling words she could not understand. She could see that even in his sleep his poor soul found no peace. With compassion, she claimed it her mission to alleviate his misery and usher him back into the world of the living. Such was her nature, for Hannah had been raised in a loving household and she knew that no man could exist without the warmth and love of those around him. In keeping with her pledge, she went to the lonely man's room each day, and sitting in a small wooden chair pulled up alongside his bed, she quietly read to him.

Hannah knew very little about the stranger, but he clearly wore the scars and sorry air of a soldier in battle. He'd been found restlessly sleeping beneath a weathered old cart, crying out in the darkness to demons of gloom. A nun, devoted to the poor and the homeless, brought him, weak and cloudy, to the open doors of the great hospital. Once assured of a bed, she reverently placed her palms together in front of her heart and bowed low to the ground. Then, making the sign of the cross, she slipped silently back into the night.

Unwilling to speak, his background and preferences remained a mystery to all. So Hannah decided to read to him from a wide assortment of newspapers, magazines, novels and poetry. She read currents and politics and articles of economics. She read gentle tales by wise old men and melodic verses passed down from the ages.

Consistently he refused to acknowledge her presence. Lying on his side, his face to the wall he remained silent and dead to the world. But Hannah persevered and continued her commitment, never knowing if he listened to her words or if his thoughts were spent elsewhere.

One day Hannah brought with her a very old book. It was large and heavy—bound tightly in deep, dark, red leather with intricately raised gold embossments, tied shut by means of two short leather straps secured on each end. It contained beautiful verses written by ancient seers of the past. It was special to Hannah for it had been given to her by the father she never knew, and knowing that it had once been his prized possession, she treasured it as she would a rare lapis stone. And now, settling comfortably in her chair, she untied the straps that bound it shut and carefully opened the yellowed, parchment sheets. Allowing the page to choose itself, she began to read from the passage that opened before her:

"I take no form.
My soul has shattered into a never-ending silence that envelops and caresses me.
I am part of no thing; and I am a part of all things.
I am at peace, at home in this vast timelessness.
And even though they seek, they shall not find,

For no one can claim my countenance or look upon me.
I take no form and I rejoice,
For I reside in the heart of eternity."

The man remained motionless as she read aloud to him. But he had been listening, enthralled by her voice. When he heard the ancient words spoken with such eloquent clarity, he felt the rush of a thousand rivers run through his soul. His eyes fluttered briefly beneath their dark lids. Each verse delivered with such well-paced precision. Each sound, a cradle in the shadowy night. Who was this woman that had been sent to placate him? A mere child by the sound of her voice. He remained on his side, his face always averted. The poem had surely touched the man's chilly heart, but he dared not speak. He did not move. He lay there in silence, denying all pleasures.

Hannah gently closed the book, taking time to carefully retie the worn leather straps. He took note of the sounds as she gave rise to leave. The familiar scraping of her chair when she pulled it away, the soft sigh escaping her lips once the visit was over, and then the gathering of her things as she turned to depart. He heard her sweet voice as she bade him farewell, promising to return again the next day. But still, he did not turn towards her or utter a word.

Finally, as he heard her walk across the threshold, then, and only then, did he turn his head to watch. He noticed how very slight she was, her hair thick and waved. Her uniform neatly pressed. And he noticed her gait, how her steps were both confident and measured. He wondered how one so young could be so calm, so self-assured.

Hannah was unaware of his observations. She did not stop to look back or pause to see if she'd forgotten her scarf, and therefore she failed to see his watchful gaze and the soft pool of tears that had welled so passionately in his eyes.

The next day when Hannah arrived, the man in Room 43 was not sleeping. He did not turn his head away from her, but instead, greeted her with just a whisper of a smile, and his eyes, although slightly averted, remained open.

"Thank you for reading to me," he said. His voice was barely audible, hoarse and dry.

"It is my pleasure," she responded, remaining poised and reserved. Hannah was thrilled to see the change in him, no matter how small. But she showed no emotion, not wanting to frighten him back into his solitude.

When he heard her voice so sure, so compelling, he found the strength to look directly into her face. He saw her warm eyes and her beautiful smile. It was as if the sun itself had broken out from behind the clouds and cast its golden rays into the dark gray shadows of the hospital room. He breathed in, filling his lungs.

And Hannah saw the man for the first time, too. Although he was only forty-five, he looked old and careworn. Life had taken its toll. Curious, she searched his face for signs of his former nature. She imagined that he had once been a handsome man with strong character and a gentle hand. Diligently, her gaze passed across his lifeless mouth, his deep, wrinkled brow, and gauntly drawn cheeks; and so it came as no surprise that when she finally looked into his dark, deep-set eyes all she saw was great sadness.

"Would you like to take a walk in the garden today?" she asked him.

"I'm afraid I cannot walk," he replied, pointing to his missing limb.

"No worry, I will push the wheelchair. I could use the fresh air and the exercise. I've been indoors all day, studying for my exams."

He hesitated, a faint smile crossed his lips, "I would like that."

"You are called, Mr. Suleman, eh?"

"Yes, but please, you would honor me if you would call me Marwan."

"Then Marwan it is. And you must call me Hannah." She tapped her name tag, it read: *Hannah Badeer.*

"Hannah was my mother's name," he said quietly, almost a whisper.

Hannah wheeled him down the long hospital corridor, past the half-opened doors of patients' rooms. Marwan could see nurses rushing in and out. Broken bodies lying in their beds, with tubes extending from their arms, reaching out like an octopus for its prey. Some had clear tents covering their faces, the oxygen released in a rhythmic pulsating motion. He turned his head away, embarrassed by the intrusion on their sufferings.

His heart began to race. Maybe this was not such a good idea after all.

Then he heard Hannah's voice behind him. She was chattering softly about the simplest of things. The sun had finally come out, she said. And she was sure that she'd seen flowers blooming already. Wouldn't it be nice to pick some and put them alongside the window in his room?

When they reached the gardens on the east side of the building, Marwan shivered with a sigh of relief. A cool breeze slipped lightly across his face, his arms tingling as the hairs stood on end. Hannah tucked a blanket around his waist and over his shoulders as he gazed upwards to the sky, watching the gentle movement of the cedar tree overhead, its wide-spreading horizontal branches reaching out to shade the dappled stone walkway. They moved farther out, into the sun, and walked between the roses they found planted along the pathway. As they moved, slowly working their way through the carefully tended grounds, Hannah chatted calmly to Marwan, her voice smooth and soothing. She pointed out the subtleties of the park-like setting: how the gardenias and jasmine were sprinkled randomly beneath the cypress trees, and where a pair of mourning doves had built their nest, huddled deep between the branches and brambles of an old bougainvillea. The warm sun and subtle fragrances were a welcome change from the cold, antiseptic smells of the hospital room. And for the first time in a very long while, Marwan, absorbing the new world around him, began to relax.

Each day thereafter, when Hannah came to Marwan's room she would take him in his wheelchair and together they would walk through the garden. Sometimes she would stop and sit alongside him on a stone bench, where she'd read books or newspapers aloud. He'd listen intently, devouring her every word, while his senses basked in the sweet fragrance and subtle breezes that enveloped the courtyard. The sounds of water cascading from the nearby fountain, or the shrilled chirpings of the sparrows overhead were soothing backgrounds to her rhythmic tenor.

Other times they would just sit and talk, sipping warm, fragrant tea made from rose hips or the leaves of freshly picked peppermint.

And they'd nibble on anise flavored cookies sprinkled lightly with crunchy sesame seeds. He'd always remark that they were the finest and tastiest *kurshellas* that he'd ever had, and Hannah would blush, for she'd made them herself.

When they'd look to the horizon and the sun's slow descent, and they'd witness the shadows of the cedar and cypress grow twice their size, she'd rise from her seat and reluctantly wheel him back to his room. She'd help him safely to his bed and tuck the white sheets in around his body.

His voice would grow louder and faster as he spoke to her, hoping that somehow she would remain a few moments longer. And knowing this, she would linger as best she could, for although he never told her, she knew that he dreaded the solitude of sleep.

Marwan began to eat again. His face filled out, and the bones that once protruded sharply through his hospital gown were now softened with flesh. The hospital administrators were pleased with his progress and amazed at the effect Hannah seemed to have on him. They smiled as they saw her walking by, and nodded their approval as she pushed his chair down the hall and out into the gardens, always chatting pleasantly, soothingly.

Marwan looked forward to her visits. If she were just a few minutes late, he'd become anxious and worried, his neck, back and shoulders growing tight and beginning to ache. But she always appeared, day in and day out, and when he saw her walk through the door with book in hand and that infectious smile upon her face, his body would relax, and he'd feel buoyant and light like the white billowy clouds that were drifting past his window.

In all the time they spent together Hannah noticed that Marwan never spoke of himself or his past. And Hannah, being a nurse and employee of the hospital, likewise abstained. Protocol and propriety required her to refrain from discussing any personal matters with the patients. However, she couldn't help feel that it was becoming increasingly difficult to limit their discussions to the same philosophical and literary topics to which they'd become accustomed.

One day while they were sitting in the garden enjoying the warm breeze and sipping peppermint tea sweetened with orange blossom honey, Marwan got the courage to speak to Hannah on a more personal level. He tried his best to sound casual, picking a leaf from a nearby jasmine plant and fingering it a while, until finally he found his voice, and then he began, "Hannah, you remind me of someone I once knew a long time ago."

He was very melancholy.

"You sound so sad," she replied. "Is it someone who has since passed away?"

"In a manner of speaking, I suppose she has," he said wistfully. "But, it's more complicated than that . . ." and his voice trailed off as his thoughts wandered back to days past. "Forgive me," he finally continued, "I should not have burdened you with this matter. It's just that . . . well . . . let's just say that I am glad to have you as my friend." He smiled up at her. "Can I call you my friend?"

"Why, of course. I would be honored to consider you my friend."

"Well, then, it's settled. I have a friend. And you, my dear, are the only one I have."

"I hope that I can be one of many," she smiled back at him.

"Tell me about yourself, Hannah. Do you enjoy school? In my day, women were rarely allowed to get an education. You are very lucky you know. The times have changed so much."

Hannah hesitated. She knew the protocol and that she should not break the hospital's rules, but she couldn't stop herself, she responded, "Yes, I do enjoy school. You see, my family is poor. I am my mother's youngest child. We were raised without a father. My mother is a *dayah* from a village far from here. She supported us with her work and she worked very hard. When I showed promise in my studies, she knew that one day she would be proud of me. She wanted me to have what she could not, and I am forever grateful to her."

Marwan nodded in silent understanding.

"This is good. This is good," was all that he would say.

He pointed to her wedding ring. "I see that you are married. I hope he is a nice young man, worthy of such a fine woman."

"Yes, he is a doctor here at the hospital and I am fortunate. I love him very much."

"Ah, yes . . . Love."

And he said no more. His eyes glazed over as he looked into the distance, and he saw things that Hannah could not see.

The days passed and Hannah and Marwan continued to share their time and their thoughts with each other. One sunny day, Hannah, on her way to Marwan's room, found him sitting in the hallway. He was in his wheelchair and had met her halfway down the corridor.

"I can wheel myself now!" he exclaimed proudly, "See, I am strong again."

"Yes, I can see that. How far you've come in such a short time!" Hannah was smiling.

"Now, my dear Hannah, you can relax and enjoy our walks, for you won't have to push me anymore."

"I've always enjoyed our walks, Marwan. But I'm glad that you are stronger now."

He smiled at her and reached out to touch her hand. She withdrew it, but only after hesitating for a brief moment, his hand on hers.

Hannah was confused and embarrassed, a strange feeling encompassing her.

Who is this man who evokes such feelings in me? she asked herself.

This was not a feeling of romance or attraction, for she was truly in love with her husband, George. This was different. A comforting sense. Like the time when she was a young girl and had not been well. Her mother covered her tenderly with a knitted quilt made by her Auntie Dora. Or when she sat in church and heard the Gregorian chanting and smelled the sweet fragrance of burning incense. The priest, in all his splendor, giving blessings and making the sign of the cross. Such was the nature of Marwan's touch. And this puzzled Hannah, for she knew of no others to whom she reacted in this way.

Unlikely as it was, he had become an engaging habit that she could not break. She felt at home, so comforted in his presence. It was obvious that his feelings towards her were the same. They laughed at like-minded things and worried together when they'd found a baby bird that had fallen from its nest. Marwan knew not to directly touch the young chick. He explained how his scent would be detected by its mother, disturbing the delicate balance of nature. He showed Hannah how to use leaves from a nearby tree to carry the fallen bird back to its nest. She admired his astute knowledge of the natural world and his sensitivity to the simple order of life.

As they spent time together, they learned that they both had an affinity for language and scholarly pursuits. Hannah loved poetry written by the ancients, as did Marwan. And they both noticed how the other sustained a deliberate way of approaching life, never rushing into expectations or chasing false opportunities. They both had a tendency to think things out carefully and thoroughly before acting or speaking. Hannah laughed, for she knew few others who had such measured tendencies as her own.

Hannah's husband, Dr. George Badeer, having heard so many encouraging tales about his wife's patient, went to visit Mr. Suleman. Although not under his care, the stories from both Hannah and his colleagues regarding Marwan's progress had clearly piqued his interest. He was impressed with the changes that had been reported. In the short time he spent visiting Marwan Suleman, George also found himself befriending the gentle man. He confided in Hannah that he, too, thought his company felt strangely familiar. Reassuring and reposed. He was pleased that Hannah had been instrumental in bringing the man back from his saddened state into one of joy. He marveled at his wife's skills and her endearing bedside manner and he knew that she would make a good nurse. She had found her true profession.

SIXTY TWO

The Last Goodbye

HANNAH WAS RUNNING LATE. Breathless, she burst into Marwan's room. She'd brought her favorite book of poetry to read to him, its rich leather cover pressed tightly to her chest. But when she saw her comrade, she stopped. Her eyes stared and her fingers grew limp as the book she was carrying slid from her hands, crashing with a thud to the floor.

Marwan was fully dressed, smiling and sitting upright on the side of his bed.

"I'm being released today," he told her proudly. "But I told them I couldn't go until I'd had a chance to say goodbye to you."

"Oh, Marwan!" Hannah exhaled the words.

"I will miss you, Hannah."

"And I will miss you, Marwan. I am happy for your good health, but sad to lose my dear friend."

"A friend is never lost, Hannah. That is something you have taught me. Something that I'd sadly forgotten."

"Such a touching sentiment, Marwan. I think you're right about that. I'm glad that I could be instrumental in helping you."

The light moisture filling her eyes began to cloud her vision. She turned her head as she slowly stepped forward into the room.

"Yes, you have. You certainly have." He was smiling to himself, a wistful smile.

Marwan had never spoken of his life outside the hospital. He'd kept his past to himself. And Hannah realized that she didn't even know where he lived or whether he had family to return to. There was no one there to pick him up and take him home. No one had ever come to visit. She became uneasy as she thought through these matters and she wanted to question him, to uncover the mysteries of his life. But she was embarrassed, not wanting to pry or offend.

Pensively she walked over to the window. She needed air, time to think. She released the latch and cranked open the panel. Immediately the sweet scent of jasmine rushed into the room, its heady fragrance caressing her senses.

He noticed her consternation.

"What is it, Hannah? What are you thinking that makes your brow wrinkle up so tightly?" He pointed to her forehead.

"Ah, yes," Hannah laughed nervously, the tiny muscles surrounding her eyes softening. "My mother always knew when I was troubled. She used to tell me that I could never lie, that the truth was clearly written upon my face. And when I'd get frustrated by my transparency, she reminded me that it was a good thing—that it meant I had a pure soul."

"Yes, an old Arab proverb. A wise woman, your mother. But then, how could I have expected anything less when I see what a fine daughter she has raised." Marwan looked at her closer, "So, tell me Hannah, what is this truth that troubles you so?"

She took a deep breath. "I'm worried about you Marwan. Where you'll go from here. You've never told me about your home, your family, or your past. Tell me, do you have someplace to go today when you leave here? I couldn't bear to think that you might be alone or even worse that you'd slip back to the sadness that you had when you first arrived."

Marwan was nodding. "You are very astute. Such a fine girl. It was truly my good fortune to have had you as my nurse. For indeed you have opened my heart and helped me to see the joy in life again."

He smiled at her, his eyes gentle, yet piercing.

She blushed and turned away. Gazing out the window she saw the massive white clouds that floated overhead. Their soft, billowy forms seemed to reach out to her as they pressed close against the deep blue sky. She exhaled softly and her shoulders relaxed as she heard his voice again.

"Permit me to explain . . . it was long ago. I once had a family and a beautiful home. An orchard, rich with fig trees and olive trees . . ."

As he struggled to find the words, Hannah turned back to look at him, he was watching her. Their gaze held for a moment, suspended in time. She searched his face, neither one able to look away.

Finally, inhaling deeply, he continued, "And then something very unfortunate happened. I learned that all men are not good. And all things are not of God. I suffered and in turn I caused much suffering. I searched to find blame until finally it consumed me. I've lived alone for many years now. Abandoning all others and trusting no one. When I came to this hospital, it was not the illness of my body, but rather the misery of my heart that brought me here."

He paused a moment, taking in another deep breath. "I'm sorry to say that long ago I'd forsaken the Lord . . . I was ready to die and have death take me where it may."

Hannah was watching his face. He was clean shaven now. His cheeks had filled out and the lines that creased his forehead had all but disappeared. She couldn't believe that he had come so far in his healing, that he could now open up and share these things with her. She was happy for him, but also very intrigued by the story he told. She wanted to know more.

"And now, Marwan? Are things right with you?"

"I think they are. I've finally put things right between myself and God. *Mashallah*, I have you to thank for that. But now I must make things right with my past. Fate gives you what it will, and each season unfolds in its due time."

He was looking down, fingering the sash tied around his waist. "It is up to each one of us to choose how we greet the life we've been given. I'm afraid that's where I made my mistakes. And now I want to make it right again."

Hannah was fascinated. Her eyes widened like a child seated at the foot of a great master. She pushed her hair back behind her ears, and sat down on the chair alongside his bed. She hoped he would continue. She was not disappointed.

"By God's grace, I once had a beautiful family. But I dishonored them . . . it was a long time ago. Entirely my fault, you see. This has been my burden to bear and my shame to carry. It was war . . . I lost my leg." He looked up at her, "But more importantly, Hannah, I lost my heart. I lost my faith in mankind . . . fwthh . . . gone." He made a twirling motion with his hand. ". . . evaporated like raindrops from a shallow pond. And then you came into my life and like a breeze from the sea, you gave me hope . . . I could breathe again."

Hannah looked down. Her cheeks flushed, she could no longer meet his gaze. She had done so little. She stared at her hands resting in her lap, her eyes avoiding his. She noticed the book that she'd brought, still lying on the floor where it fell, the pages tied shut by its leather straps.

He went on, unaware of her discomfort.

"I am forever indebted to you Hannah . . . for your kindness and your friendship. It's made me think. I could continue to blame those who instigated ill will towards me. I could do that until the day that I die. But I realize now that time is short and life is precious. The season for blame is over. The hour has come for me to accept my follies for what they were, ask for forgiveness, and move on.

"*Enshallah*, I've asked the Lord for his mercy, and I feel that I've made things right in that regard. But now I must return home and try to make things right with the ones I love . . ."

He paused. His heart was beating hard now, his chest tightening up. "If it's not too late . . . I can only hope. You see, in all my misery, I've never stopped loving them." He was shaking his head, "Such wasted time . . . such wasted time." The end of the sash was now wrapped entirely around his fingers. "I just hope I'm not too late. I hope . . ." His head was bent, his eyes cast downward. For the first time since she'd arrived, he noticed the book that Hannah had dropped near his bedside.

Tears were openly welling in Hannah's eyes. Touched by this man who had suffered, who had healed, and had finally found the strength to seek redemption. This stranger who had gone from despondency to hope. She was honored to have been a part of his destiny.

He continued. He was speaking slowly now, deliberately. His eyes never leaving the thick leather book that lay on the floor.

"Hannah, you are a fine young woman and you've opened my eyes to the value of the world. To the value of my life . . . You are someone's daughter and I'm sure that your mother is very proud of you. You make me want to know my daughter and my son, and my . . ."

He carefully bent down and reached out, his fingers slowly wrapping around the leather bound book that lay on the floor. He placed it in his lap and his hands ran lightly over the gold emboss-ments, a decorative pattern that surrounded the edges of the book. Now it was he who noticed the scent of jasmine as it drifted in through the window, the breeze warm and inviting.

"Hannah," he asked, his measured voice showing no sign of the raging beast that was now pounding inside his chest, "is this your book?"

"Yes," Hannah responded dutifully. "I'm sorry to have dropped it. It is my favorite book. A book of poetry. I've read from it before . . . do you remember? You thanked me the next day."

His deep-set gaze grew deeper still, disappearing softly into the dark hollow of his eyes. The muscles in his face tensed up, impercep-tibly, and then relaxed again. His hands were trembling.

"Yes," he said slowly, nodding. "I do remember. I remember it well. 'A Part of All Things,' eh?"

Hannah nodded. She was pleased that he remembered. It was her favorite poem. The one her father had read to her mother on their wedding night. Her mother told her that it was her treasured verse. That when she'd heard the words spoken so passionately, so tenderly from her husband's mouth, she knew their souls would be forever bound.

"This is a very fine book . . ." carefully, ceremoniously, he handed it back to her. "A very fine book indeed."

He paused, staring at her face, watching intently as she lovingly wrapped her sweet arms around the tome. He stared at her fingers, her wrists, and drank in the graceful movement of her body.

"Tell me, Hannah, how did you come by such a fine, old book?"

His voice was soft now, calm and considered. His outward demeanor belying his shattering emotions. His body was on fire; every nerve and muscle that supported his skin was ablaze while a torrential storm released its compassionate mercy. His thoughts were racing. Forward. Then back. They soared outwards to the boundaries of eternity and returned home again.

"It was my father's book," she said to him. It was her turn to be sad. "*Enshallah*, I never knew my father. My mother gave it to me. She told me that I'd inherited his love for poetry and therefore, it was rightfully mine." Now her palms were skimming the soft, thick leather, caressing it as a mother would its child. "It is all I have of him." It was almost a whisper.

"I see," he said thoughtfully. "I see."

Suddenly the door opened and Lucine Haleeba came in.

"Ah, I see you've found her," she said to Marwan.

"Yes, and now it is time for me to go. I can only thank you all for saving my life, for giving me back what I had lost and restoring my reason for living." He was speaking to the head nurse, but his gaze was still upon Hannah, her cheeks hot, flushed, as the matron looked her way.

Lucine turned back to Marwan and smiled. She held out her hand to him, "Goodbye, Mr. Suleman. We are all very happy for your recovery and wish you continued good health and all the best in life. God be with you." She turned back to Hannah, "Perhaps Nurse Hannah would be so kind as to wheel you out to your taxi? It is waiting outside."

"I would be glad to," Hannah said softly. She tried not to show her sadness. She had grown attached to this kind and measured man, and he would be sorely missed. And yet, she was happy that he was finally well enough to go home and resume his life with such renewed hope.

They moved through the halls in silence, Hannah pushing his chair one last time. As they passed through the double doors and onto the boulevard, they saw the taxi waiting, its vibrating engine spewing a cloud of gray smoke from its rear.

They turned to face each other, the hum of the noisy street disappeared like flakes of snow on a warm winter's day. The roar of cars and buses went by unnoticed, the whooshing tires that raced against the worn, gravelly pavement vanished in the wind. A mother's angry voice, prodding her children after a trying day at the *souk*, passed them without sound. And the resonant words of a vendor as he excitedly negotiated the sale of a beautiful, handmade carpet—"no other quite like it in all the world," he was saying—were lost.

Hannah and Marwan did not hear them.

The driver opened the door. Marwan motioned to give them one more moment, one final goodbye.

He turned to Hannah, taking her hands in his.

"Thank you again for all you've done. For all that you've been to me. And please, thank your husband, too. It was kind of him to share his wife with me. Indeed, you are fortunate to have found each other."

Then, surprisingly, he carefully placed a small note securely into the palm of her left hand, wrapping her fingers gently around it. It was folded up tightly, into a little square.

She did not attempt to open it, but instead, looked at him with question in her eyes.

"There is something that I must explain," he whispered quietly to her. "Long ago, I was forced to change my name, to change my identity. We were at war . . . I made a choice . . . I had to stop the cruelty. Such carnage, such butchery . . . even in battle it was indefensible. The British, they were good people, civilized soldiers." He was shaking his head, his eyes staring down at his open palms. "I made a choice."

Hannah reached out and touched his hands. They were cold, shaking.

"Please, let me finish," he begged.

She nodded and let go, the warmth of her fingers softly slipping away.

"They found out . . . the Ottoman forces. No good deed goes unrewarded they told me . . . or unpunished. I paid dearly for it."

He was breathing heavily now, thoughts tearing through his mind unrestrained, scattered. Memories of lies and deceits, clandestine missions and false reports. Treachery and treason followed by heartache, and more. Shivering, he brushed them aside.

"Things happened so quickly. I had no option. In order to survive, to protect my family, I took on a new life. Overnight. Just like that. I became this man you now know as Marwan Suleman."

He took in a deep breath and breathed out, barely able to whisper the words.

"On that paper is written my real name. I want you to have it. You see, my stay in the hospital has given me opportunity to think. I realize that life is unpredictable and one never knows how much time we have left in this world."

Hannah began to protest.

"No, wait, please let me finish," he begged, raising his hand. "In the event that things don't go well. When I return home, I mean. I want . . . no, I *need* for someone, just *one* someone in this troubled world to know who I really am. I need this for *me,*" he pounded his chest, "it's the only way I'll know that *I* still exist. I need it like I need the air to breathe. And, Hannah, my dear friend, I want that someone to be you."

She was staring at him, mesmerized. Not an eyelash fluttered, not a muscle moved.

He held both her hands in his and gazed intensely into her eyes.

"Hannah, it's no secret that I have grown fond of you over these past few months. You have given me back my life, my soul. You are more than just a nurse, you are . . . like a daughter to me. I am forever indebted to you. For your kindness and your friendship. And if one day you find it in your heart . . ."

He could not finish. He turned away.

Hannah nodded, tears beginning to well in her eyes. Sad to see him go, but even more, she was touched by his words, so fraught with sorrow, the despair overwhelming. In his voice. In his tone. Vast and powerful. She felt small and insignificant. Her life had been safely paved for her. She'd known only loving, fair-minded ways, and the guilt of it now, tore at her heart.

He was a good man, of that she was certain. What fortuneless circumstance had cost him so dearly? What pitiless fate could extol such pain? She could not fathom.

She watched silently as the driver helped him into the car. He turned back, looking one last time through the clouded glass window, his fingers pressed white against the gray smoky pane, his eyes, intense and searching, they screamed a thousand desperate refrains. She raised up her hand, it was trembling. In a voiceless whisper, she wished him good health as the driver revved up his engine and noisily drove away.

The smell of dust and burning gasoline lingered in the air, the scent of jasmine now forgotten. Hannah looked down at the palm of her hand, removing the folded paper that had been so carefully placed there. Her heart pounded as she slowly opened it. And wiping the tears from her eyes, she read the words printed neatly upon the sheet.

"I am Jabran Yusef, Abu Essam . . ."

She froze.

Motionless, her eyes could go no further, the name suspended in her mind.

Her stomach turned, twisting into a merciless knot.

She forced herself to read the words again and again, until her mind accepted what her eyes beheld. Her hands were shaking, her head reeling, until finally, reluctantly, she tore her gaze from the folded note.

But it was too late.

As she looked up, her widened eyes filled with horror—the taxi was disappearing down the street. She covered her mouth, a pained cry echoing through the air as she fell to her knees.

The head nurse appeared by her side, "Hannah, are you all right?"

Hannah could not respond; her head in her hands, she was crying passionately, desperately.

"You poor girl, it will be all right. Don't worry. My, my," she patted her back, "I know it's hard to say goodbye. The two of you had grown so close. But, it was time for him to go. You understand. Listen to me, please. I want you to leave early today. No more work, your day is over. Here, I will have a driver take you home."

She motioned to a waiting taxi.

Quickly, the vehicle pulled up in front of the two nurses.

"It's time to go home," Lucine said.

Hannah kept the note crumpled firmly in the palm of her hand as she settled in the back of the old taxi. The seat was torn and the fabric soiled. The smell of smoke pervaded the air. Cigars. She glanced in the rear view mirror at the driver's face, his reflection staring back at hers. She wondered why he was smiling. What could he possibly know of happiness?

Leaning back, her head resting against the mottled upholstery, she rolled down the window. The warm breeze greeted her, caressing her dampened cheeks. She closed her eyes and reveled for a moment in its soft embrace.

She took a deep breath, aware of the scent carried in by the wind—jasmine. It had been there all along, like sacred footprints left on the sea's sandy shore. Smiling, she raised her hand to her lips, and then softly, lovingly, she kissed the fingers of her tightly clenched fist.

-THE END-

ACKNOWLEDGMENTS

It is with heartfelt appreciation that I thank my family and friends for their support as I wrote this book. Thank you to my daughter, Michele Brosch, for reading and re-reading my work. Your feedback and keen eye helped make this the best it could be. Thanks to my son, John Fiske, for always believing in me. Thank you to my niece, Joanne Schroeder, whose never-ending input, enthusiasm and faith in having this story told kept me going. Thank you to my friend, Eileen Jennings—you were so wise when you patted my manuscript and told me that this novel would be much longer by the time it was done. Many thanks to my brother-in-law Joe Amash and my cousins, Isa and Hala Ajluni, whose personal accounts of life in Palestine helped give authenticity to my work. Thank you to my sister, Ann Amash, and my brother, William Peters, for reading and providing me feedback. You are forever a part of me. Thank you to Father Joe Highland and Mary Highland for your insights into Catholic faith and convent life. You are a living example of all that is good. Thank you to my friend, Dean Haas, for reading the entire manuscript on your vacation. Your encouragement was energizing. Thank you to Joan Vokac, you appeared when I needed you most and helped make this dream a reality. Thank you to Frankie Frey for your professionalism and wonderful design work.

Finally, I give my deepest gratitude to my husband and soulmate, Paul, who patiently read my manuscript again and again. Never doubting. Always encouraging. You are amazing. At your side, I am home.

IN THE AUTHOR'S WORDS

THE FIG ORCHARD is a work of fiction. Names, characters, places, villages, schools, businesses, houses of worship and incidents either are the product of my imagination or are used fictitiously. Any resemblance to actual persons, living or dead, structures, institutions, business establishments, events, or locales is entirely coincidental.

THE FIG ORCHARD is a fictional story of a woman's life within a time and culture. And as a storyteller, I have taken liberties with some of the historical aspects of the time.

Beit el Jebel and Dar al Qamar are fictitious villages in Palestine.

Qasr Azraq, The Blue Fortress does exist. It is located in present-day eastern Jordan. Although occupied by Ottoman forces at various times throughout history, in 1917 it housed British troops headed by T.E. Lawrence during the Arab revolt against the Ottoman Empire. The Turkish camp and the British bombing of the fortress in THE FIG ORCHARD are products of my imagination.

In THE FIG ORCHARD, the Spanish Flu hit Beit el Jebel in 1920, but in reality its greatest impact took place throughout the world in 1918.

In THE FIG ORCHARD, the Convent of the Sisters of Mercy and their university in Jerusalem are fictional, as are the hospital and university in Beirut.

READERS GUIDE FOR THE FIG ORCHARD

—Discussion Questions—

1. Who was your favorite character? Why?

2. How do you think Nisrina's life was shaped by her father's refusal to send her to school? Would it have changed her outlook on the role of a woman in her culture? Would it have affected her decisions or life outcomes? How and why?

3. Discuss Nisrina's relationship with her husband. How did it differ from her father's relationship with her stepmother, Esma? Why do you think that is?

4. How did Jabran's capture by the Turkish soldiers affect the rest of Nisrina's life? What might have made the outcome different?

5. Discuss Nisrina's relationship with her best friend, Lamia and how their paths diverged and converged. What kept their friendship strong despite their different experiences? How did their lives unexpectedly differ as adults?

6. When Jabran did not return from the war, Nisrina was given the opportunity to marry another man from the village. Her father-in-law told her that if she did remarry, by the law of their land, she could not take her children with her—they belonged to her husband's family. How do you think this made Nisrina feel? Can you think of reasons that would justify separating a mother from her children in this way? How does this differ from other cultures?

7. Nisrina had to stand up to the Mother Superior to remain in the midwifery program. What resources did she draw upon in her passionate plea?

8. How did Nisrina change while at the nunnery? What did her experiences with Magda Attia teach her?

9. Why did Sister Alodia react to Nisrina the way she did in the beginning? Discuss Nisrina's changing relationship with Sister Alodia.

10. What could the Yusef family have done differently to change the course of events that followed old Farooz's death? What role did the culture play in Najeeb's power over the family?

11. Magda Attia had been cruel to Nisrina at the university in Jerusalem. She later married an abusive man. How did Magda Attia's marriage experience change her? Did she deserve what finally happened to her?

12. In her youth, Mona suffered tragically by the cruelty of Najeeb. She later took revenge through her actions to protect Nisrina. Does rape ever justify murder?

13. When the British Colonel paid his respects to Nisrina, he recognized her husband as a soldier lost in the war. Should he have told her so? Did he make the right decision in remaining silent?

CPSIA information can be obtained at www.ICGtesting.com
Printed in the USA
LVOW05s0956110813

347261LV00003B/9/P